Praise for the Davis Way (

"Funny & wonderful & human. I
of approval."

– Janet Evanovich

"Archer navigates a satisfyingly complex plot and injects plenty
of humor as she goes....a winning hand for fans of Janet Evanovich."

– *Library Journal*

"Davis's smarts, her mad computer skills, and a plucky crew of
fellow hostages drive a story full of humor and action, interspersed
with moments of surprising emotional depth."

– *Publishers Weekly*

"Archer's bright and silly humor makes this a pleasure to read.
Fans of Janet Evanovich's Stephanie Plum will absolutely adore Davis
Way and her many mishaps."

– *RT Book Reviews*

"A whirlwind ride, filled with clever solutions to seemingly
outlandish problems and an indomitable heroine."

– *BookLife Editor's Choice Review*

"Slot tournament season at the Bellissimo Resort and Casino
in Biloxi, Miss., provides the backdrop for Archer's enjoyable sequel
to *Double Whammy*...Credible characters and plenty of Gulf Coast
local color help make this a winner."

– *Publishers Weekly*

"Davis Way is one of the funniest sleuths in crime fiction. You'll
laugh until you cry."

– Valerie (V.M.) Burns,
Agatha, Anthony, Edgar, and Next Generation Award Nominee

"Hilarious, action-packed, with a touch of home-sweet-home
and a ton of glitz and glam. I'm booking my next vacation at the
Bellissimo!"

– Susan M. Boyer,
USA Today Bestselling Author of the Liz Talbot Mystery Series

"Seriously funny, wickedly entertaining. Davis gets me every time."

– Janet Evanovich

"Fast-paced, snarky action set in a compelling, southern glitz-and-glamour locale...Utterly un-put-down-able."

– Molly Harper,
Author of the Award-Winning Nice Girls Series

"As impressive as the amount of sheer fun and humor involved are the details concerning casino security, counterfeiting, and cons. The author never fails to entertain with the amount of laughs, action, and intrigue she loads into this immensely fun series."

– *Kings River Life Magazine*

"Filled with humor and fresh, endearing characters. It's that rarest of books: a beautifully written page-turner. It's a winner!"

– Michael Lee West,
Author of *Gone With a Handsomer Man*

"A smart, snappy writer who hits your funny bone!"

– Janet Evanovich

"*Double Trouble* was an awesome story and it is the best book in this engagingly entertaining series."

– *Dru's Book Musings*

"There is so much humor and relentless action that readers will be propelled through to the explosive finale."

– *Kings River Life Magazine*

DOUBLE BLAST

4

GRETCHEN ARCHER

**The Davis Way Crime Caper Series
by Gretchen Archer**
Novels
DOUBLE WHAMMY (#1)
DOUBLE DIP (#2)
DOUBLE STRIKE (#3)
DOUBLE MINT (#4)
DOUBLE KNOT (#5)
DOUBLE UP (#6)
DOUBLE DOG DARE (#7)
DOUBLE AGENT (#8)
DOUBLE TROUBLE (#9)
DOUBLE WIDE (#10)
DOUBLE DOSE (#11)
DOUBLE BLAST (#12)
Bellissimo Casino Crime Caper Short Stories
DOUBLE JINX
DOUBLE DECK THE HALLS
DOUBLE BLUFF
DOUBLE DEEP
DOUBLE HIGH STAKES

DOUBLE BLAST
A DAVIS WAY CRIME CAPER

Gretchen Archer

ONE

The woman I was when I left my hometown of Pine Apple, Alabama, wasn't the woman who retuned seven years later. I'd changed in ways I was aware of and in ways I would soon learn. For the most part, I looked the same, in spite of leaving Pine Apple alone, unemployed, and way down on my luck. I returned happily married with three children, somewhat gainfully employed, and keeping a steady, sometimes hectic, pace on life's happiest path.

I couldn't ask for more.

The somewhat gainfully employed part was about family leave. Formerly known as maternity leave. Either way, mine was over. I'd recently returned to work as an undercover casino spy, but barely. No more than ten hours a week tracking casino cyber cheats from my home office with the baby napping beside me. The happily married part was thanks to my husband, Bradley. Bradley Cole. The three children part was about my four-year-old identical twin daughters, Bexley and Quinn, and my new baby, Bradley Hudson Cole, Jr., who, so far, Pine Apple was calling Junior.

His name wasn't Junior.

After deciding to name the baby after his father, my husband and I agreed we didn't want two Bradleys under the same roof. That would end up Big Bradley/Little Bradley sooner rather than later, especially since our little guy was giving all indications (recently reinforced at his five-month well-baby checkup where he scored in the sixtieth percentile in height) that he might lean closer to his mother's slighter stature—I'm five foot two and a half—than his father's greater height. Which was a solid six feet. The girls looked like their father: long, lean, sun kissed, with sky-blue eyes and golden curls. Our son looked more like me: almost a redhead, almost brown eyes, and probably wouldn't be the biggest boy at T-ball. Our plan all along had been to call the baby by his middle name, Hudson, which was my mother-in-law's maiden name (it was the South; we passed down names like family photo albums full of faded history, like chipped and cracked Christmas dinnerware brought over on the Mayflower, like ancient threadbare quilts), but Hudson didn't and wouldn't stick. Mostly because his big sisters had trouble with it. Or maybe they just didn't like it. The day we brought him home from the hospital the girls called him Baby Huddle. We corrected them. "It's Hudson." They corrected us. "It's Huddle." Which quickly turned to Puddle. Which was shortened to Puddy. Which somehow became Puddy Bubby. And that wasn't going to work.

Puddy Bubby Cole?

I couldn't send a child to kindergarten named Puddy Bubby Cole.

No telling how that would turn out.

It was my father, who was the very reason I was home, to fill in for him at my old job as Pine Apple police officer while he and my mother ticked off an item on their bucket list—they were really out of town because of potato salad—who'd first called the baby Junior. "Bradley Cole, Jr.," he'd said while rocking his ten-hour-old grandson. "Junior."

"Oh, Daddy," I'd said from my vacation bed, which was really a hospital bed, but if you've ever been nine months pregnant while chasing four-year-old twins, you'd understand that a night in the hospital was a vacation, "don't call him Junior."

"Why in the world not? Junior is a fine name. It carries weight."

"It carries the weight of Beryl. Or Wilbur. Or Luther."

"Those are all fine names, Davis."

"They're old man names, Daddy."

"What do you want me to call him? Is it Houston?"

"Hudson!"

"I'll never remember that," he'd said. "Junior it is."

I'd have put a stop to it right then and there had my vacation door not filled with baby blue balloons. Behind the balloons were Hudson's big sisters, there to meet him for the very first time. And I didn't think about it again until almost six months later when everyone in Pine Apple thought I'd named my child Junior. I don't think Daddy meant for it to stick, but in the town where I was born and raised—population one grocery store, one gas station, one bank, and a dozen small but shockingly competitive churches—nicknames like Chigger, Beanpole, or Junior only had to be spoken aloud once to be carved in stone. That warm Monday morning in May as I walked the two blocks from the home I'd grown up in to my first newly deputized day on the job at Pine Apple City Hall to sit behind my father's Chief of Police desk, no less than ten heads popped out windows to say, "Hello, Junior!"

"His name isn't Junior," I called back.

"Whatever you say, Davis! And welcome home!"

The children and I crossed Banana Street, and I didn't ask if they wanted to walk two blocks north and see the ratty efficiency apartment I'd lived in before I moved to Biloxi, Mississippi, where I landed a dream job on an undercover casino security team, on the beach, no less, right before I met, fell hard for, then married their father and went on to call half of the twenty-ninth floor of the five-star Bellissimo Resort and Casino my home. Although I did take a right off Main Street after crossing Banana to The Front Porch—part general store, part antique, collectible, and curiosity shop, and noontime hot spot thanks to the old-fashioned lunch counter—to pick up my deputy. The girls ran ahead, squealing, "Aunt Merri! Cousin Riley! Granny Dee!" All of whom lived above The Front Porch. My younger sister and only sibling, Meredith, her daughter, Riley, plus our grandmother and my deputy for the next two weeks, Granny Dee, lived on the second and third floors of the restored antebellum where my father was born.

Pine Apple was full of history.

Some good.

Some not so good.

I backed the stroller up three steps and pushed through the front door of The Front Porch. One foot in, I almost put the stroller in reverse. The air inside was spicy. Like the inside of a habanero pepper. I leaned over the stroller to see if the baby's eyes were watering. "Meredith." I batted through prickly air on my way to the lunch counter in the kitchen, which seemed to be the source of the hot and heady perfume, and there was my younger sister, wearing an apron featuring a huge bottle of Texas Pete Hot Sauce and not delicately eating a chicken wing. At eight thirty in the morning. "Meredith." My throat burned. "What are you doing?"

"I'm trying to win the chicken wing cookoff."

"Could you crack a window while you're at it?"

Bex and Quinn scrambled onto counter stools patiently waiting for root beer floats, which was how my sister greeted them, with carbonation, sugar, and a cherry on top. Bex coughed and Quinn had her shirt pulled up over her nose. I threw open the kitchen door so the baby could breathe, then backtracked to prop open the front door. To let the scorched air out and fresh air in. Just in time to watch a food truck roll down Main Street.

A food truck?

In Pine Apple?

In huge flaming letters, from the front bumper to the tow hitch, the converted Airstream trailer with Mobile County license plates read, WINGS ON WHEELS. At the end of the logo was a dancing chicken. The dancing chicken was on fire. I watched as the truck slowed in front of Pine Apple Bank & Trust. Then parked. Half in the street, half on the bank's lawn, straddling the sidewalk. Anyone with banking business would have to walk around, through, or over the food truck. Having not unlocked the police station door yet, I had my first official task—a parking violation. It might be my only official task for the next two weeks, because not much happened in Pine Apple. If there was even a remote chance of anything happening, I wouldn't be there singlehandedly representing all law and all order with two feisty girls and a baby. Basically, I was a warm body to answer the phone for two weeks.

If it rang.

Back in the kitchen, I said, "Meredith, is it a coincidence that a chicken wing truck from Mobile just rolled down Main Street and parked in front of the bank?"

Pushing root beer floats larger than their heads across the lunch counter to Bex and Quinn, Meredith said, "Probably not."

"What's that supposed to mean?"

"It means they're probably in the chicken wing cookoff. And they're here to set up."

"It's a week away."

"It's less than a week away."

"Whatever. Why would a chicken truck be setting up so early?"

Meredith shrugged. "Getting a head start?"

"Do you call blocking the entrance to the bank getting a head start?"

"Tell them to move."

"I will," I said, "after you tell me when the potato salad cookoff opened to out-of-towners."

"Mobile is two hours away, Davis. That's not exactly the other side of the world. And it isn't a potato salad cookoff anymore. It's a chicken wing cookoff."

I knew that, but the combination of the words potato, salad, and cookoff were so burned into my brain, they were the words that spilled out of my mouth. All our lives, and before that, probably going back to prehistoric times, Pine Apple ushered in summer and honored the three Wilcox County heroes who'd sacrificed their lives for our country in three different wars by hosting a Memorial Day Celebration. It started with a pancake breakfast and street fair on Saturday morning, ended with a parade and fireworks show on Monday, but the real deal had always been the potato salad cookoff on Sunday afternoon. Every year the same fifty women entered the competition and every year the same woman won. Our mother. She'd won so many times she could wallpaper the living room with her potato salad ribbons. A little tired of it, and on the heels of the previous year's cookoff getting out of control with the other forty-nine entrants trying too hard to knock Mother off her potato salad throne, one with a Creole Crawfish Potato Salad that tried to kill everyone who came within ten feet of it, the Pine Apple Women's Society almost unanimously voted to stop with the potato salad and usher in a new tradition with a chicken wing cookoff.

My mother was the single holdout vote.

She refused to enter a chicken wing cookoff on principle, that principle being chicken wings weren't edible. More trouble than they were worth. And only consumed by people who weren't raised right and didn't know any better. Worse, she'd said, chicken wings would attract a rowdy crowd of beer-guzzling sports enthusiasts. Was that how we wanted to honor our fallen heroes? Mother stomped out of the meeting, yelling over her shoulder, "Why not just have a chicken feet cookoff? Or chicken lips?" She marched straight to the police station where she announced to my father that she had plans for Memorial Day. She was going on the Niagara Falls honeymoon he'd promised her almost forty years earlier. He could go on their honeymoon with her or stay in Pine Apple and eat chicken elbows alone.

Which was when he called me.

The baby was six weeks old at the time and I was beginning to feel like myself again. Partly because I was only seven pounds away from being back in my jeans, but mostly because our new little guy had slipped into our lives so easily. He was the happiest, easiest, cuddliest baby ever. He almost never cried, slept through the night like an angel, and our daughters absolutely adored their little brother. We felt complete. Complete enough for my husband to consider an offer from his alma mater to participate in an alumni teaching fellowship for two weeks at Texas Law, which was actually the University of Texas at Austin School of Law, but everyone called it Texas Law. And with sports betting soon to be on the ballot in the Lone Star State, Texas Law turned to its most successful casino attorney alum for the inside scoop on gaming.

My husband.

"If I accept, I'll be away on Memorial Day, Davis."

"What did we do last Memorial Day, Bradley?"

"I don't remember."

"Exactly," I said. "Go. It will look great on your resumé."

"My resumé? Do you know something I don't? Should I be looking for a job?"

Hardly. He was president and CEO of the Bellissimo. And he made running a billion-dollar casino resort look like running a lemonade stand.

That afternoon, my father called. Could I possibly fill in for him for two weeks in May? The last two weeks in May? "Your mother's having one of her spells."

"What about?" I'd asked.

"Potato salad and chicken knees," he'd answered.

"Do chickens have knees?"

"Surely they do."

I hesitated.

He heard me hesitate.

"Two whole weeks?" I asked.

"It'll fly by, Sweet Pea," he answered.

"You have to know it's an honor that you'd ask me. And it would be wonderful to be home for two weeks. But Daddy—"

"Eddie and Bea," he interrupted.

Eddie was my ex-ex-husband, who I desperately didn't want to marry either time. Bea was his mother. And she was worse. "Yes," I confirmed.

"You won't have to worry about either of them, Sweet Pea. Not Eddie or Bea."

"I know he's working out of town, but what about Bea? I really don't want to spend two weeks with Bea."

"She won't be here. Neither will be in town while you're filling in for me."

"Are you sure?"

"I'm positive."

Not once, not ever, had my father told me something was true that wasn't. And the dates Bradley would be in Texas and Daddy needed help were only off by one. Spending two quiet weeks in Pine Apple with my sister, my niece, and my grandmother would be perfect. There'd be plenty of help with the baby. Bex and Quinn could decorate their bikes and ride them in the Memorial Day Parade. And there I was.

"Why chicken wings?" I asked my sister.

"Why not chicken wings?" she asked back.

"A chili cookoff would make more sense."

"A chili cookoff at the end of May?"

She had a hot point. She went on to tell me the Women's Society had considered a cake bake-off, but cakes were voted down because of our mother's banana pudding poke cake. Same with pies because of Mother's chocolate chip pecan pie. "So the Women's Society kept going until they found a food they knew Mother wouldn't cook?"

"That," Meredith said, "and a chicken wing food truck was in town for Customer Appreciation Day at the bank."

"Since when did the bank appreciate its customers?"

"Since never, but everyone appreciated the chicken wings. You should have seen the food truck, Davis. It was called Lord of the Wings, and the people cooking and serving the wings were dressed like little hobbits. Everyone went nuts and here we are."

"Does Mother know you're trying to win the chicken wing cookoff?" I asked my sister.

"Absolutely not."

"Does Mother know you've entered the chicken wing cookoff?"

"Of course not."

By then, she'd freed her nephew from his stroller. She gave him a good look, a kiss on the top of his head, and a baby snuggle. "Hello, there Juuuun—" she cut her eyes at me "—bug!"

Bex and Quinn danced in their seats. "Junebug! Junebug!"

"Don't start that, Meredith. His name is Judson."

Her head snapped my way, her mouth dropped open, and laughter escaped. "What did you say?"

"Hudson!" Although I'd heard myself too. With all the Junior business, then the girls yelling Junebug, the J slipped out. "The baby's name is Hudson!"

"Sure it is."

"It is!"

"One of these days we'll figure out what to call him." Meredith bounced the baby on her hip. "What are you feeding him? Biscuits and gravy? T-bone steaks? Fried pork chops?" Said the woman who'd just served my daughters ice cream for breakfast. "Not that there's anything wrong with a roly-poly baby." Said the woman who gave birth to my nine-pound niece. "Maybe we should call him Tank. Or Chunk. Or Block." Said the woman who threatened to kill me when the fascinating concept of spelling took over my second-grade life and I found the name "Edith" inside "Meredith" and called her that.

Once.

"None of those are his name and never will be—" I almost called her Edith just to make my point. "He'll lose his baby fat as soon as he starts crawling. Which could be any minute."

"He's five months old, Davis. He isn't even close to crawling."

"He's almost six months old, Dr. Spock, and between now and when he does crawl, please call him by his name."

"Which is?"

I said, "Hudson!" just as one of the root beer float twins said, "Junebug!" and the other said, "Muddy Puddy Hula Bubby!"

I threw my hands in the air and Meredith wisely changed the subject. "Isn't it wonderful having a boy in the family? We have no brothers, no boy cousins. We don't even have an uncle."

We didn't have an aunt either because our parents were only children. Which left me and only me to stand up for her when our mother found out her favorite daughter had betrayed her. Something I felt compelled to point out.

"How am I betraying Mother?" Meredith asked.

"By entering the chicken wing cookoff."

"I'm not officially entered." Just then my deputy appeared in the doorway. I did a double take, recovered quickly, and opened my mouth to say hello to my grandmother just as Meredith finished with, "You are."

I wasn't sure if I should ask my grandmother to buckle herself into her stairlift and ride right back upstairs to change clothes or if I should tackle my sister for throwing me under the bus with our mother by entering *me* in the chicken wing cookoff when a clipped summons rang in from the open front door.

"Hey," a not particularly friendly voice called out. "Is anyone here?"

"At the lunch counter!" Meredith yelled an inch from the baby's ear, which didn't bother him a bit. Thanks to his big sisters, he was very accustomed to sudden and loud noises.

In stepped a woman who'd disappeared from my life twenty years earlier. A blast from my past. A long-gone moment in time. It was Florida. Florida Simmons. Willowy, porcelain pretty, exotic, and voluptuous Florida Simmons. She hadn't changed a bit. She looked for all the world like she'd just stepped out of Spanish II and was on her way to her locker before fifth-period chemistry lab. Her family moved to Pine Apple from Prattville, Alabama, eighty miles or so up the road, when her parents acquired controlling interest in Pine Apple Bank & Trust. We were fifteen. With an eye lock during third-period geometry as Florida was introduced to our class, we became the fastest of friends. I'd grown up looking for a lifeline in Pine Apple with my sister being more popular than I was with the other four or five girls anywhere near our ages, which was still the case, and it all ended that day in third-period geometry with Florida. I'd found a friend of my very own. But it only lasted until my world caved in less than a year later.

I didn't stay in touch.

With anyone.

Including Florida.

By the time I returned to Pine Apple years later with two undergraduate degrees from the University of Alabama at Birmingham and, having just completed my officer training at Alabama Law Enforcement Academy, a new gun and fresh patrol uniforms—one of which my grandmother was wearing at the moment, and not only did it not fit her at all, it wasn't so fresh anymore—Florida was long gone. I knew she and her father, Frank, dropped off the Pine Apple map at the same time I had, and that her mother, Fiona, had gone into hiding. And that was about all I knew. That was about all anyone knew. Florida and her father were never heard from again. Fiona unhappily resurfaced after securing financing to reopen the town's only bank. The same bank her husband robbed. Pine Apple residents learned the hard way not to ask Fiona Simmons about her long-lost husband or her estranged daughter lest they be slapped outright or with hefty bank fines. And while everyone knew where Frank Simmons was (the Federal Correction Institution in Talladega, Alabama), no one knew where Florida was or what had become of her. Pine Apple didn't know if she'd joined a convent, moved to Canada to save whales, or married an oligarch and lived in a Russian palace.

And there she was.

With a teenage son.

Who was the spitting image of my ex-ex-husband, Eddie the Idiot.

Eddie, even Eddie, who took off his shoes to count on his toes if the number he was looking for went into double digits, could have done the math. The child was conceived and born while Eddie and I were married. Which stirred up zero emotion directed at him. The only thing Eddie Crawford could stir up in me was irritation. When it came to her, though, to the woman standing in front of me with a teenage boy who was the spitting image of my ex-ex-husband, I was instantly hopping mad. And my anger was pointed straight at her. I was immediately and completely furious. With her.

I couldn't and didn't speak.

Meredith couldn't and didn't speak.

Bex and Quinn didn't say anything because they were busy with their root beer floats, not that they'd have had anything to say about Eddie the Adulterer procreating while married to their mother had they not been busy with their root beer floats.

It was my grandmother, Granny Dee, swimming inside my old Pine Apple police uniform, looking for all the world like she needed to be holding a senior citizen trick-or-treat bag on her way to ring doorbells hoping for fun-sized protein drinks, who spoke up. Probably because she was decades past holding her tongue. "I'll be a monkey's uncle." She stared openly at the teenager. "It's like Eddie Crawford is a boy again. He's Eddie Junior. Hello there, Junior."

Florida Simmons pulled a folded sheet of paper from her back pocket and waved it. "What do I do with this?"

"What is it?" Meredith asked.

"My entry form for the chicken wing cookoff."

"You must be the last-minute entry."

Florida didn't confirm or deny.

Meredith held out a hand. "You can leave it with me."

Florida slammed the sheet of paper on the lunch counter. Then turned on my ninety-year-old grandmother. "His name isn't Junior."

The room stood still in their wake with the only sound being that of spoons inside soda glasses and the steam pouring from my angry ears until Meredith said, "Davis! What is wrong with you? What's it to you if Eddie has a son? It was a million years ago. Look." She dangled my son in the air between us. "Look." She gave the root beer float slurpers a nod. "Look what you have. Why do you care?"

"Girl codes," our grandmother said.

"No." I pulled a chair from under a Formica-topped luncheon table and sat in it hard. "It isn't girl code, Granny. Good for Eddie if he has a son."

"Then what?" Meredith asked.

"What, honey?" Granny added.

"The money." I looked back and forth between my sister and my grandmother. "Florida came back to Pine Apple for the money."

The silence as my sister and grandmother processed the possibility of Florida Simmons knowing the location of the money her father picked straight from Pine Apple pockets when he emptied the bank, hid the money, then disappeared into the night so many years ago, thinking enough time had passed that she could show up and retrieve the money no one had been able to locate in all that time, and under the cover of the Memorial Day festivities with me and only me in a position of authority to stand in her way, was finally broken by a muted trill. It was my phone. I patted pockets. No phone. My eyes darted around the room until they lit on the baby's stroller. My phone was deep inside the diaper bag. By the time I'd excavated it, I'd missed the call. I shook it in the air. "Daddy."

"That was Daddy?" Meredith asked.

"Samuel called?" my grandmother asked.

"How does he already know she's back?" I asked.

They shrugged.

I dialed Daddy's number. It went straight to voicemail. I counted to ten and dialed again. Same thing. After four attempts, I gave up, and was rewarded with the ding of a voicemail. From Daddy. Who would never stop one phone chore, that of leaving what must have been a mile-long voicemail, for another. That of answering an incoming call. I placed my phone in the middle of the lunch table and let everyone listen in.

"Davis, honey." Daddy's recorded voice sounded harried. "Two things. One, we've had a bit of an accident here. Not your mother. Or me. We're fine. It's Bea. She's twisted her ankle. According to her, she's broken it. Shattered to smithereens, she says, claiming she'll never walk again, but trust me, Sweet Pea, it's just a sprain. The problem is she was in Canada at the time of the accident. Your mother and I had turned in for the night, and Bea, saying she needed a midnight snack, boarded a GO Train in search of what she called a steamie, which is, as I understand it, a steamed hot dog, but promptly fell asleep and woke in Canada. She injured her ankle in her haste to exit the train as there was a steamie vendor at the train station and in her sights. Now your mother and I are in Canada with her. And we're finding the healthcare system here a little tricky to navigate. They're telling us it will be a twelve-hour wait to see a nurse. Up to three days to see a doctor. If we leave, we'll lose our place in what they call the queue. Bea's fine, other than she fully intends to wear down the overworked staff until she's given pain medication, and it's morphine she's demanding, when in fact it's your mother Bea's wearing down. We could rent a car and drive to Buffalo, New York, in under two hours to see a doctor at an American healthcare facility, but Bea won't hear of it. She's adamant that the Canadians are responsible for her life-threatening injuries and the Canadians will pay. I'll keep you posted. In the meantime, and the second reason I called, there's something I forgot to tell you."

My sister, my grandmother, and I exchanged glances. His voice didn't have the gravitas of he-knew-about-Florida-Simmons-showing-up-for-the-money-her-father-stole in it. So he hadn't heard she was in town.

Yet.

He hadn't heard yet.

"The fireworks for this year's Memorial Day Celebration—" his message went on "—are being supplied by a special events contractor out of Talladega. Flash Fireworks, a new company started by a retired police officer. Not completely retired, mind you. He works in corrections now, but still a former brother in blue. His men will arrive mid-week to set up in the empty two-acre lot at the corner of Wright and Oak Streets. The empty lot at the bottom of the hill. You know the hill I'm talking about, and let me assure you, it's as overgrown now as it was the last time you saw it. Far more so in fact. Which leads me to what I forgot to tell you. Tomorrow morning a weed control crew, another new contractor, this one from Montgomery, will arrive at seven to clear the hill. I don't know all the details, but from what I understand, the equipment will begin arriving today. So when the station phone starts ringing with brush mower and mulcher sightings, then noise complaints, tell everyone to relax. Roy Howdy Carter is in charge. I know that isn't great news, as you have very little patience for Roy Howdy, but I'm sure it will turn out fine. Keep in mind that he's just lost his only living relative and that he's all I have by way of help. Hope all is well, call me if you need me, kiss my grandchildren, two kisses for Junior if you don't mind, and don't worry about Bea."

My ex-ex-mother-in-law, Bea Crawford, was the last thing I intended to worry about, other than the relief of knowing she wouldn't suddenly show up when she heard Florida Simmons was in town with a boy who was clearly Eddie Crawford's son, making her the boy's grandmother. That showdown wouldn't happen on my watch with Bea indisposed in Canada. And if someone let Eddie the Idiot know, the man I'd accidentally married twice, it wouldn't be a problem for me either. Because he couldn't get to town in a hurry unless he swam. He was a fry cook on an offshore oil rig way out in the Gulf. Not that Bea and Eddie wouldn't find out, seeing as how gossip was Pine Apple's number one form of entertainment, but chances were neither would be able to make their way home until I was safely back in Biloxi. I looked up from the phone to my sister and my grandmother. "Mother and Daddy took Bea on their honeymoon?"

As it would turn out, the Bea Crawford news was the wrong takeaway from Daddy's message.

TWO

Meredith unplugged the air fryers, covered and refrigerated the chicken wings, then flipped the Be-Right-Back sign on The Front Porch door. Only giving the chicken wing truck to our right a sideways glance—no Florida, no Eddie Junior, no chickens flapping their endangered wings—we traipsed en masse the other way. To regroup. To process. And to put some space between me and Florida. A whole block of space. Which was about as much distance as could be put between the Bank Robber's Daughter and the Chief of Police's Daughter. Florida Simmons and I would be on top of each other for as long as we were both in town. Such was the topography of Pine Apple, Alabama.

I took my father's seat at the Chief of Police desk. Granny parked herself at my old patrol officer desk beside his. Having fallen asleep on the short ride over, the baby slept in his stroller between us, and Meredith sat in the visitor's chair. Bex and Quinn set up Little Critter shop in Pine Apple's only jail cell, tucking their bunnies in for their naps—always coinciding with their baby brother's naps—on Pine Apple's jail cell's only cot, which was actually a Tempur-Pedic twin with a mahogany headboard that my father stretched out in often. Every day after lunch often. (To rest his eyes.) So my mother kept the pillows fluffed, the sheets clean, and the hobnail bedspread neatly tucked.

I'd grabbed the folded sheet of paper Florida Simmons slammed on the lunch counter at The Front Porch. I pulled it from my own back pocket and spread it out on the desk while Granny Dee flipped the noisy metal clips of her industrial stainless-steel lunchbox and spread out what she'd prepared for our lunch on hers. There were four mini cans of Orange Crush soda, three packages of Little Debbie Swiss Cake Rolls, two thick sandwiches with gray interiors, cut in half and nestled in sandwich bags, and one big bag of Lay's barbeque potato chips she'd somehow stuffed into the concave lid of the lunchbox. She arranged everything by size.

"Granny," Meredith said. "It's too early for lunch."

"It's never too early for liverwurst," Granny said.

Meredith said, "Liverwurst?" to Granny, then giving the sheet of paper I was studying a nod, "What is it?" to me. "What's it say?"

"Liverwurst is delicious, nutritious, and works for every meal," Granny said. "Like liverwurst and scrambled eggs."

"Like she said, it's her chicken wing cookoff entry form," I told my sister. "And it doesn't say much."

"Liverwurst on rye toast," Granny said.

"Her address is a P. O. Box in Mobile, she left the space for her telephone number blank," I said, "and her surname is the same. Simmons."

"Liverwurst and fried onion."

"All it really says is that her chicken truck has a ten-foot canopy, and she needs this many volts and that many amps." I looked up. "She's supplying her own hundred-foot extension cord and plans on hooking up to the bank."

"So she and her mother are speaking again," Meredith said, to which I said, "So she doesn't plan on moving the chicken truck," to which Granny said, "Liverwurst salad with pineapple and pimento."

Meredith's face went blank. "Granny, that sounds nasty."

We heard a knuckle knock just before the police station door creaked open and Roy Howdy Carter, the man my father said I had very little patience for, filled it. He pulled off his hat. "Davis." Then he said hello to Meredith and Granny. "Ma'ams." He gave the imprisoned twins a nod. "Young ladies."

I stood. "Hello, Roy Howdy."

"Hey, Davis."

"I was sorry to hear about your uncle."

"I was sorry to hear about it too."

I wasn't sure what to say. According to my father, Roy Howdy hadn't been informed of his uncle's death so much as he'd found the body. Just then, he found the stroller between the two desks. "Well, there's Junior." He craned his neck and peered. "He's cute as a sack of puppies. Hey, there, Junior."

I was very sure what to say about that. "His name isn't Junior."

Granny leaned past me. "Davis's baby might have to move over on the Junior business, Roy Howdy, because we found another Junior and he's bigger," she said, "so he's more Junior than Davis's Junior. Not sure there's enough room in this town for two Juniors. Maybe we should call Davis's baby Chip. Like chip off the old block." She shook a crooked finger at me. "That makes you the old block." She finished with, "Liverwurst on saltines with a thin slice of radish."

"It's Hudson," I told Roy Howdy. "The baby's name is Hudson."

"You sure about that?"

"I'm his mother. I'm quite sure."

"Somebody needs to tell your daddy."

Were the next two weeks going to be nothing but telling people my son's name wasn't Junior? "What can I do for you Roy Howdy?"

"Did you get the memo about my weed control crew?"

"I did."

"Good deal," he placed his hat back on his head, "and good day." He was out the door then right back in. "Somebody just pulled up to your Daddy and Mama's place." Meredith and I exchanged a quick ask-and-answer glance agreeing we weren't expecting anyone in the silent way sisters do. "Nice truck," Roy Howdy added.

He backed up so I could step past him and look down the street one more block to see for myself. The nice truck parked behind my car in Mother and Daddy's driveway was a Bellissimo truck. A Chevrolet Silverado Double Cab work truck, one of a new fleet of twenty-five trucks painted signature Bellissimo blue, used by maintenance, groundskeeping, and anyone else at the Bellissimo who needed a truck to complete an assignment. My mind flew to my new dog nanny, the seventeen-year-old daughter of one of the Bellissimo's many accountants, who was supposed to be dog sitting our goldendoodle, Candy, and our Old English sheepdog, Cotton, in our twenty-ninth-floor Bellissimo home. Had she decided they were too much trouble? (Cotton often found trouble and trouble found him even more often.) Had she had enough and was delivering them to me? Before I could come up with an alternate scenario for a Bellissimo truck in my parents' driveway, like maybe the whole place had burned to the ground and someone was coming to tell me in person, the driver door opened and feet hit the ground. Even from a distance, the shoes looked familiar. They were shoes I knew. Valentinos. Worn by a six-foot-tall woman I really knew. It was my partner. Fantasy Erb. Acting lead of the Bellissimo Resort and Casino's undercover security team while I was on maternity leave. She slammed the truck door and started down the winding walk that cut through the sea of spikey flowers to Mother and Daddy's front door. I whipped my phone from my pocket and speed dialed. "Hey," I said. "What are you doing here? Why are you driving a work truck?"

"Open the door and I'll tell you," she said.

"Is everything okay?"

"Open the door."

"Are my dogs okay? Is the Bellissimo on fire?"

"Open the door, Davis."

"The door is open, Fantasy. You're in Pine Apple. We don't lock doors, but I'm not there," I said. "I'm behind you at the police station."

I watched her turn, weave back through the flowerbeds to the curb, and look.

She said, "I can't see you through the trees."

I stepped into the street and waved.

She waved back and started walking. By then, my whole gang had joined me on the sidewalk. Except the baby. Who was still asleep in his stroller between the desks. When Fantasy got within shouting distance, she did. "I'VE BEEN FIRED."

"WHAT?" I shouted back.

"I'VE BEEN FIRED!"

"*WHAT*?"

Beside me, my sister said, "Davis, lower your voice before everyone in town hears you," just as Fantasy let loose with, "FIRED! FROM MY JOB!"

"NO WAY!"

"WAY!"

Fantasy took over for me as lead of our undercover casino spy team halfway through my pregnancy. It wasn't like I had to train her to do my job; we'd worked side-by-side for the better part of seven years. She knew how to do my job. The problem was, we approached our jobs from different perspectives, so working solo, she looked at my job through her lens. I was stealthier than she was. In police officer terms, which was my background, you don't draw on someone with an empty gun. You load the gun first. Fantasy was more take-immediate-action than me. In prison guard terms, which was her background, stop a situation before it has time to start. If the gun wasn't loaded, coldcock the suspect with it. As a team, it worked. We worked. On my own, I might stay behind the scenes too long gathering evidence and let the perp slip through my fingers. On her own, she might blast in too soon and too aggressively, which still let the criminal off the hook after they filed assault charges. The truth was we worked best as a team. I held her off until we had enough evidence to turn a casino cheat over to the authorities, and she encouraged me to pounce before time ran out.

Together, we worked in perfect harmony.

Apart, we were capable of singing offkey.

By then she'd reached us, slowing on her final approach. She was wearing the same clothes I'd seen her in the day before when she helped me load my car and hugged me goodbye for two weeks. A day later, it was as if she'd fought a war in them. She looked disheveled, sleep deprived, and dehydrated. From crying.

"Fired?" I asked. "As in terminated? As in pack your things?"

"Just like that."

"Who fired you?"

"Your husband."

"He's in Texas."

"They have phones in Texas, Davis. He fired me over the phone."

From the corner of my eye, I could see we'd attracted an audience. Meredith saw it too and said, "What'd I tell you?" Across the street, Hazel Patterson of Hazel's Hairdos slowly swept her spotless porch. Her neighbor, Brownie, of Brownie's Hardware, stood at the curb staring into his empty mailbox waiting for mail to appear. On the corner to our left, Stan, of Stan's Heat and Air, toed the ground with a boot searching for imaginary weeds on his immaculate lawn. "Let's take this inside." I held the door and closed it behind everyone. Bex and Quinn ran for the jail cell. Meredith, unsure of what to do, followed the girls. Granny eased back into the chair behind my old desk. I sat down at Daddy's desk. Fantasy fell into the visitor's chair. And all of a sudden, the precinct was stuffed.

"When were you fired?" I asked. "And why?"

She threw her hands in the air and looked to the ceiling for where-do-I-start answers.

"At the beginning," I said. "Start at the beginning."

"Do you have coffee?" she asked. "I wouldn't mind starting with coffee."

Daddy brought his coffee to work in a thermos or walked to Bea's Diner, the same Bea who'd accompanied my parents to Niagara Falls and was giving the Canadian Health Act a run for its money, for a cup of the sludge she served. The only coffee at the police station was Sanka instant. Which in no way resembled coffee. Meredith released herself from Little Critter jail. "I just brewed a fresh pot of coffee at the Porch. I'll go get it." With one foot out the door and one still in, she turned back. "Granny, come help me." Then, "Girls," she said to her four-year-old cellmates, "come help Granny."

Meredith gently closed the door behind them.

Fantasy slapped her knees. "I'm in trouble."

"What kind of trouble?"

"Let me put it this way." She tipped her head back and closed her eyes. "If there isn't a warrant out for my arrest already, there will be."

"That isn't starting at the beginning."

Her eyes met mine. "I shot someone, okay, Davis?"

I sat straight up. "You what?"

"I shot someone."

"Who?"

"A punk."

"You shot a punk."

She nodded. "And I might have abducted someone."

"You might have abducted someone? Either you did or you didn't." I surrendered. "Help me out here. Did you or did you not shoot a punk, and did you or did you not abduct someone?"

"Yes and yes. I didn't mean to shoot the punk, and I certainly didn't intend to abduct anyone. But I might have kidnapped someone as opposed to abducting someone, because I crossed a state line. Which is worse? Which is the crossed-a-state-line one? Abduction or kidnapping?"

"Are we talking about one person or two people?"

"What?"

"Are they the same person?" I asked. "The person you shot and the person you abducted or kidnapped. Are they the same person?"

"No."

"Great," I said. "Two felonies." I covered my eyes with a hand to hide from her next answer before I asked, "Did you kill the punk?"

"Of course not!"

I came out from behind my hand. "It's a valid question. And appropriate, given the circumstances."

The door cracked open, and Meredith's face appeared. She held a thermal carafe in one hand and two Front Porch mugs in the other. She sat them down on the corner of Daddy's desk without a word, then slipped back out. I stood, poured, passed, then said, "Try again and start at the beginning. The very beginning."

Holding the mug with both hands, probably to keep it steady, Fantasy said, "Graduation."

"Who graduated?"

"Everyone graduated," she said. "The Bellissimo is crawling with graduates. Gulf Coast Community, Southern Mississippi, South Alabama, and LSU. Good Lord." She rolled her eyes. "LSU."

I knew all about LSU graduates. And the others. May was a month we dreaded because of the constant flow of graduates who poured out of chartered buses, blasted into the Bellissimo, and celebrated the end of their academic careers with wild abandon and what was surely every penny of the cash gifts they'd just received from their grandparents. And because the graduations were staggered between the schools, the traffic and mayhem that started the first weekend of May didn't end until after Memorial Day. We shooed out one graduating class while ushering another in. It was just short of unbearable. The graduates weren't there for the casino, the beautiful guest rooms overlooking the Gulf, the headliner acts in the Bellissimo theater, or the five-star dining. They were there to party, and that was all they did. They spent their days doubled or even tripled up on Bellissimo pool loungers sleeping off their all-nighters in the bars. Property damage went through the roof. The drunk tank below the casino stayed full. The complaints from non-commencement guests landed one on top of the other. The year before, answering a multitude of noise calls up and down the fifth floor of the hotel, Fantasy and I found twenty completely inebriated graduates and their hired help, four dancers from Luck Be a Lady Gentleman's Bar on Howard Avenue, slammed into a single guest room. And the graduates had just received their diplomas from Saint Joseph Seminary in St. Benedict, Louisiana.

"So the punk you shot was a graduate?"

"Yes."

"From which school?"

"Does it matter?"

I'd asked out of curiosity, or maybe to keep the information flowing from her, but she answered in a way that made me think it did matter. "Which school, Fantasy?"

She spoke to her coffee instead of me. "Biloxi."

"Gulf Coast Community College in Biloxi? They don't have graduation per se, do they?"

"I don't know a thing about Gulf Coast Community College."

"Then what school are you talking about? There isn't a four-year college in Biloxi."

"I'm aware."

The room grew deathly still until I broke the silence with, "Noooo."

She barely responded with, "Yessss."

"You shot a kid? You shot a kid from Biloxi High School?"

"A graduate, Davis. Are you listening? He was a graduate."

Not that the distinction would mean a thing to a judge or jury.

"Fantasy, tell me it was justified."

"I can't."

My mouth dropped open.

"Obviously I think it was a good shoot," she said, "but everyone else, not so much."

"Where is the kid?" I asked.

"Probably in surgery."

"Probably?"

"The bullet might have lodged, okay, Davis? I'm assuming he's in surgery having it removed."

"Lodged where?"

Her eyes rolled up and scanned the ceiling as if looking for the answer. "His backside."

I could barely hear myself when I said, "You shot a kid in the back?"

"His backside, Davis."

"The back side of his head? The back side of his neck?" I kept going down each of the kid's vertebra until she stopped me.

"I shot him in the ass, okay? His ass. He's going to be fine. And I didn't shoot him intentionally. I fired a warning shot in the air. It ricocheted off a chandelier ceiling plate, bounced off a Tesla windshield, and found a punk. All I did was fire a warning shot. How was I supposed to know it would make its way to a punk?"

And with that, the story I didn't think could get any worse might have. There was a strong possibility it wasn't just any Tesla. But I held my breath and held out hope, because with perfect timing, a punk, chandelier, and Tesla could be found at the Bellissimo entrance. Where permitted firearms were legal. Which wouldn't be so bad. Still bad, but not as bad as if it had happened in the middle of the casino. Where a punk, a chandelier, and a Tesla could have also lined up perfectly. And where firearms were prohibited.

"It was a Roadster," she said, "the Tesla."

A bit of my hope faded.

"A white Tesla Roadster."

All my hope faded.

She spoke her next words to the floor, but I doubted the floor could hear them through the mumble. I heard them because they were the three words I knew were coming. "In the casino."

It was clearly posted everywhere. Firearms in the casino were strictly forbidden. And that included us unless we were in pursuit of a credible threat. There were other exceptions, including cash couriers on their way to or from our vault with loads of cash, but last I checked, chasing a kid wasn't on the exception list. So she'd fired a shot into the air from a forbidden weapon in a packed-out casino that hit a chandelier, then the $225,000 Tesla Roadster that was to be raffled away on Memorial Day, before lodging into a high school kid's rear end. She was correct when she said she was in trouble. She was in big trouble. The only circumstance under which Fantasy firing off a round inside a crowded casino could be ruled a good shoot was if lives were at stake. It sounded very much like *she'd* threatened lives. And Bradley, my husband, President and CEO of the Bellissimo Resort and Casino, could have suspended her without pay pending an investigation, but according to Fantasy, he hadn't. And I wasn't sure I could blame him, because even to me it sounded cut and dried.

She watched me process the dire information, but all she had to say was, "Did you know Tesla windshields were bulletproof?"

I did not.

"Maybe they weren't meant to be, but they are," she said. "That bullet didn't even leave a scratch on the Tesla. Pinged right off the windshield and straight into that kid's ass. You should have seen it." She slurped coffee. "Ping, ping, thud."

Had I been there to see it, I'd have stopped her.

Then she said, "Maybe Tesla windshields are made of the same material as Tesla spaceship windshields."

I sat back. "How long do you want to talk about windshields?"

"I'm done." She stretched her long legs out. "However, I would like to talk about those barbeque chips." She pointed at my old desk. "I have a raging hungry headache. Are the chips up for grabs?"

I reached over my still sleeping son, grabbed the bag of chips, and tossed them to her. Thirty seconds later, peering into the bag, she said, "Who ran over these chips?" I told her Granny had stuffed them into the lunchbox lid. "They're chip dust." She eyed the sandwiches. "Did she sit on the sandwiches after she took a sledgehammer to the chips?"

"The sandwiches are liverwurst."

She shuddered at the very thought, and shuddered so hard, I heard a rumbling. I peeked at the baby, still fast asleep. I eyed her a little closer, wondering how long it had been since she'd eaten, wondering if the barbeque chip dust was hitting rock bottom, because I heard the rumbling again. A little louder that time. And decided it was coming from outside. Cutting my eyes to the station's commercial storefront window and seeing nothing happening on Main Street, I turned back to Fantasy.

"There's something you need to know, Davis."

I waited.

"He was packing."

A breath of relief escaped my lips. A really good attorney could argue self-defense.

"Except, as it turned out, he was packing a paintball gun."

I landed an elbow on the desk, slapped my forehead with the palm of my hand to hold my head up, and stared down at Daddy's police blotter. "What," I said to the blotter, "happened?"

"So," she said through a mouth full of annihilated chips, "Whiskey."

I picked my head up just far enough to see her. "Whiskey?" I asked. "The kid was drinking whiskey?"

"No," she said. "Whiskey the person."

"Our Whiskey?"

"The same."

"What in the world does shooting a kid have to do with Whiskey?"

Whiskey, a Bellissimo fixture, was somewhere between fifty and eighty. It was hard to tell. He reminded me very much of a penguin: he had somewhat of a dapper charm about him, he was short and portly, and he waddled. And in spite of the fact that Whiskey had a home, a home he supposedly shared with his spinster sister, his mailing address was the casino's. Because most nights he hung his hat in our drunk tank. His car was rigged with a breathalyzer after multiple drunk driving incidents, so he showed up at the drunk tank desk four or five nights a week and checked himself in with something like, "Regrettably, my vehicle is in a state of malfunction, and I would very much appreciate accommodations for the night." When it came to Whiskey, our casino staff fell into one of two groups: those who wouldn't serve him alcohol and those who served him doubles when he ordered singles. Team Save Whiskey wanted to help him sober up and was made up of bartenders who either refused to serve him or diluted his drinks to 99 percent tonic, and of servers who, spotting Whiskey, made U-turns. On the other hand, Team Shut Up Whiskey plied him with alcohol. Because anywhere near sober Whiskey was a chatterbox. He'd park himself at one of the many Bellissimo bars and start slinging obscure words around. Lots of them. It distracted both the bartenders, servers, and casino guests to no end. And last I heard, Team Shut Up Whiskey was winning, because Whiskey had learned to work around Team Save Whiskey. He taught himself to sneak up behind servers and lift drinks off their trays, talk other unsuspecting casino guests into ordering drinks for him, which wasn't too hard because the drinks were free, and when all else failed, he strolled up and down the slot aisles slamming back libatious leftovers he found between the machines. It was as if, after losing his lifelong job as a crossword puzzle constructor for *The New Orleans Time-Picayune* when it suddenly shut down, Whiskey preferred inebriation and the drunk tank to sobriety and home with his spinster sister. Several months earlier, we started receiving mail addressed to him. The mailroom call came to me. "What should we do with Whiskey's mail?" At the time, I had a two-month-old and didn't care about Whiskey's mail. "Deliver it to his cot in the drunk tank," I'd said. "Good idea," the mailroom woman said. And the beat went on.

"What about Whiskey?" I asked Fantasy.

"I was taking him home."

There were several reasons Whiskey might need a ride home. Some nights his sister would call the switchboard and have him paged every fifteen minutes because it was his turn to haul the garbage bins to the curb. Or because he'd eaten her Swanson's Chicken Parm Dinner. Or because his cat, Eight Across, wouldn't stop whining. Everyone in the casino grew weary of it. So someone or another would track down Whiskey and give him a ride home. Other nights, Whiskey wanted to go home and asked us to call him a cab. And still other nights, usually weekend nights, we sent him home because we needed his drunk tank cot. Which turned out to be the case the night before.

"It was two o'clock this morning," Fantasy said. "Maybe three. I'd just finished rounding up LSU graduates and dragging them by their Jack and Coke ears to the drunk tank, where we had a full house. I told Whiskey to get up, I was taking him home because we needed his bed, but he was still plastered after playing tequila pong all night with Southern Mississippi graduates and I didn't want my car to smell like tequila for a week. So I went to Valet to ask for one of the new Bellissimo trucks, thinking the new truck smell would drown out the tequila fumes, but I didn't have to because there was one already parked at the front door. Valet was nowhere to be found, so I couldn't exactly ask to borrow the truck for ten minutes just to get Whiskey home, but there were the keys, dangling on the Valet key board. So I helped myself."

My head shot right to give Main Street another glance out the window, because I heard the rumbling again. Closer that time. I hadn't imagined it. Was it thunder? Looking out the window and still seeing nothing but clear blue skies dotted with innocent white clouds in the distance, I rolled a keep-going hand.

"I clocked out, got my purse, then hauled Whiskey to Valet on a luggage cart." She dropped the empty barbeque chip dust bag on the floor and ran her hands down her thighs. Her dirty jeans barely noticed. "I'd just finished pouring him into the backseat when a black panel van pulled up. You know how in the movies it's always a white panel van? It was a black panel van. And it didn't roll up so much as it came in hot and slammed the brakes about an inch from the brand new Bellissimo truck with passed-out Whiskey inside. The side door of the van slid open and at least thirty naked punks piled out, all packing, and all running."

"Naked? Packing? Running?"

"Davis," she leaned in, "they all had paintball guns that looked exactly like pistols. They looked more like Smith & Wessons than Smith & Wessons look like Smith & Wessons. And they were all in front of me. I never had the chance to see the orange tag on the barrel identifying them as paintball guns. I saw naked punks with Smith & Wessons running wide open for the casino. That's what I saw."

I rolled my keep-going hand again.

"Gulfport High School," she said.

"I thought we were talking about Biloxi High School."

"We were, but Gulfport High School graduated yesterday."

It was my first hint as to the next chapter of her story, because the rivalry between the two high schools was epic.

"Last night, the Gulfport graduates were in the conference center ballroom above the casino for their graduation dance. Thirty naked Biloxi punks who wanted to paint the Gulfport Admiral blue ballroom Biloxi Indian Nation red with paintball guns piled out of the black panel van, blew through the front doors, mowed down everyone in their way, flew past security, and all the way into the casino."

"So you chased them."

"Of course I chased them. Anyone in any position of authority would have chased them. If you'd been in my shoes, Davis, you'd have chased thirty naked punks all carrying Smith & Wessons through the casino too. And you'd have identified yourself over and over again, ordering them to stop the whole time just like I did. And if none of that worked, you'd have fired a warning shot. Like I did."

The rumbling outside had gotten so loud it interrupted us, and that time I heard loud voices trying to shout over it. Raised and argumentative. Too far away for me to catch anything, but one sounded like Roy Howdy Carter and the other sounded like my grandmother. I stood to investigate, but before I could clear the desk, I thought of something. "Where's Whiskey?"

"Sleeping it off in the backseat of the Bellissimo truck."

Three things happened at once. The relief that flooded me after hearing the details of Fantasy's Bellissimo shoot, which there was a small chance could be ruled justified, especially if our surveillance footage backed her up, dissipated with the realization that Whiskey was passed out in my parents' driveway. Two, the baby woke up, saw Fantasy, and tried to jump out of his stroller to get to her. I caught him just in time. And three, the floor started shaking. The next thing that happened was the most terrifying of all. The police station's storefront windows filled. With goats. They stared at us, and we stared right back at them.

The baby was thrilled.

Me and Fantasy, not so much.

THREE

The goats were absolutely everywhere. They were up, down, and all over Main Street. There were hundreds upon hundreds of goats. There might have been a thousand goats. Across the street, Hazel's Hairdos' previously spotless porch was full of goats. Next door, the red flowering mandevilla that had been climbing up Brownie's Hardware's mailbox post was gone. Eaten by goats. And to our left, on the corner, wide swaths of Stan's Heat and Air's formerly immaculate lawn were gone, trampled and upturned by goats. So many goats.

"What in the world?" Fantasy was by my side at the window. "It looks like the Bible out there."

I could do nothing but gape in stunned horror knowing I was in charge. The goats were my problem. And I didn't have a clue as to how to solve a single goat problem. Much less hundreds upon hundreds of goat problems. The noise was almost unbearable, and we were inside. Every dog in town was barking at top volume, every cow in every nearby pasture was at its fence trying to moo the goats away, every bird was out of every tree warning every other bird in the Southeast at the top of its bird lungs, every resident and proprietor up and down Main Street was either in the middle of the goats objecting or halfway out a window protesting, and above it all, every goat was bleating. I could see Roy Howdy, who was hanging from a lamppost—halfway up, legs wrapped around—arguing with my grandmother. Who was standing in the middle of the street outside of The Front Porch wearing the tatters of my old patrol uniform, batting off the goats who were nibbling away at the fabric. I couldn't hear what they were accusing each other of for the goats. And dogs. And cows. And birds. And business owners. And residents. My best guess was that my grandmother was reading Roy Howdy his rights. I passed the baby to Fantasy, ran for the storage closet in the kitchenette, knocked traffic cones and school crossing signs out of my way, then grabbed the bullhorn. With my hand on the doorknob, I turned to Fantasy. "Whatever happens, do not step outside with my baby."

Wide-eyed, she nodded emphatically.

I said, "Stand back."

She stood back all the way into the jail cell.

I eased the door open an inch.

The goats immediately swarmed.

I put the bullhorn to the sliver of daylight and pulsed the siren.

The goats backed up.

I siren-beeped my way past them until I made it ten feet to Daddy's patrol car at the curb. I scrambled up the hood backwards, beeping goats away the whole time, but the hood wasn't high enough off the ground. One of the goats reared up and landed his two front hooves an inch from my feet, so I kept scrambling until I'd reached the roof. I tried to stand on the siren bar. By then, two goats had climbed the hood. Behind me, three goats had climbed the back bumper and were pounding their hooves into the trunk. Daddy's patrol car was in motion, like a goat-powered seesaw, so I sat on the siren bar to keep from falling and being eaten by goats. My lips to the mouthpiece, I pressed the intercom button of the bullhorn and yelled, "ROY HOWDY CARTER! WHAT THE HOLY HELL? IS THIS WHAT YOU CALL A WEED CONTROL CREW?"

Everything quieted, even the cows, with the noted exception of the goats.

Roy Howdy yelled over them. "SOMETHING'S GONE WRONG, DAVIS."

"YOU THINK?"

My sister's voice broke through, screaming at my grandmother, then I watched four goats follow Granny up three steps. The door barely opened, my sister's arm shot out, she caught Granny by the collar, and jerked her inside. It was then that I saw Florida Simmons safely under the canopy and leaning out the open window of her chicken wing truck tossing celery to goats.

She saw me too.

She waved a celery stalk at me. Grinning from ear to ear, clearly enjoying herself, she leaned all the way across the serving counter to yell, "HOW'S IT GOING, DAVIS?"

FOUR

I learned more about goats in the next three hours than I'd learned in the previous thirtysomething years. And I grew up in the country. I'd been around goats all my Alabama life. But not that many at one time. And not as hungry as these goats were. One thing I learned was they were pack animals. They stuck together. The most troublesome goats were the ones who wandered off from the horde and couldn't find their way back. Their bleats were shrill, insistent, continuous, and if I spoke goat, which I didn't, I'd have said to the stranded goats, "Pipe down. Someone will come get you in a minute." Another thing I learned was the ones with beards, the billy goats, had anger management issues. I learned that the creepy eyes on the sides of their heads, the eyes with the disturbing rectangular pupils, gave the goats almost 360-degree vision. There was no sneaking up on an animal with eyes in the back of its head. Another thing I learned was that they would eat anything not nailed down and they chewed in a roundabout way; their mouths rolled around in a disturbing circle rather than chomping up and down. And the multitude of goats in question, apparently having been on a diet for days, weeks maybe, from the looks of things, in anticipation of their weed control job, were starving. They indiscriminately ate everything in sight. They were biters. And kickers. They were jumpers. And incredible climbers. Before my sister had the good sense to call a man who raised border collies in Camden, twenty miles west of Pine Apple, there were goats who'd climbed to the roofs of carports, garages, and even homes. The loudest goat on the face of the earth was a kid who climbed two flights of rickety steps to Pine Apple Baptist's bell tower. He was stuck up there for more than an hour and we almost lost our minds. Not only was the goat, who found his way up but couldn't find his way down, crying nonstop, he kept banging into the church bell, all of which was broadcast for miles from the echo chamber

43

that was the bell tower. It was only after four border collies from Camden arrived and herded the goats into Pine Apple High School's gymnasium—a terrible temporary solution for a holding pen, but it was all we had—that we could halfway breathe. And had Pine Apple smelled any better at that point, we might've been able to breathe deeply. The unpleasant aroma was only matched by the horrific vista: mayhem and destruction. It was as if a smelly tornado had ripped through Pine Apple.

When most of the goats were locked in the high school gym, we gathered at City Hall. And by we, I meant me and hundreds of goat-battered residents and business owners. I slowly walked up the steps to address the crowd. I picked up the bullhorn.

"First of all—" I accidentally hit both buttons at the same time, the siren and the speaker, and the bullhorn broadcast an amplified screech that was by far louder than the goats. There were outcries and the slapping of hands over ears. I sat the bullhorn at my feet and raised my voice with as much of a smile as I could muster. "Hello, Pine Apple!"

Dirty, weary, and strangely accusatory faces stared back.

As if the goats were my fault.

I blew hair out of my face and kept going.

"As you all know, my father is out of town. You've got me."

There was murmuring. There were scoffs. There were sneers. I was met with a universal vote of no confidence. So much for Mrs. Nice Guy. I picked up the bullhorn again and gave it a siren beep in the air to quiet my hostile audience. When they settled down, I put my lips to the bullhorn speaker, hit the button, and slowly said, "I'm not a bit happier about this than you are. No one will be unhappier about it than my father. And if anyone breathes a word of this to him before I have a chance to get to the bottom of what happened and before we work together to clean up this mess, I'll lock you up and throw away the key. Do you hear me?"

They heard me. And the general consensus being I possessed sneaky Big City ways of taking out casino enemies using devious computer tricks, and if those didn't work, back-alley mob-style hits, had them listening.

"Roy Howdy Carter?"

He didn't make his presence known, but a wide circle around him cleared. He lifted a limp arm. "Hey, Davis."

"Don't you 'Hey, Davis,' me, Roy Howdy. March yourself to the police station and stay there until I get there."

A diagonal path cleared to show him the way.

He slinked down it.

"I need a volunteer to coordinate cleanup." There was much shuffling, absentminded whistling, and idle searching of the sky. "Bubba Jackson?" The crowd parted until Bubba was standing all by his lonesome. "You'll direct cleanup efforts." Bubba scratched his head. "Everyone else, go home. Get your brooms, your mops, your shovels, your rakes, your wheelbarrows, your wagons, and every Hefty Lawn and Garden bag you have under your sink. Anyone with a pressure washer, bring it. Anyone with a shop-vac, bring it. Anyone with a leaf blower, bring it. We have less than a week to put our town back together."

"Will your daddy be home in less than a week?" someone in the crowd called out.

"Memorial Day is in less than a week," I said.

In the melee of goats, the town had all but forgotten.

I stepped down and the crowd parted for me.

I followed Roy Howdy's path and slammed the police station door behind me. I breezed past him, holding up a wait-a-minute finger, then had a seat behind my father's desk. There was a sticky note from Fantasy on my laptop. *I took the baby to your sister's so I could check on Whiskey.* I tossed it and opened the computer. I hacked into T-Mobile, found my father's, mother's, and Bea

Crawford's phones, then temporarily blocked their phones from making or receiving calls from area code 251. It wouldn't keep them from hearing the news—for all I knew everyone in town had already called my father—but it would slow things down. I slammed my laptop closed a lot harder than I intended to and moved on. To Roy Howdy.

"Sit down." I pointed to what was previously the visitor chair. I repurposed it to the perp chair. Because Roy Howdy was in big trouble. I reached into my t-shirt and pulled out my phone, along with a stem holding the smashed dregs of wild blackberries I'd picked up somewhere along the goat way, which was almost good news, because I'd wondered what the scratchy sticky smear on my t-shirt was but hadn't had time to investigate. The dark blob was pulverized blackberries. And the reason my phone was in my bra was because the pockets of my previously white jeans had been sacrificed to goats. I was lucky I still had a phone. When it hit the ground after my back pockets turned into goat snacks, it was all but trampled. Which was when it went to my bra. I shook it at Roy Howdy. (My phone. Not my bra.) "Don't move a muscle while I check on my children."

"Any chance you'd mind me going to the little boy's room?"

"So you can sneak out the backdoor? Yes, I mind. Keep your seat."

My phone was a mess. There were countless missed calls from the Bellissimo, all, I felt certain, were about Fantasy. Four calls from my husband. The first three were probably about Fantasy. The fourth was probably wondering why I wasn't answering my phone. I shot him a quick text message saying I'd been gathering wild blackberries, which was true, and otherwise busy trying to fill Daddy's shoes, also true, and I'd call him soon. He texted back. *Don't worry about calling right away. I'm up next at the Texas Law podium. It sounds like you're having a great Pine Apple time. I'm happy for you. I bet the girls loved picking blackberries. I bet my boy loved the fresh country air. Quickly,*

Davis, I need to tell you my side of the story, actually Biloxi PD's side of the story, when you have a minute. I'm sure you've heard Fantasy's side by now. Tell her to turn herself in. Call when you can. I'd missed two calls from my father before I'd blocked his phone. That struck fear in my soul. He needed to hear the goat story from me. I needed to know the goat story before I could tell it. I didn't want Roy Howdy to hear whatever it was Daddy had to say, then blab it all over town, so I read the transcribed version of his voicemails. The first one said, *Sweet Pea, we've had an unfortunate development. Bea overheard an amputation being discussed between a surgeon and a scheduling nurse (the pinkie toe of an elderly diabetic patient) and things have escalated to an entirely new level. Bea is convinced they were secretly discussing her and intend to amputate her leg. She's demanding to be extricated by Navy SEALs. She's insisting someone put her in touch with hostage negotiators at The White House. No one can calm her. If they don't sedate her soon, I will be forced to take matters into my own hands. How? I haven't figured it out yet. If she doesn't calm down, it might take a baseball bat. I'm calling to see how the weed control is going. Let me know.* His second message said, *Sweet Pea, is there any truth to the rumor that Pine Apple's Prodigal Daughter has returned?*

It was a good thing I'd blocked his phone. Because someone had already snuck in a call to him about Florida Simmons. I opened my laptop, bypassed the block on his phone, but only long enough to shoot him a quick text. *All is well, Daddy. Good luck with Bea.*

I called my sister. "Are my children okay?"

"The girls are at the lunch counter watching *PAW Patrol* and eating chicken wings."

"They can't eat chicken wings, Meredith. They'll choke on chicken bones."

Roy Howdy piped up from the perp chair. "I wish I was choking on chicken bones."

I didn't say, "Me too," because just then, my sister said, "They're boneless."

"Surely you're not feeding the baby chicken wings."

Roy Howdy said, "I wish somebody would feed me chicken wings."

Meredith said, "Of course not."

I asked, "Is Fantasy with you?"

"I think she's still at Mother and Daddy's. Mother's flowers are gone, Davis. All her dahlias and zinnias were wiped out. And it looks like someone took a shovel to every square inch of the yard. There isn't a blade of grass left."

"What are dahlias and zinnias?"

"Flowers, Davis. The hundreds of bright red, yellow, orange, pink, and purple flowers in Mother's flowerbeds are gone."

I told Meredith we'd take care of the dahlias and zinnias before Mother returned. She said that wasn't possible unless I had a greenhouse in my back pocket, and that certainly wasn't the case because I no longer had back pockets. Meanwhile, Roy Howdy shuffled in his seat. Checked the clock on the wall. Checked his phone for messages. And apparently with chicken wings on his brain, checked out the liverwurst sandwiches still on my old patrol desk. I tossed him one and told Meredith to keep the children inside and I'd see her as soon as humanly possible. By then, thirty whole seconds later, the first liverwurst sandwich was gone. I reloaded Roy Howdy with an Orange Crush soda and the second liverwurst sandwich. I caught my breath for the additional thirty seconds it took for him to inhale both.

"Good stuff." He pounded his chest with a fist to help it all down.

"Roy Howdy." I sat back. Crossed my arms. I tipped my head back, leading with my chin, and narrowed my eyes. To finish setting the mood. "Why did my father tell me to look for brush mowers and mulchers to clear the hill at Wright and Oak Streets? How did he not know you'd arranged for hundreds of wild goats to clear it?"

"I forgot to tell him?"

"Are you asking me or telling me, Roy Howdy?"

"Are we still talking about the goats?"

I took a deep breath and spoke slower. "Did you originally hire a landscaping company to clear the hill, then change your mind?"

"My mind." He put a hand on his head. Probably to make sure his mind was still in there after losing his hat to a goat. "What's the question?"

"Was it your idea to bring goats to Pine Apple?"

"No."

"Whose idea was it?"

"I was out having lunch—" which must have reminded him of the lunch he'd just scarfed down, because he pounded his chest again "—barbeque and hot slaw and fried corn—"

I interrupted. "Whose idea was it to bring goats to Pine Apple?"

"Mine."

"You just said it wasn't."

"Not at first. But then it was. Because I got some real good advice while I was having barbeque that was way cheaper and more environment friendly."

"Someone gave you cheaper and environmentally friendly barbeque advice?"

"Someone gave me cheaper and environment friendly weed advice."

I waited.

"—while I was having barbeque."

"So the goats weren't your idea."

"Yes."

"Yes they were or yes they weren't?"

"Half and half."

I was going to lose my mind. And I had a sneaking suspicion who the other half of the equation was, because there was only one place in town that served barbeque. Very bad barbeque, I might add. Scooped out of huge Costco tubs and microwaved to near death. "Were the goats Bea Crawford's idea? Were you having Friday Barbeque at Bea's Diner and she suggested the cheaper and more environmentally friendly goats?"

Roy Howdy was genuinely impressed. "How'd you know that?"

"Where's the paperwork?"

"What paperwork?"

"Surely there's a paper trail of your agreement with the goat contractor."

He pointed at the circa 1980 Commodore 64 monstrosity covering half of my father's desk. "Should be all up in there, Davis. I wrote it down and Bea typed it all in."

Great. It would take an hour to turn on Daddy's old computer. I didn't have an hour. "Do you remember how many goats you ordered?"

He answered quickly and confidently. "Ten."

"Do you remember the name of the company?"

"Something about goats but not exactly."

"Not exactly what?"

"I don't remember the exact name."

"But you've spoken to them?"

He nodded. "Lots." He pounded his chest again. "Was that Spams?"

I picked up the station phone's cordless receiver. "What are you talking about?"

"The sandwiches. Spams?"

"Spams?" He wasn't talking about junk mail. He was talking about gelatinous canned mystery meat. "No," I said. "Liverwurst."

"Oh, hell." His head fell back. "Me and liverwurst ain't friends."

"Uhm." I had nothing. "We'll make this quick."

"Why didn't you tell me that was liverwurst?"

"Because I was checking on my children. How did you not know it was liverwurst when you bit into it?"

Roy Howdy pounded his chest again. "I already got the heartburn."

I poked a big red square along the row of buttons on the station phone base, then the speaker button. I spoke over the dial tone. "What's the number?"

Roy Howdy very hesitantly guessed. "Four?"

I leaned in. "The goat company's phone number. If you've talked to them lots you should have their phone number."

Roy Howdy held up a gotcha finger, then fumbled for his phone and began scrolling. When he found it, I dialed as he read the numbers slowly and at top volume.

A man with a testy voice answered on the first ring. "Graze Away Goat Rental, Home of Hassle-Free Brush Removal and Weed Control. This is Bobby."

"Bobby, my name is Davis Way Cole. I'm acting chief of police in Pine Apple, Alabama."

"Boy, I wouldn't want to be you right now, lady."

"Bobby, I wouldn't want to be *you*."

I went left, he went right. I lobbed, he volleyed. I pinged, he ponged. When I grew weary of his refusal to accept responsibility for the goat invasion, I threw a few litigious and negative Yelp review threats his way until he finally admitted the fault was Graze Away's. Bobby blamed his sorry dispatcher, who'd stayed up all night "honky tonking," for mistakenly sending the truck headed to Mobile to clear off two thousand acres for a "stripper mall" to us, and mistakenly sending the ten goats we'd ordered for our one-acre hill to them. According to Bobby, Mobile had it worse than we did because it was too late for them to cancel their scheduled excavators. Which he called scheduled escalators. Graze Away caught the mistake when the job site in Mobile called to ask when the rest of the goats would arrive, which was when the sorry dispatcher found the semi-truck full of famished goats who were supposed to be in Mobile on State Route 10 instead. Headed west instead of south, and at the time, less than two miles from Pine Apple. He told the driver to turn around and take the goats to Mobile. The driver tried to turn around on the two-lane road with nothing but front yards and fields on either side and ended up busting an axle after jackknifing at the Welcome to Pine Apple sign. Which upset the goats. Who the driver said rammed the gate until they were free. Which was when Bobby fired the sorry dispatcher. He finished with, "I should've waited to fire him till this mess was cleaned up, because I need my goats back."

"Please," I said, "come get them."

"Can't hardly, because the road into your town is blocked."

"By your truck, Bobby."

"I'm working on that."

"Working on it how?"

"I sent a wrecker for the busted rig. Once it's cleared, I'll send another truck."

"Send the other truck now."

"How am I supposed to send a truck if the road's blocked?"

"We're talking about twenty miles of a two-lane road, Bobby. It's okay if two trucks are on it. By the time the second truck gets here, the wrecker you say is on the way will have cleared the road."

"That's three trucks, lady, when you add on the wrecker."

"I can count," I said. "And stop calling me lady."

"Well, listen up, not-a-lady. I work the goats. Not the trucks."

He took a deep breath, either to explain goats, trucks, or ladies to me, or ask me to explain goats, trucks, and ladies to him, but I beat him to the punch. "What are we looking at?"

"Come again?"

"How long before you can pick up your goats?"

"I'd say by sunup tomorrow morning."

"Where do your trucks come from?" I asked. "Minnesota?"

"I don't know where trucks come from, lady. Like I said, I work with goats. Not trucks. I don't know where to find trucks."

"Stop calling me lady, and I don't care if you stand in the street and flag a truck down, Bobby. Have one here by sundown today," I said, "and it needs to be full."

"Lady, there ain't no way you could need or want more goats."

"I need and want turf grass, and lots of it. I need and want soil, mulch, shrubbery, and flowers in full bloom. Fill up the truck you send with grass, shrubs, and all manner of flowers. Send plenty of dahlias and zinnias," I said, "in very bright colors."

"Where am I supposed to find all that?"

"A landscaping company, Bobby. Home Depot. Lowe's. You can dig up every yard in your subdivision for all I care."

"I live in a trailer park."

"I don't care."

The line went silent for ten seconds, then he asked, "Who's supposed to pay for all that?"

"Did you not just admit that the fault was yours? You're paying for it, Bobby."

"Lady, do you think you're talking to the Wells Fargo? We don't have that kind of money. We got goats. Not money. And I got a boss who's hell on wheels. She won't go for it."

"You caused this problem, Bobby. You need to fix it. And don't call me lady one more time. My name is Davis."

"A lady named David? That's a new one."

"My name is not David. It's Davis."

I looked up to see Roy Howdy's face had gone from its usual blotchy red to pasty yellow. With a tinge of green. I pointed to the door. He ran. I didn't know where Roy Howdy was going, probably to the creepy funeral home he lived in, but I gave him plenty of time to get there before I ended the call with Bobby from Graze Away and stepped out of the police station for air, momentarily forgetting it wasn't pleasant air. It was my first panoramic view of the wreckage left in the wake of the goat storm. Pine Apple was ravaged. And it was heartbreaking.

My head snapped right when I heard a vehicle approaching from the west. It was a chicken wing truck. A bright yellow Ford E350. It had a gable roof. As it slowly circled Town Square, I could see one side of the truck had shutters over the closed serving window and the other side had a white picket fence painted under the wing menu. Bright red bouncing letters above the menu proclaimed the truck to be the House of Wings. The driver and his female passenger were mouths agape, heads on swivels, taking in the mayhem. Everyone on the cleanup crew stopped what they were doing to stare. The truck stared back, slowing at the post office. The driver put the truck in reverse, made a delicate three-point turn, then went back the way he'd come.

FIVE

That night it rained. A heavy soaking rain that lasted all night.

I didn't notice the sky above me turning dark just before sunset because I was halfway up a tree watching the border collies from Camden shoo the goats into a livestock trailer backed up to the high school gymnasium doors. I'd leased the truck from an owner-operator named Gator Macon who lived in Evergreen, thirty miles south, transferring the two thousand dollars he charged from my own savings account. Money I fully intended to recoup from Graze Away Goat Rental. Who'd stopped taking my calls.

I didn't notice the low gray cloud cover behind me as I dropped from the tree when the last goat boarded, and I didn't hear the thunder from inside the echo chamber of the annihilated high school gymnasium we immediately set about cleaning, because the unwieldy retractable bleachers the goats had stomped to near death were louder. It was only when someone opened the double doors at the other end of the gym to let the offensive goat air out and heavy winds whipped through that I realized a summer storm was on top of us. The first gust almost ripped the janitorial mop I was wielding out of my hands. But it didn't actually start raining until two hours later. Just after my sister called to say my children were fed, bathed, ready for bed, and she was exhausted. (Everyone in Pine Apple was exhausted.) She said she'd called her daughter, my teenage niece, Riley, who was away at cheer camp, and told her to hitchhike home to help with her cousins. (She didn't mean that.) She said she was on her way to my parents' house with Bex, Quinn, and the baby, and if I didn't show up soon, she'd leave them there alone. (She wouldn't do that.) Which was just after Penny Ballard, who lived on Dogwood Lane, called to say it was a boy. And he was so cute, she said, they just might keep him. Which was just after Fantasy called to tell me she'd found Whiskey asleep in a garden tub.

"Asleep? In a tub? Are you sure he didn't drown?"

"There wasn't water in the tub, Davis. I put a pillow under his head, threw a blanket on him, and left him there. In the dry garden tub."

I'd been so busy, I'd almost forgotten about Whiskey.

I'd almost forgotten about Fantasy.

Standing in the middle of the gymnasium wrestling an industrial mop with my almost-red hair propelling around my head keeping time with the wind, it all came slamming back: the casino shooting of a high schooler, my fugitive friend who'd fired the shot, and her hostage. Whiskey. They'd been out of sight for the better part of three hours, and thus out of mind.

Earlier, just after the House of Wings food truck dropped out of Pine Apple's chicken wing cookoff, I wove through cleanup efforts and made my way to my parents' house after Fantasy called to say she needed help. I found her trying to talk Whiskey off the roof. Of the house. Where he'd been for more than an hour. Now, how he got up there, I didn't know. He saw me, scrambled up another foot until his back was against the chimney, then recognition set in.

"I am acquainted with your persona," he said.

"Hello, Whiskey." I spoke calmly, lest he make a sudden move and tumble down. I had enough going on without Whiskey falling off the roof. "What happened?" I asked. "How'd you get up there? Why are you up there?"

From his perch, he told me, using the longest words known to man and assembling them in the most convoluted way possible, that he'd woken up in the backseat of the truck earlier having no idea where he was or how he got there, then, after sliding open and crawling out of the cab's back window and standing in the bed of the truck surrounded by bleating goats, had a goat epiphany in which he was advised by a speaking goat wizard to give up the devil's juice for good. I nodded along with him—yes, everyone knew about mystical goats who doubled as life coaches, when what I was really nodding along with was what everyone knew about the aftermath of tequila pong—and asked again how he'd wound up on the roof. He said he'd hitched a ride with a goat. Actually, he said, "I engaged in an unconventional equestrian endeavor by mounting a winged steed of the Bovidae variety."

"Oh," I said. "I see." What I saw was that Whiskey might be sober. Or well on his way. Saying he'd ridden on the wings of a goat to the roof wasn't exactly a teetotaler thought, so he must have started the sobering process after he'd landed on the roof. And sober Whiskey meant we'd need an interpreter. Or at least a comprehensive Oxford English Dictionary.

So how'd he get up there?

He stuck to his flying goat story.

My best guess was he'd scaled the house to the roof the same way I used to get from the roof to the ground.

I held up a be-right-back finger to Fantasy then walked around the house to see Daddy's intricate gutter work, meticulously assembled to direct rainwater to Mother's former vegetable garden—not a vegetable in sight—torn away from the brick and in galvanized steel pieces on the ground. Whiskey hadn't ridden a goat to the roof, he'd shimmied his stout self up the horizontal and vertical gutters using the galvanized elbows as steps, and the unit hadn't held under his weight. I retraced my steps to the front. I waved at Whiskey. He hesitantly waved back. I told Fantasy, "He isn't coming down the way he went up."

"Could you kindly replicate your librettos for the sake of my auditory comprehension?" Whiskey called.

"Don't worry about it, Whiskey," I yelled. "Keep your seat."

"He got himself up there," Fantasy said under her breath. "Surely he can get himself down."

"Not without help."

Whiskey wiped his sweating brow. "Could you elucidate the current state of affairs being discussed?"

I could not.

So I said, "Are you thirsty, Whiskey? Hungry?"

"Equally," he said.

"Then you'll need to get down. We'll help you. For now, stay right where you are," I said. "Don't move a muscle."

The only ladder I found in the garage was two feet too short. And Whiskey surely wasn't steady enough to navigate two feet of air. We'd need more ladder. Two members of Pine Apple's Volunteer Fire Department who could have helped were more than a mile away at Penny and Pete Ballard's on Dogwood Lane trying to coax a stubborn goat out of the kitchen, and their firetruck was twenty miles away, in Greenville, where the third and final volunteer firefighter was gathering more cleaning supplies after we'd wiped the shelves clean at our only grocery store, the Piggly Wiggly. The only way to get Whiskey off the roof was through the attic's dormer window. From the destroyed front yard, I eyed Whiskey on the roof, then the attic dormer window he was a sharp corner away from, before the sun reflecting off the bright blue of the new Bellissimo truck in the driveway almost blinded me. Catching my full attention. At which point, I realized I had not one, but two immediate problems: a career drunk who spoke crossword stuck on my parents' roof and a truck sitting in their driveway for anyone and everyone to see. "Fantasy." She swung her head my way. "You have to do it."

"Do what?"

"Go to the attic, open the dormer window, and talk Whiskey inside. Have him scoot around the corner to you, then grab him. Climb out there if you have to."

"You make it sound like you're not coming with me."

"I'm not."

"It's going to take both of us to talk him in, Davis."

"I can't."

"Why not?"

"Because." I pointed at the Bellissimo truck. "I need to destroy the board diagnostic port."

Her face was a state of confusion.

"So I can wipe the history clean."

Which baffled her more. She raised why hands.

"Because if it hasn't happened already, any minute someone's going to figure out a brand new Bellissimo truck is missing."

"Okay."

"And they're already looking for you."

"No doubt."

"Pretty soon, someone's going to notice this truck is missing." I pointed. "Two plus two equals what?"

"Tetrad!" Whiskey yelled from the roof.

Ignoring him, I said, "They'll figure out you took the truck. Then they'll ping its location. I'm going to destroy the board diagnostic port so they won't find you and the truck in Pine Apple."

She snapped her fingers and pointed at me. "That's a good idea."

It would have been a better idea if I'd thought of it as soon as she'd told me what had happened earlier, but I'd been busy fighting goats.

She took off for the front door yelling, "I'm on my way, Whiskey," and, "how do I get to the attic?" as I turned for the truck. Fifteen minutes later, when things were finally quiet on the roof and the infotainment screen on the truck's dashboard looked like I'd taken a brick to it, Fantasy walked out the front door.

"Where's Whiskey?"

He was hiding behind Fantasy.

Worried about another run-in with a flying wizard goat, I supposed.

"Come on." I opened the driver's door. "Let's go."

"Where?" Fantasy dragged Whiskey by his collar.

"To my ex-ex-mother-in-law's."

"Why? What does this have to do with her?" Then it occurred to her she hadn't seen my ex-ex-mother-in-law since she'd fugitively rolled into town in a stolen truck with a hostage. After shooting a kid. "Where is Bea?"

By then, we'd all piled in. "She's in Canada with my parents on their honeymoon. And she's injured. Somewhere between a twisted ankle and total paralysis from the ankle down." I started the engine. "We'll park the truck and Whiskey at Bea's."

"Were I to have an unfortunate encounter with a bee, it would prompt an immediate immunological response," Whiskey said.

I caught his eye in the rearview mirror. "Bea is a person. Not an insect. She has an Airbnb. You'll love it."

"She's in possession of a what?"

Fantasy looked over her shoulder to Whiskey in the backseat. "It's a nice vacation home. It's a double-wide trailer with a garden tub."

"Could you expound?" he asked.

"A garden tub is what you call a bathtub in a trailer," I said.

"And it is your intent that I temporarily sojourn at said location?" Whiskey asked.

For lack of a better answer, I said, "Yes." Because Bea was busy testing the limits of the Canadian Health Act. She'd never know. And that was when my phone rang for the millionth time. I looked before I ignored the call from the Alabama National Guard—someone must have called them about the goats—only to take the call that came in on top of the first from one of the two volunteer firefighters at Penny and Pete Ballard's on Dogwood Lane. "Could you run by here, Davis? This goat won't come out from behind the kitchen table. It's like backed into a corner and we can't get it out."

I blew out a breath of frustration and asked how three of us ganging up on the goat would be any more productive than the two of them trying to scare the goat from behind the table, to which he said it might be a situation that needed a woman's touch. "It's a nanny goat."

"And that is?"

"A female," he said. "Maybe you can woman talk it."

I sincerely doubted it, nor did I appreciate him suggesting I spoke girl goat by virtue of being female, but I told him I'd be there in ten minutes. By then, we were rolling into Bea's. I parked behind the trailer, bumper-to-bumper with her truck, then hit the start/stop button. The new Bellissimo truck said, "You have arrived at Shady Grove Mobile Home Park."

"No!" I said to the spiderwebbed infotainment screen.

"What?" Fantasy said to me.

"Whatever I thought I did to the truck, I didn't."

"*What?*"

I turned to her. "Fantasy. The truck still knows where it is."

"Now what?" she asked.

I threw open the driver door, dropped to the ground, and stomped to Bea's truck. I didn't want any part of the interior, because for all I knew Bea had a pet tarantula living in there, so I looked in the bed. Then helped myself to a baseball bat. Back at the Bellissimo truck, I said, "Everybody out." I let the infotainment screen have it that time. After three strikes, it sizzled, then died. With a single puff of blue smoke.

That oughta do it.

I told Fantasy to get Whiskey settled, called my sister to check on my children, then hoofed it to Dogwood Lane. The afternoon sun blazing down on me the whole way. No hint of rain.

The volunteer firemen said they'd tried everything to get the goat out from behind the table. "Did you try food?" I asked.

They shared blank looks.

One said, "We tried to lasso it."

The other said, "We sang it 'Baa, Baa, Black Sheep.'"

I said, "And you didn't think to feed it? The goats are starving." I swept a hand toward Pine Apple Proper. "Have you seen Main Street? Have you seen everyone's yards? That's why everything is gone. The goats are starving."

The goat let loose with a howl. Agreeing with me. I patted her head. "It's okay, girl." I turned to the volunteer firemen. "Food."

We emptied the Ballard cupboards. We gave the goat bites of every vegetable, every fruit, bits of leftover meatloaf, BOOMCHICKAPOP kettle corn, then Chips Ahoy! Chunky Chunk Chocolate cookies. All of which the goat gladly woofed down, but only the few bites I placed directly in front of her. She wouldn't follow the snack path to the door. I moved on to peanut butter, which the goat seemed to like a lot. "Come on, goatie girl." I tore off another bite of peanut butter sandwich and began laying a trail leading out. "That's a good goat," I said soothingly. When I had her a foot from the kitchen door, the volunteer firemen started celebrating too soon, high fiving each other, one yelling, "Got your goat!" and the other one yelling, "Greatest of All Time!" sending the goat right back to its kitchen corner. I threw my hands in the air, then glanced at the message buzzing in on my phone. Gator Macon had arrived from Camden in his livestock truck. I breezed past the two volunteer firefighters and the goat saying, "Good luck."

"Where are you going?" one asked my back.

I was going to the high school gymnasium was where I was going. To bid farewell to all the nanny goat's friends. I was at the end of the Ballard's driveway when the goat in the kitchen let out a horror-movie howl. A howl I recognized. Because I'd recently given birth and had heard it up and down the labor and delivery hall. I looked back to the house, wondering where my priorities should be. The goat in the kitchen who was probably in labor or her nine hundred and ninety-nine friends in the high school gymnasium.

I ran for the gym. The waning sun beating down on me the whole way. And it wasn't until that night after a long hot shower as Fantasy and I tried to fall asleep on the twin beds of my childhood bedroom that it started raining.

Bex and Quinn were fast asleep between us on a pallet made of quilts, and the baby was dreaming baby dreams in a mini crib beside the dresser. We'd both sidestepped hard truths in long conversations with our respective husbands, and we'd raided my parents' liquor cabinet finding nothing but a bottle of cheap champagne and a fifth of Peppermint Schnapps. Both still had Christmas ribbons tied around their necks. We put the champagne in the refrigerator to chill, then unwrapped the Schnapps and passed it back and forth until every drop was gone and we were left with minty fresh alcohol breath. Yet sleep still eluded us. So we whispered over my slumbering children and the hard rain. It was the kind of rain that was made for sleep, with no thunder or lightning, just a heavy downpour washing away the last of the goats, but it wasn't helping us. It wouldn't help with the ruined landscape of Main Street either—stripped bare, every other busted storefront boarded, and totally free of its former small-town picturesque hominess—but at least what was left would sparkle. We listened to the rain pour and the children sleep until she whispered, "You know how they say everything happens for a reason?"

"Yes," I whispered back. "But I'm not sure I buy into it."

"Aristotle said it," she whispered.

"Said what?"

"That there's something to be gained from hard times."

"Are you sure it wasn't Charles Dickens who said that?" I whispered.

"Does it matter?" she whispered back.

It didn't. "What?" I asked. "What's to be gained?"

"I don't know yet," she whispered. "I have to wait and see."

"I'm not sure where you're going with this, Fantasy. Is there something amazing in store for you that wouldn't have happened had you not shot a minor in the middle of the casino then ran like the wind in a stolen vehicle? With a hostage? What would it be? Your own reality show where the former prison guard becomes the inmate?"

"I wonder what reality television pays." She rolled over onto her back. "And if replacing my salary would calm Reggie down."

Fantasy's husband, Reggie, was a freelance sportswriter who worked from home, which was to say he was a stay-at-home dad for their three teenage sons whose names all started with K. I couldn't keep their names straight. And not because I didn't care about the boys. I did. It was because I'd grown up in Pine Apple only having to know a few hundred names. Not a few hundred gazillion names. So I called them Special K One, Two, and Three. Their father, Reggie, who called them by their given names, wasn't so upset about the accidental shooting, or the victim's parents all over local Biloxi television promising Fantasy was on her way to Rikers Island for life, and that they'd own the Bellissimo before it was over, because he fully understood the nature of Fantasy's job. Reggie knew that protecting a billion-dollar corporation meant protecting the public. And protecting the public came with risks. Like me, who in the end thought she had taken defensive action against what she saw as a credible threat, I think Reggie felt like there was a chance it would all come out in the wash. As far as Fantasy keeping her job, again like me, Reggie wasn't so sure. But most of all, Reggie was a way bigger Gulfport Admirals fan than a Biloxi Indian Nation fan. So he sided with the Admirals, which was to say he sided with his wife. What Reggie was so worked up about was Fantasy involving their two oldest sons. Special K One and Special K Two. One was a licensed driver. Two had his learner's permit. Barely on the road with Whiskey sleeping it off behind her, Fantasy called and woke Special K One and Two. She had them sneak out, ride their bikes two miles to the Bellissimo, retrieve her car, load their bikes in the back, then drive her Volvo to the Greyhound Bus Station on Martin Luther King Jr. Boulevard. She told them where the parking lot cameras were and how to avoid them before abandoning her car. She told them to hop back on their bikes and hustle back to bed before their father woke up, but that didn't happen, because the boys knew their mother stashed cash in the console of her car. They took themselves out to breakfast before riding their bikes home. Their father, awakened an hour earlier by the police who were looking for his wife, was waiting in the driveway for his sons. And he was mad. From my fly-on-the-wall perspective, I almost agreed with Fantasy when earlier on the phone she'd said, "They sneak out every other night, Reggie. So what if they snuck out to help their mother?" I could hear her husband's rage when she pulled the phone away from her head but couldn't make out exactly what he was saying. Although she responded, "Go ahead. Turn me into Child Welfare. If they want a piece of me too, they can just get in line."

Reggie said they were all grounded for life—Special K One, Special K Two, and Fantasy.

But it worked.

Afterward, while I'd impatiently waited for Gator Macon to return my call and tell me he and his livestock rig were on the way, I gave Daddy's computer enough CPR to bring it back from the dead. I pulled up NCIC, the National Crime Information Center, where I used my father's credentials to search for Fantasy. Right away I found a bench warrant issued by the State of Mississippi for her immediate apprehension. The charges were attempted homicide, endangering the public, and fleeing the scene of the crime. Included were her vitals—full name, birthdate, home address, and description: female,

Black, thirty-seven years old, last seen wearing dark jeans and a sleeveless white sweater. Whereabouts unknown. Approach with caution. The suspect would most likely be armed and she was most certainly dangerous. NCIC said her car, make and model listed, was found abandoned at the Biloxi Greyhound Station. She could be anywhere. But she wasn't anywhere. She was in the twin bed opposite me. Trying to fall asleep. And she was still philosophizing. Over my sleeping daughters, she whispered, "Everything will be okay in the end, Davis. If it isn't okay, it isn't the end."

Considering my old high school friend Florida had shown up to free Pine Apple of the proceeds from The Great Bank Heist of years earlier and that the Memorial Day Celebration of present day was doomed, neither of which I was okay with, I didn't respond.

She whispered, "I'm not sure who said that."

"It doesn't matter who said it, Fantasy. Neither one of us is anywhere near okay."

"Then it isn't the end."

"When my mother comes home and finds a front yard full of dirt instead of flowers, it will be the end."

"The hardest part is over," she said, "the goats are gone."

"Except one who just gave birth in a kitchen on Dogwood Lane."

"To a baby boy goat or a baby girl goat?"

"A boy."

The rain slid down the windows in sheets.

"At least the cleanup work is done." She burrowed deeper under the covers. "And now Pine Apple is taking a much needed shower. All it needs is a little sprucing."

"A little sprucing?" I raised up on an elbow. "It would take a greenhouse. A landscaping conglomerate. Every flower and every blade of grass in every lawn and garden department of every Home Depot in Alabama. It would take relocating an entire botanical garden and scattering it up and down Main Street. And last time I checked, I didn't have a botanical garden."

"Yes, you do."

"I most certainly don't."

"Maybe you don't," she said, "but Bianca does."

SIX

Salvatore Casimiro built the Bellissimo Resort and Casino in Biloxi, Mississippi, in 1996. It was just like Vegas. But with sweet tea. And on the beach. When his only daughter, Bianca, married Richard Sanders, casino control went to him. It wasn't long before the Sanderses owned the Bellissimo, including the Bellissimo offsite and award-winning greenhouses. From my laptop the next morning, armed with my second cup of coffee at my parents' kitchen table, I emailed the Bellissimo greenhouse director. Or, rather, Bianca Sanders emailed Stephen Halliday, Master Gardener and Vice President of Bellissimo Horticulture. But only after extensive Google searches like "flowers for snobs" and "rich people grass" and "ludicrously expensive gardens," jotting down notes on my mother's grocery list pad every time I came across anything that sounded pretentious. The whole time, *Bubble Guppies* blared from the television, Froot Loops flew around my head, and the baby, beside me in his stroller, cooed and kicked at his Baby Einstein Sweet Sea Dreams mobile.

Mr. Halliday, I trust this correspondence finds you well. I'll have you know it most certainly does not find me well. It finds me traumatized.

TRAUMATIZED!

As you are surely aware, I don't venture from my Bellissimo Penthouse home often, and when I do, it is with purpose. Last evening, that purpose was to join my husband and sons at Restaurant R'evolution in New Orleans. I adore their Baby Beet Mélange while my sons all but inhale the chef's world-renowned Death by Gumbo. My main course was to have been a bite or two of the delicious Butter Poached Lobster and Black Linguini, but I was so distraught, I could hardly even enjoy my Bésame, a delicious concoction of peach, basil, lemon, and sparkling wine (I prefer Champagne Perrier-Jouët), much less swallow a morsel of food.

What, might you ask, upset me so?

I was all but blinded by the garish display in the Bellissimo Gardens, which, as you very well know, includes my private ingress and egress to and from my home.

To points beyond.

Such as Restaurant R'evolution.

Located in the very heart of the French Quarter.

In New Orleans.

Mr. Halliday, I demand that the offensive display in the Bellissimo Gardens be replaced immediately. This morning would not be too soon. This evening will be too late as far as your continued employment with the Bellissimo is concerned. I am all for patriotism and love the United States of America with a passion only equal to my love for my ancestral motherland, Italy, yet I have no desire to demonstrate my devotion to my heritage by crudely attempting to recreate the red, white, and green national symbol of solidarity, the Italian flag, in a GARDEN. No more than I want to be emotionally assaulted by an entire acre of red, white, and blue mockingly representing the American flag in the Bellissimo gardens. Flags are to be proudly flown. Not clumsily recreated at ground level. To be trodden upon. Your vulgar attempts to honor the American flag have produced quite the opposite effect. It is as if the Bellissimo is DENOUNCING our national symbol of freedom and liberty.

Perhaps an illustration would be in order.

On the occasion of my recent birthday (as you probably know, I am in my very early forties), were the Bellissimo gardens transformed in my likeness to honor me? While a pleasingly artistic idea, and a propitious undertaking, would it be in any way APPROPRIATE? No, it would not. In fact, it would have been in the POOREST of taste. How could my essence be captured florally? It couldn't. How could my alabaster complexion be recreated botanically? Impossible! Just as your crude attempt at America's symbol of patriotism has sadly missed its mark.

Wherever did you find AZURE BLUE roses?

They are appalling.

Remove and replace everything.

Forthwith.

I will generously give you until tomorrow to replace the garden. When I awaken, don my dressing gown, and make my way to the conservatory overlooking the garden in my Penthouse home to enjoy my pressed coffee imported from Wallenford Estate in Jamaica, I expect to see a magnificently traditional garden. There'd better be summer shrubbery, such as butterfly bushes, abelia, clethra, chaste and topiary trees, and they'd better be perfectly groomed and/or bursting with fragrant and hearty blooms. And should you be interested in keeping your job, Mr. Halliday, the greenery had better be sitting atop a bed of hearty Kentucky Bluegrass. Not the commonplace and sad excuse underfoot at present that can only be compared to hay. Which, as you know, is for HORSES. The ridiculously offensive red, white, and blue hydrangeas occupying every other square inch of the Bellissimo Gardens? Be GONE with them. If they are not replaced by day's end with blooming and fittingly hued lantana, cannas, and celosia, you should look for employment elsewhere.

Carefully remove, pack, and deliver every single vulgar item from the Bellissimo Gardens to my personal assistant in rural Alabama. Every blade of grass, every plant, every shrub, every flower, and every accoutrement. Everything. Roots and sod intact. And at once. I shall tell her to expect it by day's end. Have you any questions, which you shouldn't, because I've stated my wishes precisely, you may direct them to the nearest employment agency.

Bianca Casimiro Sanders

Postscript: Include in the shipment a generous amount of dahlias and zinnias in various vibrant shades.

I hit send, then moved on to my second cyber chore.

Florida Simmons.

What was she doing in Pine Apple? To my knowledge, and to everyone else's, Florida hadn't been back to Pine Apple to see her mother even once. It was common knowledge that Essie Wagner, long time Pine Apple postmistress, hadn't seen even one birthday or Christmas card exchange between mother and daughter. Ever. Mother's Day had come and gone for almost two decades with FTD floral arrangements hitting porches all over town, but never Fiona's. And Shirley, at Pine Apple a Day Keeps the Doctor Away Medical Center, said there was no emergency contact on Fiona's medical record. There was nothing to indicate in the years since the bank robbery that Fiona even had a daughter. So why would Florida show up now? What had prompted the reconciliation? My fingertips were on the keyboard ready to snoop around for a few answers when Fantasy appeared in the kitchen doorway. Feet shuffling along, eyes half closed, nose in the air, sniffing, with her arms outstretched and her hands exploring surfaces, including the top of Bex's head. I assumed she was on a coffee hunt.

She found it.

She poured.

She blew across the top, then had at it. She sipped slowly at first, then with more enthusiasm, all the way to a chug. She landed her empty mug on the counter, wiped the back of her hand across her mouth, and looked over her shoulder. "Do we have flowers?"

"On the way."

She jerked open and slammed shut cabinets and drawers until she found a bowl and spoon. She scraped a chair out then sat down beside Quinn. "Pass the Froot Loops." Then to Bex. "Pass the milk." She shook cereal into her bowl. "So you're good?" She splashed milk into her bowl. "Now can we work on getting me squared away?"

I reached for the last cold sip of my own coffee. "Squared away how?"

"By investigating the unfortunate incident at the Bellissimo."

I checked the girls—still glued to *Bubble Guppies*—then leaned in and whispered, "Is that what we're calling it? The unfortunate incident?"

She didn't check on the girls, didn't lean in, and didn't whisper. "Yes, Davis. There's a warrant out for my arrest. The police are looking for me. Our boss is looking for me. Your husband is looking for me."

"They're all looking for me too," I said. "I've dodged just as many calls as you."

"With both of us dodging everyone's calls, they're going to figure out we're together. Someone's going to show up any minute and haul me off."

Honestly, I was surprised someone hadn't shown up already.

"The goats are gone." She began pleading her case. "The town is clean from the rain. Flowers are on the way. Can we not concentrate on my situation?"

I checked on the girls again. Deep into a drama of their own. The episode was "MMMystery on the Friendship Express," a kid-friendly take on Agatha Christie's *Murder on the Orient Express*. I'd seen it a dozen times. I knew who'd eaten half the cake. Bex and Quinn, who knew every line too, were nonetheless glued to it hard enough for what was probably the fiftieth time for me to safely tell Fantasy, "Yes. We'll look into it." I lowered my voice. "But first I need your help recovering the money from a bank robbery."

Her spoon clattered to her bowl. "The bank was robbed?"

Bex and Quinn's blonde heads whipped our way.

"Fantasy's teasing." I pasted on a smile.

They went back to *Bubble Guppies*.

She leaned in. "When? Last night?"

"No." I kept my voice down. "When I was in high school."

She pushed her Froot Loops away. "Let's see if I have this straight." She sat back and crossed her arms. "We can't start an investigation into the pickle I'm in right this minute until we look into a million-year-old bank robbery?"

"Before it's stolen again."

"Before what is stolen again?"

"The money."

"*What* money?"

"The money from the bank robbery when I was in high school."

She shook her head. She blinked hard.

"It was never recovered," I explained. "I always thought it was small-town folklore. I thought the money was long gone. But now I know it's still here."

She surveyed Mother's kitchen. "Here, where?"

"Here in Pine Apple."

"How do you know that?"

"Because someone's come back to collect it."

"Who?"

"Her name is Florida Simmons. I went to high school with her, and it was her father who robbed the bank. Then hid the money. Everyone in three counties has searched for years and it's never been found. Clearly, no one knew where to look. She does."

"How do you know that?"

"Because she wouldn't be here otherwise."

"Here, *where*?"

I rolled my eyes. "Pine Apple!"

She leaned all the way in. "If this Florida woman knows where money is from a long-ago bank robbery, where's she been? Why has she waited all these years?"

"Because she was hiding Eddie Crawford's son."

She tried to shake the words into her head. "Are there two Eddie Crawford's, or are we talking about your ex-ex-husband?"

"Him."

"Him, *who*?"

"Fantasy? Are you listening to me?"

"I'm trying!"

Two blonde heads whipped our way again.

"Finish your breakfast, girls." I smiled big. Then turned to Fantasy. "Did you see the chicken wing truck yesterday?"

Fantasy landed an elbow on the table, slapped a palm against her forehead, and spoke slowly to the table. "Did you just change subjects? Are you talking about the chicken wing thing now?"

I stood, reached for the baby, and settled him on my hip. "Let's get dressed. We'll drop off the children with Aunt Merri, then I'll tell you all about it."

And I had every intention of doing just that, but...mud happens.

SEVEN

With the baby in his stroller and Bex and Quinn on their bikes, Fantasy and I traded the comfort of my parents' house for mud. Had I bothered to look out a window that morning, I'd have been a little prepared.

I hadn't and I wasn't.

As my parents' garage door slowly opened, I wondered where I was.

Because it looked nothing like Pine Apple.

Or even planet Earth.

The air was crisp and clean after the gully washer of the night before, but the trade-off was mud. Without ground cover, the rain had relocated much of the soil. We sidestepped our way down the muddy driveway between devastated swaths of front yard to the muddier sidewalk. The girls aimed their bike wheels at any dark puddle that looked particularly deep, and the baby's stroller wheels, thick with mud after half a block, splashed sludge at us.

"Nine hundred dollars," Fantasy lamented as she tiptoed around a puddle.

"What about nine hundred dollars?" I skirted a puddle of my own.

"My Valentino Rockstud flats." She kept her eyes on her feet. "Does anyone in town sell shoes?"

"The Mercantile sells duck boots."

"That'll work."

"There's The Mercantile." I nodded.

The sign on the door read CLOSED UNTIL FURTHER NOTICE BECAUSE Y'ALL WIPED ME OUT YESTERDAY. THESE SHELVES IS EMPTY.

She slipped out of her Valentinos and braved the next block barefoot.

Half of Pine Apple was already awake and appeared to be hard at work shuffling mud. The other half was up, out, and congregated at City Hall. Tightly packed, one on top of the other, they saw me approach and stopped arguing amongst themselves so they could begin lobbing their complaints and demands at me. Shouting all over each other. In the mix, I heard "FEMA!" and "Another chicken wing truck has done come and gone, Davis. You'd better do something!" and one bright "Good morning, Junior!" Then I heard, "Davis, if you don't get on the stick and fix this mess, I'm calling your daddy!" That last bit was from my own grandmother. Who was at the front of the line trying to arrest everyone. I stood there long enough to admire the collection of mud-splattered rainboots attached to the protesters, wishing I'd thought to pack the girls' Barbie pink puddle stompers, then raised my voice above theirs. "I'll be back in ten minutes." I started the stroller engine again, making a run for it. The crowd didn't like it, doubling down, yelling at my back with even more energy than they'd yelled at my front.

I backed the stroller up the steps to Meredith's.

Her door was locked.

I banged on it.

"Meredith! Open up!"

"No," she said through the door. "Your children are covered in mud."

"Girls," I said, "take off your shoes."

"And their clothes," came through the door.

"My children aren't going to strip down in the street, Meredith." The door burst open.

I pushed my little people through, telling them to be sweet for their Aunt Merri, then hightailed it out of there to tackle the waiting throng at City Hall. I stood with my back against the locked door of the police station, then pointed and called out numbers like I was the deli counter. Pine Apple began filing in. One by one.

Fantasy, back in her Valentinos after taking a water hose to her feet, wanting to help move things along so we could get to her problems, passed out cups of microwaved Sanka while I listened to town grievances and jotted notes. I said things like, "I'll find someone who can fumigate your minivan, Lou Ann." And, "I don't believe a word of that, Grady. Your sunporch was falling apart twenty years ago. You've got a lot of nerve trying to blame it on the goats." And, "I'm no swimming pool expert, but if it were me, Karen, I'd drain the pool, Clorox it to death, give it a good rinse, then fill it with fresh water before I dipped a toe in it." Just before eleven, Eugenia Winters Stone, number sixteen, and the woman at the tip-top of my mother's frenemy list, stepped in and took the perp seat. She pulled a monogrammed hankie from inside the sleeve of her blouse and dabbed her forehead.

"Davis." She could drag out my name a mile. "As Community Liaison for Pine Apple's Women's Society, and in light of present circumstances, I'd like to make a motion that Memorial Day be rescheduled."

"It's a national holiday, Eugenia." I sat back in Daddy's chair. "How am I supposed to reschedule a national holiday?"

"Our celebration," she explained. "I'd like to make a motion we reschedule our celebration."

"Make a motion to whom?"

"Well, you, Davis." She crossed her Lilly Pulitzer rainboots the other way. "With your daddy out of town, not only are you our only protection against civil unrest, but you're our acting mayor."

I tapped a pencil against the desk. "No."

Eugenia's head snapped. "I beg your pardon."

"We will not postpone, Eugenia. We have the rest of the week to put Pine Apple back together in time for our Memorial Day Celebration."

She opened her mouth to argue, but I beat her to the punch with, "And that's my final word on the subject."

Eugenia inhaled sharply, stood, very insincerely wished me a good day, then stomped for the door. Mumbling something under her breath.

"What was that, Eugenia?" I asked.

She spun. She narrowed her eyes. "I've never known your father to make such a poor decision." She tsk-tsked and slammed the door. A door I locked behind her, flipping the Out to Lunch sign.

"What's her problem?" Fantasy asked.

"She's mad."

"The whole town's mad, Davis."

"She's extra mad," I said. "Her home was broken into a while back. She was fine, nothing was stolen, and as it turned out, it was her nephew who was trying to sneak in and find her car keys because she wouldn't let him borrow her car to go see his girlfriend."

Fantasy's face was nothing if not confused.

"The nephew wrecked his truck."

Fantasy's face was absolute incredulity. "So?"

"The break-in scared Eugenia. She went off on a self-defense bender. Learned jiu-jitsu, took marksmanship classes, and from what my mother told me, she can put your eye out with her thumb."

Fantasy's face was completely baffled. "*So?*"

"She wanted this job." I poked my father's desk. "She wanted Daddy to swear her in as acting chief of police. She's mad he didn't. And it's me she's mad at."

Just then the phone rang. The caller ID said State of Alabama. Had Eugenia already tattled on me to the Alabama Law Enforcement Agency?

"Pine Apple Police." My voice shook a little.

Over an incredible amount of background noise—static from a communication radio interrupting the rush of road and wind from what had to be an open window—a man said, "This is Alabama State Trooper Arlan Crow calling for Chief Samuel Way."

"This is acting chief Davis Way Cole."

"Where's your non-acting chief?"

"On vacation," I said. "What's this about, Trooper Crow?"

"A wild goose chase," he said. "I'm just west of Andalusia on my way to you to check out a fugitive BOLO for one Fantasy Erb, six-foot-tall female, wanted for questioning in a Mississippi shooting, unless you can tell me she's not there."

"She's not here."

The sound of his relief at not having to drive to Pine Apple was loud and clear over his radio static, the road, and the roaring wind. "Thank you."

"Was that about me?" Fantasy asked.

"No," I lied. "Why would you think it was about you?"

"A trooper called. And you said, 'She's not here.' Why wouldn't I think it was about me?"

Saving me from being forced to admit the call was about her, faces appeared around the Out to Lunch sign at the door. Old women faces. Pine Apple's Women's Society old women faces. Eugenia Winters Stone sent her posse. They rattled the doorknob and knuckled the glass demanding entry. I stood, slowly walked their way, but instead of letting them in, I yanked the cord to let the metal blinds tumble down to loud dissent. Not only was it time to hide Fantasy, it was time to relocate police headquarters so I could get a little work done already. Before I could, I needed to copy the hard drive from my father's computer onto my laptop. And make two calls. From the precinct phone.

* * *

While Fantasy knocked out a small chore list gathering the station supplies we might need and worked on a Gone Fishing Until Further

Notice sign for the door, I stared at the phone on Daddy's desk. Working up my nerve. Because to stave off my husband calling Mississippi's Governor, who Bradley was tight with, and asking him to send search and rescue teams to conduct a wellness check on me and the children after returning half the calls I'd missed from him that morning with quick text messages—*The girls found my mother's jewelry and are wearing all of it, hold on,* and, *On the phone with our dog nanny at home, I'll call right back,* and, *Flipping pancakes, syrup everywhere, give me a minute,* and, *My old Sunday School teacher dropped by to meet the baby and now I'm flying out the door. I'll call you when I get to the police station*—then letting the other calls go to voicemail, I had to check in with him.

All was well in Texas.

The only subject I glossed over, which was to say lied by omission, was that of Fantasy. With a hand, I shooed her away from my old desk and into the police station's kitchenette before saying, "She's not with me, Bradley." Because she wasn't. She was in the next room. "Has anyone tried her parents in Florida? She could be in Florida." Fantasy's head poked out the kitchenette door. Eyebrows up around her hairline, she slashed at her own throat with a flat hand. "On second thought, don't call Fantasy's parents, Bradley. They're old. Why scare them?"

"Are you telling me you haven't talked to her, Davis?"

"I didn't say that."

"Well?"

"She's trying to work things out."

"Where is she?"

I shooed Fantasy out of the room and clapped my hands over my eyes so I couldn't see where she went, not that there were that many places to go in the small police station, before saying, "I don't know."

"Have you told her to turn herself in?"

"I haven't. If you think I should, the next time I hear from her, I will."

"Of course I think you should."

"I will."

He inhaled, probably gearing up to blast me with more Fantasy questions I'd have to tiptoe around, so I stopped him by saying to thin air, "Come on in, Rerun. I'll just be a minute." To the phone I said, "Duty calls. But rest assured, Bradley, I believe Fantasy will do the right thing. She's probably locked up with a team of defense attorneys. Or waiting for the dust to settle. She'll either show up here, at the Bellissimo, or at the police station to turn herself in. Until then, she can take care of herself."

"I hope you're right."

"I am."

There was a beat of a pause as I waited for him to end the conversation, but he didn't. He squeezed another horrific question into our already nerve-racking conversation. "Do you have any idea why Bianca Sanders, who last I heard was in Europe, would ask Horticulture to dig up two acres of gardens?"

"That's crazy."

"Indeed."

And there went his second opportunity to say bye. But instead, I heard, "Davis? Is there anything you want to tell me?"

"Yes."

The silence was deafening.

"Go ahead," he said.

"I love you," I blurted out. "I really, really love you, Bradley, and I miss you."

And with that, he settled down enough to let me go. Or it could have been that the school bell rang at Texas Law. Either way, we said our goodbyes with promises to talk again soon. In a way, I was proud of myself for juggling so many wet cats. In another way, I was miserable about wet cat juggling above my husband's head too. And just to double down on my misery, I picked up the phone again.

Fantasy's head popped out of the supply closet. "What are you doing?"

"I'm calling my father."

"Davis, let's get out of here."

"And go where?"

"Anywhere but here. And when we get anywhere, you can call your dad."

"I need to get it over with, and I need to get it over with from this phone." I shook the receiver at her.

"And I need to go underground, Davis, and I need to be underground anywhere but here."

"I want out of here too." And just to prove my point, someone yelled through the window. "Davis! Open up. I know you're in there." I raised *see?* eyebrows at Fantasy. Then I unblocked Daddy's phone and dialed. "We're out of here just as soon as I finish this call."

All was not well in Ontario.

I glossed over a thousand subjects with him, which was to say I lied by omission all over the place. "Everything's fine on the home front, Daddy. Just watching the chicken wing trucks roll in and set up shop."

"I haven't heard a word from anyone, Davis."

"Anyone who?"

"For starters, your grandmother or your sister. Or you, until just now."

"We talked yesterday."

"Only for you to tell me we'd talk later," he said. "It's unusual that I'm not getting calls from home."

"Everyone wants you and Mother to have a nice time," I said. "They're giving you space."

"Since when was I allowed space from the residents of Pine Apple?"

Since never, so I said, "Maybe the cell service where you are isn't any more efficient than the healthcare system."

"Could be," he said, "although I've received a couple calls from Marcus Flash."

"Who?"

"Marcus Flash. The owner of Flash Fireworks."

"The new fireworks supplier from Tuscaloosa?"

"Talladega," he corrected me.

"Talladega," I said. "Got it. Was he calling about the fireworks for Memorial Day?"

"Yes," Daddy said. "Wanting to confirm we were still on. 'Considering the new development,' he said. What do you think he might've been referring to, Davis?"

My brain split into perfect halves: one half wondering how someone a hundred and fifty miles away knew about the goats and the other half searching for a reasonable answer to my father's question. I went with, "We got a ton of rain last night." Which was true. "That might explain the hit or miss calls too."

"There could be trouble at the cell tower."

"Do you want me to load up the children, drive out there, and take a look?"

"No," he said. "But send someone."

"I'll get right on it and let you know."

"Maybe call Squirrel Higgons," Daddy said. "Or Geneva Crowder. They're both close to the cell tower. And expect a call from Marcus Flash. I gave him your number."

"Sounds good," I said. "And as soon as I hear something about the cell tower, I'll be in touch—"

"Hold your horses a minute, Sweet Pea. Don't you want to know how Bea is?"

Honestly, I didn't.

"She's insisting her ankle is swollen," he told me anyway. "But in a side-by-side comparison, good ankle to bad ankle, it's impossible to tell a difference. She says I can't see the swelling because she inherited thick ankles. I wouldn't know. She certainly inherited a thick skull. And one inherently thick ankle looks no more swollen than the other inherently thick ankle to me. She says the swelling is internal. 'Inside my foot,' she insists. And to press her regarding if her injury is in the foot or the ankle is to encourage her to talk herself into the damage radiating all the way to her earlobes. And now she's developed vertigo. From ankle instability. 'I'm walking crooked,' she says. 'It's making my brain crooked.'"

"She's probably right about having a crooked brain."

Fantasy looked at me sideways.

"I don't care to weigh in on the alignment of Bea's brain," Daddy said, "but I do know the concept of the squeaky wheel doesn't cross the Canadian border. The more noise, demands, and complaints she lodges, the further down the list she goes. We are approaching the forty-eight-hour mark at the hospital. I have a good mind to send your poor mother home to her grandchildren without me—"

"Are you sure that's a good idea, Daddy?"

"She'd have an easier time with the chicken wings than she's having with Bea, Davis."

"I meant traveling alone," I said. "Are you sure you want Mother traveling alone? She won't even drive to Greenville alone, and it's only twenty miles, and you think she'd be comfortable flying home alone? Going through Customs alone? How many connecting flights would it be?"

"Too many," he admitted.

Just then, my cell phone flashed with an incoming text message from my sister. *Just took a call from another chicken wing truck. The*

Cluck Stops Here. They heard about the mud and dropped out. I'm on my second load of laundry with your messy children.

"Davis?"

"I'm here, Daddy."

Beside me, tapping an anxious Valentino, Fantasy mouthed, "*So am I.*"

I held up a wait-a-minute finger to her, still staring at the message on my cell phone. "Daddy, I have a question, then I need to let you go and check on the children."

"And the cell tower."

"And the cell tower," I repeated.

"Ask away, Sweet Pea."

"Is Roy Howdy completely in charge of Public Works?"

Beside me, Fantasy mouthed, "*Roy what?*"

I waved her off as Daddy asked, "What do you mean?"

"Is there a second-in-command?"

"Why?"

"Because I need to run something by him and he's not around."

"That's unusual. He knows it's all hands on deck this week. When was the last time you saw him?"

"Late yesterday afternoon," I said. "And he wasn't feeling well."

"That boy is as strong as an ox, Davis. I've never heard him complain about not feeling well. Did something happen?"

I didn't want to bring up the liverwurst, so I said, "Not that I know of."

"I'm sure he's fine. It's probably nothing more than lingering melancholy over the loss of his uncle."

"You think? He doesn't seem gloomy to me."

"He's putting on a brave face, Davis. Inwardly, I'm sure he's devastated."

"Daddy, Old Man Carter was a lifelong mortician who lived in a haunted house and had been in a bad mood since—" the bank was robbed, I didn't say "—forever." (I did say.) "Roy Howdy might be relieved."

"Davis."

"That came out harsher than I meant it to."

"Don't listen to town gossip."

"I won't unless the town is gossiping about who's second in command when it comes to Public Works."

Fantasy was in front of me waving like a marshaller on the tarmac leading an Airbus A380 to its parking stand.

I waved back in a much smaller fashion.

"There is a second in command, Davis, but it won't do you any good. Is this about the weed cleanup on the hill at Wright and Oak? Was it unsuccessful?"

"There isn't a weed left in all of Pine Apple."

"Well, isn't that good news?"

It was far from good news.

He followed up with, "Then what would you need from Roy Howdy?"

"Maybe I don't need Roy Howdy. What I need is to know who's in charge of the chicken wing competition."

"What do you mean by in charge?"

"Who can tell me how many chicken wing trucks are coming?"

"Last I heard, it was a good dozen," he said. "Why?"

Because I needed to know how to contact the three trucks who'd dropped out of the competition so I could talk them back in. And see what chicken wing trucks were scheduled to arrive next so I could postpone them. Not that I wanted to explain any of that to Daddy. So I pivoted to another question that might get me the answer I needed. "Where can I find a list of parking assignments for the trucks?"

"There isn't one that I know of. It's first come, first served. Which would be why some are arriving early. To get the premium spots around Town Square."

"You think? Isn't there anyone who actually knows?"

"Davis." Then my father sighed the weariest sigh I'd ever heard. "What I'm trying hard not to tell you is that Bea was in charge of lining up the competitors for the chicken wing competition. Which is something even your mother doesn't know. Bea is the one with the information you're asking for. Would you like to speak to her?"

I told him I absolutely did not want to speak to her.

"Is there anything else, Sweet Pea?"

"What do you mean?"

"Is there anything else you need to tell me?"

"No, Daddy." I died a little inside. "Everything's fine." I told him I loved him, I'd work it out on the chicken wing business and take care of Pine Apple for him while he took care of Mother and Bea, then had the 251 area code blocked from his phone again thirty seconds after we hung up. Fantasy shot out of her chair, but I was glued to mine. Staring into space. Or rather into the jail cell. Staring despondently having plunged into such deep waters by not coming clean with my father when the chances of him not learning what had happened were miniscule. And I probably wouldn't have stopped wallowing in daughter shame on top of wife shame for hours had there not been a fist pound on the station door to snap me out of it.

Then a second pound.

Then a third.

Very official sounding pounds.

Fantasy and I exchanged wide-eyed-looks-of-wonder at the demanding interruption, but before we could blurt out panicked parting words before she was taken into custody, we heard a weak, "Ms. Erb? Are you within the confines of this location?" The voice on the other side of the door wasn't anyone looking for Fantasy with

a warrant in hand, anyone from the Bellissimo there to haul her back
to Biloxi, nor was it anyone in law enforcement to toss her into the
back of their paddy wagon.

"It's me," we heard. "Cedric. Cedric Kinder."

I whispered, "Cedric Kinder? Is that Whiskey's real name?"

She crossed to the door and yanked it open. After staring at him
wide-eyed for a curious second, she pulled him inside.

He smelled like a citrus grove in a way I immediately recognized,
and recoiled from, as it was a well-known aromatic announcement
of Bea Crawford having recently bathed, but it was Whiskey who'd
bathed. (Good news.) In Bea's tangy soap. (Not such good news.)
And he was lost inside one of her Hawaiian muumuu dresses. (Bad
news.)

"About my current attire," he said.

We both cocked an ear.

"My garments were in the midst of soil contamination as a result
of my many adventures of the day prior to this."

We waited.

"With ecstatic jubilation, I happened upon an apparel cleansing
unit at my fetching, although somewhat primitive, and slightly
unkept vacation home."

Whiskey found a washing machine at Bea's.

"However, between disrobing prior to immersing myself
aquatically into the lovely garden tub for the purpose of personal
hygiene—"

Ewwww.

"—I had an unfortunate encounter with a mustelid of the genus
Mustela—"

We had nothing.

"—commonly referred to as a ferret—"

Still, we had nothing.

"—who, it would seem, dwells in the apparel cleansing unit."

We could not have been more confused.

"An ill-tempered mustelid."

An angry ferret?

"And upon the intrusion of my garments, the creature attempted to consume them."

It was a full minute before anyone spoke, and when the silence was broken, it was me. "There was a ferret in the washing machine who ate your clothes?"

"Affirmative," Whiskey said, then asked, "What might be the probability that there's an operational food establishment in this barren municipal?"

EIGHT

I parked Whiskey, who had the hairiest man legs I'd ever seen in my life, like carpet on his legs, in the perp chair. I told him he would not starve to death before I cloned the hard drive from my father's antiquated desktop computer and downloaded it to my laptop. Fantasy stayed beside the door, still peeking out between the blinds, stealing views up and down Main Street, no doubt waiting on a casino terrorism task force to roll into town and haul her off. Up until the minute we left the safety of my parents' house earlier, adrenalin and the relative obscurity of Pine Apple had somewhat tamped down her terror. The goats, my children, the Peppermint Schnapps, and the rain had assisted in distracting her. But the trooper call she knew I didn't tell the truth about, followed by listening to my end of the conversation about her with my husband, combined with the fact that she'd hit the twenty-four-hour mark as a fugitive had her anxiety level set to turbo. She fidgeted. Checked her phone at least once a minute. And her eyes kept darting to the kitchenette, as if she might actually make a cup of Sanka instant coffee and attempt to swallow it just to have something to do while she waited to go to prison. Where the coffee was probably worse than Sanka.

Without looking up from my laptop as a bar on my home screen slowly filled with new content, patting the boxy monitor of Daddy's computer, urging it along, I said, "If you're going to guard the door, Fantasy, tell me what's going on."

"Do you mean while I wait for a SWAT team to roar into town and cart me away?"

"I won't let that happen."

"I'm not sure how you'll stop it from happening."

I finally looked up. Gave a nod to the jail cell. "I'll lock you up. Claim you as my own prisoner. I'll say you're responsible for the hellscape that is my hometown. Which they will all agree is worse than shooting a kid."

From the perp chair, Whiskey's head whipped Fantasy's way. "You engaged in a firearm altercation with an adolescent?"

Fantasy said, "Shut up, Whiskey," sounding very much like her old self, and her old self must have decided what I'd asked her to do was better than drinking Sanka, because she began reporting the Pine Apple news from between blind slats while Daddy's slower-than-Christmas computer churned along. "The old ladies are in the street shooting dirty looks this way. Every kid in town is slinging mud at every other kid in town. I can only see their eyeballs. Looks like half of the work crew is still shoveling mud. The other half have water hoses, washing down the sidewalks, which is actually making more mud for the mud crew. The bakery might be reopening. There's a guy wandering around who isn't dirty. And a hair-pulling mud wrestling match between two women in front of your sister's store, one of the women is your grandmother, Davis, the other is a hefty and heavily tattooed fifty-year-old bleached blonde. Your grandmother is about to take her down." Four or five peeks later, she said, "So far no feds to extradite me back to Mississippi."

I slammed my laptop closed for the second time that day—finally—then stood. "Let's go."

"Where?" both Fantasy and Whiskey asked.

"To our new hideout."

"Which of you might have cause to hide?" Whiskey wanted to know. "And whom, may I ask, would said person or persons be hiding from?"

"I meant to say our new office."

Whiskey looked skeptical.

"There's food," I added.

Whiskey nodded and stood, ready to go. He smoothed his muumuu. "I sincerely regret there were no alternative wardrobe options at my vacation rental."

Fantasy said, "We regret it too."

We left the police station through the back door.

"Which way?" Fantasy asked.

"I'm trying to decide," I answered.

"What is the anticipated distance to our new destination?" Whiskey asked.

"You two be quiet. I'm trying to think."

We needed to cross Main Street without crossing Main Street through throngs of disgruntled and muddy Pine Applers. We'd have to circle around. I looked right. The way I wanted to go. But it was nothing but backyards that looked like swamps. I looked left. The way I didn't want to go. One path would require hiking over a steep hill, if the steep hill hadn't been washed away by the rain after the goats cleared it—Fantasy's Valentinos would never make it—but the other path might scar us for life.

Hiking it was.

We rounded the corner at the end of the block and landed at the intersection of Wright and Oak Streets, which put us at the edge of the empty lot below the hill that should have been cleared for fireworks by the goats. Only to see that it hadn't been. And just like my father said, the hill was ten times as overgrown as the last time I'd seen it. The goats didn't do the very job they were hired to do, and there would be no stomping up, then down, a steep hill through thick kudzu vines up to our knees.

Hiking it wasn't.

Because snakes.

Scarred for life it was.

Because we couldn't very well fly over Main Street.

I marched that way.

My troops followed.

We rounded the next corner on Wright Street, which landed us just behind busy Town Square, full of muddy children, hopefully my daughters not among them. We hurried across the street in the opposite direction and took cover beneath overgrown red maples hiding a tall iron gate.

I tried the gate.

It didn't budge.

Fantasy, a semi-devout Catholic, took one look through the iron bars and crossed herself. "No way, Davis."

Whiskey chimed in with, "I would prefer not to traverse a graveyard."

I gave the gate a hard kick and was rewarded with an ear-piercing scream of iron-on-iron. I stepped in, saying, "You chickens come on."

Whiskey, who wasn't Catholic at all that I knew of, crossed himself too, or maybe he diamonded himself, asking, "What lies beyond this place of final rest?"

I stopped between two crumbling headstones and looked back to see that neither had moved.

"I want to know too," Fantasy said. "Where are we going?"

"Bea's," I told them. "Bea's Diner."

"The individual graciously extending hospitality to me?" Whiskey asked.

The same.

That Bea.

Bea Crawford.

My ex-ex-mother-in-law Bea.

Airbnb Bea.

Swollen ankle and crooked brain Bea.

"What about ghosts?" Fantasy was rooted to the sidewalk.

"Since when do you believe in ghosts?" I asked.

"What if there's instability from the amalgamation of earth and water and we inadvertently plunge into an interment?"

"You think we're going to sink into a grave?" I'd just about had it with both of them.

Whiskey was hanging on Fantasy's arm.

She was trying to shake him off. "Isn't there an easier way to get to Bea's?"

"Yes," I said. "Straight down Main Street where the whole world will see us. I'll be stopped every two inches. Everyone in town will see you to say, 'She went that way,' to anyone with a badge who asks. And you," I looked at Whiskey in his muumuu, "never mind. So you two can either come with me the back way or march down Main Street and meet me there. I don't care." Then I took a Mother-May-I leap onto a relatively mud-free grave marker, hopscotched my way to the next one, passed the crumbling old funeral home on the hill—a sight that horrified Fantasy and Whiskey—and cleared the small cemetery. Four minutes and a dozen muddy graves later, we were staring at Bea's Diner. Our souls seemingly intact.

A block south of everything and everyone else, Bea's was set back from Main Street by a deep front yard. Hundred-year-old oaks at the curb provided additional cover. And the gapped path leading to the diner—the concrete sidewalk cracked, raised, and nonexistent at regular intervals thanks to runaway roots from a nearby willow tree—was a winding obstacle course. The diner wasn't easy to get to; you had to want to go. Very few did when it was open. No one would with it closed. Which made it the perfect place to hole up.

"Can you believe this?" Fantasy, barefoot again with the heels of her Valentino slides poking out her back pockets, jumped over a dirty puddle between chunks of sidewalk.

"Believe what?" I hopped the mud gap right behind her.

"I find the entire predicament difficult to comprehend." Whiskey wasn't watching where he was waddling and landed a loafer in the middle of it.

"All the weeds that Bea calls grass look like they're right where she left them." Fantasy reached the front door first. "Why didn't the goats eat here?"

"No one in their right mind eats here." I joined her, my shoes helping themselves to the welcome mat, leaving long smears of dirty gifts. "Including, it would seem, goats."

Whiskey brought up the rear. "The marriage of soil and moisture has created a mire that I find myself weary of traversing." He was out of breath and bent over, palms to knees, studying his shoes. A dark puddle radiated around his right loafer. "Does this region regularly experience atmospheric anomalies that produce sludge?" He tried to squeeze more out of the muddy shoe by placing his dry shoe on his wet shoe, thus standing on his own foot. Wobbling like a bowling pin. And still wearing a muumuu. "Do either of you know if the meteorological conditions we find ourselves in are archetypal for this geographic location?"

Neither of us bothered to respond because, first of all, we barely understood a word of it, and second of all, we were busy reading the sign on the door. "OFF ON A HONEYMOONS. WHEN I GET BACK ALL PLATE LUNCHES WILL BE ON SALE A DOLLAR OFF. MAYBE THREE DOLLARS OFF. DEPENDS ON HOW LONG I'M GONE AND IF THE DEEP FREEZE HOLTS UP. DAMN DEEP FREEZE. IF THE DEEP FREEZE DON'T HOLT UP THERE'LL BE A ALL YOU CAN STUFF IN YOUR FACE LASAGNAS SPECIAL."

The front door was locked.

I took off.

"Where do you think you're going?" Fantasy asked.

"Around back," I answered.

"I'm not walking through more mud," she said.

"Whiskey," I said over my shoulder, "give Fantasy a ride."

She was taller than him. He was stouter than her. It took them a minute. Her long legs were everywhere. The extra weight produced a deep slurping noise with his every step, and the mud ate both his loafers before we made it around back to a terrifying sight riddled with broken kitchen equipment, busted dining room furniture, and a beaten-up collection of garbage cans under a metal canopy in various states of tenancy. Scarier than that, we found the backdoor not only unlocked, but ajar. I held Fantasy and Whiskey back with one hand and reached behind me for my old service revolver with the other. I announced myself. No response. I clicked on the flashlight mounted to my gun, stepped in an inch, sprayed a beam around the room, and scared up a screeching cat. Whiskey, barefoot and high stepping in a circle, splashing mud everywhere, yelled, "Whoop! Whoop! Whoop!" when the cat, who most likely lived in the kitchen under the guise of pest control, circled his muddy legs before whizzing past him.

"The cat smelled your soap. Or maybe it saw your dress," Fantasy said. "Thought you were Bea." She stepped in, batting for a light switch, until I caught her hand. "Right," she said. "We're hiding."

We made our way through the gelatinous cold grease smells of the kitchen to the rancid sour mop smells of the dining room by the light of my service revolver's flashlight. I clicked it off, trading the blaring announcement that someone was nosing around the closed diner for the modicum of daylight peeking above and below the pulled shades.

"This restaurant isn't operational," Whiskey said. "How are we to find sustenance without a staff to prepare and serve?"

"Dig around behind the front counter," I said. "It's help yourself day."

He spun that way, mud caked on his hairy legs to mid-calf, the ruffled hem of his muumuu spinning too. "I am at an unfortunate disadvantage in the food preparation department."

"Look in the coolers under the grill. Find something you don't have to cook." By then, I'd landed on one side of a lunch booth farthest from the front door. Fantasy took the bench opposite me.

"The miniature refrigeration unit is bare of all but one container of mustard," Whiskey let us know.

With a tug, I raised the rolling window shade a foot—dust danced through the air—giving me a broader view of the twisted sidewalk leading to Main Street with a sliver of a view of the action there. "Then make yourself a mustard sandwich."

"I'd prefer breakfast," he said. "Farm raised eggs. Over easy. With warm buttered biscuits and sausage gravy."

Our heads turned in time to stare him down.

Whiskey raised both hands in the air as if to keep us in our seats. "I'll continue my nourishment quest and find a suitable alternative."

I opened my laptop and navigated to Daddy's swiped hard drive. My eyes landed on a folder marked Memorial Day. I clicked it, did a quick search and found fourteen additional Memorial Day folders, and with two more clicks I'd combined and sorted them by date. I minimized everything. Tucking it all away for later. Because in addition to Fantasy drumming her fingers on the table, she had a muddy foot going. I needed to take care of her first.

"What manner of foulness might this be?" Whiskey plopped a plate on the counter sending mysterious liquid splashing. On the plate was something round and limp. It was various shades of unpleasant colors ranging from pea-soup green to fungal brown.

"That might have been a head of lettuce at some point," I said.

"Don't eat it," Fantasy added.

I logged into NCIC again, the National Crime Information Center, and used my father's credentials to get to the good stuff.

"Here we go," I said, as the database of reported criminal activity and apprehensions appeared.

The top half of Fantasy shot up and across the table to have an upside-down look. "What's it say?"

"I don't know." I sat back. "I can't see through your head."

I scooted to the window to make room for her to sit beside me. She did. I placed the laptop between us. She zeroed in on the busy screen so loaded with cryptic law enforcement communique, then pushed it right back to me. "Go, go, go, Davis."

I went, went, went, narrowing the website's search clock to the past twenty-four hours, then narrowing down to the state of Mississippi, then Harrison County, then typed *Bellissimo Resort and Casino* in the search bar. Before a list could populate, from behind the counter, Whiskey said, "Is this a prepared steak of the pork variety?"

Fantasy craned her neck for a closer look. "Do you mean ham? Ham isn't white. And it doesn't have big holes in it. I don't know what that is."

Without looking up to see for myself, I said, "Toss it, Whiskey."

NCIC reported two vehicular incidents during the night at the Bellissimo, one in the parking garage, the other at the main entrance, and four D&Ds. (Drunk and disorderly.) Nothing was posted about a reward being offered for Fantasy's hide, which meant so far the Bellissimo hadn't thrown her under the bus.

"Go back and search my name."

"I don't want to, Fantasy. Yesterday you were a new listing. Plenty of bored precincts might have clicked out of curiosity. Today you're old news. If anyone's paying attention, a second click from the same precinct will be noticed. One more click would track the hit to an unauthorized device. As in my laptop. I'd go to prison with you. Do you want me to go to prison with you?"

"Yes."

"No. But I'll tell you what I will do."

"Tell me."

"I'll buy you a little time."

"Buy me a lot of time, Davis."

I opened a new screen and busted through Biloxi Police Department's firewall. And not for the first time. In my defense, I only breached their system when I needed answers to questions they didn't have time to answer. The way I looked at it, wouldn't they rather I look it up myself as opposed to bothering them with endless phone calls? I clicked the outstanding warrants tab. Knowing Fantasy's would still be active, since she was right beside me rather than in custody, and not wanting her to see the gory details, I clicked through to get to the police reports behind the warrants. I found her case and clicked the evidence tab. The boys were naked, so there were no personal effects confiscated past eight senior rings and two smart watches, but all the paintball guns were in an evidence locker. On a longshot whim, three clicks later, I'd ordered ballistics tests on the paintball guns. For authorization, I borrowed our favorite detective, Sandy Marini's, credentials. Something I felt certain Biloxi PD and especially Sandy would prefer me not do, but desperate times and all.

"Ballistics on paintball guns? Sandy's going to kill you, Davis."

"She's going to need to get in line."

"For sure, you're going to prison with me."

From behind the counter, Whiskey said, "I hereby volunteer to be your incarceration associate solely for the three-square-meals amenity. Because the peanut butter at this locale is both a strange consistency and an unfortunate hue not native to the peanut." He landed the open end of a day camp-sized container on the counter for our inspection. It was shiny. And gooey. And gray. Dark gray. Almost black.

"Check the refrigerator and the freezer in the kitchen," I suggested, as I toggled back to NCIC and clicked ALABAMA from the pull-down menu on the home screen looking for anything that might be happening closer to where we were, like maybe the offices of Graze Away Goat Rental, Home of Hassle-Free Brush Removal and Weed Control, had burned to the ground during the night. No such luck. Although Graze Away could still be further down the list, because the main event was so spectacular. And not in a good way. There'd been a prison break at Federal Correction Institution in Talladega. Three male inmates were on the lam. Everything else that had happened in the great state of Alabama during the past twenty-four hours was run of the mill by comparison, if multiple vehicular fatalities, even more vehicular thefts, even more drug and gang related incidents, seven solicitation arrests, six major property damage reports, five grand larcenies, four new missing persons cases, three suspected kidnappings, two significant fire events, and one confirmed homicide could be called run of the mill.

From the kitchen, Whiskey called out, "There is a large bright orange container labeled 'Home Depot' in the refrigeration unit," he said. "Its intent could be to hold paint. Although it contains what might be coleslaw. Or a pasta salad of some sort. It could very well be a chilled spinach dish."

"Don't eat it," Fantasy yelled. "In fact, stop looking at it."

"Try the freezer," I suggested, as I opened a new window and navigated to *Biloxi Sun Herald*'s website to see what the news had to say about Fantasy the morning after only to find she wasn't the headline. Well, she was and she wasn't. The lead story was more about the parents of the boy she'd unwittingly sent to surgery, Bumper Bartlett, son of Butch and Boofie Bartlett, in that he'd been released from the hospital after minor surgery to repair a flesh wound "to the right lower rear of his trunk" and that his parents had officially lawyered up. In a big way. I grabbed her arm. "Good news." I tilted the screen.

She leaned in and gave the accompanying photo of the parents surrounded by steely-eyed attorneys on the courthouse steps half a glance before pushing the laptop right back to me. "How is this good news?"

"The kid."

"Whose parents have hired fourteen lawyers. Again, Davis, how is this good news?"

"Second of all—" I shot out two fingers "—the 'repairing a flesh wound' part means that the doctors slapped a few stitches in his rear end. Which is hardly surgery. He's already been released. But first of all—" I shot out one finger "—his name." I pushed the laptop back in front of her. "If he weren't eighteen, his name wouldn't be in the paper."

She zoomed in. Before she could celebrate the victory—according to the *Sun Herald*, the kid wasn't a kid, and the paper's fact checkers would've confirmed it before risking a lawsuit themselves—something else caught her eye. She tapped the screen. "The driver."

I squinted. "No, that's the father."

"Then he's the father and the driver," she said. "He was the man driving the van full of naked kids with paintball guns."

My jaw dropped halfway open with the promising implications—the father fully sanctioned and, in fact, aided and assisted with the risky prank on Bellissimo property, and Bellissimo Surveillance would prove it—until Whiskey called out from the kitchen.

"I have unearthed a discovery of note!" His voice had risen several octaves. "You need to observe this, Mesdames Erb and Cole!"

"Observe what?" we both asked.

"There are human remains ensconced in the freezer. Remains that transitioned into the realm of the deceased long ago."

After a pause for stunned silence, I yelled, "WHAT?"

"A DEAD MAN," Whiskey yelled back in people words as opposed to crosswords. "IN THE FREEZER."

NINE

I elbowed Fantasy. "Go look."

She elbowed me back. "You go look."

"What do you want me to do?" I asked. "Go see a frozen dead man or save you?"

"Both."

"Go," I said.

"No," she said. "I've just traipsed through a cemetery. I will not go look at a dead man." Instead, she raised her voice in the direction of the kitchen to say, "It's probably roadkill, Whiskey. A deer. Or a wild boar."

"WELL, THIS WILD BOAR WAS IN THE MILITARY."

Fantasy's head tipped back. "YOU JUST SAID HE WAS IN THE FREEZER."

"I'M AT A LOSS TO STATE IT IN SIMPLER TERMS. THERE IS A DEAD MAN DRESSED IN MILITARY ATTIRE IN THE FREEZER MODERATELY HIDDEN UNDER FROZEN ITALIAN ENTRÉES."

Fantasy and I looked at each other.

"FROZEN WHAT?" we both asked.

"LASAGNA!"

"Fantasy," I said, "go see."

"Davis, I'm a little more invested in what you're doing on the computer than in whatever's in Bea's freezer. Whiskey isn't in his right mind to begin with, and he's a notorious source of bad information. The man talks in circles. And to goats." She turned away from me. "LOOK UNDER THE LASAGNA AND MAKE SURE YOU'RE NOT HALUCINATING, WHISKEY."

"I WILL ATTEMPT TO—" Whiskey finished his sentence with a tremendous thud.

"Whiskey?" I called out.

No answer.

"Did he just drop a frozen lasagna?" I asked.

"Did he just drop a dead body?" she asked back.

I yelled, "WHISKEY, DID YOU DROP THE BODY?"

Still no answer.

With an enormous sigh, she finally exited the booth and was in the process of dragging her feet behind me to the kitchen when the unmistakable sound of a truck slowing to a grinding halt on Main Street rattled the dirty windows. I shot right back into the booth. I couldn't see a thing. I scrambled to standing, stepped onto the table, and met up with a solid inch of congealed and greasy dust on the shade casing before I saw the front end of an eighteen-wheeler flatbed truck rolling to a stop. A fenced flatbed truck. I could see the cab, the trailer, and green. Green, green, and more glorious green, stacked at least eight feet high and dotted with shades of red from blush to candy apple, shades of blue from arctic to cobalt, and pure white.

The contents of the Bellissimo Gardens.

A sight for very sore eyes.

"That thud?" It was Fantasy in the doorway between the kitchen and the dining room. "It was Whiskey. He passed out."

"Throw cold water on him."

"What are you looking at?"

"A truck," I said. "With a fifty-foot trailer. From the Bellissimo."

"Well, you'd better stop watching that and come watch this."

"This what?" I was busy watching the driver door of the first truck open and the driver drop to the street to be immediately surrounded by curious Pine Apple residents.

"Whiskey was right."

"About?" The passenger door of the truck opened. I couldn't see who climbed out.

"There's a dead man."

"You're sure?" I couldn't see the passenger rounding the cab through the cover of the oak trees.

"I'm positive," she said. "Past dead. Bones and such."

The passenger who'd exited the truck rounded the cab, barely coming into my line of sight. "And you're absolutely positive it's human remains?"

"Yes, human remains. You've got a grave robber in Pine Apple who dug up a body during the night and dumped it here, then tried to hide it under three industrial-sized frozen lasagnas. And he's Air Force. Looks like he was a decorated pilot."

My eyes swam, my breath left my lungs, and my heart dropped to the floor.

For two reasons.

I didn't have a grave robber in Pine Apple—well, the deep freeze was saying otherwise, so I probably did—but more than that, what I had was a once-removed bank robber. Because the long dead Air Force pilot's body that was relocated to Bea Crawford's freezer and hidden under frozen lasagna had to be USAF Command Pilot Eli Atwell. Former best friend of bank-robbing Frank Simmons. Alibi to Fiona Simmons. Bailer-outer of Pine Apple Bank & Trust. Why would someone dig up his grave? Because the money everyone had been looking for all these years must have been buried with him.

But that was only half of it.

The other half was the passenger from the truck. Standing in the middle of Main Street was our boss. Mine and Fantasy's. It was Jeremy Covey. Vice President of Security for the Bellissimo Resort and Casino. And he didn't need a megaphone when, feet planted wide and fists on hips, he tipped his bald head back and yelled my name to the heavens.

TEN

The diner had seven booths along the front wall. Each booth had its own grimy window and its own mini jukebox. All in various stages of inoperable. (The windows, the jukeboxes, and half of the booths.) Opposite the booths, twelve duct tape-decorated stools marched along the lunch counter at regular intervals. There were no mini jukeboxes, but there were plenty of condiments. Including a scattered assortment of salad dressings. At room temp. One directly in front of me had my attention. It had clearly been in residence for at least a decade, held less than an inch of what might have been petrified product inside, and it was labeled Green Goddess. Which I'd never even heard of.

There was an odd four-top table past the far end of the counter where diners weren't welcome. It was Bea's office. Where she held court, negotiations, and interrogations. Where, unless otherwise occupied burning food, she listened in and butted in on lunch conversations. And on the wall just above where she sat, she proudly displayed a framed copy of her most recent report card from the Alabama Department of Public Health. Why she took pride in her score of 47—overwritten on the scoresheet in huge numbers with a thick red marker, then circled, and underlined twice—who knew. Just like no one knew why she displayed her Yelp score of 1.3 at the other end of the counter. Beside the cash register.

There was a four- by seven-foot-wide aisle between all the corroded chrome, chipped Formica, and ripped pleather, giving our boss plenty of room, fifty feet one way and fifty feet the other way, to pace the length of the diner. Or stomp, rather, between the three of us.

Fifteen minutes had passed since, defeated and having no other choice, I'd called him and told him where to find me. Ten minutes had passed since he'd pulled three chairs from Bea's office table and

106

placed them strategically, one at one end of the room, one at the other end, and one in the middle, then seated us by pointing. With Whiskey in the middle. Five minutes had passed since he'd spoken to us with, "Don't move a muscle. Don't even blink." Since then, he'd traveled between us. He'd stop and stare, just to ratchet up the tension, but didn't say anything for the longest. Then finally, the interrogation started. With Whiskey. "Cedric? Do you realize you look ridiculous?"

"I'm fully aware."

"What are you doing here?"

Whiskey noisily rubbed his sandpaper chin. "I'm unable to provide a definitive answer."

"How is it, Cedric, you don't know why you're here?"

"I surely have been posing the same question to myself."

"Do you remember arriving?"

"My recollection is somewhat shrouded," Whiskey said, "but I do remember meeting a herd of ill-tempered goats."

"No Hair—" I interrupted to answer for Whiskey in English, and to keep him from telling No Hair the flying goat story, only to be immediately cut off with a stop-sign hand.

"That moniker sounds pejorative," Whiskey stage-whispered to me. "Are you not concerned he'll take offense? Why would you risk increasing his ire?"

No Hair spun back to Whiskey. "Because she doesn't know any better."

"I speculate it might have more to do with the fact that you do not sport hair."

No Hair towered over him. "I'm going to sport you in a minute, Cedric, if you don't stop talking."

Whiskey zipped his lips.

Next up, Fantasy. After another two minutes of pacing, our boss, feet planted wide, arms crossed, steam coming out of his ears—I'm kidding—stopped an inch from her and demanded, "What were you thinking?"

She tried to scoot her chair back to put more space between them, but there was nowhere to go. "Which part?"

"Don't get smart with me, Fantasy."

"I wasn't thinking, okay, No Hair? There wasn't time to think."

Whiskey piped up again. "Is that your pet name for this glabrous gentleman too?"

No Hair cut his eyes at Whiskey.

Whiskey zipped his lips again.

To Fantasy, he said, "Explain yourself."

"There isn't a doubt in my mind that you know as much about what happened as I do, No Hair," she said. "You've probably watched every angle of video Surveillance could give you until you were almost blind from it, you've talked every witness blue in the face, and you've probably already started negotiations for a settlement. The only thing left for you to do is officially fire me. Which is why you're here. So go ahead."

"You've already been officially fired, Fantasy."

"So why are you here?" she demanded. "To rub it in? Go ahead, No Hair. Get it off your chest."

I leaned past Whiskey and barely said, "Fantasy. Stop."

She leaned past Whiskey and boldly said, "No, thank you."

Then she slapped her knees with her hands, took a deep breath, and stood to her full six feet. Almost eye-to-eye with No Hair. "You want an explanation? I was doing my job. The job *you* taught me to do." She stabbed his chest with a finger. "And you'd have done the same thing."

He caught her finger and held it tight. "You might be right, Fantasy, except I wouldn't have run. Like a girl."

"I fear there is no tolerance for misogyny in today's workplace," Whiskey said.

"And I believe I told you there's no tolerance for you speaking," No Hair shot back.

Whiskey zipped his lips. Again.

No Hair turned back to Fantasy. "You might be right. But I'd have found hella better backup." He gave Whiskey a nod.

Whiskey waved.

No Hair saved the best for last, slowly stomping my way. Each footfall more menacing than the one before. I squirmed in my seat. When he spoke, it was with less fury. And more curiosity. "Davis? How have you managed to destroy your hometown in two short days?"

"That's a long story, No Hair, and one I had nothing to do with."

"Of course you didn't," he said. "I can't remember the last time you took responsibility for an iota of the havoc and chaos that seem to follow you everywhere you go."

"That's not true. When it's my fault, I own it."

"Are you harboring a fugitive from the law, Davis?"

"No."

He threw his arms in the air. "See? There you go again." His arm shot out to display Exhibit One at the other end of the room. "You are most certainly harboring a fugitive. And not taking responsibility for it."

"It's not like I called Fantasy and said, 'Hey, did you shoot a kid in the casino? Come hang out with me. I'll hide you.'"

"True," Fantasy said. "And turns out, he isn't a kid."

"You shut up," No Hair said to Fantasy. "In fact," he warned, "all three of you keep quiet." And with that, he pulled his phone from his pocket and dialed. The next thing we heard was, "Brad? I've got her."

I stopped breathing.

"Yes," No Hair said to my husband, "she's here too."

I might never breathe again.

No Hair looked at me. "Where are your children?"

"With my sister."

"Did you hear that?" Apparently, Bradley heard that. Then No Hair said, "I'll let her know," and ended the call. Not looking up from his phone as he dialed again, he told me, "Your husband says don't call him, he'll call you."

Great.

Just great.

"Samuel?"

My father? No!

"You were right. But it's worse than either of us imagined."

After thirty of the longest seconds of my life, No Hair said, "I'll tell her."

He slid his phone back into his pocket. "Your father asked that you undo whatever it is you've done to his phone."

I was thinking that there was absolutely no way the situation could get any worse, when it was actually more specific than that, there was no way my *life* could get any worse than it was that very minute, when a voice rang out from the kitchen. "Say." It sounded very much like Roy Howdy. "Anybody here?"

Definitely Roy Howdy.

I tipped my head back and yelled, "Get out of here, Roy Howdy!"

"That you, Davis?" he called out. "Did you know old Eli Atwell was in this here freezer? He's supposed to be in my root cellar. What's he doing here?"

No Hair's eyes rolled back in his head. "Who is he and what is he talking about?"

"That's Roy Howdy," I explained. "He runs the funeral home and makes voodoo candles. There's a dead body in Bea's freezer."

No Hair's mouth dropped open.

"I don't know what a root cellar has to do with anything."

Fantasy leaned in. "I don't even know what a root cellar is. Or a voodoo candle, for that matter."

Whiskey piped up. "A root cellar is a subterranean room with the primary purpose of storing perishables. Although I share your curiosity regarding candles possessed with voodoo."

No Hair said, "Shut up. All three of you."

ELEVEN

The Gulfstream G280 with the Bellissimo logo splashed across the fuselage landed two hours later at a private jet strip adjacent to Montgomery Regional Airport. I thought it best I pick up my husband even though No Hair pointed out what I already knew, which was we could have a limo on the tarmac to pick him up with a quick phone call. But it wasn't a limo driver who had to face the music. It was me. I considered bringing the girls and the baby with me, knowing the music wouldn't be so loud, but I didn't. I left them with my sister.

"Fine," she said, "but take Granny. I can't handle the kids and Granny. One or the other. You choose."

"I can't. I have to go alone."

"You're killing me, Davis."

"I'm killing myself, Meredith."

"So Bradley knows everything? And Daddy knows everything?"

I could barely hear her even though we were a foot from each other. My children were climbing all over me. The girls were telling me about their day without taking breaths, everything from making mud pies, mud cupcakes, and mud cookies in the creek behind The Front Porch, catching baby frogs Aunt Merri wouldn't let them keep because their frog mommy would miss them too much if they came to live with us, then swimming in their cousin Riley's upstairs bathtub that had bear feet and was as big as a pool, then playing dress up in the Vintage Clothing room of Aunt Merri's store, and having a tea party for lunch. With memento cheese sandwiches they didn't like and cluecumber sandwiches they did. The whole time, the baby patted my face, pulled my ponytail, and made all his baby noises at top volume. Wanting in on the conversation. "I'm not sure what all Bradley or Daddy knows, Meredith," I tried to say over the children.

"Clearly Bradley knows enough to drop what he was doing, charter a plane, and fly here to kill me."

"Do you talk like that in front of your kids all the time?"

I hit the road for Montgomery.

When I arrived, Bradley's plane was still seventeen minutes out. That, according to Flight Aware. I parked, found a cup of coffee and a seat in the small passenger waiting area of the small terminal, then checked my phone. I'd received a text message from Fantasy that was so long it scrolled through three screens.

Are you okay? Is he tossing around the D word? You know I'm kidding about that. He would never. Reggie and I toss around the D word over toast, but not you and Bradley. Just hang in there. It'll all work out. And speaking of my husband, and speaking of speaking, Reggie is speaking to me again. He's still mad, more than anything else because it's the bitter end of the school year and he's having to hustle the boys through their final exams alone because of their fugitive mother, but at least the two patrol cars that have been glued to our house finally left. That's because I've turned myself in. While No Hair and I waited on a crime scene team at the diner, your grandmother scared up the only attorney in town, Smearl. I'm sure you know him. Smearl T. Webb. To whom I paid a $1 retainer. Then we had a video call with the judge. I agreed to show up for questioning on the shooting within twenty-four hours and pled not guilty to the fleeing-the-scene business in spite of the fact that I'm very guilty of fleeing the scene. I've been remanded into No Hair's custody until my court appearance tomorrow afternoon. No Hair asked Smearl T. Webb if he was licensed to practice in Mississippi and Smearl said, "Where?" He asked Smearl to file a continuance to give me until after Memorial Day anyway, and Smearl T. Webb said, "A what?" Then the man I saw earlier when I was peeking through the station blinds, the one who wasn't dirty, showed up looking for you. He's the owner of the fireworks company and he needs to talk to you. He's worried you're going to cancel. Really worried. Which is good news, I *guess, considering all the chicken wing trucks running for the hills. Not this guy. He's not a bit worried about the goats or the mud. Then the county coroner showed up. As far as I know, No Hair's still with him. He had to track down your grandmother again to sign off on the body being transferred to the crime lab, because she's the only one left standing with a badge. A badge that looks like it's from a Halloween costume, I might add, but she was THRILLED. And dragged it out for an hour. Now No Hair has me helping Roy Howdy supervise the unloading of the Bellissimo truck—a form of punishment, or torture, I think, because he knows exactly how blazing hot it is, and couldn't care less that my Valentinos are TRASHED—and unloading a truck is way slower work than you'd imagine because it's packed so tight. After a solid hour, we're only ten feet in and now up against a virtual wall of grass. Bales and bales of rolled lengths of grass, dirt side out, tied with thick twine. I can't even see what's behind all the grass except it's a big metal container of some sort. What was in the Bellissimo Gardens that would need to be packed in a big metal container? Your children are fine, but your sister is at the end of her rope. I think she was okay until I dropped off Whiskey and begged her to feed him. Since then, she's texted every ten minutes. "This is above and beyond. I can't handle these kids and this nut." "Any sign of Davis?" "Can you take this guy back?" "Is this man some sort of linguist?" "Do you know if this man has CLOTHES?" Now, Davis, this Roy Howdy person, my truck unloading buddy, he's interesting. I asked about his name, and he told me he was an eleven-pounder at birth. Everyone said, "Boy, howdy!" because he was so big, which morphed into Roy Howdy, and that's why the poor guy has such a stupid name. Although it suits him. Not only is he as strong as an ox, when he tells people they can't have a hedgerow—whatever that is—until they're all off the truck and he counts them so he can distribute them evenly (not his words...his words were more like, "You wait your turn and don't be greedy or no telling what might happen to you"), they listen. I couldn't figure out how one man wielded enough Pine Apple power to the point of no one arguing with him, not even Sherriff Eugenia Woman, then he explained the voodoo candles. He's running a voodoo candle business out of his basement. And his basement is under the FUNERAL HOME because he LIVES in a funeral home. That creepy house on the hill in the cemetery? I guess you know all this. I thought you were kidding when you told No Hair he made voodoo candles. He learned voodoo from his uncle who raised him. He says voodoo is his legacy. These people are scared to death of him and his legacy and now I understand why. I'm trying to stay in his good graces so he doesn't cast a voodoo spell on me, because I have enough probs as it is. I asked him outright if he'd put some manner of voodoo on you, since things aren't going all that well for you, and he said no. Saving the worst news for last, two more chicken wing trucks have rolled into town only to roll right back out. That's three dropouts just today. Makes me wonder why your old high school friend, who I haven't seen hide nor hair of, is still here. Or if she's still here. No one has seen her or the boy this whole town is calling Eddie Junior. I haven't heard details, just bits and pieces, but they're both hot topics. Along with the dead Air Force guy. And the hedgerows. Just...call when you can. Good luck with Bradley.*

I didn't have a clue as to why no one had seen Eddie Crawford's son, but I had a good guess where my old high school friend, Florida Simmons, was. Sleeping off an all-night grave robbing. For all I knew, she could have already left town with the long-lost money. And Eddie Crawford's son. I was wondering if I had enough time to text Fantasy back and tell her just that when I looked up to see the terminal doors open and my husband storm through them.

His eyes found mine and held them as he breezed right by.

I guess that meant we were leaving.

I hopped up.

His first words to me were in the parking lot. "I'll drive."

I tossed him the keys.

Here's the thing about my husband—he loves me. And I love him. We were a perfect match when it came to our marriage, parenting, finances, lifestyle, our five-, ten-, and fifty-year plans, plus vaguer things. Like our values and beliefs, and that neither of us particularly cared for cilantro. More than anything else, we were happy. Happily married. It sounded cliché. It also sounded impossible, unattainable, and at the very least hard, to hear most married couples tell it, but the truth was the only hard part of our marriage was work. And it was only one of us whose work got in the way.

Guess which one.

Ninety-nine days out of one hundred, our work boundaries were clearly defined. He was the President and CEO of a billion-dollar casino. And even though I led an elite security team for the same casino, I was many rungs down the Bellissimo ladder. A fact I'd never resented, mostly because I wouldn't want Bradley's job. It was hard enough for me to keep up with two employees. I'd never be able to keep up with five thousand. I had trouble answering to one boss. I'd lose my mind if I had to answer to a casino owner and a board of directors. If I had Bradley's job, I'd drag myself to the office, tell my assistant to hold my calls, then lock the door, put my head on the desk, and cry until it was time to go home. He, on the other hand, was fascinated with my job. I'd never asked him to explain balance sheets, dividends, prime-plus whatevers, or tell me what it took to run the food and beverage division of a billion-dollar resort. And I never would. Because I truly didn't want to know. He, from day one, had been exceptionally curious about my job. He found it fascinating and wanted to know as much about it as he could. In the beginning, I think it was to allay his fear for my personal safety. He didn't like that I was, as he put it, so casual with firearms. Like he thought I might shoot myself. So rather than talk him off that cliff every time I strapped on a hot gun, I taught him how to expertly wield one himself. Because knowledge was power. And it was a power he'd regrettably had to call on more than once. He calmed down. Then started worrying about takedowns. So I taught him everything I knew about evasive maneuvers and delay tactics, the elements of which he went on to apply to the never-ending media frenzy that came with his job. I taught him criminal tells, which was a very handy trick to have up his sleeve when a parade of Tang suits and mirrored Ray-Bans surrounded by personal bodyguards carrying titanium briefcases blew through our front doors, marched into our high-stakes poker room, and began splashing obscene amounts of cash around. While watching me do my job, he learned the finer points of witness interrogation. Once he knew how to ask a specific question to solicit a specific answer, it saved him countless unwise upper-management hires. At one point or another in our years together, he'd made it his job to be privy to everything I knew about law and order. Then applied the basic principles to his own job. With full understanding that when it came to actually dealing with the criminal element, as opposed to interviewing a new casino manager, I couldn't always take the straight and narrow path to a justified end that he could. While he never had to resort to it within the confines of his job, I was often forced to employ deceit to properly do mine.

He *knew* that.

It was when he felt like he was on the receiving end of deception-by-me that we hit a marriage bump. Our problems happened when he felt like he was being misled. By me. His own wife. Until I could calm him down and explain the steps I took to protect him, our children, Fantasy, and my hometown, then explain why I took those steps, I would remain in the marital hot seat having presumably undermined what the two of us had above all else: trust.

And that's where I was. Miserably staring out the window having an untrustworthy pity party as Bradley used the car's navigation system to get us from the airport to I-65 rather than ask me for directions on a route I'd grown up on. Because I'd broken his trust. And there was no telling how long he'd have given me the silent treatment had I not slapped the dashboard with both hands and screamed. "STOP. BACK UP!"

"DAVIS!" He swerved to the shoulder and slammed on the brakes. "WHAT IS WRONG WITH YOU?"

"There." I pointed up a hill. "Take me there."

He had to dip my way and look out my window—I wanted very much to touch a lock of his hair—to see what was so urgent. "I don't see a Starbucks."

"There isn't one. Do you really think I'd ask you to stop for coffee as mad at me as you are?"

He spoke to the rearview mirror as he waited to merge back into traffic. "Davis, you ask me to stop when you see a Starbucks unless you have a hot Starbucks in your hand. And even then, you've asked me to stop because there's either too much or too little cream in your coffee. But there is no Starbucks. There's a goat rental company." By then, we were approaching a median. "Only in Alabama do people rent goats."

"You'd be surprised," I said. "As it turns out, goat rental is big business."

He turned into the next median and stopped. "Maybe you and Fantasy can look into that."

"Look into what?"

"Opening a goat rental business."

We were in the middle of a highway. So rather than go down the precarious path of defending my job, or Fantasy's, or even ask him what he thought goats were supposed to eat on the Gulf—seagrass?—I asked, "Are we going to sit here until someone hits us?"

He took the left and merged onto US 80 again. But going the other way. Backtracking. He took another left at the median which pointed us at Graze Away Goat Rental. Home of Hassle-Free Brush Removal and Weed Control. He punched it between cars, we shot across US 80, and were halfway up the hill passing acres of empty goat pens on both sides when he said, "You might be right."

"About what?" I was staring at the empty pens, wondering where the goats were.

"Look at the car parked at the employee entrance."

I wasn't much of a car person. "What about it?"

"It's a Lamborghini Revuelto."

"And?"

"You might be right about the money."

I was lost. Thrilled he was speaking to me in civil tones, but lost. "What about the money?"

"There could very well be money in goat rentals."

We parked beside the Lamborghini.

I made my move to exit the car, saying, "I'll just be a minute."

"Do you need me to come with you?"

Which meant he wanted to come with me. "Would you?"

He graced me with the sliver of a weary smile. "What am I going to do with you, Davis?"

TWELVE

The office was ramshackle. Behind the front counter that ran almost the full width of the room was one woman, two battered desks, four beat-up filing cabinets, and some manner of console against the back wall that probably once held an impossibly large television but at present was home to what looked like a decade of paperwork on both sides of a two-decade-old Mr. Coffee. The only thing out of place in what might otherwise pass for a construction site office was the woman. She was ten years older than me and twenty years slicker. She looked like she'd been around the block a thousand times or two, staring down the barrel of fifty, trying hard to hang on to thirty-nine. She had long jet-black hair piled up on her head, thick eyeliner, blood-red lipstick, and was wearing a floral silk dress under a denim vest. I couldn't see her feet, but I'd have bet they were in ankle-high cowboy boots. I was dealing with a bona fide Alabama native—not a problem unless things went adversarial—who raised thin eyebrows above rhinestone embellished reading glasses.

I stepped up to the counter. "Is Bobby in?"

"Bobby's gone."

The way she said it let me know Bobby wasn't coming back. "That would be why he hasn't returned my calls."

"Which would make you Davis. From Pine Apple."

She said it so accusatorially, things went adversarial. Already. So I dispensed with the pleasantries, such as they were. "You don't know me."

"Fourteen messages on the answering machine?" she said. "All from Davis in Pine Apple? I believe I know enough."

I opened my mouth to add a fifteenth message because the answering machine's timer had cut me off the other fourteen times just when I'd gotten to the good stuff, but she stopped me with, "Save your breath." She raised a finger with a bright idea. "And let me save you a little time." She reached under the counter and I immediately jerked, my right hand sliding up my hip, which led her to believe I was carrying when in fact I wasn't, then her hand reappeared holding a business card. She said, "Settle down." She waved the business card, then slid it across the counter. "Here's my insurance information." She reached for a second business card and landed it on the first. "And here's my attorney." She pulled a third business card from somewhere inside her denim vest, and with a flick, sailed it through the air like a magician. It hit its mark, landing on the other two. I reached for the last one. She was Summer Dalton, Owner. Of Graze Away Goat Rental, Green Thumb Landscaping, and Pave the Way Asphalt. I held it out for Bradley.

He said, "This explains the Lamborghini."

She took half a seat on the edge of the desk behind her. She crossed her arms. "Go ahead," she said. "Sue me."

Bradley gathered the other two business cards, tapped them on the counter, then slid them into his jacket pocket to join the first. "We'll be in touch."

"I'm sure you will."

We took a step for the door. Before we could get on the other side of it, she said, "A little advice?"

We turned.

She toggled forked fingers at us. "Work out whatever it is going on between the two of you before you come after me for an unfortunate incident that will no doubt be ruled a simple mix-up. A mistake. A regrettable mistake, but in the end, just a mistake. And while you're digging into the details of the errors and omissions clause of my umbrella insurance, just keep in mind that a jury of my Alabama peers is going to have a hard time hammering down on little ole me, a hard-working female business owner employing hundreds of my Alabama neighbors, over grass that will grow back before poor

Pine Apple, with the full weight of a big fat Mississippi casino in its back pocket, can even whine about it to a judge."

I don't think either of us blinked.

"What?" She was suddenly coy. "Cat got your tongue?"

Beside me, Bradley—always wearing his lawyer hat above his casino CEO suit—took in a sharp breath to spout statutes and limitations at her. I put a quiet hand on his arm to stop him. Because it wouldn't do a bit of good. She knew what she knew. I met her hard eyes head on. "Where are the goats?" Expecting threats and ultimatums from me, the seemingly innocent question threw her. "What?" I could do coy too. "Frog in your throat?"

She smirked.

I smirked back. "What did you do with the goats?"

"I fired everyone," she said. "Including the goats."

Silently back on US 80 just a mile from the entrance ramp to I-65 that would lead us to Pine Apple, Bradley took an exit.

"Where are we going?"

He pointed. Starbucks. "If you're going to explain what just happened, Davis, and what it has to do with you not telling me the truth about Fantasy—" he slid into the drive-through lane "—you'll need coffee."

I wasn't sure there was that much coffee.

Before the Welcome to Pine Apple sign came into sight almost an hour later, my throat completely dry, despite the coffee, from spilling the whole truth and nothing but the truth, we passed a chicken wing truck going the wrong way. The West Wings. The truck was red, white, and blue—stars and stripes and such—with a Statue of Liberty hood ornament.

"That's four," I said.

"Let it go, Davis."

"No," I said, "not yet. Not until I try to talk them back into the cookoff. I still have time."

He pulled into my parents' driveway as dusk was descending. He cut the engine. His eyes wandered, incredulously, all over the yard, landing on Daddy's gutters in ruins and scattered in the side yard. "Davis, the chicken wing cookoff isn't going to happen. Face that fact. Then prioritize what you can make happen. Fulfill your promise to your dad to answer the station phone while you spend time with your family and take care of our children, say goodbye to Fantasy and wish her luck, then concentrate on supervising the restoration of this otherwise picturesque model of rural tranquility that you call home. And do it before your parents return. Stand down and let the feds solve the mystery of the disturbed grave. Keep the peace in Pine Apple, which shouldn't be hard to do after the dust settles, and focus your energy on restoring your mother's yard."

"What about the money?"

"What about it? Do you truly believe someone dug up a grave for money?"

I believed it completely before he shot holes in all my quick judgements.

"Money stolen twenty years ago is long gone," he said. "The only thing left is folklore."

"How can you be so sure?"

"I just listened to the whole sordid story, Davis. I'm very sure."

"I'm not."

"Has anyone asked the former bank owner? The father of your old high school friend who you say is the mother of Eddie Crawford's love child? Has anyone bothered to ask that thief what he did with the money? Ask him. He'll tell you where the money is. It's nowhere. It's long gone. Spent. Used to pay off his own debts. Or his partner ran off with it. You can't hide that much money for twenty years in a town this small."

I'd never considered that Frank Simmons might've had a partner back in the day. Nor had I ever heard anyone suggest anything close to it. It was an interesting theory, because last I checked, bank robberies were almost never solo endeavors. But I stopped myself from going down that speculative road, because for one, my head was about to explode, and for another, it wasn't nearly as appealing as Bradley's earlier advice. Reiterated just then with, "Davis, this isn't your problem. Let it go."

The thought of letting it go sounded wonderful. I'd done all I could for Fantasy, I'd arranged two acres of greenery to replace the goat damage in my hometown, and if nothing else, I could switch the chicken wing cookoff back to a potato salad competition in a heartbeat which would thrill Pine Apple's Women's Society because one of them would finally take the crown from my mother. The Memorial Day Celebration would go on with a parade and fireworks like every other year—and doing nothing but planting flowers in my parents' yard until then sounded like heaven. I could see the baby napping in his Pack 'n Play under a shade tree while the girls and I turned the tender Alabama earth, and it sounded like a vacation in and of itself, because Bradley was right. I couldn't save the world.

"Davis, let's go get Bex, Quinn, and my boy."

"That's another thing."

"What?" He was instantly alarmed.

"Your boy."

"What about him?"

"Hudson. Your boy's name is Hudson. Everyone here is calling our son Junior. Having heard it a hundred times since we rolled into town, the girls are even calling the baby Junior."

"They are not."

"Well, they're calling him Junebug. Their version of Junior. Which is cute and worse at the same time."

"We could put a stop to it if the two of us could land on what to call him. Like the goat lady said. Work it out between us first."

"It is worked out. His name is Hudson."

"Hudson *isn't* working out, Davis."

I threw my hands in the air. "Do we not get to name our own child?"

"Yes," he said. "And that part is over. We have named him. What we have to land on is what to call him. The world is full of people who don't go by their given names. How about your Roy Howdy?"

"He isn't my Roy Howdy, thank you. The baby has nothing in common with Roy Howdy."

"See? You don't even call him Hudson, Davis. You tell other people to call him Hudson when you don't. Anyone listening to you long enough would think we named our son The Baby."

"He's only five months old," I said. "Give it time."

"He'll be six months old next week and time is something I have too little of," he said. "Especially now that my dreams of becoming an adjunct professor are dashed—"

"Since when was it your dream to be an adjunct professor?"

"I was kidding," he said. "Although I'm not kidding when I say that with my academia career cut short, I should be behind my desk in Biloxi. Not only do I have the fallout from Fantasy's last stand in the casino—"

"What do you mean by last stand?"

He looked away from me. Stared at the destroyed yard. "You know I'll try my hardest to do right by Fantasy, the Bellissimo, and everyone else involved, Davis, but I can't tell you what that will look like in the end."

"Why not?"

"Because I don't know."

He impatiently tapped the steering wheel. I didn't know if it was because he'd woken up expecting another day in Texas, but by late afternoon found himself in Alabama, or if I'd overloaded him. Probably both. "When will you go home?"

He checked the time. "I want to see the children for a little more than hello and goodbye. So let's say tomorrow. We'll leave for Biloxi tomorrow."

"Who is we?"

"Me, Fantasy, and I suppose we should put Whiskey back in the Bellissimo drunk tank where he belongs."

"Whiskey's sober."

"He is not."

"He is, Bradley."

"Finally," he sighed, "some good news."

Not such good news, because sober Whiskey babbled relentlessly, but I didn't go there, because Bradley had left one Biloxi player out. "What about No Hair?"

"He's driving."

"The eighteen-wheeler he rode in on?"

"No. We'll take the new Bellissimo truck Fantasy commandeered."

I didn't go there either.

I expected his next words to be, "Davis? Did you take a baseball bat to the computer of the new Bellissimo truck?" but they were, "Davis? Who's the woman in the rocking chair?"

And there in the shadows behind the latticework of the wraparound porch was Florida Simmons.

THIRTEEN

I remembered fun, competitive, and brilliant Florida Simmons. She had an innate knack for the sciences: physics, chemistry, and biology. Our junior year in high school she won first place in the Alabama State Science Fair with something about constructing or deconstructing or reconstructing RNA molecules. Maybe it was DNA. It was so long ago, I didn't remember. Although I did remember her scoring a perfect 36 on the ACT. The last time I saw her before everything blew up in both our lives, she was flying down Main Street on her way to my house waving a sheet of paper above her head like a victory flag. She'd received Early Action Admission to MIT and was on her way to Cambridge, Massachusetts.

I wondered how that girl wound up driving a chicken wing truck.

But then again, I knew.

Everyone knew.

Because a week after she'd received the coveted MIT letter, just seven little days later, her life fell apart when her father robbed Pine Apple Bank & Trust. At the time, my young life had suddenly plunged into such shambles for reasons unrelated to Florida, I barely noticed when she vanished in the aftermath of her father disappearing with both teller drawers, every dime in the vault, every stock and bond certificate, and every item from every safe-deposit box at the bank, which was after he sold and cashed in on every mortgage the bank held on every inch of land Pine Apple had entrusted to him. And it was barely a bleep on my life radar when Frank Simmons confessed his crimes three days later after a statewide APB turned him up at VictoryLand Casino in Shorter, Alabama. With less than a hundred dollars in his wallet. I'd been long gone from Pine Apple by the time he was convicted of a Class A felony under Alabama Code Title 13A, sentenced to ninety-nine years in prison for the robbery, an additional year for endangering the welfare and livelihood of an entire town, with a "no money, no parole" clause tacked on because Frank refused to give up the location of his ill-gotten gains. The judge's last words to Frank Simmons before the gavel smacked were, "Cough up the money and we'll talk."

I wasn't around to witness the details of Frank's wife, Fiona, playing the role of Suspect Number One either. I later learned her life was turned completely upside down. She'd been endlessly interrogated by the authorities, badgered by destitute Pine Apple residents, harassed by angry local businesses, and evicted from the historic Colonial that had been the Simmons family home on Banana Street after learning her husband had sold the mortgage out from under her, trading it for a rundown one-bedroom clapboard rental with iffy plumbing on the edge of town. Away from the anguish. Away from the accusations. Away from the anger. She surely would have disappeared too had she not been under a court order to stay put. And things didn't get better for Fiona until six weeks later when Eli Atwell, her being-held-without-bond husband's best friend, stepped forward with an alibi for her. Just as she was about to be arrested for aiding, abetting, conspiracy, and possession of stolen property, Eli Atwell told the authorities Fiona had been at The American Inn on the Camden bypass at the time of the robbery. And sure enough, the owner of the rundown no-tell motel on the side of the road identified and placed Fiona at his establishment on the night before, the night of, and the night after the bank robbery.

General consensus said Fiona and Eli had been together. General consensus went on to assume that his wife having an affair with his best friend was plenty of motive for Frank to rob his own bank and run. And when Pine Apple had no choice but to accept that Fiona hadn't been in on the robbery and truly didn't know where the money was, general consensus decided Frank had hidden it. And the treasure hunt began.

Years later, when I returned home and was sworn in as a Pine Apple police officer, the treasure hunt was still on. The money had yet to be discovered. And not for lack of looking.

I'd been back almost a year when I asked my police chief father, "Why is this still a thing?" I waved another fishing expedition incident report I'd been working on steadily for two days.

He shrugged. "Small town boredom?"

At least once a month, I had to placate the new owners of the old Simmons home when they woke to a new dig under their barn. I issued citations at least every six weeks after catching search teams digging around the bank property in the dead of night. I left Pine Apple as a teenager knowing three things: Florida was gone, the bank had been robbed, and the money hadn't been recovered. I returned as an adult and the same three things were true. The case had never been solved.

"What happened?" I asked.

"What do you mean?" Daddy answered.

"Frank Simmons practically turned himself in."

"He was captured, Davis."

"He was hiding in plain sight."

He stood. "How about a cup of coffee?"

I stayed seated. "How about you start at the beginning? Start before the robbery. Help me understand what we're dealing with."

"It's over, Davis. We aren't dealing with a thing."

"We're dealing with ongoing property destruction." I waved the incident report again. "Tell me why."

Daddy said, "There's nothing to tell."

"There's nothing to tell about Frank Simmons or Eli Atwell? There's nothing you can tell me about Florida? Can you at least tell me how Fiona ended up running the bank her husband robbed? Daddy, tell me what happened."

"No one knows exactly what happened." He made a move for the door. "Let it go, Davis."

"Let it go?" The ink was still wet on my Criminal Justice degree. I didn't want to let it go. "Don't you want to know what really happened, Daddy? Don't you want to know where the money is?"

"No," he said. "I don't. What I want is a cup of coffee." He had one foot out the door when he turned back to say, "If you want to try to find your friend Florida, go ahead. Otherwise, don't poke a sleeping bear, Davis. Leave the bank robbery alone."

It wasn't a suggestion.

That afternoon, and very much without my father's blessing, I quietly requested the trial transcripts. I pored over the court documents for weeks when I wasn't otherwise occupied being miserably married to Eddie the Idiot for the second time or honing my school guard crossing skills. I landed on what felt like one truth right away: the alleged affair wasn't nearly enough motive for what Frank Simmons had done. In addition, according to the trial transcripts, Fiona's alibis, the no-tell motel owner and three other motel guests, who turned out to be nosy motel residents, thus reliable witnesses, all agreed they'd noticed someone slipping in and out of Fiona's room each of the nights, but were never asked to identify the someone as Eli Atwell. More than that, I realized reading through Eli Atwell's testimony, he never said he was there. Only that he knew for certain Fiona was. And it was as far as I could get on my own. So I turned to my grandmother. Who couldn't resist what she called scuttlebutt. On my day off, I treated her to lunch in Greenville. Bates House of Turkey. Her favorite.

"Granny." We were just past the Welcome to Pine Apple sign with twenty miles of road ahead of us. "Tell me about the bank robbery."

"So that's what this is about?"

"This is about spending time together."

"Uh-huh."

A quiet mile later, Granny said, "Davis, honey, the bank robbery almost ruined Pine Apple. No one wants to open that old wound."

"I've noticed."

"If what you've noticed is your daddy not wanting to beat that dead horse, just remember, most of his job is keeping the peace. Stirring up the bank robbery business will ruffle feathers again. Maybe you should leave it be."

Five quiet miles later, and barely above a whisper, Granny said, "Frank Simmons was a dicer, you know."

I knew she'd crack. "A whater?"

"A dicer," she said. "He rolled the dice."

Ah.

"Where is there in Pine Apple to roll dice?" I asked.

"There isn't," she answered. "There's Wednesday Night Bingo with the Presbyterians and that's it. He closed the bank at noon on Fridays and hit the riverboats in Mississippi."

That made sense too. I didn't think a thing about it at the time, because I was a teenager who didn't think about anything that wasn't directly in my face, but Florida's father was never around on the weekends.

Granny leaned across the console to take me into her confidence even though we were the only two people in my squad car. "And I've heard tell he was a bookmaker on the sly too."

A bookwhater?

Granny explained that legend had it Frank Simmons went from dice to sports betting. He made so much money betting the ponies, his Pine Apple friends wanted in on the action. Within six months, he was taking bets from all over Wilcox County. Mostly on horse races, but on SEC and NFL football too. On the World Series. On The Masters. On Wimbledon. Granny said she'd heard it told that back in the day he'd have given odds and taken bets on a game of stickball.

"I know nothing about gambling, Granny, but I doubt there's much middle ground. It sounds to me like that could only have gone one way or the other for Frank the Bookmaker."

"Half the town thinks it's one way," she said, "that he had more money than God."

"That makes no sense. If he had all that money, why would he rob his own bank?"

"That's what the other half says."

We passed Moose Harwell on his tractor. He waved; I beeped.

"The other half says what?" I asked.

"That it went the other way. And that Frank robbed the bank to pay off Biloxi thugs before they gave him a pair of concrete boots and sent him swimming with the fishies."

"That makes more sense," I said. And was an excellent motive to rob one's own bank, I didn't say. Nor did I say it was a reasonable explanation for him to hole up in a ratty casino barely an hour from Pine Apple, immediately confess, and not lift a finger in his own defense. Frank Simmons needed the protection of federal prison. And although I had no way of knowing it at the time, I'd just taken my first step down Casino Detective Lane.

"What about Fiona?"

"Strange bird, that Fiona. What about her?" Granny asked. "Where is she?"

I didn't particularly care where she was, but with the thought, I realized I hadn't seen Fiona in weeks. But then again, I hadn't been to the bank in weeks either. And Fiona sightings around town were rare.

"If you want to know what Fiona's up to, or if you want to change your checks from cute little kittens to a big smiley face background, or even if you want to say 'Boo' to her, you have to go through Courtney."

Courtney Carr. Pine Apple Bank & Trust's only teller and Fiona's only friend, and a woman who'd lost her way in 1978. The year *Grease* hit the big screen. Courtney knew every line in the script, every song on the soundtrack, and to that day still dressed in a rotating *Grease* wardrobe that could have come straight from the set. I'd never seen it live, but I'd heard she dressed as Blanche Hodel, Secretary at Rydell High, every year for Halloween.

"Courtney says Fiona's working from home," Granny said, "but I heard she had her face lifted and she's hiding out till it calms down some."

"Why would someone who never shows her face have it lifted?"

"Like I said. Strange bird, that one."

"So who's running the bank?"

"Courtney," Granny said.

"Is Courtney qualified or capable of running a bank?"

"Well, she used to run the Hallmark store at the Greenville Mall. And you know it had to be busier than the bank."

"Why did Courtney leave her Hallmark job? I thought she loved it."

"The Hallmark store closed down," Granny said. "So Fiona hired her."

"Back up a little," I said. "I wasn't really asking what Fiona's up to now, because I really don't care." I'd gone to see her when I first rolled back into town to ask about Florida and it hadn't gone well. In fact, it had gone miserably. She'd opened the door, taken one look at me, and slammed it in my face without speaking. It was as if the very sight of me triggered a panic attack in her. I'd seen her several times around town since then, each time eliciting the same fight, flight, or flee reaction. Why? I had no idea. And enough time had passed that I'd stopped worrying about it. The bank robbery, on the other hand,

I continued to worry about. "What I want to know is how she ended up running the bank her husband robbed."

"Have you asked your daddy?"

"I have, Granny, and he shut me down."

"I'll tell you if you won't tell him I told you," she said. "There's a reason people say to let a sleeping dog lie."

"I won't say a word."

My grandmother explained that after Eli Atwell saved Fiona from being burned at the stake in Town Square, Pine Apple had to accept her back into the fold when Eli went on to singlehandedly save Pine Apple Bank & Trust. He did it by moving the assets of Atwell Aviation—a third-generation manufacturing facility located another small city away, Prattville, employing more than three hundred southcentral Alabama residents—from Regions Bank in Conecuh, Alabama, to Pine Apple Bank & Trust. To include all the financial transactions resulting from the adding of polyurethane blocks to aluminum frames, covering the units with fire-retardant fabric, topping them off with cloth or leather, then shipping the finished seats to Boeing, Airbus, Gulfstream, Cessna, and Learjet to be installed in airplanes. All that money landed at Pine Apple Bank & Trust, along with the then-unheard-of practice of direct deposit payroll, thus keeping the Pine Apple cash flowing. And all under one condition. Eli would keep Pine Apple alive if, and only if, Fiona Simmons was absolved of all responsibility related to the heist the feds had already declared she had nothing to do with, never asked again where the missing money was, and allowed to run the bank full of his money. Because Fiona was the only officer of the bank left standing. If Pine Apple wanted to stay on the map they were barely on to begin with, they had to agree: Fiona Simmons was innocent and she would run the bank.

They agreed.

And six weeks after that, just two weeks after his second deployment to Kuwait, Eli was killed. Months of red tape later, and after a twenty-one-gun salute service at Alabama National Cemetery in Birmingham attended by all of Pine Apple, Eli's remains were quietly shipped home to Wilcox County, then quietly laid to rest at Carter's Funeral Home and Cemetery.

"What about Florida, Granny? Where's she been all this time?"

"No one knows," she'd said. "That girl took off and, as far as I know, hasn't been seen or heard from since."

Until a dozen years later when she showed up in a chicken wing truck.

With Eddie Crawford's son.

And there I was too.

Wondering why Florida Simmons was on my parents' porch.

FOURTEEN

With a sigh, I sat down in the rocking chair beside her. She passed me a plastic wine glass, then a wine bottle. It was Boone's Farm Fuzzy Navel. I couldn't help but laugh, barely recognizing the sound, because laughter had left me two days earlier. Boone's Farm had been gone from my life for almost two decades.

I poured.

We clinked.

I almost choked on the first sip. "How old is this?"

"I bought it this morning."

"No."

"Yes," she said. "They still make it. But now it's twelve dollars a bottle."

"Inflation."

I tried another sip. It was no better than the first.

"Keep going," Florida said. "Third sip and it'll taste like high school."

Third sip, it didn't. To me, high school tasted like Wednesday lunch: chopped beef steak drizzled with brown gravy, green beans, mashed potatoes with more brown gravy, yeast rolls, and chocolate icebox pie. The cheap wine tasted like peach baby food stirred into sour orange juice. And on the subject of all things tasty, I said, "I guess you brought Cheetos?"

It was her turn to laugh. "Oh, how soon they forget. The deal is and has always been that I steal the Boone's Farm, you bring the Cheetos."

I turned to her, making direct eye contact. "Did you steal this wine?"

"No, Mrs. Law Enforcement. I bought it up the street."

Up the street in Pine Apple was the next small town over. "Camden?"

136

"Camden Fine Wine."

"To fine wine."

We clinked again.

The soundtrack of our reunion was the rhythmic creaks of the wood porch slats beneath the rocking chairs and crickets. That's how long it took for the real conversation to start. Half a bottle of Fuzzy Navel and crickets out in full force. And they were singing from the trees. Probably because they had no bushes to hide in. It was a sound I hadn't heard in the longest—crickets—and at that point, I'd had just enough Boone's Farm for my mind to wander, trying to remember if I'd ever heard a cricket in Biloxi. Mississippi felt like home. I'd married there, had three babies there, loved where we lived, loved my job there, but it took crickets and cheap wine to make me finally feel at home again in Alabama.

She kicked things off. "I see you've replaced me."

"Fantasy," I said. "She's the very best."

"Who's she hiding from?"

"What makes you think she's hiding?"

"She's in Pine Apple. Why would she be here otherwise?"

I didn't want the conversation to end before Florida told me why we were having it, so I didn't ask who she was hiding from.

"Where'd your husband go?" she asked.

"To my sister's," I answered.

"Good."

"You'd like my husband." Even to my own ears, I sounded defensive. "Everyone likes my husband."

"I was thinking more of Meredith." She swirled her wine in the glass and gave it a hard look before finishing it off. "Her hair is probably on fire after three days of juggling four-year-olds and a baby."

"I've been a little busy."

"Yes, you have," Florida said. "Where's Meredith's daughter? I haven't seen her helping chase children."

"Riley?" My favorite niece. My only niece. "Cheer camp at Alabama."

"Roll Tide Alabama?"

"The same," I said.

"Bad timing for her to be away."

"As opposed to good timing for you to be present?"

We rocked.

She said, "Your children are beautiful, by the way."

I said, "So is yours."

"I can't take credit."

"You should. Where's *he* hiding?" I asked.

"He isn't," she said. "He's spending time with my mother."

"And she's a hider."

"Exactly."

"Florida?" I turned to her. "What happened to your mother?"

"What do you mean?"

"Way back when—"

"Do you really want to go way back when, Davis?"

Truthfully, no part of me wanted to go way back when. I had quite enough present day to deal with. Although had I stepped through that ancient door, I'd have asked if she knew what I'd ever done to her mother to deserve having a door slammed in my face. But I didn't. So we rocked until she said, "I can't get over how everyone thinks he looks like Eddie Crawford."

I had several options. I chose, "And you don't?"

"Maybe I did when he was born, but that was twelve years ago. I never look at him and see anyone else. He's his own person. Your daughters don't look a bit like you," she said. "Is it in the front of your brain at all times that they look like someone else?"

Bex and Quinn got almost every ounce of their DNA from Bradley. And what Florida said made perfect sense, although I'd never had the occasion to realize it. I thought about how much they looked like their father and how little they looked like me often when they were newborns, seeing my husband in their sky-blue eyes, but it took no time for them to grow into their own little people. Not mirrored extensions of Bradley. "You're right," I said. "It isn't something I ever think about unless someone brings it up. But if I were introducing the girls to a town of four hundred busybodies where everyone knew Bradley, and the girls looked just like him, I wouldn't be so surprised if people noticed."

She didn't respond.

"In fact, Florida, I might have planned it that way."

"Why might you have done that?"

"To get it out there," I said. "To get it over with."

"I came back because I had to, Davis, not to get anything over with. Besides," she added, "a lot of people look like Eddie. Dark hair, dark eyes. And it's been a million years."

"You just said it'd been twelve."

The tinge of frost trailing off my voice settled over us. And her next word would be her first and last acknowledging I was married to Eddie at the time his son was conceived. "Davis—"

"Don't." I stopped her. "It didn't matter then, Florida, and it doesn't matter now."

I meant every word.

She knew it.

So we rocked.

I wasn't quite sure where to go from there. I chose, "How is your mother?"

She stopped rocking. "I tell you what. We'll talk about my mother for a while, then we'll talk about yours. Or we could skip the mother talk." She held out a crooked pinkie finger.

I pinkie promised to skip the mother chat, which might not have tasted like high school, but it sure felt like high school.

We rocked.

"Florida?"

"Yes?"

"Did you come here to tell me you're dropping out of the chicken wing cookoff?"

"Not so much." She split another four inches of Boone's Farm between our glasses. "Why would I drop out? Because every other food truck is dropping out? My plan is to wait until I'm the last truck standing. Then I win."

"I remember that about you."

"What?"

"That you love to win."

"Says the winner of life."

"I'm not sure what you mean by that."

"Look at you," she said. "The gorgeous husband. The beautiful children. The big house, big job, big money, big life."

"How would you know how big my house is?"

"For one, I practically live next door."

Biloxi and Mobile were an hour's drive apart.

"And for two," she said, "I spend a week in Biloxi every year."

"Oh, really?"

"Cruisin' the Coast? The collector car show?"

"I'm familiar."

"You can find me in the food truck park at Edgewater Mall."

"So you really are in the chicken wing business?"

"Did you think someone loaned me a chicken wing truck?" she asked. "Yes. I'm in the chicken wing business. I'd been hired to conduct a study on strategies to optimize poultry nutrition—"

She kept going with something about the negative economic viability of poultry farming, which was why the co-op that hired her paid her with a chicken wing truck, but I was only half listening because I realized the chicken wing cookoff had been a setup. Pine Apple Bank & Trust, who in no way appreciated its customers, planted the chicken-wing seed by bringing in a food truck at the height of the Women's Society's potato salad-cake-pie dilemma. It had nothing to do with my mother's winning streak and everything to do with sneaking, or luring, Florida back to Pine Apple in her chicken wing truck. Not wanting to give her information she might not have, I didn't go there. Instead, I went with, "Do you even like chicken wings?"

"I do not."

"So tell me again why you drive a chicken wing truck?"

"After you tell me how you ended up living in a casino."

"That's a long story."

"Same here," she said. "A long story."

"What's the long boring story called?"

She tilted her head my way.

"Your story," I explained. "What's the title of your story?"

She said, "Babies change lives."

That they did.

We rocked.

"So you've seen my house?" I asked. "How'd that happen?"

"I didn't break in and tiptoe through while you were sleeping, if that's what you're thinking. Mr. Google told me your husband, his wife, and their children lived at the Bellissimo," she said. "And it's the biggest house I've ever seen."

"I have a lot of housemates."

We rocked.

"So you come to Biloxi once a year, knowing I live there, and have never stopped by to say hi."

"I thought it best to not dredge up old ghosts."

"Yet here we are."

We rocked.

We drank Boone's Farm.

"I have a question for you, Davis."

I had another one for her too. "Shoot."

"How is it you tangled with Eddie Crawford for years—" nearby, an owl hooted, probably celebrating her finally getting to the good stuff "—years and *years*," she went on, "even marrying him *twice*, and came out of it unscathed? Meanwhile, there's me, who didn't speak ten words to him in high school, and I have to live with him for the rest of mine."

Just then, the Boone's Farm kicked in. "Are you kidding me?" I slapped the arm of my rocker. "Is that why you're here? You're moving in with Eddie? You're going to live in the middle of the Gulf?"

Her Boone's Farm kicked in. Her head fell back with wild laughter. I remembered that about her too. "No!" Her head came down. The laughter didn't stop. "I hope I'm never in the same room with Eddie again. I couldn't live with him for five minutes. How does that man even live with himself?"

"I don't know how he made it through the birth canal. So I don't have an answer."

We rocked.

"Do you think it's Bea's fault?" she asked.

"Is what Bea's fault?"

"How pathetic Eddie is. Isn't it always the mother's fault?"

I tucked that away for later—Florida blamed her mother, for what, I wasn't sure—to say, "I'm not sure I'd call Eddie pathetic. He has a room-temp IQ, he's never met a social skill, and he won't stop stealing cars from me, but how can he truly be pathetic if he doesn't know he's pathetic? Doesn't there have to be some level of awareness?"

"Maybe you're right and he's not pathetic," Dr. Boone's Farm, Therapist in a Bottle, said. Then went on to say, "Maybe there are parts of our pasts when we were pathetic, and we associate him with those times, and pathetically project it onto him."

"Deep thoughts."

We rocked.

"He looks just like Eddie, Florida."

"Established. And thank the Lord."

"He'd be just as cute if he looked like you."

"His feet look like mine." She shot out a muddy flip-flopped foot as evidence. "And I didn't mean it that way," she said. "I meant he could have looked like Bea. Or Eddie's dad. That huge nose on that man." She snapped her fingers having found the corner of her brain where Eddie's father's name lived. "Melvin. What ever happened to Melvin, by the way?"

"You haven't heard?" I asked. "It's old news. Seems like someone would have told you."

"I haven't spoken a word to anyone in Pine Apple in all these years. Who would have told me?"

"Someone told you Meredith has a daughter," I said. "My niece, Riley. So you must have a Pine Apple connection."

"I do," she said. "Facebook."

"Is that how you found out about the chicken wing cookoff?"

She rolled her head in a yes-and-no way.

"How did you know Eddie had moved out of town?"

"Facebook."

"How did you know Bea would be out of town?" I answered my own question. "Facebook."

She nodded. "The Pine Apple Neighborhood page."

"Stalker."

She laughed.

And we rocked.

"So what did happen to Melvin?" she asked.

"He left Bea, moved to Austin, married a man named Randy, and as far as I know, is living happily ever after."

"That is unreal," she said, "and not on Facebook."

We rocked.

"You know what else wasn't on Facebook, Davis?"

"No."

"That your father would be away, and you would be here in his place."

"If it helps any," I said, "I was just as shocked to see you as you were to see me."

"Here's to shockers."

We clinked.

"Davis, there's something else I can't find on Facebook."

"What?"

"When will Bea be back?"

"I think you're in the clear for the next few days."

"Has something happened?" she asked.

"Why? What have you heard?"

"I haven't heard a thing. But she stopped posting pictures of every bite of food before, during, and after she's eaten it." Before I could find a way to tell her the Crooked Bea Brain story in the shortest way possible, Florida decided she didn't want to hear it. "Just tell me if she's on her way."

"No," I said. "She isn't."

"Will she be back before Memorial Day?"

That, I couldn't be sure of. "How about if I let you know the minute I hear she's coming home?"

"That'll work."

We rocked.

"I have a question for you, Florida."

"Just one?"

"Just one."

"Okay."

"Did you come back for the money?"

After a minute that felt like ten, she said, "Pass."

"Do you know where your father hid the money, Florida?"

"I passed on the money question, Davis."

"So you don't think he hid the money."

"You're not going to let this go, are you?"

"I want to, Florida. I really do."

"Maybe this will help," she said. "My mother doesn't think he hid a thing. And since she's had plenty of time to find it, that's good enough for me."

I'd love to have said, "That's good enough for me too," but it most certainly wasn't. So I said, "I thought you didn't want to talk about your mother."

"I don't. Final question."

"Did you dig up Eli Atwell's grave?"

Which she had a ready response for. Not an answer, but a comeback. "He wasn't in a grave. Not in the ground anyway. He was in the crypt under the funeral home."

"There isn't a crypt under the funeral home." As soon as the words left my lips, it came slamming back, what Roy Howdy had said earlier about a root cellar. Specifically, Eli Atwell's body was supposed to be in his root cellar. He'd been serious? I thought he was just being Roy Howdy. "Florida." I grabbed her arm. "Is there a crypt under the funeral home?"

She turned her face to me. Stunned. "Where have you been all day? Yes, there's a crypt under the funeral home. They just found it."

"Who is they?"

She shrugged. "The very large bald man your bestie calls Hair and the dead body police."

"We call him No Hair." I held out my plastic glass. She loaded it. "Are we talking about an actual crypt? A mausoleum? Full of tombs? Or are we talking stacks of dead bodies in Roy Howdy's basement?"

"I wouldn't know."

I asked, "How many bodies are in the basement crypt?"

She answered, "Don't know and don't want to."

"And Roy Howdy *knew* he was living on top of dead bodies?"

"That's a trick question," she said. "On the one hand, how could he not know? And on the other, Roy Howdy doesn't know what day of the week it is."

"Still," I said. "Hard to believe."

"Only in Pine Apple."

We rocked.

"I wonder if Roy Howdy was authorized to live on top of bodies. Surely there are...rules."

"One would think."

"I wonder if my father knows there are dead bodies in Roy's basement."

"Another thing I wouldn't know."

We rocked.

I cut the cadaver silence with, "So?"

"No," she said. "I didn't break into the crypt." She let a full minute pass before slowly adding, "But I'm worried sick my mother did."

I heard cricket necks snap our way with the breaking news. Before I could decide how to respond, or if I even should respond, Florida breaking our pinkie promise to not discuss our mothers for the second time brought mine around. My phone interrupted the still night with an incoming text message from her.

"Is that your phone?" Florida asked.

"It is." I dug for it.

"It sounds like a fire alarm."

"It's the text alert and ring tone I've assigned to my mother."

"That bad?"

"It's worse." I didn't click on the incoming message right away because I was busy preparing myself for my mother's barely decipherable voice-to-text message. "If it's nothing, she calls. If it's horrible, she texts."

"It isn't going to read itself."

With a sigh, I clicked.

Davis Way, you glisten to me and you glisten ghoul. Your farther needs yelp. Bee is a illegal Fabian. She has been Arrested Development and is in the illegal Fabian detonation. We diddle nose she diddle have a gas port. The hospitable went to clack her in for an extermination and assed for her gas port. She diddle have one. Now she is a illegal Fabian. Halp us. And fixture your farther's Fone.

I passed my fone—I meant phone—to Florida. "I see what you mean." She passed it back. "Whatever it is, it sounds horrible."

We rocked.

"What's it say?" she asked.

"Bea has been detained in Canada for entering without a passport."

She dropped her head. Her shoulders shook. She laughed out, "How'd that even happen?"

"She got on the wrong train and wound up in Canada. Apparently without a passport."

"Why would Bea Crawford have a passport to begin with? Has she even crossed the Alabama state line in her life before now?"

"All the time."

"Oh, really?"

"Really," I said. "She shows up on my Mississippi doorstep regularly."

"So you didn't get stuck with Eddie but you got stuck with Bea?"

"So it would seem."

We rocked.

"Davis?" Her voice was soft. Almost pleading. "Go easy on her."

Every ounce of me wanted to reach for her hand and give it a reassuring squeeze that I wouldn't skin her mother alive. But I knew better than to even hint that I'd look the other way if Fiona Simmons had, indeed, upended Eli Atwell's final resting place.

So we rocked.

"Florida?"

"Hmmm?"

"What's his name?"

"Who?"

"You know who."

"It isn't Junior."

"I heard that," I said. "Really. What's his name?"

"I don't want to tell you."

"It's a secret?"

She said, "No. I just don't want to tell you."

I said, "Tell me anyway."

"It's Cole."

"Cole Simmons." I tried it on. "It's a great name."

"It's worked out well for you."

"It will work out well for him too."

After a quiet moment of contemplation in which she found two more drops of Fuzzy Navel in the bottle and split them between our glasses, she asked, "What's your son's name?"

Staring into my wine glass, wondering if the lone drop at the bottom was worth the tip of the plastic glass, I said, "I'm not sure."

FIFTEEN

Before I let my father swear me in to keep the peace in Pine Apple for two weeks, I had him send me the precinct's police blotter for the previous twelve months. I studied it for three weeks as if my life and the lives of my children depended on it.

Because they did.

What I'd learned was the past twelve months had seen an uptick in crime, law enforcement activity, and public safety callouts in Pine Apple, Alabama. Murder and manslaughter counts, zero. Deaths by natural causes, two. The first, Mary Beulah Hawthorne's great aunt by marriage, Jane-Jane Hawthorne, age 107, who didn't wake up from a nap one afternoon. The other, Roy Howdy's uncle, age 82, who didn't wake up one morning. Rape, zero. Robbery, two: one bicycle and one chainsaw. Grand larceny, zero. Breaking and entering, one, the incident that sent Eugenia Winters Stone down the Delta Force Drive. Aggravated assault, two, up from one the year before, and both charges were against my ex-ex-mother-in-law, Bea Crawford—her again—over altercations with customers at the diner. One where she smacked a man upside the head with a hot skillet for complaining about her goulash. She paid him off rather than face him in court. Two hundred and fifty dollars in small bills and free corndogs for a month. Property crimes the year before, fourteen, most of those charges were filed by Emma Stamper against her neighbor, Dill Barter, for crossing his property line to hers with his weed whacker, endangering her arborvitae, which wasn't the real problem. Dill Barter weed whacking in his birthday suit was the real problem. Property damage the year before? Five incidents. All mailboxes mowed down by strangers passing through on their way to somewhere else. Motor vehicle theft, zero. Parking violations, twenty-two (up five), traffic stops, thirty-seven (up eight), but most of those were Daddy pulling over his buddies to shoot the breeze.

Disturbing the peace calls, multiple, just like the previous year, but nothing more serious than a ten-person food fight in the produce section at Pine Apple's only grocery store, Piggly Wiggly, fondly referred to as The Pig. And on the fire side, there were three incidents. All three grill fires, all contained immediately with no substantial damage, and all three at (again) my ex-ex-mother-in-law's diner.

In light of what I'd learned, which was nothing new at all, I'd decided filling in for my father wasn't exactly putting myself or my children in harm's way. And with my two least favorite residents out of my hair—Bea Crawford and her son, Eddie—I thought my time in my hometown would be a cake walk. I knew going in I was committing to oversee the Memorial Day Celebration, but that was 49 percent of the draw. It was traditionally the most fun that could be had in Pine Apple. My sister, niece, and my grandmother were the other 51 percent. Meredith, feeling very aunt deprived with almost two hundred miles between us, signed up to care for my children while I sat behind Daddy's desk for three or four hours a day, something we'd both looked forward to. Me? The mommy break. Meredith? The pitter-patter of little feet in her house again and a baby to rock. And no one had been more excited than my grandmother, who'd been so looking forward to her job as deputy. None of us could've foreseen the goats, the torrential rain, Fantasy showing up with Whiskey in tow, Florida Simmons popping up out of nowhere driving a chicken wing truck with a boy who was very clearly a product of Pine Apple, or a dead body snatched from what turned out to be a crypt, which turned out to be nothing more than a root cellar. In my wildest dreams, I couldn't have imagined any single one of those events. Much less all of them. Within forty-eight hours. And I said as much later that night when I found myself in the hot seat at my mother's kitchen table.

My people were angry.

Very angry.

At me.

Bradley and I parted ways in my parents' driveway two hours earlier and he'd been fine. Much better than when I'd picked him up at the airport. He'd even wished me luck with my old friend on the porch and kissed me bye. But he'd gotten himself all worked up again when, ten minutes later, he found my dazed grandmother, sitting on the sidewalk outside of The Front Porch staring into space and sipping from a pint jar of watermelon moonshine singing an inebriated version of the theme song to *Fancy Nancy*, one of Bex and Quinn's favorite television shows, and knew my grandmother couldn't take one more minute of our children. Then he found Meredith. Without a marble left in her head after single-handedly caring for Bex, Quinn, and the baby since early that morning. "Why don't they take naps?" she'd asked Bradley. "WHY?" Then she'd cried. Real live tears of exhaustion. "Even the baby, Bradley, *he* doesn't nap." After prying the moonshine from Granny's bony fingers, then strapping her in her stairlift and sending her upstairs to bed, he helped Meredith put her house and store back together after twelve straight hours of a kid tornado. Then, with all three children in tow, he'd dragged Joe, of Joe's Automotive on Cherry Street, away from his supper table to the site of the Bellissimo truck he intended to make his Pine Apple getaway in the next morning with No Hair at the wheel and Fantasy and Whiskey in the backseat, only for Joe to proclaim it good for nothing but scrap. Because the cost of replacing the computer I'd destroyed, which had 100 percent to do with the truck running, was just as expensive as buying the truck again. Joe had said to Bradley, "I'll buy the tires off you for two hundred each." And in the process of traveling from my parents' house to Meredith's, then to the dead truck behind Bea Crawford's mobile home, he'd seen what had been in the ground and flourishing in Mississippi that morning in buckets and bales scattered all over town awaiting planting in Alabama the next. But it was something about the very sight of the eighteen-wheeler flatbed still in the middle of Main Street that had truly set him off. What? I didn't know. But he was fuming.

No Hair was furious with Fantasy. For everything. For breathing, for being a Biloxi headline, and for forcing him to stop what he would otherwise be doing to hire her replacement. Because, he said, her dismissal was, "...permanent. Etched in stone. Don't bother to clean out your locker, because I'm going to burn it all as soon as I get back." He was even madder at me for asking the Biloxi Crime Lab to run unauthorized ballistics tests on the paintball guns Fantasy had chased through the casino the night of the incident. Which No Hair claimed was a delay tactic on my part and a waste of the city's valuable time and resources, not to mention I should rest assured he did not have a word to say in my defense when Detective Sandy Marini called him to protest my unsanctioned use of her credentials. He'd had to stop what he was doing to talk her down, which was traipsing through the mud with the Wilcox County coroner through the small cemetery Fantasy, Whiskey, and I had already visited that day, without finding an unearthed grave. Only to learn Eli Atwell's body had been in Roy Howdy's basement. Something Roy Howdy claimed to have nothing to do with. That was all his uncle. No Hair went on to learn all manner of other things he didn't want to know. Such as, Alabama allowed burial on private property, which Roy Howdy's funeral home actually was, because (news to everyone) Roy Howdy wasn't a licensed funeral director. Therefore his funeral home wasn't a licensed funeral home. When No Hair confronted Roy Howdy with the ominous news, he'd said, "For real? I gotta have a license?" But mostly No Hair was as mad as a hornet about the fact that he wasn't in Mississippi doing his own job, because he was in Alabama doing mine.

I didn't know what was wrong with Fantasy. I'd asked as we'd assembled. She'd snapped, "What's it to you, Davis?" I backed off, chalking it up to her fugitive predicament, fatigue, and the death of her Valentinos when she was forced to drop them in one of the many dumpsters still scattered around town.

All that anger combined had the three of them almost accusing me of carelessly risking everything I held dear by agreeing to come to Pine Apple and fill in for my father in the first place. To which I responded I most certainly had not, having done my homework and finding no risk to mine or my family's safety. They weren't impressed. Hinting that I'd allowed everything to happen. Or somehow caused it. Or at the very least, didn't stop it.

My boss was to my right. In Mother's seat. "No Hair? How could I have stopped Fantasy from showing up if I didn't know she was coming?"

"Don't you two have clairvoyant ESP tracking devices on each other's brains?"

"There's no such thing as clairvoyant ESP tracking devices on brains."

Fantasy was to my left. In Meredith's chair. Wearing Liberty overalls she'd cut off to Liberty capris over a tank top featuring jumping frogs, both of which she'd helped herself to after breaking in the backdoor of Pine Apple Mercantile and digging through the damaged and returned goods bin. Where she'd also acquired new footwear. Duck mocs. Which were duck boots without the boot part. They were an unfortunate shade of orange. "I called you, No Hair," she said. "I called you from the casino floor while I was chasing naked gun-toting punks. I wouldn't have had to run if you'd answered your phone. I called you again to tell you I was on my way to Pine Apple, and you didn't answer that time either."

"It was the middle of the night, Fantasy."

"As long as I'm on record as having called you first."

He said, "Duly noted," but he didn't sound like he gave a flip. Or maybe he sounded like it didn't matter. Because at that point, after firing her so thoroughly, it didn't.

"No Hair." Fantasy slapped the table. "Do you think I'm happy about this? Any of it? Look at me. I've been here two days and I've already turned into an Alabama redneck. I'm wearing a frog shirt."

I probably should have stayed out if it, but I jumped right in with, "That you stole."

She narrowed her eyes at me. "Because the store wasn't open."

"That's generally true of small-town retail at ten o'clock at night."

She said, "It was seven o'clock at night and I left a note."

No Hair said, "You two shut up."

Fantasy redirected her wrath back at No Hair. "Stop acting like I've been on some kind of vacation. I've been on a nightmare." She stabbed the table with a finger. "It's been a total nightmare." Stab, stab, stab. "For all that's happened here, I'd have been way better off staying home and letting Biloxi PD lock me up. Or turning myself over to the punk's parents. Because being here has been like being in hell. I don't know what's left for Davis to do to Pine Apple other than burn it to the ground."

"Hey," I snapped.

"I'm not necessarily blaming *you*, Davis," she said. In a very blaming way.

"But you are, Fantasy."

"Well, why don't you run it by your best friend Florida? See if she thinks what I said was blaming you."

My jaw dropped.

"Fantasy," Bradley, who was directly across from me in Daddy's chair, spoke up. "The only thing Davis is truly guilty of, other than hiding you and withholding information from me, is bankrupting her hometown, destroying a brand new truck, and wiping out the Bellissimo Gardens."

"How have I bankrupted my hometown, Bradley?"

"Let me rephrase."

"Please do."

"When it's all said and done, the cleanup of Pine Apple is going to cost tens of thousands of dollars."

Well.

Bradley landed his elbows on the table, clasped his hands together, and leaned in. "Considering the only fundraiser on the annual books isn't on track to make a dime, does the town have enough money tucked away from last year's Memorial Day Celebration to clean up this year's?"

Well.

"Do we?" He steepled two fingers and rocked them back and forth between us.

Well.

"We could help," I offered. "A little. Then pay ourselves back when the town gets a settlement from Goat Woman."

He shook his head in decided disagreement. "If the case isn't immediately tossed out of court on the merits of the contract someone here surely signed, Pine Apple will lose a lawsuit against the goat woman after a long drawn-out court battle. And you and I won't be in a position to help for a decade, Davis."

I found that a little hard to believe.

We had savings, didn't we?

"We owe the Bellissimo thirty-seven thousand dollars for a truck," he said.

Well.

Our savings would take a hit.

"And upwards of a million dollars for the Bellissimo Gardens."

"*What*?" I must have misheard him. "A million *what*?"

"Upwards of a million dollars, Davis," my husband said.

"For *flowers*?"

"Yes," he said. "For flowers. What were you thinking? That because the directive to destroy the Bellissimo Gardens was supposedly from Bianca, accounting would sweep the expenses under a rug?"

Well.

At the time, I wasn't thinking that far ahead. But had I been, yes, that's what I would've thought. Rather than go there, I said, "*Flowers?*"

"First of all," he started, "the value of the greenery you had stripped from the gardens, flowers being the least of it, was a hundred thousand dollars. The cost of what was flown in to replace it was two hundred thousand dollars. The labor it took to rip up and replace the gardens in a day, bringing in landscaping contractors from all over the Gulf, was almost three hundred thousand dollars. Then throw in the biggest ticket item of them all. The slot machines. Both the production cost of and in revenue lost." He finally sat back. "And that puts the total just over the million-dollar mark."

The kitchen grew so quiet, we could hear Whiskey softly snoring on the sofa in the den. Had the girls, sleeping upstairs, rolled over in their beds, we'd have heard their little legs rubbing against the sheets. Had the baby hiccupped, we might have all jumped out of our skins, so still was the kitchen as the gravity of the moment when the amount of money we owed the Bellissimo was served up at the table.

I broke the silence with a whispered question. "What slot machines?"

As it turned out, the metal container on the flatbed truck was home to fifty proprietary slot machines. Double Blast. A fun game intended to digitally explode with glorious fireworks for the fifty veterans who'd qualified to play in the Bellissimo's Veteran's Tournament in the Garden Pavilion on Memorial Day. And when I, posing as Bianca, had instructed Stephen Halliday, Master Gardener, and Vice President of Bellissimo Horticulture, to ship every single thing in the Bellissimo Garden to Pine Apple, he'd assumed I meant the slot machines too.

Forget the chicken wing cookoff.

We could have a Memorial Day slot tournament in Pine Apple.

Except private gaming was against Alabama law.

I'd have to find a workaround.

Just as soon as I got the ludicrously expensive flowers in the dirt from one end of town to the other.

Then figured out what to do with the bodies in Roy Howdy's basement.

And found the money stolen from Pine Apple Bank & Trust all those years ago.

Before it was stolen again.

If it hadn't been already.

SIXTEEN

We slept all over my parents' house.

Meredith had seven bedrooms in the antebellum our father was born in, but no one wanted to bother her. So we stayed put and made do. The children were in my old bedroom. No Hair was assigned to Meredith's old room. Fantasy got the velvet settee in the dining room, just a buffet sideboard away from Whiskey's den sofa, and the narrow settee wasn't particularly suitable for sitting. Much less sleeping. Not to mention Fantasy had legs out to there. Bradley and I took my parents' room, but when I tiptoed in, the bed was empty. I eased the door open to my old bedroom and found him asleep in my old twin bed, with Bex and Quinn in the other, and the baby softly sleeping in his Pack 'n Play. The light from the hall through the cracked door fell on my husband's troubled face but didn't wake him. I quietly closed the door and tiptoed back down the stairs to the kitchen in search of a cracker. Or a crumb of a cracker. Because had I been a food journal person, I'd have logged endless cups of coffee, two bites of Quinn's Froot Loops, and half a bottle of Boone's Farm Fuzzy Navel for the entire day. I was starving. I didn't find a cracker, but I did find Fantasy.

I sat in my father's chair, mostly because she was in mine. "Can't sleep?"

"Could you sleep on a concrete slab a foot shorter than you that was ten feet from Whiskey?"

"I doubt it."

"Trust me, you couldn't. Because slab of concrete aside, Motormouth talks in his sleep."

"Oh, really?" I noticed that most of her animosity aimed directly at me earlier in the evening was gone. She was still a little chilly, but I also noticed a warm red glow in the middle of the oven panel. I knew the red glow. It meant the oven was preheating. "What's he saying?"

"Nothing decipherable. Lone odd words."

The only light on in the kitchen was the nightlight above the stove. It shined a spotlight on a square Pyrex dish wrapped in a mile of foil sitting atop a cookie sheet. Fantasy had pulled something from the freezer.

"Like old crossword puzzle words," she said. "I heard what sounded like pill garlic several times. Do you think that's garlic in pill form?"

"I bet he was saying pilgarlic. It sounds the same but it's one word. And I think it means bald," I said. "He was probably sleep talking about No Hair. What's in the dish?"

As if on cue, the oven dinged readiness.

She did the honors.

After trapping the Pyrex in the oven, she said, "King Ranch Chicken."

"Which is delicious. How long?"

"Right now, it's a frozen brick." She sat back down. "What do you think? Forty-five minutes?"

"What do you want to do for the next forty-five minutes?"

"What do I want to do?" She tapped her chin and studied the ceiling. "Find a car. Sneak home to see Reggie and the boys before I turn myself in tomorrow. Take one last hot shower at home to wash the rest of the flower dirt from under my fingernails. Find something a little more appropriate to wear to my bond hearing."

"Take my car."

She sat statue still.

"Leave the car seats," I added.

Imagining the possibilities, she didn't move a muscle or say a word.

I tried again. "Take Whiskey with you?"

She almost laughed. "I can't do that. You know I can't do that. No Hair would skin me alive."

"He's not all that attached to Whiskey."

"You know what I mean."

"For the best, I guess, because I doubt I could get the keys out of Bradley's pocket without waking the children, which would wake the whole house. And considering everyone's had a day, we should probably let them sleep."

"You know what we could do?" she asked.

"What?"

"Hotwire a chicken wing truck. I could drive it home."

We sat through a moment of extreme silence.

"Don't be mad at Florida, Fantasy."

"Don't let her use you, Davis."

"Use me for what?"

"Cover."

Mother's cookie sheet, feeling the heat, popped in the oven.

"Cover for what?" I asked.

She tapped the table. "We were sitting right here having breakfast this morning and you said she was back to collect the money from a long-ago bank robbery."

"Was that really just this morning?"

"And you said, Davis, it was the only reason she could possibly be in Pine Apple after all these years. To collect the stolen money."

The cookie sheet popped again.

"If you were right," she said, "and it sounded to me like you believed every word you were saying, then your cocktail hour on the porch was nothing but her cozying up to you so you'd look the other way when she disappears with the money."

"I'd hardly call Boone's Farm cocktails."

And there went the cookie sheet again.

"Listen, Fantasy."

"I'm all ears." She sat back and crossed her arms. "Explain it to me."

"Florida has made mistakes."

Fantasy blinked.

"Haven't we all?"

Fantasy studied her cuticles.

"Big mistakes?"

Fantasy sniffed.

"With big consequences?"

Fantasy took a sharp breath, held it, then let it go.

"But she didn't come here tonight to cozy up to me so I'll look the other way while she rides off into the sunset with the money her father stole."

Fantasy huffed.

"She came to tell me where to look."

Fantasy raised an eyebrow. "She told you where the money was?" She tipped forward as if to push away from the table. "Let's go."

"She didn't tell me where to look for the money, but she sent me in the right direction."

Fantasy sat back. "And you believe her? This isn't your old friend sending you on a wild goose chase?"

"No." I shook my head. "Definitely not."

After the cookie sheet popped again—what was wrong with Mother's cookie sheet?—Fantasy said, "How much money are we talking about, anyway?"

"The cash from the teller drawers and everything that was in the vault back in the day. Plus the proceeds from mortgages her dad sold."

"Which was how much?"

"Somewhere between two and three hundred thousand."

"That isn't exactly a fortune."

"Obviously we're not so impressed because we're used to casino numbers. We see that much money being wagered just walking through the casino. But three hundred thousand dollars was a fortune to a small town twenty years ago." I rose from the table. Started a pot of coffee. Might as well. "It's still a lot of money to the small town he almost ruined. And at this point, maybe it isn't the money so much as it is feeling violated by a man they trusted."

"Wasn't the money insured?"

"It was," I said, "up to a hundred thousand for each depositor."

"I thought it was more than that."

"It is now," I said. "It wasn't then."

"But everyone got their money back."

"Yes." The coffee dripped along. "Eventually."

"And they caught the bank robber."

"Yes," I said again. "At a casino."

"Are you lying?"

"No." I split the two inches of coffee that had already dripped, as dark and strong as espresso, into two mugs. I passed one to her. "A statewide APB turned him up three days later at a casino eighty miles from here where he confessed everything at a five-cent Double Diamond slot machine as soon as he was approached. He was charged and convicted of robbing the bank, then sentenced to ninety-nine years with no parole for refusing to tell the judge what he did with the money."

"It sounds very wrapped-up-with-a-bow, Davis. Everyone got their money back, the bank robber went to prison, and the town was saved."

"Except the money was never recovered."

"It might have been today," she said.

"What makes you think that?"

"What other reason would someone have for busting into their father's best friend's casket? Obviously, the money was buried with the Air Force man. Why else would she dig him up?"

I leaned in and spoke slowly. "Florida didn't do it."

She leaned in and spoke slowly too. Or, rather, she spat, "Of course she didn't."

"You don't know her."

"Are you sure you do, Davis? Dead bodies and bank robberies aside, she blows back into town with your ex-husband's *son*, conceived when you were married to him, and she gets a pass?"

We'd had our disagreements in the past, but never going all the way to the line before then. We listened to the second hand tick on Mother's rooster clock on the wall for at least five minutes without saying another word, because I think we scared ourselves. I knew I wasn't willing to cross the line, and neither of us wanted to go any further down the Florida Simmons road, so we listened to the clock tick long enough to take a breath and a step back. I ended the stalemate when I whispered, "If you're serious about making a run for it, Fantasy, you could take Bea Crawford's truck."

She gave it half a thought before she said, "That would only add to my problems. No Hair would leave me barely alive and step aside so Bea could finish me off."

"Speaking of Bea." I looked around the kitchen, even though I knew my laptop wasn't there. I wasn't sure where it was, but it wasn't there. "She's been detained by immigration in Canada."

"Are you lying to me again?" Every word was hanging on a laugh.

"I've never lied to you, Fantasy."

"The state trooper call this morning?"

"I was protecting you from an ugly truth. That's different than lying."

"Okay," she said. "Are you protecting me from an ugly truth about Bea?"

"You've met Bea. That's all it takes to know all her ugly truths."

"You didn't think to mention this new ugly truth earlier? We could have used the comic relief of it all."

"It got lost in the shuffle." I looked around the kitchen again. My laptop still wasn't there. "I bet I left my laptop at the diner when I left to pick up Bradley."

"You did," she said. "I knew you didn't mean to, so on my way to unload the flower truck I dropped it off at the police station."

"Thank you."

"You're welcome."

I glanced at the oven. "How much longer, do you think?"

"I don't know." She shrugged. "I can't smell King Ranch Chicken yet. Can you?"

"I'd say it needs at least another thirty minutes. Then five more minutes without the foil."

"Okay," she said. "Your point?"

"Go with me to the police station to get my laptop."

"Why?"

"So we can Google Bea. Screenshot her mug shot."

"No way."

"Because I need my laptop."

"Still, no way."

"By the time we get back the casserole will be almost ready."

"Again, no way."

"It's barely a block."

"It's two blocks," she said. "In the dark."

"It's Pine Apple."

"Are you about to launch into a speech about how nothing happens in Pine Apple? Because I beg to differ."

"I want to see if the ballistics report is back on you, Fantasy. Okay?"

That got her.

We eased out the kitchen door and around the side of the house, sidestepping Daddy's gutters on the ground by the flashlight of my phone, proclaiming the earth, after a day of roaring sunshine, to be on the road to mud recovery. We walked the quiet sidewalk of Main Street by the glow of the streetlights, the American Flag banners attached, placed weeks earlier in anticipation of the Memorial Day Celebration and high enough to have survived the goats. One directly above our heads caught a gust of air and snapped in the still night. At the same time, the streetlamp above the banner flickered with an electrifying buzz. Scaring us to death.

Fantasy, trying to tear my arm off, also trying to drag me back to Mother and Daddy's, said, "Let's go back."

"Let's get my laptop." I pointed. "There's the precinct. It'll only take a minute."

"This place is spooky at night."

"This place is quiet at night," I said. "That's all. We live in a city where there's always noise. It's the quiet here that's unnerving."

"I tell you what's unnerving."

We were almost at the station. "What?"

"Look." She pointed.

On the door someone had penned *Go Back Where You Came From, DAVIS* in bright red spray paint.

I said, "This is where I came from."

I snapped several pictures of the warning before unlocking the door and creaking it open. Rather than turn on a light, I used my phone's flashlight. My laptop was right where Fantasy left it. On Daddy's desk. Sitting on my laptop was a sealed envelope with my name handwritten and underlined. Below it, in all capital letters, the word URGENT. I grabbed it along with my laptop.

"Who's the letter from?" Fantasy asked.

"I don't know," I answered.

"What's the warning about, Davis? Who wants you to leave town?"

"At this point I'd say everyone."

I locked the door, and we ran. Safely back at my parents' house with the deadbolt thrown, we let the door hold us up. Still trying to catch her breath, Fantasy said, "Do you really believe her?"

Florida. She was talking about Florida. "I do," I panted. "She didn't have a thing to do with the robbery."

"And Eddie Crawford's kid?"

We locked eyes.

"I don't care, Fantasy. I truly don't care."

She nodded.

"If you spent five minutes with her," I said, "just five minutes, you'd understand."

The kitchen timer almost scared us to death.

Her next words were ten minutes later and spoken to a dinner plate. "You were right. This is delicious."

To which I agreed, then said, "You're not going to believe this." I took another bite before spinning my laptop around so she could see it.

"What?" she asked. "I don't know what I'm looking at."

"The ballistics report for the paintball guns."

"What about them?"

"One isn't a paintball gun."

Her fork stopped halfway between her plate and her mouth. "What is it?"

"A Smith & Wesson twenty-two magnum."

We didn't have time to pick our jaws off the kitchen floor before the kitchen door filled with Whiskey. Still wearing a muumuu and looking for all the world like Mr. Whipple, the Please Don't Squeeze the Charmin man. When he was working undercover. Whiskey yawned, eyed the casserole, and scratched his belly. "Where might the tableware accoutrements be located in this happy domicile?"

"The what?" Fantasy asked.

"The cutlery and crockery."

"The what?" I asked.

"Forks," Whiskey said. "And plates."

SEVENTEEN

Roy Howdy answered my six thirty call the next morning with, "What? What! Who died?"

"Roy Howdy, it's Davis. No one died. That I know of. But I need you at the police station at sunup."

"That's, like, tomorrow."

"That's, like, in a few minutes."

"Is this about the root cellar? Because I haven't been anywhere near it. When somebody tells me they'll throw me under the jail if I go to the root cellar, I don't go to the root cellar. I've only been there once in my whole life anyway, and I'm not going again. No siree, Bob. That root cellar was all my uncle. And nobody can talk to him about the root cellar because he's *in* the root cellar."

"This isn't about the root cellar." Not yet it wasn't. "It's about the hill above the empty lot at Wright and Oak Streets. The hill we don't want to go up in flames during the fireworks show. The goats didn't clear it. You need to."

"I need to what?"

"Clear it."

"Clear what?"

"The hill."

"The whole hill? How am I supposed to do that?"

"I don't care. Use a machete and hack through. Use a backhoe and dig. Mow the hill down with a bulldozer if you have to."

"I don't have none of that stuff, Davis."

"Do you have dynamite?"

"No," he said. "But I might know where I can get some homemade. Why?"

"Because you could blow the hill off the face of the map for all I care, Roy Howdy, just get it done."

"You don't really mean that, do you?" he asked. "The dynamite part? Wouldn't that be like cutting off my face to make my nose mad?"

It was way too early for Roy Howdy.

"Get rid of the kudzu, Roy Howdy, and I don't particularly care or want to know how you do it, but you have until sundown today to get the hill cleared."

"Or what?"

I thought it was a little early for threatening him within an inch of his life—he was in enough trouble all on his own—and I didn't want to tell him about the decidedly unfriendly letter left at the police station by Marcus Flash with Flash Fireworks, who'd driven all the way to Pine Apple to leave a note saying he didn't appreciate me not taking his calls—I never answered unknown numbers—and that if I didn't get the hill cleared he'd be happy to set up fireworks shop in the middle of Main Street, so I kept going. "Paint the door of the police station first."

"You're saying if I don't blow up the hill then I have to paint the station door?"

"No. I need you to do both. I'm saying paint the station door first."

"Why?"

"Because it needs to be painted."

"What color?"

"The color it's supposed to be."

"It was white yesterday."

"Well it isn't white this morning. So paint it." I was tired of sounding so harsh so early, even though it was Roy Howdy, who didn't respond to anything else. Except maybe food. And when I'd tried that Monday, it hadn't worked out well. So instead I added, "Please."

"Then blow up the hill?"

I took a deep breath of patience. "Paint the station door first. Then before you start clearing the hill, round up everyone from yesterday to help plant the grass, bushes, and flowers today. Then *clear* the hill."

"Some people got jobs, Davis. Lots of people who didn't go to work yesterday to help clean up the mud has to go back today."

"Tell them it's their civic duty to take another vacation day."

"Their what?"

I skipped repeating myself to say, "It's going to take everyone. Start rounding everyone up."

"It'd help if somebody'd get that big truck out of the street."

He was talking about the eighteen-wheeler flatbed from the Bellissimo. Still with the metal container full of slot machines we had no way to unload and still blocking Main Street.

"You're right," I said. "You'll need a forklift—"

"I don't have a forklift."

"Find one."

"Where am I supposed to find a forklift?"

"Try the toothpick factory. You know they have forklifts. Or Yonder Apple Farm. They do too. Just find one."

"Then what?"

"Drive it back to town."

"Can I drive a forklift on the two-lane?"

I rolled my eyes. Tapped a foot. "How about if I promise not to cite you for driving a forklift on the two-lane?"

"Not to what me?"

"Give you a ticket."

"That'll work," he said. "Then what? Blow up the hill?"

"Use the forklift to carefully unload the metal container on the truck," I said. "Carefully."

"Why?"

"Because we can't move the truck until we unload the container."

"And do what with the container?"

That was a good question. I knew I'd probably need the slot machines at one of our many churches in order to skirt Alabama gaming laws. With only three of the churches on Main Street, the one closest to Town Square and the Memorial Day festivities would be Pine Apple Baptist. "The Baptist church parking lot."

"For real?"

"Yes, Roy Howdy."

"Have you talked to Brother Gene about it?"

"I will."

"Where in the church parking lot?"

"Close to the Fellowship Hall."

"In front or behind the Fellowship Hall?"

"I don't care!"

"Then somebody will move the truck blocking Main Street?" he asked.

"Yes," I answered. "You."

"I don't drive big trucks, Davis."

"You do today."

"What happened to the real driver?"

"Long gone."

"Why?"

"Because he had other loads to haul. He couldn't wait around for us to unload the truck that still isn't completely unloaded."

"If his truck is still here, how'd he get out of town? Did he hitchhike?"

"DOES IT MATTER?"

Roy Howdy took a second to decide it didn't matter. "Where is it I'm supposed to put the eighteen-wheeler?"

"Park it in the empty lot at the corner of Wright and Oak Streets. The empty lot at the bottom of the hill."

"Before or after I blow it up?"

"Roy Howdy, hold on."

"Why?"

I gently placed my phone on the table, stood, walked to the sink, then threw open the kitchen window. I took a deep breath of daybreak air, calmed down, then went back to my phone. "Where were we?" I didn't wait for him to answer. "Park the eighteen-wheeler in the lot at the corner of Wright and Oak Streets."

"But that's where the fireworks truck is setting up, Davis. And they're going to be here today or tomorrow."

"Which one is it?"

"I don't know because I haven't figured out which day is today yet."

"It's Wednesday, Roy Howdy. Not that it matters except to say that you need to hurry and clear the hill. Then park the eighteen-wheeler sitting in the middle of Main Street in the lot. There's plenty of room for two trucks."

"Why?"

That time I tapped my foot, then rolled my eyes. "Why what?"

"Why park the big truck in the empty lot?"

"For the same reason the fireworks truck is parking in the empty lot, Roy Howdy. Because it's the only place in town with enough space to park an eighteen-wheeler."

"It'll fit in The Pig parking lot."

"Roy Howdy—"

"Okay," he interrupted. "Have it your way."

"And hurry," I said.

"Let me get this straight," he said. "Hurry up and paint the station door, then hurry up and blow up the hill—"

"—*clear* the hill, Roy Howdy—"

"—then hurry up and steal a forklift—"

"—do not steal a forklift—"

"—borrow a forklift, then hurry up and drop a metal thing at the church—"

"—do not drop it, Roy Howdy. Move it carefully—"

"—carefully drop a metal thing, then hurry up and move a big truck. All by my lonesome and all by sundown."

Finally. I'd gotten through.

"Davis, do you get that my Public Works job is supposed to be two hours a week on Saturday? Not two hundred hours a day on whatever day this is? I got a voodoo candle business and a funeral home to run, you know."

"About that." I woke up my laptop that had fallen asleep from listening to my boring conversation with Roy Howdy. I minimized the Biloxi Crime Lab ballistics report on the paintball guns and maximized the email I'd received during the night about the funeral home. "You have a meeting with the Death Investigation Discipline of the Alabama Department of Forensic Sciences at the police station at nine."

"The who?" he asked. "Is *this* about the root cellar?"

I wondered what gave it away.

EIGHTEEN

After my disturbing call with Roy Howdy, which I shouldn't have been beating myself up about, because every interaction I'd had with Roy Howdy since the playground had been unsettling on some level, I went back to my laptop to access my financial situation. Considering my circumstances, I found it grim.

I wasn't flat broke, or close to it, but I certainly couldn't begin to pay the Bellissimo back unless accounting would be willing to deduct it from my paycheck every other Friday. For the rest of my life. I didn't want the debt hanging over my head until I was ninety years old, and I didn't want the debt hanging over Bradley's head for even ninety more minutes, so I logged into Pine Apple Bank & Trust and opened a new checking account. Something I hadn't done in years. Then I applied for a personal loan. Something I'd never done.

I left the University of Alabama at Birmingham with two degrees, one in Criminal Justice, the other in Computer Information Science, without ever applying for a student loan. Thanks to my parents. And thanks to my grandmother, who bought me my first car, I'd never applied for a car loan. I'd never applied for a home loan because I'd never owned a home, a truth about myself that surprised me when I thought it out loud. I'd made it almost to my forties—yikes—without ever owning a home. So if I'd never applied for a school, auto, or home loan, it only stood to reason I'd never applied for a personal loan. Before I moved to Biloxi and landed a dream job at the Bellissimo, I'd been too broke to qualify for a personal loan. Since then, I hadn't needed one. But there I sat at my parents' kitchen table, the sun barely up, the house so quiet around me with everyone still sleeping off the day before, downloading a personal loan application. And trying to fill it out.

Having been in the same Biloxi job for so long, I had to start with the last four digits and backtrack my way to my full Social Security number as I typed it, because my fingers didn't have the muscle memory. I was married to the Bellissimo's President and CEO. Human Resources filled out my paperwork. And while I knew the casino's street address—875 Beach Boulevard, Biloxi, MS, 39530—I had to look up the five-digit number identifying my specific address on the twenty-ninth floor, because Bradley's PA moonlighted as my personal assistant too, attending to each and every detail. Like my precise mailing address. And when it came to my annual salary, it was a real shocker that I had to go into the Bellissimo's system and actually look up the ridiculously large amount of money I earned. Or maybe I should say the outrageous amount of money I was paid. By the end of the personal loan application process, I could barely hear the house waking because my own personal wake-up call was so loud.

I was spoiled rotten.

Not only that, I'd packed my spoiled rottenness like my toothbrush and driven my pampered life to Pine Apple never doubting I could do my father's job just as well as he could.

I was wrong.

I'd been in Biloxi for so long, knew my job so well, knew every nook and cranny of the grounds, trusted my well-oiled team, and stayed ready for anything. I knew casino cheats, scams, and hijinks as well as Dunkin' knew donuts. Yet I found myself in the kitchen I'd grown up in realizing I no longer knew my hometown. So far, I'd been blindsided right and left. In spite of everything I thought I'd done to prepare, I was totally out of my element, and worse, I'd let everyone down. My husband, my father, my sister, my best friend and partner, my boss, and every resident of Pine Apple. No Hair was right when he said I didn't take responsibility for what was mine. More than that, I did *not* possess my father's nuances for the job, his steady hand, his patience, and his foresight. I'd been operating in my own capacity, doing things my way, thinking I was younger, sharper, and that I knew better. But I didn't. And it was time for my ego to step aside and clean up the mess I'd made. And I would. Just as soon as I said good morning to my little people—two of whom, the blonde ones, had raced down the stairs and climbed into my lap in the middle of my fit of self-awareness—and secured a personal loan.

It was a start.

Bradley, holding the baby, hesitated in the doorway, wondering if it was safe to enter after how we'd said goodnight. Which, technically, we hadn't.

"Sorry," I said. "I'm sorry. And good morning."

To which he said, "I'm sorry too. And I love you."

"I'll make this right, Bradley."

"We'll work it out, Davis."

And just like that. I didn't say how I planned on making it right and he didn't say how we'd work it out, but that would come.

Twenty minutes later, the children and I were dressed for the day and bacon was sizzling on the stove. From the toaster, where he caught an airborne waffle with a fork, Bradley said, "Go, Davis. Do what you need to do." He told me if he didn't see me before, he'd see me at two that afternoon to hand off our children when the limo would arrive to take him, No Hair, Fantasy, and Whiskey back to Biloxi. I kissed the tops of little heads, grabbed one waffle and two slices of bacon, stepped into my Keds, and left for the police station. My optimism, determination, and newfound humility only made it a block before I stopped cold.

The police station door was red.

Roy Howdy painted the door red.

Christmas red.

Taylor Swift lips red.

Blood red.

The paint was so tacky red, I must have just missed him. There'd be no painting it white again anytime soon or it'd end up a pink door. So I opened the wet red door and stepped around it carefully. I left it cracked and opened the backdoor wide, creating a draft to help the red paint dry faster, then sat down at Daddy's desk with purpose. I checked the Alabama Crime Database from his computer finding nothing of note in Pine Apple's immediate area except a carjacking gone wrong south of us in Beatrice, Alabama, when a carjacker sped off without noticing the angry German Shepard in the cargo area of the Lexus GV80 SUV he'd swiped, a massive reward posted for the three Talladega prison escapees still on the run, and a domestic disturbance north of us in Ackerville that sent three feuding sisters and their husbands to jail. The report said the altercation was over macaroni and cheese. Next, from my laptop, I submitted a gun trace request with the Mississippi Bureau of Alcohol, Tobacco, and Firearms on Fantasy's behalf for the twenty-two magnum that had been hiding with the paintball guns on the ballistics report from Biloxi PD. Then I checked my email to see that my personal loan appointment had been confirmed for three o'clock that afternoon. After all that, I called my sister.

"How are you?"

"All better," she said.

"How's Granny Dee?"

"Wearing me out."

"Why?"

"She doesn't want to ride to Tuscaloosa with me. She wants to stay here and arrest people."

"Who does she want to arrest?"

"I don't think she cares. And it isn't so much that she wants to arrest people, it's you, Davis. She wants to be with you. Where all the action is. She thinks she'll miss something if she goes with me. She had to officially sign something yesterday, and to hear her tell the story it was the proudest moment of her life."

"No proud moments to be had in Tuscaloosa?"

"Not a one."

"Why is it you're driving to Tuscaloosa?"

"Because cheerleading camp is over."

Ah. My niece. Riley.

"Send Granny to the police station with a cup of coffee for me. I'll keep her busy."

"Busy how?"

"I'll think of something."

"I'd rather you keep an eye on her than keep her busy, Davis."

"I'll do that too."

"No, you won't. Unless you woke up with a third eyeball, you don't have one to keep on Granny. I took my eye off her for ten minutes yesterday and she got into moonshine."

"I can take care of Granny, Meredith."

Maybe leaving the red door open wasn't such a good idea.

Because it filled with Otis and Eileen Atkins.

Otis said, "You got a minute, Davis?"

Eileen said, "I like the red door. It's pretty."

Travis and Odette Boyd fell in line behind Otis and Eileen.

Travis said, "If I could run something by you real quick, Davis."

Eileen said, "Davis, did you paint the door red for good luck?"

It was seven thirty in the morning.

I invited them in with a wave, then held up a wait-a-second finger. I turned my head away, and whispered to my sister, still on the phone, "Have Granny meet me at the barber shop."

"Frank's?" she asked. "Is he open?"

"No."

"Oh, you and Granny are going to hide at Frank's."

"Right."

"So Granny and coffee at Frank's," she said. "Do you need her to bring anything else?"

Every single thing she knew about Pine Apple Funeral Home and every single thing she'd heard about Fiona Simmons—Pine

Apple Bank & Trust President, bank robber Frank's ex-wife, and Florida's mother—since the last time I'd picked her brain. But I didn't say that. Instead, I thanked my sister for all she'd done for me, promised again to take care of Granny, hung up, and gave the two couples in front of me exactly what they deserved: my undivided attention. Five minutes later, I passed the Atkinses my debit card and told them to go to Home Depot in Greenville and buy all the mulch they could fit in their truck. I didn't say, "Hurry, before the account is empty." Five minutes after that, I had an easier time passing the Boyds my credit card, because for the time being, I had more wiggle room on the credit card, then asked them to go to Camden Feed and Seed and try to rent a pull-behind lawn roller. Something I'd never heard of. Odette Boyd said, "Think of it like a big rolling pin to smooth out little hills and little valleys the goats and the mud left in our yards so the grass will lay flat." Which meant others would need an industrial rolling pin too before they could roll out and plant sod. After the two couples left, I grabbed a big fat black Sharpie and wrote a note to tape on the lucky red door window with my cell phone number, and underneath that, I basically said, "I'm all yours, Pine Apple. Call me if you need me."

I hiked my messenger bag on my shoulder and crossed the street.

I hugged my grandmother. "How are you feeling this morning, Granny?"

"A little wobbly," she said. "Must have been my meeting with the county coroner."

"I want to hear all about it."

A look of concentration washed over her face. "I gave him the what-for."

I had no idea what she meant by that, so I said, "Thank you for filling in for me."

"Just doing my job, Davis. Just doing my job."

We sat in the two soft leather barber chairs that faced Main Street. We reclined them enough to put our feet up. We opened Granny's thermos full of hot coffee, poured, and clicked our mugs.

"Here's to our little town, Davis."

"Here's to our little town, Granny."

We admired the police station's new red door while watching our little town go green. We were two sips in when Granny said, "Look at that." She shook a crooked finger. She was pointing at the taillights on Florida Simmons's chicken wing truck.

"I wonder where she's going," I said.

"I wonder if she's got Eddie Junior with her."

We wondered away until eight thirty when half of the sod grass from the Bellissimo Gardens was on its way into Pine Apple yards. The other half was somewhere in the trim, transport, or placement stage. Sod grass being new to everyone, we could see gaps where home and store owners had mopped themselves into yard corners. The blank spaces were randomly filled with juniper bushes, boxwoods, or something called sweetspire that looked like a knee-high bush wearing white caterpillars to me, but landscaping beggars can't be choosers. By our second cup of coffee, the Atkinses returned from Home Depot and began distributing the mulch, which made a world of difference in the flower beds we could see, and the Boyds returned with the industrial rolling pin. Travis Boyd hooked it up to his riding lawn mower, driving it up and down Main Street smoothing front and back yards, preparing them for sod grass, and had we just finished the final round of a Mr. Pine Apple pageant, he'd have been wearing a crown and cradling a dozen roses.

At ten minutes until nine o'clock, I told Granny I'd be right back and asked her to save my barber chair. She'd finished telling me the long Pine Apple Funeral Home story and was just getting to all the Pine Apple Bank & Trust good stuff I'd missed. "Don't forget where we were, Granny."

"That weirdo Fiona Simmons," Granny said.

"Right."

I sent a text message to Roy Howdy, reminding him it was time, then crossed the street to meet with two representatives of the Death Investigation Discipline of the Alabama Department of Forensic Sciences.

They were twelve minutes late.

They didn't want Sanka.

I listened to the clock tick.

They listened to the answering machine take the calls as I dialed the funeral home number again and again.

I disengaged the phone's speaker. "Clearly, Roy Howdy's forgotten, or he's tied up." I clasped my hands on the desk. "What's the bottom line?"

Investigators working through the night found one empty casket—Eli Atwell's, of which I was more than well aware—and four caskets full. One was positively identified as the former funeral home owner, Roy Howdy's uncle, and the lab team was in the process of both determining his cause of death and attempting to identify the other three.

I said, "Mr. Carter died of natural causes."

The woman, Holly Reed, who was wearing enough jewelry to open a boutique, said, "Forgive us if we don't exactly take you at your word." She sat back and crossed her legs. "Preliminary autopsy reports indicate otherwise."

I cleared my throat. "What do the preliminary autopsy reports indicate?"

"What do you think they indicate?" she asked. "Foul play."

The clock ticked in time with the blood pounding through my temples. "Why don't we wait on the final results." I kept my voice steady. "There isn't a doubt in my mind that the preliminary reports are wrong."

But suddenly there was a doubt in my mind.

What happened to Old Man Carter?

"You'll be the first to know when the cause of death is determined," she said, "but that isn't why we're here. We're here about corpse abuse." She hit the last two words hard. "Now the other three bodies, we know when they died, and we know the cause of death, or causes of the deaths, if you will, but we don't know why the bodies were interred in a root cellar."

"So, when?" I asked.

"When what?" the man, Luther Pratt, asked. And he was wearing enough cologne to open a shop next door to Holly Reed's.

"When did they die?"

"August," she said.

"Two thousand five," he said.

I surrendered with both hands. "There you go."

"Where is it we're going?" The drippy white beads of Holly's earrings jangled.

"Where are you from, Ms. Reed?" I asked.

"Philly," she answered.

I turned to the man. "Where are you from, Mr. Pratt?"

"I transferred to Alabama from Idaho," he said. "Boise."

"August of two thousand five was Hurricane Katrina," I said. "This town drowned. The bodies you found are those of brothers Charles and Colin Osborne, and their cousin, Wesley Snyder."

They waited for further explanation.

"I was here." I tapped Daddy's desk. "I was a patrol officer. I'll never forget it. They died on Brantley Lake. Off County Road 63. Katrina reached us as a tropical storm with winds up to a hundred and fifty miles an hour, and those three went fishing. In a tropical storm. I was at the triple funeral. Clearly, with the graveyard flooded from the hurricane rain, their caskets were stored in the root cellar to be buried at a later date."

They stared at me. The jewelry woman and the cologne man.

"But obviously weren't," I added.

"And no one bothered to ask why?" Cologne asked.

"I guess not," I said. "Everyone assumed that, at some point, the bodies were buried. Go to the cemetery. You'll see their grave markers. I don't think anyone knew they weren't officially buried. Including Roy Howdy."

"How do you know that?" Jewelry asked.

"Because he didn't know there were bodies in the root cellar until his uncle died."

"When was that?" Cologne asked.

"Recently," I said. "In the past few months." I'd heard it from my mother and read it on my father's police blotter when I studied it, but I didn't exactly remember. "Maybe three months ago."

"And you believe your Roy Howdy person?" Jewelry asked. "He didn't know he was living above dead bodies?"

"Not until his uncle died. And yes, I believe him."

"Why?" Cologne asked.

"Because I know him. I know this town. I know these people. And I believe Roy Howdy."

"Believe what, exactly?" Jewelry asked.

I sat back down to explain what had been explained to me by my grandmother just fifteen minutes earlier. Roy Howdy didn't know about the root cellar through a small door on the back wall of the basement in the massive home built in the 1930s, much less the dead bodies it contained, until he read the note his uncle left to be opened after his death. It forbade Roy Howdy from burying his body in the ground. Something about the voodoo going away. The uncle's last wish was to be laid to rest in the root cellar instead. That was when Roy Howdy discovered the four additional caskets.

"Why didn't Mr. Howdy alert the authorities?" Cologne asked.

"I wouldn't know." Although I did. Roy Howdy would have alerted my father. Who was all the authority Roy Howdy recognized. But I wasn't about to throw my father under the Death Investigation Discipline bus, because I didn't believe for a minute Roy Howdy had bothered to mention it to Daddy. Because Daddy would have already taken care of it.

"What about the empty casket in the root cellar?" Jewelry asked. "What happened there?"

My eyes cut across the street to Frank's Barber Shop where my grandmother waited to tell me the rest of the Pine Apple Bank & Trust story. "I'm looking into it."

Jewelry stood. Cologne stood.

One passed me a cease and desist letter against Carter's Funeral Home and told me the remaining bodies would be picked up after the holiday weekend.

The other passed me a federal warrant to serve Roy Howdy for improperly storing human remains.

I showed them the red door.

They promised to be in touch with fines, levies, and additional criminal charges.

I promised to shut down the funeral home the rest of the way and to make sure they never found Roy Howdy.

Jewelry looked at me like I'd lost my last marble. "Why would you willfully obstruct justice?"

"Because he's innocent," I said, "and I won't let a resident of this town face criminal charges for something he didn't know about and wasn't responsible for."

When they were safely past the Welcome to Pine Apple sign, I said, "Roy Howdy? You can come out now."

The storage closet door creaked open.

His head appeared, his face whitewashed.

"What happened to your uncle, Roy Howdy?"

"Maybe I don't rightly know?"

NINETEEN

By the time everyone broke for lunch catered by the Methodist church—fried baloney and tomato sandwiches, Pringles, and Hawaiian Punch—I'd made rounds all over town, spoken to everyone, and solved the world's problems. Maybe not the world's, but as many of Pine Apple's as I could. At one point, I detoured home to change into my last pair of Keds that weren't caked in mud, the pair I'd packed for Memorial Day, red with blue daisies, and ran into the Atkinses and the Boyds. They'd come to return my debit and credit cards. They stayed to get Daddy's gutters out of the yard and back on the house. And I'd kept an eye on Granny by sending her on Special Assignment to the Baptist church.

"I'll need a gun, Davis."

"We're not going to shoot the preacher, Granny."

"He won't do it unless I tell him I'll blow his brains out if he doesn't. Slot machines in the Lord's House?"

"Slot machines in the Lord's Fellowship Hall. Big difference."

"He still won't go for it."

"He has to, Granny. It's the only way we have to pay for the goat cleanup. Which means it's charitable," I said. "Drive that point home. Every dime will be for charity."

Granny shook her head. "Not going to fly, Davis."

"It will, Granny. It's the 'Chuck E. Cheese Law.'"

"The who?"

"It's an Alabama law that exempts currency-operated amusement machines under special circumstances. And what we have here are special circumstances."

"How do you know all that, smarty pants?"

"Because I work in the gaming industry."

She gave me the point. "Let's say Pastor Gene buys it. Gloria won't."

186

Gloria. Pastor Gene's wife. Who wrote all his sermons and passed the offering plates during services—mental finger snap—helping herself to whatever she wanted when she counted it afterward. I'd forgotten all about Gloria. We had dirt on Gloria. "Even better," I told Granny. "Forget Pastor Gene. Go straight to Gloria."

"Oh." Granny nodded. "*Oh*!" Granny's eyes grew wide. "You're telling me to twist Gloria's arm."

"Twist it off if you have to."

"Then what?"

"Then you'll be the casino manager."

Granny batted at the barber chair arms. "Get me out of this contraption, Davis."

I tried to check on No Hair and Fantasy twice. They were supposed to be at The Front Porch, where I found the CLOSED sign flipped and the front door locked. So I used the backdoor. The first time, No Hair, who'd turned Meredith's lunch counter into a satellite Bellissimo office, put his call on hold with the casino manager in Biloxi to tell me Fantasy was in the next city over shopping for clothes because she couldn't go to court that afternoon looking like something the cat dragged in.

"Camden?" I asked.

"Who?"

"Camden is the next city over."

"So?"

"How'd she get there, No Hair? It's twenty miles."

"Don't know, don't care."

"Where's Whiskey?" I asked.

"Again," he said, "don't know, don't care." Then he went back to his call.

The second time I stopped by, almost an hour later, No Hair put his conference call on hold with the casino accountants to tell me

Whiskey was at Bea Crawford's Airbnb, he had no idea why, and that Fantasy had returned from Camden, but he didn't know where she was.

"What was she wearing?" I asked.

"How would I know?"

"Did you bother to look at her?"

He rolled his eyes and clicked back to his call.

I rolled my eyes and clicked back to running Pine Apple.

Making another loop around town to see if anyone needed me, I admired the red, white, and blue Bellissimo flowers bursting, in full bloom, from the half-barrel planters around Town Square and up and down Main Street. I mediated a few arguments, swapped spades, hoes, and rakes between neighbors, relocated potting soil from those with too much to those with too little, stopped by the Ballard's to say hello to their newborn goat, helped with a fence, and called to have the last dumpster at the edge of town picked up. By the time I'd come full circle, Roy Howdy had moved the eighteen-wheeler. A huge improvement. And by the time I broke for lunch, most yards and storefronts along Main Street looked like yards and storefronts again. If I squinted my eyes to very little vision, everything looked good. Eyes wide open, the lawns looked more like patchwork quilts, without much rhyme or reason, but as the day wore on, I discovered a surprising secret weapon. Willa Walters. She was Pine Apple High School's librarian until her early retirement after the unexpected death of her husband. I barely remembered it. I barely remembered her. I did remember how quiet she was. And I remembered her being a walking encyclopedia with a ready answer to even the most obscure of questions. But I didn't remember her having ten green thumbs.

There was a tap on my shoulder with a, "Pardon me. Davis?"

At the time, I was stomping through my parents' yard trying to stay clean enough for my personal loan appointment while placing buckets of bright spiky flowers where Meredith and I intended to plant them late that afternoon. A plan we hatched over lunch at The Front Porch without Fantasy, still MIA, but with my niece, Riley, home from cheer camp, Bradley, the children, and Whiskey. Because none of us wanted anything to do with the fried baloney or the Hawaiian Punch. "Mrs.—" it took me a second "—Walters." I swiped the back of a dirty gardening glove across my damp brow. "Hello."

"Dear," she tapped her own forehead, "you have a little something." She kept tapping until I figured it out. She went on to politely tell me, in her librarian voice I had to lean in to hear, what everyone was doing wrong. Namely planting foxglove, or what she called digitalis purpurea, a plant with blue, pendulous, bell-shape flowers resembling trumpets, which were, according to her, toxic to humans and animals alike. She feared for everyone's safety. "Might you have a word with those who surely aren't aware?"

I didn't have a word or a second to spare. Much less all the words and time it would take to go all over town trying to identify pendulous trumpet flowers. So I said, "Might you?"

Two bright pink spots appeared on her cheeks. She didn't want to have a word with anyone. She'd just spoken more words than I heard her speak throughout all of high school, and I'd say it had taken her all morning to work up the nerve to spit those out. I said, "Excuse me, Mrs. Walters." I stepped away from her and yelled, "WHISKEY!"

I had custody of Whiskey, because, as I'd been informed at lunch, it was my turn. And after an hour of Whiskey worrying me to death, following me and my wheelbarrow back and forth from Town Square as I filled my parents' driveway with buckets of what would be their flowerbeds, the whole time him peppering me with what he called sesquipedalians, which he explained was a big word that meant big words, I parked him on my parents' porch swing and told him to pipe down and stay put. In his fresh muumuu from Bea

Crawford's closet. Waiting on two o'clock. When he, Bradley, and No Hair would leave for Biloxi, supposedly with Fantasy. Who was still nowhere to be found and not answering her phone. Whiskey yelled back, "'Tis the hour of our departure, Mrs. Cole?"

"Not yet." I turned back to smile at Mrs. Walters, then back to Whiskey, I yelled, "Think you could help me for a minute?"

"Most certainly." I heard the porch swing creak. "I am, if nothing else, your humble servant." He ambled down the steps, coming to an abrupt halt at the walkway when he saw Mrs. Walters. Two bright spots popped up on his cheeks too. "How—" he gave a little bow "—may I be of assistance?"

He was speaking to Mrs. Walters.

Not me.

I introduced the librarian to the crossword puzzle man. Whiskey explained away his "current state of attire," and Mrs. Walters told him his appearance was "truly explicable considering his Mustelidae dilemma." They seemed to understand every single word the other spoke. He happily agreed to be her Cyrano de Bergerac and apprise the "unaware of their potential peril from the beautiful yet deadly digitalis purpurea," and off they went. Passing—finally—Fantasy. Headed my way wearing a crisp denim shirtwaist dress and espadrilles. Walking side-by-side with Florida Simmons. And not just walking. But chitchatting too. And smiling. At each other.

So that's where Fantasy had been.

With Florida.

And that's how she'd gotten to Camden.

In a chicken wing truck.

I stared holes through both of them.

"What?" Fantasy came to a stop in front of me. "You believe her, and I believe you. More than that, I can't leave you here without backup."

I studied the curiosity of the two of them.

Wondering who broke the ice.

And why.

Until the fire alarm ringtone of my mother calling cut through the thick afternoon air. I reached for my phone. "It's my mother."

"I know," Fantasy said.

"I know too," Florida said.

"How do you know?" Fantasy asked Florida.

"That same siren went off when we were drinking Boone's Farm."

"Ah," Fantasy said.

"It's nothing." The fire alarm sounded again. "If it were something bad, it would be a text message." The next word I spoke was, "Mother?"

The next word I heard was, "Daddy."

"Daddy." Adrenalin shot through me. "I'm so glad you called."

"Are you, now?"

I could count the times my father had used a cynical tone like that with me on one hand. "Daddy, let me explain—"

"Davis, I don't have time for you to explain."

"Why? Are you on your way home?"

Florida's head jerked.

"No," Daddy said.

I shook my head no at Florida.

She puffed out a breath of relief.

"Can I ask one more question, Daddy?"

"If you make it quick."

"What can you tell me about the day Old Man Carter died?"

"Nothing," he said. "For one, I spent a good part of the day meeting with the new fireworks contractor and didn't know anything was amiss with Mr. Carter until later, and for another, I truly don't have time. Bea's been arrested, Davis."

"I thought she'd been detained."

"She was. Now she's been taken into custody."

"Why was Bea arrested? What'd she do?" I pulled my phone from my ear and pushed the speaker icon. Everyone loved a good Bea story. And I didn't want to have to repeat it.

"What didn't she do would be the better question," Daddy said. "As her reluctant representative based on my law enforcement status in the States, I was allowed in the observation room during Bea's interview with Immigration, Refugees and Citizenship. You can't imagine what I observed. First, her backpack." He inhaled sharply. "Davis, they searched the backpack Bea had with her when she illegally crossed the border. In addition to several bratwurst sausages and a toaster, of which one isn't allowed and the other considered a fire hazard, along with Chinese deer horn knives, which are deemed deadly weapons, the immigration authorities found a large amount of cannabis edibles."

"Wait," I said. "What?"

"Davis, it is against the law to cross the border with even one of those items."

"I don't even know what they *are*."

"You know what bratwurst is, Davis, and you know what a toaster is—"

"Who drags a toaster around in a backpack?"

"She bought a used toaster at a roadside market. She said it was a good deal."

"Toasters are already good deals, Daddy. She could have bought a toaster at Walmart in Greenville for ten dollars."

"It's Bea, Davis."

"I get that. What I don't get are the deer horn knives," I said. "Are you talking...Kung Fu?"

He hesitated before saying, "You're on the right track."

"Where did Bea even get Kung Fu knives? And how did she get through the Atlanta airport with them?"

"She purchased all of the items, including the unseemly amount of cannabis edibles, at the same roadside souvenir stand. And the souvenir stand was in Niagara Falls, New York. She illegally crossed the border to Niagara Falls, Canada, with the items."

"Cannabis edibles?"

"Candies laced with a high concentration of marijuana," he explained.

I knew what they were. What I couldn't believe was that Bea knew what they were. And that Bea would do something so stupid, considering medical marijuana dispensaries were legal in Alabama and there wasn't a doctor in the state who wouldn't write her a prescription as fast as humanly possible just to get her out of their office. Meanwhile, on my left, Fantasy was laughing so hard no sound could escape. It would've been the same had she dropped a brick on her big toe and was waiting for the scream. She was turning in a slow circle, batting an arm through the air then slapping her hand down on her thigh, head bobbing, and trying to catch her breath.

I smacked her arm.

"Then, Davis," Daddy said, "Bea, as is her way, became argumentative with the Canadian immigration authorities. Insisting she was a victim. Claiming she was being railroaded by Canucks. Threatening the immigration agents. Threatening their families."

With that, Fantasy, unable to stand on her own two feet, made her way to Mother and Daddy's mailbox where she used it as a prop. The top half of her draped over it, head down, repeatedly banging the mailbox with a closed fist until the little door flew open and mail spilled out. Florida had a hand pressed over her mouth, trying to contain her amusement, but it wasn't clear if it was the Bea or the Fantasy situation entertaining her.

"She went on to describe herself as an American Patriot," Daddy said, "and too heavily handed to the point of an immigration agent asking outright if she considered herself a domestic terrorist. At which time, Bea climbed over the table, or shot over it, rather, got in the man's face, and asked if she looked like a domestic terrorist."

I glanced over at Fantasy and wondered if she needed oxygen.

"Which she did," Daddy said. "She looked very much like a terrorist. Davis, Bea has been arrested."

A call beeped in from Pine Apple a Day Keeps the Doctor Away Medical Center. I ignored it. "Okay, Daddy. What can I do?"

"From what I understand, you have enough on your plate."

"That doesn't mean that either Meredith or I couldn't fly up there and bring Mother home if you feel like you need to stay with Bea." The beep of the first incoming call stopped, only to start again immediately. The second call the same as the first, from Pine Apple a Day Keeps the Doctor Away Medical Clinic. "Daddy, I need to put you on hold."

"Sweet Pea—"

"Just for a second."

I switched the call over. "What?"

"Davis, it's Shirley at—"

I cut her off. "What, Shirley?"

"It's Roy Howdy."

"What about him?"

"I called for an ambulance to come get him," she said. "Thought you ought to know."

"What happened to him?"

"He was clearing that hill back on Oak and Wright and he's very allergic."

"To what?"

"Turns out there's poison oak under all that kudzu on the hill. He's all swolled up, he's drooling buckets because he can't swallow, and he's babbling nonsense about fireworks."

"Do you not have an EpiPen, Shirley?"

"Sure," she said. "A whole drawer full."

"Have you given Roy Howdy a dose?"

"No."

"Well, do it."

"I can't. Dr. Urleen says I can't give out medicine or I'll get sued."

"By whom?"

"By him," she said. "He says if I give somebody so much as a baby aspirin, he'll sue the pants off me."

"Where is he?"

"Don't know. But I'm going to wait on the ambulance."

"If Roy Howdy's that allergic, Shirley, he won't make it until an ambulance gets here."

"Davis, I don't want Urleen suing my pants off me."

"Get an EpiPen ready. I'm on my way."

Urleen—what a quack—could sue me all day long if he wanted to. Considering what I owed the Bellissimo, there'd be nothing for him to get. I ran down the middle of Main Street, passing my husband and children on the sidewalk on the way to my parents' house.

"Davis!"

"Mommy!"

Over my shoulder I yelled, "I'll be right back!"

My husband yelled, "I'm leaving in fifteen minutes!"

"I'll be back by then!"

I kept flying. I already had a ton of explaining to do to my father if he ever made it home from Canada, and I wasn't about to add the death of a citizen to the list. I flew through the door of Pine Apple a Day, busted into the single exam room, yanked the EpiPen from Shirley's shaking hands, and stabbed Roy Howdy in his tree-trunk thigh.

Ten minutes later, I was still panting when the children and I stood in the driveway waving until we could no longer see the Bellissimo limo as Bradley, No Hair, and Fantasy left for Biloxi. I wore my brave face. Whiskey did not. He openly wept. Quinn patted his arm. "It's okay, Mr. Whiskey. Daddy promised he'd be back for the parade."

"Young lady." Whiskey wiped away tears. "You should know by now that paternal figures often fall short of fulfilling commitments."

"Whiskey," I warned him.

"My sincere apologies, Mrs. Cole, for speaking out of turn, but bidding adieu often puts me in a state of cognitive dissonance." A hand disappeared into the pocket of his khaki pants. "I find goodbyes challenging. Comparably approaching the challenging tasks the lovely Mrs. Walters and I have on our imminent temporal horizon." His hand came out of the pocket with a cotton handkerchief with the initials WRW. William Robert Walters. My old librarian's deceased husband. And as Whiskey blew his nose, sending the girls back several feet and surely dislodging a few of his brain cells, my old librarian patted Whiskey's arm. "There, there, Cedrick. The prevailing circumstances are destined to ameliorate."

Whiskey, in a dead man's starched plaid shirt, laid a hand over hers. "Do you incline toward such an estimation?"

"I do."

And for the life of me, she said the two words as if she were at the altar of The Little White Wedding Chapel in Vegas.

Whiskey blew his nose one more time then turned to Mrs. Walters. "Come, my dear. We have a slate of laborious undertakings awaiting our diligent attention."

I wasn't exactly sure what he meant by that, or what either of them meant by any of it, but I did know that together they were going all over town tweaking haphazardly planted Pine Apple yards into showstopping works of art, so I didn't care what they meant. As long as they kept giving yard advice no one understood, but were more than happy to step aside to let the two wordsmiths show, not tell.

After they left, Bex said, "Mommy, are they from Irish?"

"Do you mean Ireland?" I hiked the baby up my hip an inch. "I don't know. Wherever they're from, they're sure good at yardwork."

We watched them until they passed the police station. The girls watched out of curiosity. I watched, wondering if Whiskey would be a permanent Pine Apple fixture. In a way, he'd fit right in, because Pine Apple made a place for everyone, but just looking at them gave me a headache between my eyes. Or I might have been in the throes of caffeine withdrawal. And the best coffee in town was at my sister's. "Let's go to Aunt Merri's." Because everyone needed a strong cup of coffee before their first personal loan interview.

Bex and Quinn raced off squealing. The baby and I followed at a much slower pace admiring Pine Apple in full bloom.

I was proud.

So proud.

And not of myself, but of everyone else.

Granny Dee was in her rocker on the front porch, her Jitterbug phone against her ear. She gave me a wink and a thumbs up in the middle of, "I do too know how to be a casino spy, because Davis taught me—" to whoever was on the other end of the line. So she was staffing the Baptist church casino. That'd keep her busy for a while. I leaned over and kissed the top of her blue-white head whispering, "Great job, Granny." As I walked through the front door, I heard the pound of little feet on the steps as Bex and Quinn raced upstairs with their cousin, and I found my sister at the lunch counter. I saddled up to the bar. "Pour me a strong one."

She landed a steaming coffee mug on the counter. "You're going to need it."

"Why?" Every muscle in my body tensed. "What's happened?"

"You're on your way to a meeting with Fiona Simmons, right?"

"I am," I said. "How'd you know that?"

"There are no secrets in Pine Apple."

Oh, but there were.

And Fiona Simmons was sitting on them.

TWENTY

The bank was dressed much like Fiona.

Beige.

And dismal.

The air was stagnant, the silence absolute, the furnishings worn, and there was no natural light past the front door. The overwhelming mood was bleak. I took a step in, vowing to liven things up a bit.

Knowing full well I was there, because the front door chime announced my arrival, Fiona Simmons didn't look up from her desk through the plate glass walls of her corner office. The only other person in the room, the lone bank teller and Fiona's mouthpiece, Courtney Carr, former Greenville Mall Hallmark Gold Crown store manager currently channeling her Sandra Dee school outfit of butter-yellow swing skirt and matching cardigan, said, "You're early."

I wasn't.

She pointed at the ancient grandfather clock holding up the wall behind me as evidence.

I pulled my phone from my pocket and checked the time. "It's three o'clock, Courtney."

She pointed above my head. "We go by the bank clock, Davis."

I took one of the metal folding chair seats on each side of the old bank clock that was eighteen minutes slow. The chair closest to Fiona's office. Where she could see me. Were she to look up.

Ten minutes later, Fiona Simmons waved me in. She still hadn't raised her eyes from whatever it was on her gargantuan desk that had her so mesmerized, but she managed to wag a finger at the two low chairs on the other side. I chose the chair on the left. It was a quicker escape route should things get really ugly. I cleared my throat and opened innocuously with, "Thanks for making time for me, Fiona."

She finally made eye contact. It was a blank stare more than anything else. Then she slowly leaned back, crossed her arms, and looked down her nose at me. With nothing. She was every bit as unhappy with me as she had been a dozen years earlier. Fiona Simmons wasn't a happy woman to begin with. And she certainly wasn't happy to see me.

She wasn't so surly back when Florida and I were high school friends. In fact, compared to my mother, who was constantly complaining about something, usually me, Fiona Simmons struck me as role-model happy. She was ten years younger, ten miles cooler, and ten infinities more fun than my own mother. She sang. And danced. She kept a radio in her kitchen window tuned to Magic 101.1 in Montgomery, a Top 40 station my mother forbade, and knew every word to every song. On any given Tuesday, Florida and I could bust through the backdoor after school and find Fiona having a party for two: herself and Britney Spears. But what I liked most about Fiona Simmons back in the day was that she didn't care what Florida and I did. She never said our shorts were too short. Not once did she ever stomp her foot and point up the staircase with, "Get that stringy hair out of your face, young lady. You look like a hippy. You're not leaving this house without two neat braids. Say something and I'll get my scissors." Fiona didn't care how we wore our hair. Or how much noise we made, how late we stayed up, how messy we were, or that we lived on a steady diet of Dr Pepper and Hostess orange cupcakes. And she never said a word when we regularly snuck out Florida's bedroom window. Then around the house to the driveway. Where we put Fiona's Mazda Miata in neutral, rolled it out to the street, and popped it off in second halfway down the hill. She didn't say anything the time we watered down her vodka to almost nothing after pouring the straight stuff into our Sonic limeades. Which was after we drank the limeades down to the last loud inch. (Or maybe she figured we'd punished ourselves enough that night. And all the next day.) I remembered thinking when I was an old lady mother, I wanted to be just like Florida's mother. Cute, bouncy, and willing to look the other way.

I'd since become a mother and had changed my mind.

And in retrospect, it was easier to understand my own mother's approach to parenting—not in practice, but rather in theory—than Fiona's just-don't-make-me-bail-you-out-of-juvie method.

What happened to that happy carefree woman?

Some I knew: her husband robbed the bank and went to prison, her only child abandoned her in the aftermath, the town turned on her, she allegedly had an affair with her husband's best friend, and he died soon after during a routine training mission on an aircraft carrier somewhere near Kuwait. Add all that up, and Fiona Simmons had baggage so heavy she'd been forced to keep what she had in Pine Apple after the bank bailout, or settle for an anonymous life of burger flipping somewhere else. Sitting in a small room rife with Fiona's bitterness, I wondered if she'd made the right choice. Clearly, Fiona's ghosts had all but driven her mad. One of them spoke up to say, "What do you want, Davis? Why are you here? You and I both know you don't need a personal loan."

She'd be surprised.

"Are you here to ask me where the long-lost money is hidden?" And at the mention of the money her husband stole, in what was clearly a nervous tick, she began tapping the business end of a thin silver mechanical pencil on her desk. The rapid staccato clip filled the space between us. "If so," she said, "you're wasting your time and mine."

I stayed silent.

So she'd keep talking.

Which she did.

"I didn't know where the money was then, I don't know where it is now, and at this point, I'm not sure I believe there ever was any hidden money." She dropped the mechanical pencil on her desk with a dull thud. "And you can forget a personal loan. I'm not in the business of loaning money to people who don't need it." She picked up the pencil again and trained it on the door. "So good day."

I thought the first part of my meeting with Fiona Simmons would last a little longer, that we'd go through the personal loan motions for more than a minute before she cut me off at the knees, but if she wanted to get right to it, fine by me. With a sigh, I pushed myself out of the chair and gathered my mental reins. I crossed to the door, but instead of going through it as she'd suggested, I gave it a nudge. The glass slid across its well-worn path in the threadbare carpet and swished closed. Much to Courtney Carr's disapproval. I took deliberate and slow steps back to Fiona, and rather than take my seat again, I stood. Right in front of her. "I don't believe you, Fiona."

She was forced to look up. "I don't care, Davis."

"I think you care very much. Clearly not about me, and what I've done to offend you so is a mystery I might never solve, but don't say you don't care about the money. I believe you found the money your husband stole from his neighbors, and with nowhere safe to hide it, you buried it with Eli Atwell. Then Florida showed up out of the blue with Eddie Crawford's son, so you violated that poor man's final resting place because you needed the money. Then you relocated both. The dead man and the money. What I want to know is why. You had to have had a pretty good reason to put yourself through that kind of horror. Moving a decayed body? In the dead of night? Through pouring rain? Why would you *do* that, Fiona?" I yanked the mechanical pencil out of her hand, mostly because I couldn't listen to it for one more second, then pointed it at her. "Where's the money?"

She shot out of her seat and reclaimed the mechanical pencil, jerking it out of my hand. Then pointed it at the narrow door of a supply closet to her right. A supply closet with a jimmy-resistant deadbolt. "The only Pine Apple money I have, the only Pine Apple money I've ever had, is right there. If you want it, take it."

So that's where Fiona kept the bank's money.

Not in the vault.

Just then the ancient grandfather clock interrupted with three ridiculously loud and excruciatingly slow gongs. I waited the reverberations out, then toned it down to say, "Again, Fiona, I don't believe you."

"Again, Davis, I don't care what you believe."

I toned it down yet another notch. Just short of sympathetic. "I think you lost your whole family in one fell swoop. You didn't respect your marriage enough to keep an eye on it and your husband went to prison. You didn't pay enough attention to your daughter and lost her too. Until now. Florida showed up, with Eddie Crawford's son no less, effectively forgiving you for whatever, and all of a sudden you have a second chance at happiness. I think you've been sitting on the money you swore under oath you knew nothing about waiting for just this day when you could make a run for it with your patched-up family and Pine Apple's money."

She didn't break eye contact.

"But you still had a problem, didn't you?"

I wasn't sure she was breathing.

I leaned in and landed, "And it wasn't Eddie Crawford."

Her cheeks flushed.

"Because Deadbeat Eddie would be better at deadbeat dadding than he's been at any other deadbeating in his life."

Her eyes narrowed.

"Your problem was his mother, right, Fiona? The battle for the future happiness of your second-chance family would be when Bea Crawford claimed her grandson. Which was why you dropped off Eli's body at the diner. To implicate Bea. To keep her tied up long enough for you to finally leave this little town with your long-lost daughter, Bea's grandson, and this town's money." I leaned in until we were all but nose to nose. "How am I doing?"

"Get out." Her voice held no emotion. "Go back where you came from, Davis."

Word-for-word, the same red advice I'd found on the police station door late the night before. "Give the money back to this town and I will."

Just then, Courtney Carr reminded us we weren't alone, yelling, "Do you want me to call the police, Fiona?"

Fiona's head snapped in Courtney's direction. "She is the police, you idiot."

Courtney yelled back, "Ya'll are making me nervous! Okay?"

Everything reset when Fiona and I said the same words on the same beat: "Then leave."

Courtney grabbed her purse from somewhere behind the teller counter and flew out the front door. Then it was just me and Fiona. Who stood to her full height and spat, "Who do you think you are, Davis? Blowing back into town like you own the place. Nosing around my life so full of yourself. So self-righteous. So quick to judge me. So sure you've figured it all out." Shaking her head slowly with scorn for me filling every deep worry line on her face, she finished with, "You have no idea what you're talking about."

I'm not sure where we'd have gone from there—cat fight?—had my phone not interrupted. I didn't bother to look until it stopped ringing, then immediately started again. I opened my mouth to deliver a parting shot along the lines of if I was right and she intended to sneak out of town in a chicken wing truck in the dead of night with her daughter and grandson, she'd better not take a single Pine Apple nickel with her, when my phone started ringing for the third time in a row.

Considering how many smoldering fires I had burning, I had to look. It could have been my sister about my children, my husband with an update on the Fantasy fiasco, my father with news from Canada, or the impatient fireworks man asking about the hill at the corner of Wright and Oak Streets. But it was my grandmother with, "Davis, you'd better get to the church quick." I could hear Pastor Gene's wife, Gloria, yelling in the background.

Which was fine.

I'd had all I could take in the stuffy bank full of Fiona's rage.

I hiked my messenger bag on my shoulder and turned on my heels. I stopped at the door to meet her eyes one last time. "She's going to find out she has a grandson, you know."

Fiona stared a hole through me.

"And when she hears," I said, "if she hasn't already, she'll hitchhike back to Pine Apple if she has to. Like you, Fiona, Bea Crawford has a hole in her heart as big as a bus. A hole a grandchild she never thought she'd have would fill. And she'll make it her mission in life to have him all to herself."

I thought I saw her right eyebrow twitch.

"She'll sue."

I thought I heard a small noise from deep in her throat that wanted to be a scoff.

"You're right," I conceded. "Even Smerle T. Webb, Esquire, will laugh her out of his office, but not before pointing out that while there isn't a court in this state that would take the boy away from his mother to award custody to his paternal grandmother, they'd all be sympathetic to his wronged father. The father, denied his parental rights for all these years, could sue for custody. And what would custody mean to Eddie, Fiona? Child support. What would child support mean to Eddie? The thing he loves most in the world. Something for nothing." I lowered my voice to one click above a whisper. "Are you up for that kind of fight? Bea Crawford will make yours and Florida's lives living hells." I let that sink in before slowly adding, "And where will that leave Cole?"

She fell back into her chair and started the engine on her mechanical pencil.

And my phone began ringing again.

"For what it's worth," I said in parting, "I'm sorry about how things turned out for you."

It felt like she opened her mouth to say something substantial, but quickly thought better of it. "Get out."

TWENTY-ONE

On my way to the Baptist church, I tried to shake it off. I might as well have been trying to shake off a broken leg. The enormity of Pine Apple's darkest day climbing out from the rock under which it had been hiding for two decades, and on my watch, combined with Fiona's baffling and bone-deep resentment of me, clung to me like another layer of skin. Add to that, very few of the darts I threw hit the Fiona board. Her denials of my accusations were absolute, leaving me to wonder what in the world was going on with her. She wasn't innocent by a long stretch, although I left the bank without a clue as to what she was guilty of. So I detoured to pop my head in my sister's backdoor. Seeing her, my children, and my niece might help sweep away the anxiety, frustration, and heartache of it all.

I found Bex and Quinn at the lunch counter on both sides of their cousin, Riley. Each girl had a stack of bright pink construction paper, safety scissors, and their own tiny container of Elmer's glue. Between them were three bowls: one full of brightly colored pom poms, another with googly eyes, and a third holding a rainbow collection of shiny sequins. They'd be busy for hours. I kissed the tops of heads and asked Riley where the baby and her mother were.

"On a walk?" she said. "Try Town Square."

No doubt I'd run into them.

And I did. On the front porch of The Front Porch. Meredith was in a rocker. My sleeping baby boy was in her arms. She immediately held a finger to her lips. I stepped over, touched my baby's sleeping head, and pantomimed walking with my fingers. Then praying.

Meredith whispered, "You're going to heaven?"

"Church," I whispered back.

I tapped my wrist where a watch might be and held up ten fingers. As in ten minutes.

She nodded.

207

I tiptoed down the first step only to turn back when she whispered, "Wait. How'd it go with Fiona?"

I rolled my eyes.

"Did you ask her why she hates you so much?"

I rolled my eyes the other way.

"Tell me later."

I gave her a nod.

On the sidewalk, I ran into Courtney Carr making her way back to the bank. She didn't slow down when she angrily hissed through her teeth, "Leave Fiona alone, Davis. She's been through enough."

"She's trying to finish what her husband started, Courtney."

Courtney stopped. And spun. "She's trying to keep it from happening again."

"What's that supposed to mean?"

Her face flushed.

She stomped off.

"Courtney!" I yelled at her back.

"Mind your own beeswax, Davis. Okay?"

I might have run after her, but my phone stopped me. Probably my grandmother to tell me she'd solved her own problem by hanging Pastor Gene's wife from the sanctuary's highest rafter, but it wasn't Granny. It was Roy Howdy. Who last I'd heard was busy receiving intravenous antihistamines at the Regional Medical Center of Central Alabama in Greenville.

"Roy Howdy?"

"Hey, Davis."

"How are you feeling?"

"Okay, I guess."

"Good."

I waited.

"Great," I added.

He still didn't respond.

So I tacked on, "Wonderful."

He cleared his throat in my ear to say what he'd obviously been working up to. "Thanks for saving my life, Davis."

"Anytime, Roy Howdy."

"And I mean both times you saved my life today. Once with those people—" he was talking about the representatives from the Death Investigation Discipline "—and then you saved my life even harder at Dr. Urleen's."

"Really, Roy Howdy, I was just doing my job."

By then, I had a foot in the Baptist church parking lot.

"Could you save me one more time?"

"It's four in the afternoon," I said. "How many times is your life going to be threatened today?"

"Come again?"

"What is it you need?"

"A ride."

"A ride to where?"

"Home."

"From where?"

"The hospital," he said. "The ambulance that gave me a ride here says they don't give rides home. I'm not calling those yuber people because I don't want to get robbed."

"Of what?"

"Come again?"

"Never mind, Roy Howdy."

"So you'll give me a ride?"

"Can't you think of anyone else in town who might have a little more free time than me?"

"Maybe Dill Barter. But you have to ride with him."

"Why is that?"

"Because you're my responsible part."

"Excuse me?"

"The part responsible."

"Responsible for what?"

"The hospital ain't free, Davis."

Did Roy Howdy not have health insurance? Of course he didn't. He didn't have a high school diploma, he didn't have a funeral home license, and he barely had a lick of sense. "How am I responsible for the bill, Roy Howdy?"

"They asked me what happened, I told them about the poison oak on the hill you made me clear, and the lady said that made you responsible for my allergic reactions. Then a little bit later she asked me who was responsible for my party, and I said, 'You just said Davis was responsible,' then she said, 'For what?' then I said, 'For everything,' then she said, 'Then she needs to pay this invoice,' and I said, 'I'll call her,' and this is me."

I waited.

"Calling her," he said.

The door to the Fellowship Hall was open.

"Her is you," he clarified.

I could hear my grandmother and Gloria going at it, and I could see small clusters of slot machines scattered in twos and threes around the room. Still packed in huge crates. "Roy Howdy, where's the forklift?"

"Are you talking to me?" he asked.

"Is your name still Roy Howdy?"

"Last I checked."

"Yes," I said. "I'm talking to you. Where's the forklift?"

"What forklift? The one I borrowed from Yonder Apple Farms? That forklift?"

"That forklift."

"Are you thinking I can drive it home? I didn't even bring it."

I counted to three. "Roy Howdy, I'm asking if you returned it."

"To Yonder Apples?"

"Yes."

"No."

"Where is it?"

"Not here. Why?"

"Because we still need it. I'll come get you and pay the hospital bill—" if my debit card would let me "—but I need you to work when we get back."

"You know, Davis? You're what they call a workhorse. You know what a workhorse is? It's somebody who works somebody else like they're a horse. If I was a horse, I'd need a ride home from the animal doctor's in Ackerville. Not the people doctor's in Greenville. Your daddy's never seen the day when he worked somebody as hard as you work somebody."

"Who saved your life twice today?"

"Okay," he said, "you win. Come get me. And could you bring two Whoppers with bacon and cheese and a big Coke?"

I hung up.

What I was really hoping was to wind up my Pine Apple day and work in my parents' yard until sundown. Not drive to Greenville.

I stepped into the Fellowship Hall. Gloria and Granny slowed down long enough to mark my presence. Granny said, "Tell her, Davis."

"Tell her what?" Having just been through my own tug of war with Fiona at the bank, I had no desire to get in the middle of Granny and Gloria's, but there I stood between two old women hurling insults and accusations at each other between yelling their sides of the story all over each other and directly at me. The surface fight seemed to be about placement of the slot machines in the Baptist church's Fellowship Hall. But the underlying problem was money. I wondered why it was that the underlying problem was always money.

"We'll line three walls with slot machines," I said. "Twenty on each of the long walls, ten machines on the back wall. And I will empty the cash boxes. Not you, Granny, because they're too heavy." (No, they weren't.) "And not you either, Gloria."

"Why not?" she demanded.

I didn't tell her it was because she had sticky fingers, but I did tell them both to take a break and that I'd meet them back at the church in an hour. Then I sent a text message to my sister to tell her something had popped up, I'd be another hour, while on my way to the station to grab the keys to the patrol car to drive to Greenville. Then all my plans flew out the window when I opened the blood-red door and found the biggest mistake of my life sitting at my father's desk.

It was Eddie.

Eddie the Idiot Crawford.

My ex-ex-husband.

"Well, lookie who it is." He smirked.

"What are you doing here, Eddie?"

"That's none of your business."

"I beg to differ."

"Beg all you want." He tipped back in Daddy's chair. "I love it when women beg."

"How'd you get here?" Truthfully, I couldn't have cared less. I was stalling. Still standing in the open door. Hoping someone would walk by and see him—huge news—then word of his return would spread like wildfire. All the way to Florida. (The person.) (Not the Sunshine State.) "Did you swim here?"

"That's none of your business either," he said, "but I could've if I'd wanted to."

"You couldn't swim a hundred and twenty-five feet, Eddie. Much less a hundred and twenty-five miles."

"That's exactly how far out in the drink I was," he said. "Glad to know you're keeping up."

"You wish." Although I was momentarily irritated at myself for letting him know I knew exactly where he was in the Gulf, but it was more along the lines of knowing where the landmines were before crossing the field that had to be crossed than keeping up. Something I didn't bother to explain to him because it just didn't matter. What mattered was the news of his surprise visit reaching Florida. At some point, she had to deal with the paternity issue. It was only right to resolve it. But did it have to be today? And without warning? "Why are you here, Eddie? What do you want?"

He rubbed his bristly chin for a full minute before sing-song drawling, "Well, a few days ago when I was having a little trouble with some boys on the rig, I called my good buddy Roy Howdy to hit him up for a little voodoo."

Roy Howdy could find his own ride home from Greenville.

"Got my voodoo business done with him, and I asked if everything here was the same as I left it. I was mostly talking about my truck I left at his place, but turned out things were nothing like I left it." Eddie tipped his head back to study the ceiling. "I decided I'd better come home and see for myself. So I asked my boss for a few personal emotion days off."

"A few what?" My eyes darted across the street where I saw Mrs. Mobly, who spent her daylight hours on her porch swing crocheting mile-long multi-colored blankets and keeping an eye on the police station like it was her job, drop her binoculars. Next, she dropped the blanket she'd been crocheting. Then she raced down her porch steps. "There's no such thing as personal emotion days."

"I can see where you might think that, Davis, because you never met a personal emotion. I, on the other foot," he patted his chest, "do have personal emotions."

"And?"

"And my old dragon lady boss said no. So I tricked her into firing me."

"How'd you manage that?" Out of the corner of my eye, I watched gossipy old Mrs. Mobly poke her head in the door of Frank's Barber Shop, and with that, I took my first full breath.

"I don't kiss and tell, Davis. But it may and might not have had something to do with tuna melts that shut down production for two shifts."

"Aren't you clever."

His head snapped up. "Thank you, Davis." He landed his feet on Daddy's desk. Then he crossed his ankles, clasped his hands behind his head, and looked me over from head to toe. "And since you said something nice to me, I'm going to say something nice back to you."

I couldn't wait to hear it. And spotted Mrs. Mobly again, who apparently couldn't wait to get through the door of Pine Apple Pies & Cakes. Which meant she only had to spread the word of Eddie's surprise return a block and a half more before she reached the chicken wing truck in front of the bank. Hopefully it would be before I strangled him, because just then he said, "I always thought you'd be one of those pudgy mamas with a big wide ass." His hands came from behind his head to demonstrate the vast width of my rear end in his imagination. "Which is only one of the reasons I didn't have kids with you."

The nerve.

The absolute nerve.

"But you wear it pretty good," he said. "I mean, you don't look like you just popped one out of the oven. I bet your homo husband is happy about that."

I had to either take a breath or shoot him.

I took a breath.

"Speaking of rugrats." In a heartbeat, he landed his feet on the floor and leaned in. "Did you hear the news? I got a kid too." He dusted the phantom lapels of his Fuel Solutions t-shirt. "I'm a proud papa."

"Did you hear the news, Eddie? Your mother's been arrested in Canada."

His brows drew in on themselves.

His eyes darted right and left.

He hadn't heard.

"And since you've heard there's a young man in town who Roy Howdy thinks bears a slight resemblance to you, and why you'd consider Roy Howdy a reliable source is a total mystery to me, I guess you heard his mother's here too."

"Where else would she be?" He asked it while poking on his phone. And because his voice had lost most of the bravado attached to every previous word he'd spoken, I presumed he was either trying to make contact with his mother or looking for news about her arrest. "I'm about to go see her." He looked up from his phone. "And we're going to have a little talk about why she never told me she was knocked up."

His bravado was back.

So was mine.

"Leave Florida alone, Eddie, or I'll lock you up."

"I got no beef with Florida. Other than she's a stone-cold bitch too."

Too? Did he mean in addition to me? I wasn't quite following, but then again, it was Eddie. Who stood with, "Like mama, like daughter." He crossed in front of Daddy's desk and breezed by me. "And it's the mama you'd better lock up. For her own good. Because I'm about to mop the floor with her old ass."

He made his exit.

I don't know how long I stood frozen in place before I slid down the door frame and let the floor hold me.

Fiona Simmons wasn't the boy's grandmother.

Fiona Simmons was his *mother*.

I didn't have time for Mrs. Mobly to spread the word another block, and I didn't have time to dig through Daddy's desk and find Florida's chicken wing cookoff paperwork with her phone number so I could warn her to run. And hide the brother she'd raised for her mother. But Pine Apple Bank & Trust's number was on a laminated card under the phone. When I gathered enough equilibrium to stagger to the desk, I dialed with a shaky finger. Courtney Carr answered.

"It's Davis. Let me speak to Fiona. Right now."

"Do you seriously think she wants to talk to you, Davis?"

"I don't want to talk to her either, but you'd better lock the front door because Eddie Crawford is about to blow through it."

TWENTY-TWO

Friday showed up at twelve a.m. as regularly scheduled.

It found me wide awake in my mother's swivel glider I'd dragged across the rug to the middle of the den, so I'd have a direct line of fire to both the front and back doors with just a pivot. I'd tossed the contents of her two armchair caddies—reading glasses, a movie theater box of Junior Mints, cuticle cream, and multiple Large-Print Word Search books—and replaced them with my old Beretta 92 service pistol, a taser gun, and a sledgehammer I found in the garage. The armchair caddy with the sledgehammer was drooping a little bit. Dragging the floor, in fact. In my lap, I had my cell phone and Daddy's personal weapon, a Ruger LC9. I didn't know who I was going to kill—almost anyone would do at that point—but I was ready.

Fiona Simmons was upstairs in Meredith's room.

Florida Simmons and her brother—I still couldn't believe it—were next door to her in my old room.

The house was quiet, so presumably, they were all asleep, if they could sleep after what we'd been through any more than I could. They could be staring at the dark ceilings in wide-eyed wonder unable to sleep. Like me. Except my eyes were darting back and forth from the street to the back porch. In wide-eyed alert.

The house was dark, the only light from the glow of a lit candle on the stove.

And the house was on edge, waiting for what might come next. I was on edge with the house, so when I heard the third step from the top of the staircase creak, I almost jumped out of my skin. Thirteen more steps and whoever it was would be in the kitchen. I barely moved a toe and had the glider aimed at the kitchen stairwell landing, halfway holding my breath because I wasn't up for another visit with Fiona and had no idea what I'd even say to young Cole if it were him, when I was rewarded with Florida.

"Don't shoot me."

I almost laughed.

She spotted an empty champagne bottle on the kitchen table. "Courtney?"

"You guessed it."

"Did she drink the whole bottle?"

"She did."

By then, Florida was in the den doorway. "Can we turn on a light?"

"It'd be better if we didn't."

"Is there any Dr Pepper?"

"No."

"Coffee it is," she said. "Where are the filters?"

Ten minutes later, after she'd made coffee by candlelight and I'd dragged Daddy's recliner next to Mother's glider in the middle of the den for her, she settled in, and we clinked coffee mugs.

"Why do you have a sledgehammer?"

"Just in case."

"What now?" she asked.

"We wait," I answered.

We waited for our coffee to cool was what we waited for.

"Fiona and Eddie," I said.

"I know," she said. "Sick."

"I've heard all manner of sick tonight."

"Worse than my mother and Eddie Crawford? What could Courtney have told you that was worse than that? What else did she tell you?"

"I'm hoping everything."

"I'm sure she did. We had to tell her everything, Davis, and she's not one to hold back."

"But everything from her is secondhand. Not from your mother's perspective. Or yours."

Florida was quiet.

"Let's hear it," I said.

Florida was even quieter. If that was possible.

"Okay," she said. "But first I have a question."

"Shoot."

"I already asked you not to shoot me."

"What's your question?"

"What are we going to do about Eddie?"

"For now, we leave well enough alone. Start talking."

TWENTY-THREE

After busting through the bank doors ready to burn it to the ground the afternoon before, Fiona had wisely asked Eddie to step into the vault so that they might have a private conversation before the whole town learned their secret—the whole town learned their secret anyway—then slammed the vault door behind him. Which was where things stood when I rushed in like a wild woman. Courtney Carr was standing guard at the door with an umbrella. She barely missed me. Fiona, ghastly pale and shaking like a leaf, was frozen in place at the vault door. Angry dissent filtered through from the other side. It was Eddie the Neanderthal Crawford beating on the inside of the vault door and making muffled threats.

I patted my heart back into my chest with relief.

Short lived relief.

Maybe two seconds.

Fiona grabbed my arm and whispered, "The vault isn't secure."

"What do you mean?"

"I don't use it. The vault hasn't been operable in twenty years. All Edward has to do is roll the interior spindle and the door will open."

"*What?*"

"Frank turned it into a safe room, Davis. Safe rooms have exits. The vault door only locks from this side. Not that side."

"A safe room? Like bottled water, Army blankets, and doomsday food?"

"More or less," she said, "emphasis on less," she added, "and more," she threw in, all the while trying to wring her own hands off her wrists. "Frank was in all kinds of trouble back in the day. He built a safe room. Since then, I've used it as a storage room."

My eyes darted around the grim lobby outside of the surprise safe room. "Can you lock down the bank?"

Her eyes flew to the front door. "Of course."

"And you have an operating alarm system, right?"

"Yes."

"So if and when he finds his way out of the vault, which chances are he won't, because it's Eddie and he won't think to try the door, he'll be locked in the bank."

"Which won't stop him from hurling a chair through the front window or busting down the door."

"Well, at least the alarm will let us know he's escaped."

"Then what? What do I do after that?"

"I don't know what to tell you to do after that, Fiona. I've been a little blindsided by your—" I threw my hands in the air hoping to catch the right word "—your *life*, so I'm somewhat at a loss to advise you. Or solve your personal problems. Of which there seem to be many."

"For what it's worth, Davis, I'm sorry." She looked straight into my heart when she clapped her hand over her mouth and muffled, "I'm so sorry."

"Fiona," my voice was gentle, "we don't have time for you to be sorry."

The front door chimed, Courtney let out a yelp, and then we were four. Five, counting Edward the Maniac, who was pitching a fit in the vault, but I never counted him. Florida, I counted.

She and Fiona locked eyes across the room, both seemed to deflate, then I witnessed mother and daughter silently acknowledging that the day they'd sacrificed so much to keep from coming had arrived. Florida slowly crossed the room and took Fiona's hands. They tipped their heads together in a quiet moment of solidarity. When they'd had enough time—because we had a pressing issue in the vault—I cleared my throat, and none too gently, to get their attention. They parted quickly, slowly turning to me. Florida's eyes sought mine and found ice. "I didn't lie to you, Davis. I never said Cole was my son."

"And you never said he was your brother either."

* * *

We dispatched Courtney to Fiona's house on Adams Street where she would retrieve Cole and quietly take him to my parents'. I told her to lock all the doors, stay in an interior room, don't answer the door, her phone, or my parents' phone if it were to ring, don't breathe a word of anything to anyone on the way, and wait for me. Then I turned on mother and daughter.

"Davis—" Fiona started.

"I don't want to hear it."

"You have to understand—" Florida tried.

"I don't, Florida." I cut her off. "I don't have to understand. And I don't care to understand. What I want to know is how fast you can get your brother out of town." I spoke the next words slowly. "And never come back. Ever. Go somewhere far, far away, get a family attorney, and handle it from somewhere else. Anywhere else. What made you think you could come home with your brother in the first place? He's just a child! And look what you've put him in the middle of! Did either of you think there was a snowball's chance it wouldn't end up right where it did?" I swept an arm in the direction of the vault door upon which Eddie the Deranged was beating and yelling threats at the top of his lungs.

Florida's eyes narrowed as she spoke slowly. "Do you think we wanted this?"

"Then *why*?" I demanded. "Why?"

Fiona tried to speak but only stuttered. And staggered a little.

Florida shot left, grabbed a low chair from her mother's office, dragged it back, then all but pushed her mother into it. "Sit down before you pass out, Mom." She opened her mouth to say something to me but changed her mind, leapt back through her mother's office door, grabbed the second little chair, and returned with it. She placed it beside Fiona's. She pointed.

I barely raised an I-don't-think-so eyebrow.

She said, "You'd better sit down."

"Say what you're going to say, Florida, and say it fast."

She tried to, but she had to wait on the muted string of the profanity-laced threats issuing from the vault that distracted her and made me want to pour straight Clorox into my ears. It was when Eddie the Deranged paused to fill up his lung tanks she squeezed in, "Three prisoners escaped Talladega Federal."

As far from what I expected to hear as could possibly be.

And it rang a distant bell.

I'd seen the notifications about the escaped prisoners on the National Crime Information Center's log. But it wasn't until just then that I made the connection that Talladega Federal was home to Frank Simmons. Her father. Fiona's ex-husband. And Pine Apple's favorite bank robber. At which point I gladly took the low chair beside Fiona, preparing to hear Florida say the words, "My father escaped prison, and he'll be here any minute," while seated. By then, Florida was pacing a small circle. She started to speak, stopping herself twice, as if I didn't know full well what her next words would be. She took so long that it dawned on me I'd brushed by the escaped prisoners' names and took good looks at all three intake photos, and I'd have definitely noticed had Frank Simmons been one of them. Maybe I didn't know what her next words would be. But when Florida opened her mouth for the third time with no luck, Fiona did the honors and barely shocked me to my very bones when she said, "Davis, Frank told his cellmate about the silver."

The question my brain wanted to ask was if one of the prison escapees was the cellmate, but the question that passed my lips was, "What silver?"

They both opened their mouths to answer, but before either could speak, Eddie the Village Idiot Trapped in the Village Vault let out another war cry just as something hit the door with a thud.

I turned to Fiona. "What's in there?"

"Boxes? Old file cabinets? A few pieces of furniture from our old house on Banana Street?"

"Weapons?" I asked.

She shook her head decisively.

"Anything he could use as a weapon?"

"Boxes? Old file cabinets? A few pieces of furniture from our old house on Banana Street?"

"If you'll give me a minute, I'll tell you the whole story," Florida offered.

And way too late. She could have told me the night we drank Boone's Farm. Or the first day she rolled into town. Even earlier that very day would have worked. "No." I stood. To the ranting of Eddie the Raging Maniac, who'd found a sliver of daylight at the side jamb where the vault door met the frame, and with his mouth pressed to it, threatened to kill Fiona, Florida, and me, before taking his boy to the Congo jungle with the monkeys, and so deep in the jungle no one would ever see either one of them again. Except maybe his Ma. Because no one told her about her grandboy either. I walked over to the same side jamb on our side and yelled back, "Shut up, Eddie!" To Florida I said, "Save it. What we need is out of here." I pointed at the vault and lowered my voice. "And a way to keep him in."

Fiona's gargantuan desk would most likely barricade the vault door should Eddie the Idiot try the spindle and find freedom to kill us all on his way to the jungle, as promised, but only if the three of us could maneuver the solid oak desk out the office door.

"We could bust it through the glass," Florida said.

"How will we pick it up to get it through the glass?" Fiona asked.

"Come on." I blazed a trail. "We'll push it."

After ten minutes, we gave up, having moved it no more than an inch with what felt like a mile to go. The two-window teller counter would work if we had a way to tear it from two walls and the floor. Which we didn't. The remaining furniture in the bank combined—five chairs and two side tables—wouldn't even slow him down. Much less stop him. But just then, the grandfather clock that was so much part of the fabric of the bank that it might as well have been part of the wall it held up let out a single half-hour peal. Five minutes later, we had the chairs and side tables six feet to the left of the clock. To break its fall when we tipped it over. So we didn't smash it to smithereens. Which he could plow through with the weight of the vault door. Only for us to soon learn that our strength combined couldn't tip the clock any more than we could move the desk.

"So much for girl power." Fiona pulled up her t-shirt to mop her brow.

"All the weight is in the middle with the mechanics," I said while studying the grandfather clock to the lovely tunes of Eddie the Spineless Congo Jungle Snake snorting and slamming himself against the vault door. Like a deranged bull. "And that's where we're pushing. We need to push it from a higher vantage point where it's hollow."

Florida and I tried to stand on the two metal folding chairs that had flanked the clock, one I'd sat in a mere hour earlier waiting on Fiona to grant me permission to enter her office, the same Fiona who was behind us trying to hold the chairs steady, but all we managed was to rock the old clock and almost break our own necks. Because our footing wasn't stable enough.

"Be quiet," I whispered.

"What?" Florida whispered back.

"Do you hear that?" I dropped from my chair perch to the floor. And pointed to the quiet vault.

"Is he dead?" Florida whispered.

"Maybe he's just asleep," her mother whispered back.

"Maybe he's figured it out." I didn't whisper.

"FIGURED WHAT OUT?" came through from the vault. "WHAT?"

Florida tossed the metal chairs out of our way. Feet planted wide, she dropped to a squat a foot from the old clock. "Come on, Davis."

"Come on, what, Florida?"

"Hop up," she said. "Rah-rah style."

It wasn't a bad idea at all, but it gave us no more height to push past the mechanical weight housed in the clock's middle than standing on the chairs had. We untangled, I climbed on one of the chairs, then up to Florida's shoulders. And with that move, one we'd made repeatedly back in the day to scale fences and trees, I truly was transported back to high school.

After five long minutes of her staggering under my weight, grunting things like, "You are so much heavier than you look," and me repeatedly crashing my upper body into the old clock grunting things like, "Childbirth is easier than this," Coach Fiona finally gave us the idea that would work with, "You need to get a running start. Hit it with your combined weights and with momentum."

We caught our breath, passed a bottle of water between us, backed up as far as we could, and reloaded, which was me climbing on Florida's shoulders again. Ten feet later, after slamming into the old grandfather clock with one final tackle, it went crashing to the floor. Blocking the vault door. We'd gone down with the clock. Fiona rushed to help us up, and we were rewarded with Eddie the Blasphemer repeatedly breaking one of the Ten Commandments along with a pounding fist to the bank door almost scaring us out of our very skins.

We stared at the front door.

Florida and I were still panting.

Then we heard, "Davis? Are you in there?"

It was Roy Howdy.

"I've got this here hospital bill for you."

I held a finger to my lips. If I let Roy Howdy in, I'd ring his neck. He was the very source of the predicament we were in. But if I throttled the very life out of him, which I could have done just then, my father would be disappointed past the point of no return. If I hadn't already crossed that line. So I didn't.

Next we heard, "Okay, Davis. I'll go look for you someplace else."

We took the back back way to my parents' house, through weeds and thistle up to our knees, dodging hubcaps, climbing over a discarded and threadbare loveseat that had lost its cushions, until we reached the gate behind what used to be my mother's vegetable garden. We stumbled into the house picking twigs and leaves out of our hair, where we met up with Courtney Carr and a terribly frightened boy. Who ran straight into his sister's arms. I gave Courtney a nod toward the kitchen to give both the small family privacy to break the news to Cole, and me time with her.

TWENTY-FOUR

I closed the kitchen door.

I pointed to the kitchen table.

Courtney dutifully sat down.

"Start talking." I said it as I reached for and dialed into the old metal breadbox on top of the refrigerator, which was really Daddy's gun safe, and retrieved his off-duty weapon. A Ruger LC9. Shiny, clean, and with a full clip. From the kitchen table as I was checking the chamber for a round, I heard a proclamation: "I don't do guns."

"I'm not going to shoot information out of you, Courtney." But rather than tuck it at my waist, I sat down across from her and landed it in front of me. Since she'd shown me a kink in her already thin armor, I'd use it to scare the story out of her. Because I needed to hear it fast. "What's this about silver?"

While trying to scoot her chair away from me and the gun, possibly all the way out the backdoor—the barrel was aimed at the stove, the safety was on, the gun wasn't going to spontaneously fire—Courtney said, "It's not my story to tell."

I sighed. "The time for keeping Fiona's secrets is over. Do you understand that lives are at stake?"

"Yeah." She scooted her chair back another inch. "Right now, mine."

"I'm not going to shoot you."

"If I tell you what I know, Fiona will shoot me."

"Fiona cares about one thing right now, and that's the safety of her children."

"And I care about my head staying on my neck."

"Courtney!" I slapped the table; the gun clattered; she jumped a mile. "Start talking."

She couldn't stop shaking long enough to start talking other than sputtering out, "I promise you, Davis, I don't know a thing."

I stood, used the heel of my left hand to rub the space between my eyes, and with my right hand picked up Daddy's weapon.

Courtney slapped her hand over her mouth dampening a shrill scream.

I held my hands up in surrender, barrel looking at the ceiling, then slowly tucked the gun at my waist—out of sight; out of mind—while she patted her heart back into her chest. I walked to the refrigerator, grabbed a bottle of cold water from it, placed it on the kitchen table, then scooted Courtney and her chair back to it. I took my seat again, crossed my arms on the table, and leaned in. "Let's start with an easy question."

She hesitantly nodded.

"Earlier today on the sidewalk in front of my sister's, you told me Fiona was trying to keep it from happening again."

She nodded. "I've got a big mouth sometimes."

"What did you mean by that, Courtney?"

"I meant I say things I don't mean to say."

"What did you mean earlier when you told me Fiona was trying to keep it from happening again. Keep what from happening again?"

She stared at the bottle of water. "Do you have anything stronger?"

I went back to the refrigerator and returned with the chilled bottle of Barefoot Bubbly Brut champagne that Fantasy and I found in the liquor cabinet. I sat it in front of Courtney, who sliced the silver foil off the neck in one smooth move with the jagged edge of a broken thumbnail on her right hand. Then the bottle dipped below the table as she slid the neck under the hem of her blouse and gave the cork one quick twist. It popped open with a dull thump. Must have been a party trick. The way she drank straight from the bottle was impressive too. After she poured what felt like half of the champagne straight down her throat, she returned the bottle to the table. She delicately dabbed at the corners of her mouth with the fingertips of her left hand and I noticed another broken nail, which was when I realized it was Courtney who'd busted into Eli Atwell's coffin. I wondered how she could be afraid of a firearm in competent hands but not afraid of a cadaver.

"Well." Courtney wrapped her hands around the base of the bottle. "Do you remember Old Man Carter?"

"Roy Howdy's uncle? Who died a few months ago?"

"The same."

The weight of the Simmons family secrets she'd been carrying began pouring out in a hushed voice, her eyes darting right to make sure the door to the den was still closed, starting with, "Old Man Carter had old Adeline Jenkins on his death slab after she went flying off that wild horse she was trying to break. You and Florida were kids. Do you remember that?" Without waiting for me to answer, she said, "And if you ask me, seventy-year-old women should leave the wild horse breaking to the young people. You remember her, right? She and your grandmother were friends. Well," Courtney leaned another inch closer to her champagne, "remember how she wore those Granny Clampet clothes? Those long dark swishy skirts? Those nasty lace-up boots?"

I didn't, really, but I nodded.

"Old Man Carter was about to pump her full of death juice—"

"Formaldehyde?"

"That's it," Courtney said. "But he had to get her out of her disgusting Granny Clampet clothes first." Courtney shuddered at the thought. "He pulls off one of those nasty boots, and a silver coin fell out. Turned out it was a silver dollar from way back when."

"How far back?"

Courtney shrugged. "Dinosaur times?"

"There's no such thing as prehistoric minted coins, Courtney."

"A long time ago, okay? The coin has a woman on it with long hair. And it's worth all the money in the world."

"All the money in the world?"

"A lot of money, okay? Like thirty million dollars."

She went on to tell me Old Man Carter was a finders keepers flavor of undertaker who promptly placed the silver coin in his Pine Apple Bank & Trust safe-deposit box so his nephew wouldn't stumble across it and toss it in Brantley Lake on a wish. On his way out the door, feeling Frank's eyes on his back, he spun around and stopped dead in his tracks with an unspoken warning for Frank to leave his safe-deposit box alone. That was all it took for Frank to know Old Man Carter had placed something of value in his bank. That afternoon, as soon as the old grandfather clock struck four, Frank locked the front door, pulled the front curtains, and found the silver coin. He stole it from Old Man Carter. He waited until dark, then buried the coin deep in the base of the hill at Wright and Oak Streets, with Old Man Carter, who'd been kicking himself for thinking the coin would be safe with Frank at the bank in the first place, watching through binoculars from the funeral parlor family viewing room.

He promptly stole it back from Frank.

Several months later, Frank found himself in somewhat of a financial crunch after a streak of bad luck with his bookmaking side hustle. Tired of borrowing money from his best friend when his personal finances went sideways, because Eli Atwell didn't mind the money so much as he minded what Frank was doing to his family, subsequently forcing him to sit through lectures about being a good husband and responsible father before he handed over the money he knew he'd never see again, Frank decided to sell his life insurance policy instead. Turned out he just thought he was selling his life insurance policy to the highest bidder, in fact the only bidder, who said, "How much do you need for it?" What he'd done was sign a predatory loan note. When he realized his mistake, he went for his real life insurance, the coin he'd buried, but the coin was gone.

He worked up his nerve to confront Old Man Carter, who'd stolen it first, then stole it again from Frank, who'd stolen it from him, and after they agreed that they'd both stolen the coin, they split custody—one month in Frank's vault, the next in Old Man Carter's root cellar—until they could unload it. Only to learn that wouldn't be anytime soon. The marketplace for rare and valuable coins was nowhere near Pine Apple, and the verification process to authenticate the coin took time. And money. Money neither had. Meanwhile, Frank's loan shark note came due. Old Man Carter didn't have the money to buy Frank out of his half of the coin, so Frank made one final and failed attempt to gamble his way out of the dilemma with disastrous results. He went to Eli Atwell one last time, who agreed to help Frank, but only if he confessed all to Fiona and either closed the bank or turned operations over to the only other officer of the bank, Fiona. Frank didn't like those terms, which left him no way out but to rob his own bank. Only to learn at the end of the month it took him to plan the heist—selling mortgages, depositing every dime coming in into his own account, pawning safe-deposit box family heirlooms, and hoarding every penny he could get his hands on—his loan shark debt had doubled. The money he'd stolen wasn't nearly enough. His only choice was to run. He hid half of the cash, telling himself it was in case Fiona and Florida were to need it one day, and that's how good Frank was at lying even to himself. Because he was really socking it away in case he somehow pulled out of the mess he'd made of his life. He used the other half of what he stole for getaway money. It was at the Pine Apple city limits sign where he was sandwiched, then run off the road by two cars full of loan shark debt collectors. With brass knuckles. And baseball bats. Frank had the advantage of familiar territory, cut through four acres of Higgly Farm's cornfields, and lost the thugs. For three whole days. Three days he waited for Old Man Carter to sell the stupid silver coin to the first collector who'd take it and give him his half already. But before that could happen, the heavily tattooed debt collectors caught up with Frank at VictoryLand Casino ninety miles from Pine Apple, where once again Frank had tried to gamble his way out with the getaway money he'd stolen from Pine Apple, and was down to almost his last nickel when he spotted the loan shark collectors entering the small casino. He slipped to a payphone, dialed 911, and told the operator exactly where to find the man who'd robbed Pine Apple Bank & Trust. So he could go to prison. Where he'd be safe.

Almost twenty years later, which more or less brought us to present day, while whiling away the endless prison hours watching news in the day room, Frank Simmons saw a feature story that would change the trajectory of too many lives. It was about the highest price ever paid for a silver dollar—thirty million dollars—and he was so shocked at seeing an image of the coin that was the exact coin he'd held in his hands all those years earlier, he'd blurted out that he knew where another coin exactly like it was. His cellmate, sitting beside him, said, "Sure you do." Frank insisted he was telling the truth, throwing in enough detail to keep his cellmate awake that night. The next day, the cellmate relayed it all to his favorite dirty guard in exchange for a new used mattress, three cigarettes, and twenty dollars in his commissary fund. The dirty guard researched Pine Apple, verified everything he could, then paid Old Man Carter a middle-of-the-night visit.

Old Man Carter wouldn't give up the coin or its location.

Instead of leaving, the dirty guard found a comfortable tombstone and waited until the house went dark. He crept in and up to the old man's bedside. He held him at gunpoint and gave him one last chance. Old Man Carter told him to go to hell. So the dirty prison guard held the old man's head in a vice grip, then tipped three drops of straight mercury into his ear. The mercury burned through to his brain, instantly evaporating and leaving no trace, and Old Man Carter didn't wake up the next morning.

Convinced the coin must be somewhere in the dilapidated funeral home, the dirty guard resumed his prison duties, recruited three of his favorite gang members, and plans for The Big Pine Apple Coin Heist were set in motion. Execution date? The only three days on the calendar strangers were allowed in town. Memorial Day weekend.

The first thing the dirty guard and his posse of three did was beat the stew out of Frank Simmons in the prison laundry room. Frank pointed the killers in the right direction—straight to the root cellar of the funeral home—in exchange for his, his former wife's, his daughter's, and his grandson's (news to Frank) lives. The three gang members barely kept their end of the bargain on the sparing of Frank's life's part. It took the prison staff a week to track down Frank's only child, Florida, to tell her if she wanted to say goodbye to her father, who was in a medically induced coma, she'd better hurry to the intensive care unit at Citizens Medical Center. It took Florida a minute to get to Frank. She wasn't about to take her brother, her mother couldn't raise Pine Apple hackles by closing the bank in the middle of the week with no notice to rush to Mobile and take care of her son, and by the time Florida made arrangements for Cole and got to her estranged father's bedside, Frank's vital signs and brain function had improved. He was brought out of the coma. When Fiona saw her father for the first time in almost twenty years, he was somewhat alert, shackled to a hospital bed in the Head Injury hall, and totally blind. He confessed all to Florida. Who, from the hospital parking lot, called her mother and told her to get her local affairs in order. Her Pine Apple clock had run out. Fiona, after being separated from her son since the day he was born with the exception of a few stolen weeks a year, on top of her miserable existence in Pine Apple, was more than ready for the next chapter of her life. Mother and daughter laid the groundwork by procuring new identities and housing in Bellevue, Nebraska, but they vowed to not make the move before they warned Pine Apple Chief of Police Samuel Way what a dirty prison guard and three soon-to-be escaped convicts had planned for Pine Apple's Memorial Day Celebration. The day of their reunion and planned getaway arrived only for them to learn Chief Way was out of town.

They got me.

"How do you know all this, Courtney?"

"Because Fiona trusts me."

Nah. I shook my head. Not buying it.

"If Fiona didn't have somebody to talk to, the top of her head might blow off."

That I somewhat bought into, but then again, I didn't.

"She wanted someone to know the whole story in case something happened to her."

A little more believable.

"I know a guy who sells Social Security numbers and driver's licenses. He used to be the manager at Orange Julius at Greenville Mall. Okay?"

That, I believed.

"Why did you disturb Eli Atwell's body, Courtney?"

Her head jerked back. "Who said I did?"

"Answer the question."

"I was looking for the silver coin."

"I get that the root cellar information was beaten out of Frank Simmons, but how did you know where the root cellar was?"

"Roy Howdy told me."

"When?"

"After his uncle died."

"Was it in the middle of a casual conversation? Roy Howdy was at the bank cashing a voodoo check and just let it slip? 'Oh, by the way, Courtney, I have a root cellar full of dead bodies.'"

"Something like that."

"Did you find the silver coin?"

Her sigh answered for her, amended with, "But old Eli might've had it. We'll never know."

I tilted my head quizzically.

"I never got to dig in his pockets because Roy Howdy came stomping down to the basement to work on his voodoo. He had two mother-in-law candle orders."

A novel idea, mother-in-law voodoo candles, and a typical Courtney move, not checking his pockets before hauling his dead carcass out of a casket. "Did Roy Howdy ask what you were doing in his basement?"

"Not so much."

I found that odd, but then again, it was Roy Howdy. "So what'd you do?"

"Well, I had to distract him."

"I wouldn't imagine it would be too hard to distract Roy Howdy, but distract him to the point of him not noticing you dragging a dead body through the basement? And this after he found you there? How'd you manage that?"

Two bright spots popped up on her cheeks.

I raised an eyebrow.

She barely smiled. A small coy smile.

"Gross, Courtney."

"Judge not lest you be judged, Davis Way. You don't know what it's like living in a small town with slim man pickens."

Oh, yes, I did. He was locked in a bank vault as we spoke. "Skip that part," I said. "Skip the Roy Howdy part altogether. Get to the why-you-moved-the-body part."

"Well, after I got rid of Roy Howdy, I couldn't get Old Eli back in the casket. I tried to stuff him back in real quick but stuffing a body back in a casket is harder than getting one out."

If lightheadedness were a thing of mine, it would have paid me a visit just then. "How did you get him out in the first place?"

"I grabbed him by his war clothes."

Lightheadedness tapped on my shoulder.

"He didn't weigh nothing," Coutney said. "He was all bones and teeth and a little bit of hair. But I couldn't get him back in because I couldn't find his knees."

Lightheadedness and I dropped our heads and held up wait-a-minute fingers until our vision returned from its swim. When it did, I said, "Then?"

"Then I grabbed a gurney, tossed old Eli on it, and hightailed it out of there so I wouldn't get caught."

"You've been caught."

"I know! Okay?"

I rolled a hand in a keep-going way.

"We went out the basement door and across the street to Bea's."

"We?" I asked.

"Me and Eli."

"Right." I cleared my throat. "Why Bea's?"

"Because it was raining cats and dogs, and because Bea's was close by and she was gone on her honeymoon."

"Then you hid the body?"

"Yes."

"Why?"

"Because I figured Roy Howdy was back by then and waiting on me."

"I told you I didn't want to hear about you and Roy Howdy."

"That's part of the story, Davis. I sent Roy Howdy to my house to get our Twister game, and by the time I got all that done with Eli,

I had to get back to Roy Howdy's. It's not like he could play Dirty Twister all by himself. Okay?"

I was about to go for Daddy's gun and she knew it.

"Okay!" She held up stop sign hands. "Okay! And you're no fun!"

"Back to Bea's Diner."

"I'm never going there again."

I slapped my own forehead with a palm in frustration.

"Not that I really went there before," she added.

My hands, of their own accord, clenched into fists.

"Bea's," Courtney rushed out. "Back to Bea's. No one was supposed to find old Eli before I could go back over my lunchbreak the next day and find the coin. Then sneak him back to Roy Howdy's. But you found old Eli first. Now we'll never find the silver coin."

If the coin was, indeed, hidden in the root cellar, it could have been in any of the four caskets. Or under a rock. Or in a shoebox. And had the coin been on Eli's person, there wasn't a doubt in my mind that Wilcox County's coroner would have bagged it as evidence and notified everyone. Including me. Which he hadn't. "What about the money?"

"What money?"

"The money Frank supposedly hid for a rainy day."

She shook her head. "He hid it good, Davis. No one's ever going to find that money."

She was probably right about that. "One last question, Courtney."

"Go right ahead. Not like I have a secret left to my name."

"What's in this for you?"

"What do you mean?"

"I get that you're Fiona's only friend in the world, but does friendship really go that far? Exhuming, transporting, and hiding corpses far?"

"Well, for one thing, Fiona didn't know about me tossin' Eli's casket till after. And what's in it for me is the bank."

"Excuse me?"

"Like you said, I'm her only friend in the world. After all I've done for her? I'll get the bank."

I think my mouth dropped open.

"Who else would she give it to?"

Bank charters didn't work that way. ("Bye, Courtney. Thanks for everything. You can have the café curtains in my kitchen, my souvenir spoon collection, and the bank.") Not that it mattered. I felt certain Pine Apple's banking days were over.

Just then the door leading to the den, a door my parents never closed, creaked open. It was Florida. Her hands rested lightly on Cole's shoulders. He didn't look up. Florida whispered, "Someone needs a minute. Do you mind if we go to your room, Davis?"

"Not at all."

Courtney and I watched them disappear into the stairwell.

I stood.

I stepped over to my mother's amazingly tidy junk drawer and pulled out her grocery list pad and a pen. I placed them in front of Courtney. "Go talk to Fiona," I said. "I'm sure she needs you." I gave the pad and pen a push. "It's probably best that Fiona, Florida, and Cole stay here with me tonight, so she might want a few things from her house. Make a list. She'll want her toothbrush. A change of clothes. She may even want you to grab important documents. Just ask her what she needs for herself, Florida, and Cole. We'll gather it all up, then I'll drive you home."

"Okay." She was up, pad and pen in hand, and on her way into the den.

"And Courtney?"

She turned.

"Whatever it is you need to say to Fiona, say it now."

"You don't think they'll take off for Nebraska tonight, do you?"

"I have no idea what's going to happen tonight."

* * *

Fifteen minutes later, I wished I'd given Courtney a timeframe. Like, "Say what you need to say, but wrap it up quickly." So I spent the time thinking about my children. Their laughs. How sweet they smelled when they woke up. How much I missed them when they were just down the street. When it occurred to me I could call and check on them, even talk to the girls, it also occurred to me that I hadn't checked my phone in three hours. That had me digging for it. And it was loaded.

First up, thirteen missed calls from Eugenia Winters Stone, President of Pine Apple Women's Society. She'd left a six-minute voicemail. No telling what that was about. But it could wait.

I scrolled through the many text message notifications I'd been completely unable to read for hours on end, much less respond to, the last one from my sister only half an hour earlier. Where was I? Why wasn't I answering? Did I hear Eddie rolled into town? Did Florida know? The baby was already asleep, and the girls were barely awake. If I didn't text right back, everyone was going to bed. And would I PLEASE call Eugenia Winters Stone. I texted her back. *Kinda tied up. Kiss my babies and I'll call you as soon as I can.* I kept scrolling, spotting a text message from Daddy, the first line of which was *We will be home Tuesday...* I didn't know if we meant Mother and Daddy or if we meant Mother, Daddy, and Bea, but I saved the rest of the message for later anyway. For one, Tuesday was an eternity away. And for two, chances were it was about Bea Crawford. I was already dealing with her son. No one should have to deal with both at the same time. I slowed down at a message from my husband, along with a picture of my dogs, Cotton and Candy. *We miss you.* I gave it a heart. Thinking that didn't show anywhere near the amount of love I was feeling, I texted back three big red hearts with, *I miss you guys too.* For good measure, I added another heart. My thumbs were poised to ask him if he had a minute for a phone call, that I was sitting on information I needed to share, but I couldn't with Fiona and Courtney in the next room and didn't want to start the "Who are Fiona and Courtney? Why are they in the next room?" business just then, so I decided it could wait until I had Courtney squared away. Why scare him before I had to? The remaining text message notifications had nothing to do with Fiona, Florida, or even Fantasy, so I figured I might as well get it over with. It wasn't like I had anything better to do while I waited on Courtney to wind it up with Fiona already. I clicked the tiny phone receiver icon to listen to Eugenia's message, which, I'd already decided, probably had something to do with Saturday's Memorial Day Kickoff Pancake Breakfast. The Pine Apple Women's Society was in charge of the event, which meant she was in charge, and it was probably a six-minute lecture on maple syrup. Only Eugenia could talk about maple syrup for six solid minutes. I hit the speaker icon, then the play button.

Daaaaavis, she huffed my name, *I certainly hope your evening has been highly entertaining. I can't imagine you shirking your sworn responsibilities to our beloved community for anything less than your own personal pleasure. Perhaps you needed, as they say, a little Me Time. Would that be why you've been unavailable to the citizens of Pine Apple since late afternoon? Was it a warm scented bath, perhaps with flickering candles, a soothing concerto on the record player, and a nice Cabernet that had you shirking your civic duties? If so, how lovely for you. And me, you might ask? How has my evening been? I had guests over for dinner. In spite of how much I have on my personal plate, I invited Willa Walters, who you might remember from your Pine Apple Pulp days, if, in fact, you ever set foot in the library, and her new beau, Cedric Kinder. Who I'm sure you know, as he hails from New Orleans, yet, as he shared with me, resides at your gambling hall in Biloxi. A charming gentleman, which, as you are surely well aware, is a scarce commodity in Pine Apple. Thus my attempt, as busy as I am, to welcome him to town with a lovely dinner. After we finished our appetizers of bourbon-glazed bacon-wrapped figs, then moved on to our salad course, Caesar, with my own white wine vinaigrette dressing, and were just finishing the highlight of our meal, garlic shrimp over fettucine with my famous white vodka sauce, we were interrupted by yet another oversized transportation trailer. Davis, Pine Apple wasn't large enough to accommodate the massive vehicle you had parked in the middle of Main Street for the better part of two days, and it still isn't large enough for the second obtrusive transportation truck you have blocking traffic, both foot and vehicular. And this new truck of yours is seemingly in need of new braking equipment. I can't imagine you could have possibly missed the heinous noise that echoed through our valley and was surely heard for miles in every direction as the hideosity screeched to a stop. I'll have you know I lost a Wedgewood Florentine serving platter in the melee. At the time of the vehicle's abrupt and intrusive halt, I'd just shaken, poured, and passed beautiful after-dinner espresso martinis and was in the process of clearing the table of serving ware. The Wedgewood platter I was holding clattered to the floor and shattered into a million pieces. The Wedgewood has been passed through the Stone family for four generations, and thanks to you, future generations will not have a platter upon which to serve their holiday turkeys. And I won't bother you with the aftermath of pasta, swimming in my signature white vodka sauce, landing on my hand-knotted wool dining room rug amidst the shards of my irreplaceable Wedgewood. As you've probably guessed by now, I was unable to reach you by phone to speak to you about the horrid, oversized truck arriving so late in the day, "after hours" as they say, and let me go on record as stating I do not appreciate being ignored. Nor do I appreciate Roy H. Carter refusing to take my calls either. Who did that leave to handle the situation? Me. I daresay when your father hears of this, on the heels of all the other turmoil you've caused, he will rue the day he chose you over me to keep law and order in our no-longer-charming little city. Davis, let's get one thing straight. A good leader does not treat their third-in-command as you've treated me. Your mother will be downright appalled when she hears of it. And believe me, she'll hear of it. If you intend to be, as they say, "out of pocket," leaving me to, as they say, "cover for you," I expect forewarning, details of pending events to include ill-timed arrivals, and open communication throughout. Your friend Cedric was kind enough to leave my dinner table, as I was otherwise occupied lightly dusting my hand-knitted wool rug with cornstarch in an effort to save it from my signature white vodka sauce, to welcome our latest "big rig" visitors, which brings me all the way to the purpose of this voice message. And please know that I find leaving voice messages just as demeaning an activity as talking to one's own wall, and leaving a message for you feels downright futile to boot, but I implore you to listen carefully, nonetheless. It has been more than three hours since Cedric left my home on my behalf to kindly request the oversized vehicle relocate, and he has yet to return. Willa, as you can well imagine having already suffered through the pain of losing her husband, is distraught at Cedric's unexplained disappearance and is blaming herself. It took me the better part of an hour—interrupted at regular intervals in my attempts to communicate with you—to calm her nerves. If and when your pedicure dries at the end of your personal evening of relaxation and rejuvenation, might you be bothered to look for your friend Cedric? That, Davis, is all. Goodbye.*

Where would I even start to look for Whiskey? There were no ditches for him to stumble into and sleep it off. There were no bars for him to saddle up to and keep his liquor party going. There was

GRETCHEN ARCHER

no package store with a posted emergency number for him to call and say something like, "Might I humbly implore you to unlock your esteemed establishment after hours so that I might procure additional libations to compliment the spirit-riddled meal I just consumed?" Eugenia plied a barely sober alcoholic with bourbon, wine, and vodka. There wasn't a doubt in my mind poor Whiskey had fallen off the wagon. And I wasn't necessarily in a position to search for the wheels. Now the eighteen-wheeler in the middle of Main Street? I had no idea. For all I knew, Eugenia had a few too many nips while whisking vodka into her signature sauce and she'd dreamed it up. Because I would have noticed a big truck on Main Street. Surely, in spite of it all, I'd have noticed.

I rose from the kitchen table, knuckled the den door, and said, "Courtney? It's time. I'll be in my car."

Ten minutes later, me drumming my fingers on the steering wheel the entire time, just about to beep the horn, Courtney opened the passenger door.

She'd left most of her mascara with Fiona.

I waited another excruciatingly long fifteen minutes in Fiona's driveway while Courtney went inside. When she finally returned with two overflowing tote bags, I gently lectured her on our way to her house. Not one word to Roy Howdy or anyone else. Don't answer any unknown calls on her phone, don't answer the door, and I'd be in touch the next morning.

"What about the bank?" She sniffed. "We open at nine."

"Take the day off."

That perked her up. "Thanks, Davis!"

And speaking of the bank, I drove by it slowly after I dropped her off. Then by my sister's. I circled around and checked behind the bank and Meredith's. All was dark and quiet at both. I kept driving. Looking for Whiskey. I even drove by Bea's Diner and Bea's Airbnb, thinking Whiskey might have wandered to either.

No Whiskey.

It was on the way home, taking the long way, patrolling around town, that I passed the intersection of Wright and Oak Streets and came to a stop. Roy Howdy had parked the eighteen-wheeler from the Bellissimo in the gravel lot at the base of the offensive hill so sloppily and at such an angle, there wasn't enough room left to park a bicycle. I put my car in reverse and peeled out, headed in the direction of the funeral home, which was another location Whiskey's alcoholic subconscious might have directed him—through the graveyard. If there was a single light on in the creepy house on the hill, the house I'd just learned Old Man Carter was murdered in, I intended to let Roy Howdy have it once and for all. But by the time I arrived, I'd half changed my mind—Roy Howdy had already had a long day—and changed my mind the rest of the way when I saw what was blocking the long funeral home driveway. It was the eighteen-wheeler that had ruined Eugenia Winters Stone's hand-knotted rug. At Roy Howdy's. It was the fireworks truck. Flash Fireworks. And it wasn't a big rig. It was a delivery truck. Like a box truck. Granted it was a big box truck, but still a box truck. Unable to park in the gravel lot that was full of the Bellissimo eighteen-wheeler, the driver of the fireworks truck crossed the street and parked in the funeral home drive. I'd forgotten the urgent letter threatening to park the fireworks truck in the middle of Main Street. I'd forgotten the fireworks altogether. I'd just about forgotten Pine Apple's Memorial Day Celebration.

I made one more loopy pass through town looking for Whiskey—still no Whiskey—checking on the bank and Meredith's one last time while I was at it—all was as I'd left it—before calling it a night.

And what a long night it had been.

About to get a lot longer.

TWENTY-FIVE

Back at Camp Way, with the Simmons family upstairs, I made the calls that had to be made.

My first four calls were to the police stations along all four routes in and out of Pine Apple—Camden to my west, Beatrice to my south, Furman to my north, and Greenville to my east. In an effort to stop the prison runaways before they reached Pine Apple, I told them all the truth. That I had a non-custodial parent threatening abduction of a minor. (Which was true.) I had him detained, but he was of the slimy variety. (Very true.) And so were his friends who were most likely on their way to Pine Apple in an attempt to spring their buddy. (Not so true, since Eddie the Deranged had so few friends.) Could they be on the lookout? All four agreed to post unmarked vehicles with eyes-wide-open officers for as long as I needed, looking for anything or anyone suspicious on the way to Pine Apple.

It was the Alabama way.

Next, I called my husband.

After I talked for five solid minutes barely stopping to take a breath, his response was, "I'll send a plane immediately, Davis. Get yourself and the children packed."

"Bradley, I have to stay. I can't let four hundred people be ambushed by three escaped convicts."

"Then scoot over. I'll be airborne in twenty minutes and I'm bringing an army."

My weary head dropped. "You can't."

"Davis!"

"I'm not saying you can't come, Bradley. Of course you can come. But you can't come in a big Bellissimo jet. There's nowhere to land it. You're better off in one of the big helicopters. And don't bring an army." I stopped to count up how many guns I might need lying in wait in Roy Howdy's root cellar when the escaped convicts rolled into town, then said, "Bring no more than four," I said. "Not an army."

"Get the children packed," he said. "I'll stay with you, but they're going home."

"By themselves? Two four-year-olds and a six-month-old baby? What kind of a plan is that?" He fumbled through a response naming almost half of his Bellissimo staff of five-thousand-plus—maybe not that many names—but all capable of caring for our children, each word a little less confident than the word before until he finally fizzled out. I listened to him breathe hard. "Bradley. If I'm going to catch three prison escapees who won't even be here until Saturday, I have to keep things as close to normal as I possibly can between now and then. You know I don't want to put the children in harm's way, and I won't. But you landing in a big Bellissimo helicopter airbus on the baseball field, piling out with what will look like hitmen, then hustling the children out of town would be the same as me hanging a Welcome, Prison Runaways! banner in Town Square. I have all day tomorrow to stop them, and that's beside the fact that I've already alerted the authorities all the way around Pine Apple, which is beside the fact that the prison escapees are coming for a *coin*. Not me, the children, or anyone else. Trust me to keep our children safe until you get here, and we'll both keep them safe when you do. If you'll give me just a minute to do my job, no one will get hurt, least of all our children."

"How is it you're going to stop three prison escapees in just a minute, Davis?"

"The dirty prison guard is the key, Bradley. As soon as I can identify him, which might take ten minutes and it might take ten hours, because I don't know his name and will have to look at every Talladega Federal guard, I'll track his phone and financial activity. The escaped prisoners don't have resources. The dirty guard will be footing the bill to get them here. Even tracking when and where the dirty guard is spending money on gas will tell me everything I need to know. If I can figure out the plan based on the dirty guard's activities, I can stop this before it starts."

After a beat of hesitation, he said, "I'll be there in an hour."

"No," I said, "it'll be more like three hours. You're coming in quietly. You need to land at the airstrip behind Atwell Aviation in Prattville. Have your pilot call the after-hours number to let someone know you're coming, and tell them you'll need to borrow a car. Take the back roads if you don't want to get arrested on your way into town—"

"What's that supposed to mean?"

"I just told you I've already alerted the authorities. Unmarked cars are posted on the main roads in and out of town looking for anything suspicious. Five big men stuffed in an Atwell Aviation loaner car late at night looks suspicious. Not to mention I'm assuming you'll have weapons. Take the back roads. Which means you'll be on the road longer than you're in the air. Park one of your team at Meredith's where our children are. Drop off another one at the police station. Bring one to Mother and Daddy's to watch our backs. Send the last one to the bank."

"Why the bank?" he asked. Then, "Never mind. I'm on my way."

"Bring my laptop. The one I keep in the bottom drawer of my desk."

"Which desk? Your home office or your office downstairs?"

"Home."

"Why?"

"Because I'll need a little cyber privacy to sneak into the prison."

"What prison are you planning on sneaking into, Davis?"

"Prison records, Bradley. At Talladega Federal. To find the dirty guard."

I heard a drawer slam. "Got it."

"And could you possibly bring Fantasy?"

"No," he said, "but I'll bring Baylor."

Baylor. Just Baylor. Like Batman was just Batman. The third member of my covert spy team at the Bellissimo Resort and Casino. A blend-in-with-the-crowd sort, a take-no-prisoners type, and best of all, a sharpshooter. Baylor could shoot a petal off a daisy from up in a tree three thousand yards away.

Perfect.

Next, I called my sister. I filled her in.

"Got it." She hung up.

Fourteen long minutes later, she sent a text message.

We're fine, doors locked and barricaded, we're camping out in the bunk room under the kitchen where the cowboys used to hang their hats. Granny is already snoring up a storm. The kids slept right through me moving them. Eddie's going to kill you, and would you PLEASE call Eugenia Stone.

Seven minutes later, I'd gathered my arsenal and moved Mother's swivel glider to the middle of the den to wait on Bradley and his posse. And in spite of the fact that sleep was out of the question, I might have rested in the still and quiet dark until he arrived, but the urgency with which he'd received the news made it so much more urgent for me, and my nerves were shot. I could have easily unloaded the Ruger when I heard the third step on the stairwell creak.

Ten minutes and a mug of coffee later, Florida began telling me her version of the story. Which didn't contradict Courtney's, but it definitely packed an emotional punch hers hadn't. Florida's version of the same events Courtney had relayed contained more detail, more eyewitness testimony, more joy, and so much more sorrow. Courtney wasn't particularly angry about anything. Florida was. Courtney didn't have to wait several beats for her heart to catch up with her story. Florida did. Courtney's chapter about Cole Simmons could be titled Fiona's Fiasco. Florida's chapter would be The

Wonderful Boy Who Would Be Mine. The most comforting to me was the fact that Florida didn't resent her mother or her brother for her life being derailed all the way to a chicken wing truck. "Don't get me wrong," she said. "I hung up on her when she told me she was pregnant, and I thought I'd die on the spot when Cole was born looking just like the devil himself."

I was stunned. "You didn't know?"

"I knew the baby wasn't Frank's, because at the time he'd been in prison for years."

"And she didn't tell you?"

"Davis, when I left Pine Apple, I had no intention of returning. I left everything and everyone behind. I didn't speak to my mother for almost four years, and when I did, it was only because she called the Dean of Students at MIT leaving a family-emergency message for me to call immediately. That was when she told me she was eight months pregnant and needed my help. I never asked who the father was. A few weeks later when Cole was born, I figured it out on my own." She went on to tell me that of all their life-altering options, Fiona showing up a few days later in Pine Apple with Eddie Crawford's newborn son being the worst of them, they landed on Florida dropping out of school for a semester and caring for her newborn brother at least until I left town, because at that point, I'd been married to Eddie and patrolling Pine Apple streets for more than a year.

No wonder Fiona slammed the door in my face.

She thought I knew. And was there to confront her.

"How did you know I'd leave Pine Apple again, Florida?"

"Because you were meant for far more than Eddie and you had so much more to give than this little town could take."

I almost couldn't breathe.

Florida's six months with her baby brother turned into a year.

The year turned into twelve.

And there we were.

One thing Florida said that I'd never forget was when she was talking about her brother as a toddler. He was three years old when he realized it was just him, Florida, and occasionally the woman he knew as his grandmother, Fiona, who held him too tight and cried all the time. He asked Florida, in three-year-old speak, if he had a father. "Whose am I?" he'd asked. "You're mine," she'd answered.

Five quiet minutes later, Florida whispered, "What is it we're waiting on?"

"The cavalry."

"That ought to work."

"The cavalry and my laptop."

"Your laptop's in the kitchen," she said. "I just saw it."

"I need the laptop Bradley's bringing. I can't get through the Talladega Federal firewall on the laptop in the kitchen without getting myself and my father in trouble. I can get through on the laptop Bradley's bringing."

"What will you do when you break into Talladega Federal's system? Check next week's menu? Sign up for arts and crafts? Reserve the basketball court?"

"Hopefully I'll find the name of the dirty prison guard."

"Flash?"

The blood pumping through my veins stopped right where it was. "What did you say?"

"I'm sure that isn't his real name, but Frank called him Flash."

Flash.

As in Marcus Flash.

As in Flash Fireworks.

The three prison escapees were already in town.

Worse, they were already at the funeral home.

And even worse, they had Whiskey.

"Florida? Do you know how to shoot a gun?"

"I've never held a gun in my life."

"Have you ever held a sledgehammer?"

"Not that I remember. But I'm sure I could manage."

I called Courtney. "Get ready. I'm coming to get you."

"Why? I just put my curlers in."

"Because you know your way around Roy Howdy's basement."

Then I called Eugenia Winters Stone.

"What? Hello? What?"

Aww, I'd woken her. I felt so bad.

(I did not feel bad.)

"Eugenia, it's Davis."

"You'd better be waking me from a restful slumber to apologize."

"I'm not. I'm calling to tell you it's time to lock and load. I'll be there to pick you up in ten minutes. Bring your highest caliber, a backup, and plenty of ammo."

I turned to Florida. "Let's go."

TWENTY-SIX

Bradley was en route. Although our attempts to communicate as he was on his way to me and I was on my way to Courtney's were spotty at best. His words "satellite" and "Bluetooth" broke through, leading me to believe something was up with the helicopter's Wi-Fi, which had Bradley bouncing in, out, and off signals from ground cell towers. After three tries, the calls dropping every time, I gave up and tossed my phone at Florida. It hit the wooden handle of the sledgehammer in her lap and landed on the floorboard.

"Why are you throwing things at me?"

"Grab my phone. Try to get the Air Traffic Control Tower in Birmingham on the line."

"Like I'm supposed to know their number?"

"Florida, just try!"

Courtney was watching from her living room window. But it was a middle-aged Frenchy Facciano, Beauty School Dropout, who raced out the door in her slumber party getup. Or Courtney's version of it anyway. She was wearing a short pink silk nightie set, pink house slippers hidden somewhere under pink feather poms the size of cantaloupes, with a pink silk scarf over spongey curlers wrapped around her giant head. She piled into the backseat. "What's this about?"

I turned to look at her by the light from her front porch. "I'll give you two minutes to get dressed. Not that we have two minutes to spare."

"I am dressed," Courtney said. "I'm wearing pajamas. Because it's bedtime."

"You look absolutely ridiculous," Florida told her. She'd said it mid-conversation with Siri, who said back, "Hmm. That's rude."

Courtney snarled a lip at Florida.

I threw it in reverse.

"NO!" Florida angrily poked my phone.

I cut my eyes her way.

"Siri gave me the number for Delta Reservations."

Three minutes later, I was slamming the brakes in front of Eugenia Winters Stone's perfect little bungalow. From the backseat, Courtney said, "You didn't say where we were going, Davis. I thought we were going to your house. I'd have at least put on my black leather capris if I'd known we were going out. I sure hope I don't run into Roy Howdy with curlers in my hair."

"Courtney, did I not say I was coming to get you because you know your way around Roy Howdy's basement? Wouldn't that mean we were going to Roy Howdy's basement?"

Florida said, "NO!" to the phone again, then to me, "That was Passenger Support at Birmingham International. With an expected wait of one hour and forty-two minutes."

I said, "Try one more time."

"Why are we doing this?" she asked.

"So Air Traffic Control can contact the helicopter and divert it."

"From?" Florida asked. "To?"

"From Prattville to Pine Apple."

"That sounds like fun," Courtney said. "Flying around in a helicopter."

Eugenia stepped out her front door. I took one look and said, "Oh, dear Lord."

Florida twisted in her seat to ask Courtney, "How is it you know your way around Roy Howdy's basement? And why would he care if you have curlers in your hair?"

To which I said, "I can't do this."

"Do what?" Florida and Courtney asked.

I pointed.

Eugenia Winters Stone stood at the top step backlit by security floodlights strung across her front porch like outdoor party lights on steroids. She was dressed in old lady camouflage, wearing old lady combat boots, her hair stuffed in an old lady combat helmet, with a long-barrel Desert Eagle pistol in a holster over the bulging cargo pocket on her right leg, and what looked like an AK-47 strapped across her back.

I rolled down the window. "Eugenia! We're not going to war! What are you doing with an assault rifle?"

She clomped down the steps saying, "I'm exercising my Second Amendment right, thank you."

Courtney lost her mind at the sight of the weapons.

Florida screamed into the phone, "I do NOT want to speak to Airside Operations!"

My head hit the steering wheel. Had I been with my own team, the entire ride would have been silent. We'd all know our assignments. Who would knock on the front door and ask everyone there to look at pictures of her lost puppy (Fantasy), who would drop in through a side window and gather evidence (me), and who would sneak up from behind and finish the takedown (Baylor). The deal would be said and done in fifteen minutes. But I wasn't with my team. So instead of taking a right for the funeral home, I took a left.

For Bea's Diner.

* * *

We busted in through the front door, flipped on all the lights, and piled into the middle booth. There was no need to hide, because by then it was one in the morning. Pine Apple was fast asleep.

Courtney was studying a children's menu with the contents of a four-pack of crayons spread out preparing to draw Roy Howdy's basement. "The kid's menu is the same as the adult's menu. What's up with that? Do your kids eat Hell, Fire, and Brimstone Salmon Patty Nachos, Davis?"

I said, "Flip the menu over to the blank side, Courtney. Work fast."

"Do you want it fast or cheap or good?" she asked. "You can only pick two. Like I used to tell my brides ordering wedding invitations from those big huge books at the Hallmark. I can get it here fast and cheap, but they won't be good, or I can get it here fast and good, but they won't be cheap, or—"

"Courtney!" I snapped. "Draw!"

Eugenia, minus her fifty caliber anti-armor sniper rifle that was currently keeping company with my spare tire, her head on a swivel, said, "What is that *odor*?"

Florida was on my phone finishing a middle-of-the-night call to Fantasy asking her to do the Air Traffic Control Tower honors. It was no more than a minute after their call ended that Fantasy texted me with *Done. They're making contact. What's going on*?

I texted back, *1-400*—I used a casino security alert code—*talk later.*

She texted back, *Someone's trying to cash a bad check?*

I texted back. *2-400.*

She texted back. *Someone's passed out on a roulette table?*

I gave up and stood up, catching Fantasy's next text on my way out of the booth. *Air Traffic just called back. Too late. Bradley already landed in Prattville. Why is Bradley in Prattville? Prattville what? Alabama?* I didn't take the time for that long answer, but I did respond to her last text asking if Florida was with me— *Yes*—before I proceeded to do the No Hair pace, back and forth down the length of the diner's aisle, just as he'd done days before.

"Is she okay?" Courtney whispered.

"She's thinking," Florida didn't whisper.

"Draw, Soldier." Eugenia tapped the menu in front of Courtney.

After two passes up and down the diner aisle, I tried my hardest to explain the situation in the simplest of terms without sending any of them out the door and running down Main Street screaming, "Save yourselves!" I took a deep breath. "There are three unsavory characters at the funeral home." I spun on my Ked slip-on heels and looked at my crew. "They don't belong here." I let that sink in. "In fact, they're wanted by the authorities." I turned to pace the other way. "They're here because they believe there is a coin in Roy Howdy's basement worth millions." I turned. And paced. "And they want the coin. They don't want us, and I don't believe they want to do our town any harm. They want to find the coin and leave with it. What we want to do is stop them. The easiest way to stop them is by apprehending them. Without violence. If it doesn't look like it's possible to take them down without anyone being harmed, we'll take a different approach." I turned to march the other way. "We'll say we know where the coin is."

Courtney's head popped up from her crayon drawing. "Do we know where the coin is?"

Florida said, "Would we be sitting here if we knew where the coin was?"

"No questions during an operation briefing," Eugenia said.

"No, Courtney," I said, while wondering if Eugenia was stable. "We don't know where the coin is. Telling them we do would be a stall tactic."

"Like to keep them busy?" Courtney asked. "Why?"

"Don't interrupt, Boot," ordered Eugenia.

"I'm not wearing boots," Courtney said.

"Oh, my God." Florida slumped against the wall.

"I just want to know why we're stalling," Courtney mumbled.

"Permission to answer?"

I waved a weary hand at Eugenia. Granting her permission.

"Waiting on munitions and reinforcement."

"She's half right," I said. "We are waiting on backup."

Courtney's head whipped around. "Who else is coming?"

I took the floor back with a loud, "Stay on track. It could go quickly. If we get to the funeral home and all three men are in the same place, we'll have a good chance at apprehending them."

Courtney raised her hand. "Didn't you say they were in the basement? Isn't that the same place?"

"Draw, Jarhead," Eugenia said.

Courtney patted the silk scarf covering her curlers. "That's so mean."

"Hey," I snapped. "First, we'll run surveillance on the funeral home basement to see if we can breach it. We'll only breach the basement if all three men are there, are in very close proximity to each other, and we're reasonably certain they don't have weapons."

Courtney raised her hand. "What kind of weapons are we talking about?"

I said, "The standard variety of weapons."

Eugenia said, "Nuclear and ballistic missiles. Biological and chemical agents."

Florida scooted as far away from Eugenia as she could, mumbling, "Someone's been watching too much cable news."

"It might go fast and easy," I said, "because chances are they won't have weapons." I didn't say because Flash, former police officer, current dirty prison guard and start-up fireworks entrepreneur, was smart enough to know the first thing they'd do would be to shoot each other. "But if we do find them armed to the teeth—"

"We wipe them off the face of the earth!" Eugenia slapped the table.

"Eugenia, did you not just fuss at Courtney for interrupting?"

I kid you not, she saluted me.

"If the three men are armed, we'll back off and find a way to make contact with them. If we're unsuccessful in convincing them we know where the coin is, therefore gaining entry so we can take control of the situation, we'll wait for backup. Hopefully, it won't get to that. Because we need in that basement."

"Do we really? I mean, if backup is on the way, and we're clearly out of our league here, why wouldn't we just wait?" Florida asked.

"Because of our second problem," I answered.

Courtney raised her hand. "What was our first problem?"

"Permission to address?" It was Eugenia. Well, in a way it was Eugenia. In another way, it was Rambo.

I nodded. Out of exasperation.

She leaned over the children's menu that, so far, was a blue rectangle separated by yellow lines with a few scattered red squiggles and a green tail. "Three assholes are at Roy Howdy's. We need to destroy them." She dusted her camo lapels and gave the floor back to me with, "Commander."

After squeezing my eyes closed, wondering just how large a mistake I'd made in bringing Eugenia—I always knew she'd snap one day—I said, "Our second problem is two possible hostages."

Before Courtney could ask what I meant by hostages, and before Eugenia could rip off her old-lady camo shirt to show us a suicide bomb she had strapped to her chest and volunteer to sacrifice herself for the good of peace on earth, or peace in Pine Apple, as it were, or before Florida could say, "This has been a ton of fun, but I think it's time for me to scoot on out," Courtney's arm shot up in the air with the children's menu. She waved it. "Ta-da!"

We huddled over the menu.

"These here are the walls."

"Perimeter," Eugenia corrected her.

Florida said, "Shhh."

I said, "Keep going, Courtney."

She cleared her throat. "This here," she tapped the menu with the blue crayon, "is a driveway going down to the basement where the ambulances drop off the dead people." She tapped again. "This here is the stairs to get down to the basement from the chapel. Those are the only ways in," tap, tap, "and the only two ways out."

"Not a single window?" I asked.

"Sure, there's a window," she answered.

"Windows are entries and exits too, Squid," Eugenia said.

Courtney shot up and got in Eugenia's face. "Stop calling me names!"

I gently pushed Courtney back into her seat. "Tell us about the window, Courtney."

She stopped glaring at Eugenia long enough to find her red crayon. She pointed at Eugenia and said, "Zip it, old lady," then went back to her menu drawing. "The window is in here." She drew a tiny box. "It's a basement kind of window. High up on the wall. Like you can kinda see out the top half during the daytime, but the bottom half is the ground. Like a little line of grass..." she went for her green crayon "...and under the little line of grass, dirt." She sighed in utter defeat after inventorying her crayons and not finding a brown one to draw the dirt. "Just use your imagination on the dirt."

I zoomed in. "It looks like you've drawn the window inside a yellow box. The yellow is hard to see, Courtney."

She painstakingly traced over the yellow box in red. "It's the undertaker room. It's like a little car washer in there." She picked up the green crayon and scribbled a circle in the middle of the room. "That's a drain in the floor," she told us. "And over here," she drew a slash, "is a washer wand hooked to the wall." She looked up. "And the window is in the undertaker room because Roy Howdy says it gets a little smelly." She pinched her nose.

Florida's whole body said, "Ewww."

Eugenia slapped her arm. "Mind over matter, Grunt."

"Watch it, Eugenia," Florida warned.

I said, "Keep going, Courtney."

"This here—" Courtney tapped the largest space "—is Roy Howdy's playroom part of the basement."

"Who in the world plays with Roy Howdy?" Florida asked.

Courtney stiffened. "His friends?"

"What friends?" Florida asked.

"Moving on," I said.

"Maybe his *girl*friend," Courtney squeezed in.

"Please." Florida rolled her eyes.

"Troops!" Eugenia slapped the table.

"Everyone be quiet," I said. "Keep going, Courtney."

She stuffed a dangling curler back into her scarf and with a snarl said, "Where was I before I was so rudely interrupted?"

"Oh, my gosh, Courtney!" The blood drained from Florida's face. "You and Roy Howdy? Is that even legal?"

"That's none of your beeswax, Florida."

"That is the nastiest thing I've heard since my mother and Eddie Crawford."

Eugenia Winters Stone's hands smacked the table. Her mouth dropped all the way open, and her eyes were about to pop out of her head. She began noisily and slowly sucking in air until I thought her lungs might burst.

I did what I had to do. I smacked the back of her head. "Eugenia! Snap out of it!"

It was then and there that I should have loaded the three of them up and taken them right back where I found them. And I would've, if Roy Howdy and Whiskey weren't being held by three escaped prisoners. I tapped on the map. "Don't either of you—" I toggled fingers at Florida and Eugenia "—say another word until Courtney finishes."

Courtney, vindicated, gave Florida and Eugenia a victory smirk. "This here," she said with newfound confidence, "is the kitchen—"

I interrupted that time. "There's a kitchen in the basement?"

"Yeah, but it's only for cooking voodoo candles."

"What's that big thing?" Florida asked.

Courtney zoomed in. "That's the stove."

"What's the big thing on the stove?" Florida asked.

"That's the wax bucket," Courtney said. "For the voodoo candles. Stay away from it, because Roy Howdy keeps it on low all the time, cause his orders come in one on top of the other 'specially around SEC playoff times. He gets Tennessee Vols and Georgia Bulldog voodoo candle orders right and left, and—"

"Courtney!"

"Geesh, Davis!" Courtney patted her curlers. "Calm down, okay? Where was I?" Courtney pointed her curlers at the map. "And this here," she tapped what looked like a short fat green snake attached to the basement, "is the root cellar." She looked up. "I've just been in it the once. It's not all that big," she said, "and the door is real little. Like you have to scooch down to get in. And it isn't all that big once you get in either. And kinda crowded. If you got claustrophobic problems, you maybe shouldn't go in there."

"How many dead soldiers on the premises?" Eugenia, who'd come back around after the bombshell news about Fiona and Eddie, or Courtney and Roy Howdy, or both, rubbed her hands together in anticipation.

"What are the chances there's a Dr Pepper here?" Florida took a look around the diner.

"Davis? Do you mind if I use the little girl's room?" Courtney pushed up from her bench seat. "I'd like to freshen up before we go to Roy Howdy's."

I called it.

There was no way I was going in with those three.

I pulled my phone out of my pocket to send Bradley a message telling him to give me a heads up when he was ten minutes out, and that I'd meet him, Baylor, and the other men at the gate of the graveyard, only to see I'd missed a message from him while pacing the floor and trying to keep the peace among my motley crew. *Put the chopper down in Prattville. No car. We are truly in the middle of nowhere. Sit tight. We'll figure something out.*

Prattville was an hour away at top speed.

If they had a car.

Which they didn't.

And even if they had a car, they wouldn't be coming in hot because I'd already told Bradley to take it easy on the road. Don't draw attention to himself. Lest he end up in Alabama lockup. For a week.

I eyeballed the three women in the diner booth. Against my better judgement, when in fact I was using no good judgement whatsoever, I said, "It's time. Let's go."

I grabbed the map.

My troops fell in line behind me.

TWENTY-SEVEN

We stepped out the door of Bea's Diner to fog. A misty Alabama fog I remembered well. A fog that would burn off at daybreak. And a welcome fog, because it solved two problems at once. It both provided cover for us traipsing through the graveyard and up the hill to the funeral home and, with the eerie mood it set, scared Florida, Courtney, and Eugenia straight.

We crossed a sleeping Main Street quietly, with the noted exceptions of the muted thud of combat boots and the loud clip of house slippers. We slowed down when we reached the gate to the cemetery. I had to tug Eugenia's camo arm to get her attention so she'd follow us in. She was busy fuming at the Flash Fireworks truck backed into the funeral home driveway that had cost her a serving platter.

We hiked the graveyard hill, dodging grave markers and tombstones, and stopped ten feet from the ugly old house with the worst of the traverse being when Florida almost knocked Courtney's head off while slinging the sledgehammer off one shoulder and onto the other.

Florida, Eugenia, and Courtney gathered around me in the dark.

"No questions," I said, "just listen."

They nodded.

"Chances are high the three men are in the root cellar looking for the coin. It's also likely the two hostages are restrained. And if it were me, based on the map, I'd restrain them in the undertaker room. So our first priority is to locate the hostages in hopes of freeing them. At the same time, if the three wanted men are in the root cellar where they believe the coin to be, we need to trap them there. Florida, if all goes well, you and Courtney will free the hostages. Eugenia, you and I will close and block the root cellar door. All that depends on us finding a safe way in." I took a deep breath. "Stay behind me, don't make a peep, and let's go."

We went.

I stopped everyone ten feet from the basement window and crawled on my belly toward the dim light. The window was old, cracked, loose in its frame, and too dirty to see through. I rubbed a silver coin-sized peephole and saw that the undertaker room was just as bad as I'd imagined. The room was small, no larger than a bedroom. Roy Howdy and Whiskey were strapped to gurneys on both sides of the open door. I knew they were alive, because I could see them struggling under their restraints. I couldn't see their hands, so I had to assume they were belted to their sides, and I couldn't see their faces. Both of their heads were covered with ski masks, on loan, I would imagine, from the prison escapees. I rubbed decades of dirt off the top of the small window in a two-inch-deep line from left to right until I could see past the undertaker room. And found the situation beyond so much worse than I'd imagined. In the large room Courtney called Roy Howdy's playroom, the one thing I hadn't counted on was occupying the sofa. His back was to me. I could see a military haircut, his feet on the coffee table, ankles crossed, and his arms stretched out along the back cushions. In his left hand, a beer. In his right hand, a gun. He was waving the gun in the air and speaking to someone to his right. In the general direction, according to Courtney's map, of the root cellar. He finished the beer, tossing the empty can through the air. He stood, still waving the gun. He was wearing a uniform. A Talladega Federal guard uniform.

It was Flash.

My head dropped.

My heart dropped with it.

What would the next step be if it were me, Fantasy, and Baylor?

We wouldn't breach the basement because the odds were stacked against us. We wouldn't try to free the hostages from the undertaker room, because not only would it be hard for even me, the smallest of our three, to get in the basement window unnoticed with the door wide open and Flash ten feet from said open door, it would be beyond difficult to get Whiskey out the same window and Roy Howdy's head wouldn't even fit through it. Much less the rest of him. Fantasy, Baylor, and I wouldn't have been able to free the hostages. So what would we do? We'd leave one gun at the window with a clear shot at the door to protect the hostages, the other two would disable the getaway vehicle, then we'd contrive a way to run the criminals out. We might cut the power to the house. We might look for an alarm system, and if we found one, trip it. Maybe we'd beat on the basement driveway door claiming to have a body to drop off. Anything that would send the bad guys running for their fireworks truck. That we'd disabled. And where we'd be lying in wait. That's what my team would do. It would be hard to put the same plan in motion with my new team of misfits because I was the only shooter. Courtney was terrified of guns, Florida had never held a gun, and Eugenia might kill everyone in the basement, including the hostages, before accidentally shooting herself. So stationing myself at the undertaker window while they disabled the fireworks truck was our only path forward. Unless the cavalry showed up in the next five minutes.

* * *

The cavalry didn't show up in the next five minutes.

Worse, neither Bradley nor Baylor answered my calls. Wherever they were between Prattville and Pine Apple, they didn't have cell service.

We stealthily made our way through the fog and down the hill to the graveyard gate, then across the street to reconvene under the cover of the willow trees again. I was busy catching my breath. Florida was busy letting the sledgehammer hold her up. Courtney was busy picking dirt out of the huge poms on her house slippers. And Eugenia was busy listening. "Do you hear that?" she asked. "I hear hammering."

It was then that I remembered what was on the other side of the willow trees.

Florida and Courtney realized where we were too.

"I don't hear anything," Courtney said.

"Neither do I," Florida said.

"It's a pounding noise," Eugenia said. "It sounds like it's coming from inside the bank."

"Maybe it's just your blood pounding in your ears from the adrenalin, Eugenia," I lamely suggested, while hustling everyone across Main Street toward Bea's Diner. Away from the rhythmic thud that did indeed sound like hammering coming from inside the bank. Once we got to my car, then gathered behind it, it still took me, Florida, and Courtney a minute to get our terror out of the bank vault it had been hijacked to and back to the funeral home where it belonged.

"What now, Commander?"

"Eugenia, my name is Daaaaaavis." I dragged it out the same way she did.

"What now, Daaaaaavis?"

"We get a step ahead of them," I said. Then I laid out our only option short of calling in the Alabama National Guard. And if Bradley, Baylor, and the guns with them didn't arrive soon, I'd be forced to call the Guard. "Does anyone know how to cut brake lines?"

Light from a streetlamp at the corner filtered through the mist and cast long shadows on the three stumped faces around mine.

Eugenia said, "My car is serviced by Mercedes-Benz in Montgomery."

Courtney said, "I don't even know what brake lines are. Do they connect the brakes to...something else?"

Florida said, "Are you thinking we cut the brakes to the fireworks truck so that when they leave the steep funeral home driveway, they plow through everything on Main Street?"

Scratch that.

I asked a more direct question. "Does anyone know how to disable a vehicle?" I knew how to destroy board diagnostic ports of brand new Bellissimo trucks, but that's where my disable-a-vehicle knowledge started and stopped.

Eugenia said, "We could shoot out the tires."

Wouldn't work for two reasons: they'd hear gunshots ringing through the night, and they'd happily drive out of town on the rims.

Courtney said, "We could pour a cup of sugar in their gas tank."

Wouldn't work. Because it was a myth. Sugar fell straight to the bottom of the gas tank where it settled in for a nice long nap.

Florida said, "Swipe the spark plugs."

We were all a little stunned. (In general. And specifically, that Florida delivered the line so matter-of-factly.)

"Keeping in mind it's not a perfect solution," she said. "If it's a diesel truck, forget it. And if it has a manual transmission, there's a chance they can start it without the spark plugs. In that case, though, it would misfire. Or the engine would surge. Or—"

"Aren't spark plugs small?" I asked. "How would we find them in the dark?"

"If it's a four-cylinder engine," Florida said, "they'll be lined up on top. Same thing if it's six cylinders. Unless they're on the side, but still easy to find. Now if it's a V8—"

"Could spark plug failure cause my radio to jump from one radio station to another of its own accord?" Eugenia asked.

"V8 like the vegetable juice?" Courtney asked. "I always put a can of V8 in my vegetable beef soup. One of those baby cans."

"What are the chances it'll work?" I asked.

Florida answered me first. "Ninety-nine percent." She answered Courtney second. "No." She answered Eugenia last. "No."

I took the time to ask a follow-up question out of curiosity. "How do you know all this?"

"Because I keep an Airstream Interstate Touring Coach running."

We stood silently and let the fog swirl around us. "Ladies." I shot a hand out in the circle. Florida landed her hand on mine. Eugenia slapped hers on Florida's. Courtney followed with hers. "I'm going back to the funeral home."

Eugenia said, "I'll back you up."

I shook my head no.

She didn't argue.

Courtney said, "If you see Roy Howdy, tell him I said hey."

Florida said, "I'll take care of the spark plugs."

* * *

When we reached the Flash Fireworks truck—the whole time I mentally tried on and peeled off different ways I might run the crew out of the house and to the inoperable truck, which would be after rescuing Roy Howdy and Whiskey, without ever finding the right fit—I held my hand out to Eugenia. She kept a blank look on her face, as if she had no idea what I wanted when she knew full well what I wanted. I shook my hand. With a huff, she unholstered her Desert Eagle pistol and plopped it in my waiting hand.

Courtney took a giant step back.

First, I clicked the gun to its safe position with a quick glare at Eugenia for not having the safety on in the first place and a quick thanks to the heavens above that she hadn't shot her own foot off before killing us all. I released the magazine, dumping the contents into the pocket of my t-shirt, then replaced the empty magazine.

I pulled back the slide and ejected the round in the chamber. I passed the empty gun back to Eugenia. I held the single round out to Florida. "Do not give it to her unless it's a life-or-death situation."

Florida nodded.

Eugenia huffed again while holstering her useless firearm.

With a loud thud.

"What was that?" I asked.

"Nothing," she answered.

"Eugenia, do you have another gun on you?"

"No, it's a smoke bomb grenade, thank you."

"No. Thank *you*, Eugenia." I relieved her of the grenade, tucking it away for safekeeping. I held my empty hand out again. "I need something to dig with." She rummaged around in the deep cargo pocket of her left camo pant leg and produced—I kid you not—a three-inch-wide folding bayonet inside a black leather case.

Courtney said, "What is that?"

Florida said, "You are a strange woman, Eugenia."

Eugenia said, "I hope you're happy, Davis. Now I am completely unarmed. I could fall prey to a predator and have no way to defend myself."

I hooked the leather case of the bayonet onto a belt loop. "When all this is over, we're going to have a long talk, Eugenia." My eyes left hers, then found Courtney's, and finally Florida's. "As soon as you have the spark plugs, let me know. Then go straight back to Bea's Diner, all three of you. Lock yourselves in and wait on me." The smoke grenade wasn't sitting well in my pocket. And accidentally detonating it inside our small circle wouldn't help a bit. I gingerly pulled it out to readjust it and my car keys came out too, falling at Eugenia's feet. "Keep them," I said. "If you don't hear from me and I'm not back in half an hour, call the Alabama National Guard and get yourselves to my sister's. You'll find her, my niece, my grandmother, and my children in the bunk room under the kitchen."

I was two steps into the foggy graveyard when I heard the pound of footfall behind me. "Davis, wait." It was Florida. She held out the sledgehammer. "Just in case you need it." We fell into a bear hug, the likes of which we hadn't shared since the day she came running up the street waving her MIT acceptance letter.

* * *

After crawling the last ten feet to the window again, I found all the players right where I'd left them. Roy Howdy and Whiskey were still straining and squirming, with decidedly less enthusiasm, but they were alive. Flash was still on the sofa with a different beer in his left hand and the same gun in his right, as he continued to bark orders in the direction of the root cellar, but with decidedly more enthusiasm. It would seem, based on the tension covering his blood-red face like a blanket he was yelling through, that he wanted the job over and done with.

So did I.

I maneuvered myself and the bayonet into a prone digging position and started relocating earth away from the window. Still soft from the torrential rain days earlier, it went quickly, with the only mishap being when I hit a rock, and in the process of dislodging it, got a face full of dirt. Not wanting the blade to scratch glass, which would have sent me scrambling for cover when Flash's head whipped around to locate the source of the noise, I flipped the bayonet and used the leather handle to move the last of the dirt away, where I discovered I wasn't dealing with a single-hung or even a double-hung window. It was a hopper window. Like an awning window, but it opened out instead of in. And it turned out to be a single large pane below all the dirt. Large enough for even Roy Howdy to escape. If I could dig a deep enough trench, I could pull it all the way open and lay it down flat. I still couldn't stand up, for fear that I'd send shadows bouncing off the basement wall, so flat on my belly it was. I batted around for the bayonet I'd dropped in the dark, crawled back two feet, and went to town. By the time I finished and rolled onto my back, my shoulders were on fire, I couldn't feel my elbows at all, and I was wearing dirt mittens. I lay there panting, fog rolling around me, thankful I hadn't unearthed any stray graveyard bones, and knew if I didn't get moving, I might never move again. I was weary. I was heartsick. And I was scared. I was scared for my husband, my children, myself, Florida, Courtney, Eugenia, and everyone else in Pine Apple until my phone buzzed in my back pocket. The vibration was so unexpected, I thought I'd been tazed. I flipped over, in hopes of the earth keeping my heart in my chest, blew dirt out of my mouth, and went for my phone. The message was from Florida. *Courtney and I are back at Bea's. Eugenia's right behind us. I think. She's all upset about our failed mission to disable the truck. Davis, the fireworks truck is a diesel. No spark plugs. I couldn't bust into the locked cab because windshield smashing isn't exactly a quiet science, so I tried to go in through the back of the truck—not locked—to get into the cab and swipe the fuses, but the back of the truck is full. Of fireworks. I've never seen so many fireworks. There's no daylight in the back of that truck and it's going to take hours to unload. I hope you're having better luck than me.*

It was the kick in the pants I needed.

I had to move.

It had to end.

And it was over in seven minutes.

Smoke bomb grenade in hand, I crawled back to the window and tried to pull the hopper window open, but it wasn't going anywhere. The window hadn't been all the way open in decades.

Sledgehammer it was.

And Florida was right.

Glass shattering didn't go unnoticed.

Flash's head swung wildly looking for the source of the noise as I traded the sledgehammer for the smoke bomb grenade. I pulled the pin and lobbed it as far as I could through the open door. I dropped in the window and hit the glass-shard floor, watching Flash's eyes dart from me to the grenade rolling across the floor. While he took the split second to decide which of us to shoot, I reached right and left pulling off face masks just as the smoke bomb detonated with the loudest blast I think I'd ever heard in my life. As the large room in the basement filled with smoke, extreme language, and blind rounds from his gun thudding into walls with one whizzing past my head, I sliced through canvas straps on gurneys with the bayonet. Roy Howdy said, "Davis?" I could barely hear him through the smoke bomb blast echoes roaring through my ears as I helped him sit up. "This is three times you've saved my life!" I hauled him off the gurney and shoved him toward the window. "Now I'm like your slave forever!"

I pointed to the window. "GET OUT!"

Roy Howdy shoved the gurney he'd been strapped to beneath the window, locked the wheels, climbed out the window, then dropped to his knees to help Whiskey out. Whiskey was mouthing off in his usual way, his long words spilling out one on top of the other, packing a little more punch than they usually did, but I wasn't listening as I scrambled up the gurney and out the window behind him. I was an inch from freedom when a vice grip wrapped around my left ankle and yanked. I felt it all the way up my leg and into my hip. I kicked with my right foot and with everything I had, connected—I'm not sure who released the primal guttural grunt, or maybe we both did. My left slip-on Ked slipped off before I could escape.

By the time I made it out, the smoke from the grenade had filled the undertaker room and was following me in whisps. Roy Howdy and Whiskey each grabbed an arm of mine and were dragging me away when the distant wail of a fire engine reached my ears. There wasn't a doubt in my mind it was my husband roaring into town. He was still several miles out, but in the country sound traveled. And occasionally disappeared. Like my hearing did just then when Eugenia Winters Stone, who'd freed her AK-47 from the trunk of my car, emptied an entire cartridge of thirty rounds into the getaway truck. Full of fireworks.

The sky literally exploded.

The three of us stopped at the first row of headstones, fell to our knees, then collapsed on the ground. We rolled on to our backs and watched the show.

TWENTY-EIGHT

It was five thirty in the morning before the fire engine Baylor found, hotwired, and confiscated from a sleeping volunteer firehall four miles from Atwell Aviation, along with Pine Apple's three volunteer firefighters and every other volunteer firefighter and all available equipment within a thirty-mile radius—they'd all heard the blast—finally extinguished all the little fires. Thanks to the fireworks. Eugenia had blown out the thin metal sidewall of the box truck and the ignited fireworks inside did the rest. There was nothing left of the truck but the smoldering cab. Pine Apple was left with scattered scorched-earth debris, especially on the west end of town, and the air was singed with sulfur, which was only slightly less offensive than the smell of the goats. But having only lost one garage way out on Collins Road, far from ground zero of all the pyrotechnics, all in all, we'd dodged a fire bullet. Which would have fulfilled Fantasy's prophecy from what felt like weeks ago, but was really only days ago, when she said all I had left to do was burn my hometown to the ground.

It was five forty-five in the morning when the Talladega Federal prisoner transport bus rolled into town to cart home their three wayward residents. At the detonation of the smoke bomb grenade, one of them had slammed the root cellar door closed. With a little too much enthusiasm. Considering it was an ancient rustic wood door housed in a thick wooden frame built into the side of a hill that had swollen with the rain. The three prisoners were trapped. With the dead bodies. Talladega Federal's wayward guard, Marcus Flash, on the other hand, was on the run. He'd escaped the smoky basement by crawling up the stairwell, leaving a wide trail of candle wax in his wake after tipping over then falling in the contents of an eighty-quart stainless steel stockpot full of the hot stuff. We could see the outline of his feet cast in deep wax near the stove, and past those, where he'd landed face first in hot wax trying to outrun it.

After I found my shoe in the undertaker room, Roy Howdy and I, not on one of the little-fires-everywhere crews, followed the trail of hardened wax by flashlight. Up the stairs, then out the front door, down the driveway, and all the way to the empty lot below the hill at the intersection of Wright and Oak Streets. Where the haphazardly parked eighteen-wheeler from the Bellissimo wasn't.

"Roy Howdy?" I was all the same color—head to toe—a hue that was equal parts dirt and soot. "Did you leave the keys in the eighteen-wheeler?"

"Maybe."

That was a yes. "Why?"

"I figured you'd get mad if I lost them."

"You lost the whole truck. And bonus, you let a—" I didn't think it was the time or place to break the Old Man Carter news to Roy Howdy by calling Flash a murderer, so I went with "—deranged madman escape."

After a thoughtful moment passed, which didn't happen often with Roy Howdy, he said, "When is it your daddy's going to be back?"

"Tuesday," I said. "I think." I never read the rest of his text message, and my phone was long gone. Probably somewhere in the graveyard. Or trucking down the road in an eighteen-wheeler with Marcus Flash, who I immediately radioed in a BOLO for so the manhunt could get underway. He had a head start, but it wasn't easy to take Alabama backroads or hide from state troopers on the highways in a wanted big rig. Especially if you'd just bathed in eighty quarts of 130-degree wax and driving big rigs wasn't your day job. So it wouldn't be long.

It was six o'clock in the morning when Bex and Quinn settled down enough to sit down. With their father. They, along with everyone else near and far, took to the streets at four in the morning to watch the spectacular fireworks blunder, except my family had taken to an attic window. My sister wouldn't let the girls or my grandmother leave the house. "And Junebug," she said, "slept through it all."

The baby was still asleep. In Bradley's arms. And I was way too tired to tackle the Junebug business.

"Where's Eugenia?" Meredith asked.

"Probably asleep."

"Where's Courtney?"

"Probably the same."

"Where's Florida?"

Any other time I would have said, "On the other side of the state line," but I said, "I'm sure she's asleep too."

"Now, what's this about a coin?" Meredith was perched on the double vanity between the two small sinks, yelling at me as I finally took a shower already. "They were looking for a coin? Did they find it?"

I poked my soapy head out of the shower to tell her that not only were the prison escapees' denials of finding the coin credible, as credible as a felon's denial could be, we'd wanded them to death with a metal detector only hitting on belt buckles and prison dental work.

"And you believe them?" Meredith asked.

I poked my soapy head out again. "Meredith, if you separate three criminals and question them individually, at least one is going to turn on the other two. Every time. And I'm beginning to think the coin is long gone if there ever was a coin to begin with."

"Get back in the shower," my sister said. "You're dripping mud on my floor. Now, what's this about Eugenia?"

I yelled the story from under the hot spray.

"Davis, you have to be making this up."

I stuck my head out of the shower again. "Who could make that up?"

And just to get Meredith going again, insisting that I'd hallucinated every Eugenia word, at seven that morning, while we sat on The Front Porch steps with hot mugs of coffee, Eugenia Winters Stone and her Women's Society friends marched down Main Street ready to flip Memorial Day pancakes. Eugenia was dressed in her Talbots finest red, white, and blue. With her right arm resting in an American flag scarf sling.

Ah, recoil. Thy name is Eugenia.

She slowed in front of us.

"Davis."

"Eugenia."

"Meredith."

"Good morning, Eugenia," Meredith said. "What's wrong with your arm?"

"A touch of bursitis." She turned to me. "How are you this fine morning?"

"I'm well, Eugenia. Your touch of bursitis notwithstanding, how are you?"

"Other than the rude interruption of the premature fireworks display that was nothing short of a massive explosion disturbing me at such an ungodly hour, which your father would've never let happen, I'm looking forward to a lovely small stack of blueberry pancakes."

She barely winked at me.

When the women were out of earshot, Meredith said, "I knew you made all that up."

"What I need is to get up." I sat my coffee mug down and slapped my knees. "And open the police station."

"I'd hang a Gone Fishing sign if I were you."

"I can't," I said. "Daddy would never forgive me, because it's go time. Our Memorial Day Celebration is here. People are starting to pour in for pancakes. The street fair vendors are setting up. We need police presence."

"No one needs police presence to eat pancakes or buy light-up necklaces, Davis."

"Good," I said. "I'll open the station and get a nap in the jail cell."

Five quiet minutes later and I had yet to move a muscle. Meredith grabbed my arm. "Davis?"

"Hmm?" Sleep was barreling toward me.

"What about Eddie?"

Sleep stopped, waved bye, and sprinted the other way.

We ran, with me bringing up the rear, because I was wearing clean shoes of Meredith's that were a size and a half too big. The last time I'd been anywhere near the bank was when Roy Howdy and I were tracking wax. It was still dark then, the fog had firework smoke reinforcement, our heads were down, our eyes trained on the beams of the flashlights, and as soon as we passed the back of the dark bank—which, honestly, didn't even register at the time—the missing Bellissimo eighteen-wheeler had commanded all our attention. Hours later, in the light of a new day, I saw what I'd missed behind a willow tree. Eddie the Insane had managed to beat a two-foot-tall and two-foot-wide square opening into the back wall of the vault.

I dove in up to my waist, blocking daylight and plunging myself into semi-darkness. I wrangled an arm out. "Give me your phone."

It landed in my hand. "Is he in there?" she whispered. "Is he dead?"

Shining the beam of the flashlight around the room as far as the light would reach, I didn't see Eddie. More than that, my skin wasn't crawling. So I knew he wasn't there. Odd furniture that might have been placed in somewhat of an orderly fashion the day before was strewn about, piled haphazardly, and mostly demolished. Legs were broken off small tables, a dresser was missing its drawers, and a mirror had been pulverized for its metal framework.

Seven years of bad luck for Eddie.

Boxes that had probably been full had been emptied. Clothes were strewn everywhere. A stretch of old safe-deposit boxes had been ripped from the wall, then mutilated. But the most interesting was an inset on my left that looked like a small utility room. From my vantage point, I could only see a blue pedestal sink. Scattered with what looked like white rocks. White rocks of wax. Marcus Flash had been there. How had we missed it earlier? Because he'd picked up his waxy trail right where he left off after his detour to the vault on his way to the eighteen-wheeler. We hadn't seen where he'd veered off the path in the dark. He'd probably hidden in the vault until the chaos of the emergency vehicles gave him enough cover to make his getaway.

So where was Eddie?

Eddie the Idiot was probably driving the eighteen-wheeler.

But that wasn't the worst news.

The worst news was, Flash wouldn't have passed up an opportunity to rob the bank.

I shouted over my shoulder. "Meredith!"

She smacked me. "I'm right here. Don't yell."

"I think the bank's been robbed."

"AGAIN? Davis, Daddy's going to disown you."

By then, I was stuck. I couldn't twist my arms back through the opening far enough to push myself out. Meredith pulled me out by my legs.

I dusted myself off and poked through the contacts on her phone. "You don't have Courtney's number?"

"Why would I have Courtney's number?"

I found Roy Howdy's. "It's Davis. I need Courtney's phone number. Right now."

"Davis, I was up all night." Like I didn't know. "I'm trying to sleep till the pancakes are ready."

"The number, Roy Howdy."

He gave me Courtney's phone number.

"Say, Davis, do you know if we're having bacon at the pancake breakfast? Last year it was just sausage. And not sausage patties. The link kind. Me and sausage links ain't friends."

I hung up on him and dialed Courtney's number.

"*What*?"

I might lose my mind. "Roy Howdy? Are you at Courtney's?"

"Yes. My place is a big mess."

Another tidbit he was sharing as if I didn't know.

"When I asked for Courtney's number, you could have just—" There was no reason to waste my breath. "Let me speak to Courtney."

"She's sleeping. She was up all night too."

Someone save me.

"Roy Howdy—" It was a threat.

"Alright, alright, hold on."

When I finally had Courtney on the line, I asked for the security code to the bank's front door keypad. She said, "I'm not supposed to tell."

"Courtney—" Another threat.

"Nineteen-nineteen. Okay?"

Roy Howdy and Courtney were a match made in May-December romance heaven.

Everything inside the bank looked exactly like it had the last time I'd seen it—Courtney's teller drawer wasn't in broken pieces on the ground, Fiona's desk hadn't been touched, and the small locked door in her office where the real money was hadn't been tampered with. Nothing about the bank said, "I've been robbed!"

Relief, relief, relief.

But it also meant any evidence left by Marcus Flash was inside the vault. And short of taking a wrecking ball to exterior wall, I didn't have access. The problem was the grandfather clock. It was in the way, and it wasn't going anywhere. Tipping it over to block the door was one thing. Standing it up to gain access would be quite another. So I sat down where I stood. In the middle of the lobby. Flopped down might be more like it.

"Davis, honey," my sister sat down beside me, "go to Mother and Daddy's. Climb in bed. Get a few hours of sleep. We'll figure it out."

"I don't think you understand what all I'm up against, Meredith."

"Yes, I do." She lobbed an arm across my shoulders and pulled me in. "You're up against our Memorial Day Celebration. We have a pancake breakfast to get to, then we have the street fair to go to, then we'll spend the rest of the day getting ready for—"

I picked up where she left off. "—the chicken wing competition that isn't happening." I hauled myself up.

"Where are you going?"

Crazy, was where I was going. "I'm going to the police station to put out an APB letting everyone chasing Marcus Flash know that he probably has a passenger. Then I'm sending Granny to the police station to man the desk and answer the phone for a few hours. Because I'm taking your advice. I'm going to lay down before I fall down."

"Davis, Granny is at her casino. Baylor and the men who came with him are helping her set everything up."

I'd forgotten all about the casino in the Fellowship Hall at the Baptist church.

"Did you hear what they found when they unpacked the slot machines?"

I threw my hands in the air. "Dead bodies?"

"Silver dollars! The slot machines pay silver dollars! Baylor says they're uncirculated, so anyone who wins one silver dollar is really winning twenty-five dollars."

I stared at her, blank-faced—I couldn't take anymore—and turned for the door.

"Wait!" She ran after me. "Don't leave me here by myself!"

On the street, she peeled off at The Front Porch. "Why don't I check on Bradley and the kiddos? I'll let them know you need a little...quiet time."

I nodded.

Somehow my leaden legs made it to Town Square. There were hundreds of people at picnic tables with plates piled high with pancakes. I went straight through the middle to the large tent with four flat-top griddles on the left, condiments and drinks on a long table on the right, and in the middle, huge portraits of Wilcox County's three fallen soldiers on easels. Eugenia was standing beside Eli Atwell's image in deep conversation with two women I didn't know. I tapped her shoulder. Her good shoulder.

"Davis?"

"Could you take over for me at the police station for a few hours?"

She smiled at the two women. "Could you excuse us?" They scattered, and she turned back to me. "Certainly."

"No funny stuff, Eugenia. I mean it."

She nodded. "Understood."

"Do I need to define funny stuff?"

"You do not."

I turned to slink away, but Pine Apple's finest hour, full of laughter, energy, and the retelling of the fireworks fiasco at every other banquet table draped in red, white, and blue, stopped me. I turned back around. "Eugenia?"

"Davis?"

"Get the word out. We're having a potato salad competition tomorrow."

"Of course."

At the edge of Town Square, I heard the squeals of delight as she shared the news with her devoted Women's Society followers. I made it to the police station where I unlocked the door for Eugenia and kept going. I don't remember the two-block walk to my parents' house, but I do remember seeing them. My mother was standing in the middle of her dirt yard with her mouth wide open. She saw me and started screaming. "Davis Way! WHY IS MY YARD IN THE DRIVEWAY?" I said, "Mother, you'd better get to the kitchen. The potato salad business is back on." My father let me get to the mailbox before he said, "Sweet Pea? Are you okay?" I said, "Is it really Tuesday already?" Then I saw Bea Crawford rounding the car laden with enough overstuffed mismatched luggage for a six-month cruise. "Oh, hey, Bea," I said. "You have a grandson. Fiona Simmons is his mother. They're inside." I didn't turn to look on my way in the door, but it sounded like she'd dropped six months' worth of overstuffed mismatched luggage.

Nope.

She'd passed out.

Inside the front door I found a ghastly pale Fiona with her hands on Cole's shoulders. "What do I do, Davis?" she whispered.

I passed her on my way to bed. "Take your son outside to meet his grandmother."

TWENTY-NINE

My husband woke me seven hours later with the glorious Biloxi news that Butch and Boofie Bartlett had dropped their lawsuit against Fantasy. Something about Butch not having a permit for the gun he sent his eighteen-year-old son into the Bellissimo with, plus all the other parents filing Contributing to the Delinquency of a Minor charges against him. Somewhere in all the media frenzy and scrutiny, his partner in the drywall business got spooked and turned himself in for tax evasion, which was, in effect, turning in Butch too. The Bellissimo internal and police investigations of Fantasy's role in the dustup were still open and in progress. The Bellissimo was still mad at having to swap out the controversial Tesla in the middle of the casino floor, but the huge expense of a defense attorney and the ordeal of a long-drawn-out trial wasn't going to happen.

"So she's back at work?"

"I didn't say that."

There was a knuckle on the open door.

It was my father.

"Sweet Pea?"

"Hi, Daddy."

He said, "You missed the pancakes."

Bradley kissed the top of my head. "I'll let you two talk."

Daddy pulled out the desk chair I used to sit in to memorize spelling words. I took the furry vanity stool where I'd learned to—mouth all the way open—poke myself in the eye with a mascara wand.

Daddy kicked things off with, "Who picked red?"

"What?"

"The police station door. Who decided to paint the door red?"

And the thin father ice I'd been skating on turned to solid ground.

"Why did you tell me you'd be home Tuesday?" I asked.

"You must not have read my entire message. I said I'd be home Tuesday unless the charges against Bea were dropped. I went on to say if the charges were dropped, we'd be on the first flight home. Which we were. We left Buffalo at six thirty yesterday evening, landed in Atlanta at nine, retrieved your mother's car from long-term parking, got on the road, stopped and rented hotel rooms in LaGrange, Georgia, slept, then drove the rest of the way early this morning."

"Canada let her go?"

"She wore them down, Sweet Pea."

Bea could wear down The Supreme Court.

"The authorities confiscated her souvenirs, she's never to set foot in Canada again, and she's landed herself on an international travel watchlist which will most likely prevent her from ever acquiring a passport. Although I'm not so sure she'll ever want to leave Pine Apple again. So all in all, she received a slap on the wrist considering what she put everyone through." He sat back. "And for the record, I tried to call you repeatedly. On the way to the airport in Buffalo, again when we landed in Atlanta, and even this morning."

"I lost my phone."

"Ah." He sat back. "So, what all have I missed?"

I laughed.

"Davis." He leaned forward in his seat, elbows on knees, and let me know important news was on the way. "Eddie ran the confiscated eighteen-wheeler off the road in Fort Deposit."

I knew they wouldn't get far. Fort Deposit was another small Alabama town north of Greenville. Larger than Pine Apple, for sure, but not a metropolis. "What about Marcus Flash?"

"When the authorities arrived at the scene, they found Marcus Flash unconscious on the floorboard of the cab. He was apprehended, and he's currently at Regional in Greenville being treated for second-degree burns covering most of his torso in addition to a thorough truck beating."

I raised an eyebrow. "A truck beating?"

"Eddie's never driven an eighteen-wheeler," he said, "and his passenger wasn't buckled in. Apparently, Eddie took the curves pretty hard and found the brakes tricky. Marcus Flash almost went through the windshield."

"So he's in custody? Handcuffed to a hospital bed?"

"And shackled," Daddy said. "With officers posted at the door."

"Really? Do they think a banged-up man with second-degree burns is going to chew through the shackles?"

"No," Daddy said. "But there was a small problem."

I raised both eyebrows that time.

"Or maybe I should say there was a large problem."

My eyebrows stayed where they were.

"Bea."

"*What*?"

He told me Bea called Eddie to break the glorious news—she was a grandmother. He congratulated her with breaking news of his own—he was a father. He went on to tell her he was being held for questioning by the Alabama Bureau of Investigation concerning his road trip with Marcus Flash. Then told her he'd been imprisoned at Pine Apple Bank & Trust before being kidnapped by a human candle with a buzzcut. Bea immediately drove to Greenville and busted Eddie out with, "I watch Blues Bloods. Either charge him or let him loose." She and Eddie went straight to Regional Hospital so she could have a word with the buzzcut human candle about treating a new father so poorly. Hospital security called it in to the police, saying Bea was posing a threat to one of their patients, when we could have told them to give her a minute, because Bea posed a bigger threat to herself than anyone else.

"Does anyone believe Eddie?" I asked. More like croaked. "I mean, kidnapped by a candle man? Imprisoned at the bank?"

Daddy hesitated, weighing his answer, and I hoped he wouldn't weigh it for too long, because I was holding my breath. I slowly let it out when he finally said, "Bea certainly believes him. Me?" He studied the ceiling. "I'm not so sure."

Whew.

"Where are Bea and Eddie now?" I asked.

"Trying to talk their way out of disturbing the peace citations," he answered.

"They'll probably talk themselves into more trouble."

"Which is why they've called their attorney."

"Daddy, please don't tell me they called Smerle."

"They did. Pine Apple's own Smerle T. Webb, Esquire, is on his way to Greenville to spring them."

"They'll all three end up in jail."

"We can only hope."

We both laughed.

"What about Marcus Flash?" I asked.

"He'll be charged with first-degree murder along with aiding and abetting a prison escape by video conference later today."

"So you know about Old Man Carter."

"I've been busy catching up while you were sleeping."

"How caught up are you?"

"Oh, I don't know. I've inspected the funeral home crypt I knew nothing about, and I've spoken to Roy Howdy."

"How'd he take the news about his uncle?"

"Let's see." Daddy crossed his arms. "I believe his words were, 'Well he's dead either way, Chief Way. Did you hear what I did there? Way-way?"

We both laughed. Sad and weary laughs. Maybe just relieved laughs on Roy Howdy's behalf, but laughs.

"Who caught you up on all the news?"

"Mostly, my twin granddaughters," he said. "What they didn't tell me, your grandmother the casino manager did. Eugenia Winters Stone filled in a few of the blanks, giving you surprisingly high marks for your problem solving and leadership skills."

"Oh, really?"

"Did you two have a meeting of the minds while I was away?"

My head rocked. "So to speak."

He checked his watch.

"Before you go, Daddy, what about Fiona?"

"Hopefully she'll be the last of my catchup conversations. I'm on my way to speak to her now."

"Are you?"

"We're meeting at the bank."

"I thought the bank was closed today."

"Odd that the bank would be closed on a regular banking day, don't you think?" He spoke slower when he added, "Other than the gaping hole in the back of the vault, of course."

"Yeah." I looked away. "There's that."

"I think you should join us."

His words were even, not charged with any emotion or urgency, but I had the feeling that beneath his gentle suggestion was a firm request. My guess was he wanted to talk to both of us about Eddie's claim of having spent the night in the bank vault. Although his next words made me wonder. "Fiona wants to get her affairs in order, including the bank, which she intends to close, before she consults with a family attorney."

We sat quietly until it was my turn to deliver a hard line gently. "You knew, didn't you, Daddy?"

He smiled a weary smile. "I knew she had a child that she hid away, Davis. And that was all I knew."

After those words settled, we were both talked out. He stood first. I followed. "Let me catch my breath and change clothes." I gave my sister's two-sizes-too-big shirt a pluck. "I'd like to see my children for just a minute, then I'll meet you at the bank. I'll tell you everything."

"I don't know if I want you to tell me everything, Davis."

"I promise to tell you everything you need to know."

He patted my cheek, kissed me on the forehead, then turned for the door. Where he stopped. "So, goats?"

I raised both hands in incredulous surrender.

I closed the door behind him and fell against it.

Twenty minutes later—talk about being transported back to high school—I was still trying to talk myself into going downstairs, where I could hear my mother banging away in the kitchen. She couldn't have been too terribly mad at me, or at least wanted me to die in clean clothes, because she'd washed and ironed mine while I'd slept. Even my Memorial Day Keds slip-ons looked like I'd just taken them out of the box. The red ones. With the blue daisies.

I took a deep breath and let the third step announce my pending arrival.

"Davis?" she yelled up the stairs. "Is that you? Get down here."

I hit the last step bracing myself for what was coming next, but it was, "Will you look at this?" She pointed out the window. "Do you remember your old librarian? Willa Walters?" She didn't wait for me to answer. "Look what she and her new beau have done with my flowerbeds."

I took a look, and while I'd never let the words pass my lips, not even whispered to Bradley in the middle of the night, on a remote island, an uninhabited remote island, on Mars, Mother's flowerbeds had never looked better.

She covered peeled and sliced celery and slid the bowl into the refrigerator between four covered bowls of potato salad.

How long had I slept?

Mother moved to the stove. "Grab me a kitchen towel from the drawer to cover these potatoes, Davis, then let's go get a lemonade at the street fair while they cool. Let's stop by the Baptist church and see this casino nonsense your grandmother won't stop yammering about." Immediately followed by, "Sakes, alive, Davis, I can't believe Bea's a grandmother. She can't either. Passed out cold on the sidewalk. We couldn't rouse her for nothing. Eventually your daddy had to get the water hose after her, and just as soon as he did, here comes Fiona and that handsome boy of hers. Bea started crying and almost crushed that boy to death." Mother stopped her kitchen work to look at me. "Can you believe Fiona? Can you even believe it? Now I do give her credit for finally clearing her conscious by getting it out there, because having a secret that big has almost eaten that woman alive, but the poor boy." She emptied steaming potatoes into the colander waiting in the sink. "Bea going on and on about how she was going to decorate his room in Mickey Mouse and Donald Duck. Until Eddie called. In trouble again. I told her she ought not be driving after swooning in the driveway, but there she went. I'll give her a call later. Or maybe not." She pulled off her apron. "I've had about enough of Bea for a while."

So had I. And I'd seen her for thirty seconds.

* * *

Main Street was a tapestry of sun, patriotism, community spirit, and long-held tradition. The air was thick with laughter, music from a bluegrass band in Town Square, and...tacos?

I was starving.

Bex and Quinn spotted us right away and came flying up the street waving cotton candy swords. Bradley, right behind the girls with the baby in his arms, picked up his step. Bex wrapped her arms around my legs, Quinn wrapped hers around Mother's, then they

traded. I tipped Quinn's blonde head back. "You look beautiful!"
The girls had been to the facepainting booth. Their faces were
wall-to-wall four-year-old American flags. We'd have some face
scrubbing work later that they wouldn't like. Bradley caught up. My
baby's arms were wide open. Reaching for me. I took him into my
own arms, buried my face in his baby neck, and wished I could stop
time. Place my little family in a snow globe right where we stood in
the middle of Main Street with the sweet spirit of my small southern
hometown swirling all around us. Forever. But maybe minus the
funeral home. Bea's Diner. And Pine Apple Bank & Trust.

I told Bradley I had one last chore.

He nodded. "Think you'll be long?"

"I hope not."

"Girls?" he said. "Let's show your grandmother the carousel."

"I'll be at the bank," I said to his face. "I'll keep the baby," I said
to his back, as he was already chasing Bex and Quinn. Who were
dragging their grandmother to the carousel.

THIRTY

The bank door was unlocked. I half knocked anyway as I pushed in to the sound of Cole. I'd never heard him speak. His audience of Daddy, Fiona, and Florida were listening intently to the boy's retelling of meeting his grandmother. Fiona didn't find it the least bit funny. Daddy was trying not to laugh. Florida was all but rolling on the floor. She couldn't even catch her breath. Daddy said, "Look who's here! It's—" he came to a screeching halt "—my grandson!"

I pulled up a chair beside Daddy and passed him his grandson.

Fiona told us she'd contacted Alabama's banking commissioner that morning and gave notice that she intended to close the bank. State regulators would arrive Tuesday to help issue receiver's claims to all depositors, and to ensure all banking activities—check processing and ATM card functions specifically—would carry on as usual until Pine Apple Bank & Trust's few assets were liquidated and the doors closed for good.

"What will you do then, Fiona?" By then, the baby was at Daddy's feet. Or I thought he was at Daddy's feet. I'd taken my eye off him for two seconds and he'd somehow scooted between us.

"I have appointments with three family law attorneys next week."

All our eyes went to Cole.

His eyes were on the baby.

"Oh, he knows all about it." Florida lobbed an open hand on her brother's head like a hat. He knocked it off. "He's tougher than he looks."

"I'm not tough enough for a pet ferret named Fester who lives in a washing machine or a Disney room in a trailer," he said. "And why does she have orange hair?"

"She dyes it that color," I said.

293

"It looks like she glued Cheetos on her head. And I'm not calling her MawMaw either."

"Call her Bea," I suggested. "Like the rest of us do. On good days."

"After meeting her, I'm scared to death to meet my dad."

We looked at each other, like, *say something comforting,* but no one could come up with anything.

Daddy cleared his throat in a way that let us know it was time to move on and discuss the gaping hole in the vault wall. But before he could nail us, I had to find the baby, who'd scooted out of my sight and had pulled himself up to standing on the back of Daddy's chair. Which scared and thrilled me.

Florida said, "Cole, play with the baby."

"Play with him?"

"Keep an eye on him," she said.

"Start at the beginning," Daddy said to us as soon as Cole stood and stepped away. "And don't leave anything out."

Fiona, Florida, and I started stammering all over each other. Soundbites from the next ten minutes, all of which Daddy sat through with a dazed look on his face, his eyes hopping between us, included Florida saying, "If you ask me, the whole thing was Courtney's fault," Fiona saying, "He wouldn't stop calling me a lying polecat," and me saying, "He asked for it, Daddy." We might have gone on for another hour, because I could see with everything we were lobbing at him as fast as we could, my father was losing interest in charging us with kidnapping and imprisonment, until Cole interrupted everything.

"Hey," he said, "this baby—" The baby had scooted himself all the way to the grandfather clock. Which, lying on its side, was as tall as a coffee table, making it a perfect baby height. And my perfect baby had pulled himself up to a wobbly stand. Then plopped right back down. Thrilled with himself. He immediately reached his chubby hands out to do it again.

Florida said, "Stand behind him, Cole, and be ready to catch him." I made a mental note to remember to write it in his baby book—*Pulled himself up to standing on an old grandfather clock*!—then got things going again. "Daddy, don't forget that Eddie's a liar. You know that." I wondered, since the baby had been in my sister's care for five days that felt like five weeks, if she already knew. Had he pulled himself up to standing for her first? Florida roped me back into the matter at hand. "Does he have a criminal record, Mr. Way? If someone held a gun to my head and said, 'Do you think Eddie Crawford has a criminal record?' I'd say yes." She turned to her mother. "That will help you in court." Fiona rolled her eyes. She knew what Daddy and I knew as well, and what Florida wasn't admitting to herself. Or at least trying to protect her mother from. Which was Eddie could have a criminal record stretching from coast-to-coast, but that wouldn't make the court look more favorably on what she'd put both her children through.

"Hey." It was Cole again. "This baby's found something."

The baby had somehow turned the grandfather clock corner and was at the crown, partially hidden behind the intricate woodwork of the arched façade. I jumped up to scoop him out of what could be harm's way when we heard a loud click. A block of wood shot up and I couldn't see my baby at all. I flew. Daddy, Florida, and Fiona were right behind me. The baby's chubby little hands had found and depressed a barely protruding wooden square. It must have looked like one of his ABC blocks and he'd reached out to play with it. What he'd thought was an ABC block on the old clock was actually a trigger that released a panel. Startled by the contents of the interior pouring out, the baby plopped down. On money. So much money.

Florida, hands on hips, said, "Well, look at you, Cash."

It would be ten minutes after we emptied the hidden compartment of money that we found the 1794 Flowing Hair silver dollar taped to a small inside wall of the clock's crown, but it would be from that moment on my son would be called Cash.

Cash Cole.

EPILOGUE

Word spread quickly about Granny's Little Casino, which we ended up calling Granny's Little Cash Cow. It brought in more traffic than Pine Apple's Memorial Day Celebration had ever seen. And it was profitable enough for the town to purchase the slot machines from the Bellissimo to stow away for many Memorial Day Celebrations to come.

Eugenia Winters Stone amended the Potato Salad Cookoff rules to make it a blind competition—mostly because her right arm was in no shape to pen her usual calligraphy nameplates—anonymously numbering each entry and serving the salads to the judges in identical patriotic bowls originally purchased for chicken wing sauces so no one would recognize anyone else's Pyrex. In spite of my mother's delicious entry, she had no way of tipping the scales in her favor with dirty looks and veiled threats should anyone consider not voting for her potato salad. Pine Apple's newest resident, Cedric Kinder, won with his Loaded Twice-Baked Potato Salad.

(Who knew Whiskey could cook?)

(Or would take Roy Howdy's place as Daddy's Public Works sidekick?)

The 1794 Flowing Hair silver dollar was returned to descendants of Adeline Jenkins. Who immediately had it appraised by a rare coin collector in Birmingham. He offered to take it off their hands for thirty dollars. As it turned out, the news feature Frank Simmons watched in the prison common room was about the sale of the very first 1794 Flowing Hair silver dollar struck in the United States. Not any of the thousands of Flowing Hair silver dollars that followed. Hundreds of which could be found on eBay in the fifty-dollar range.

Having no way to evenly distribute the money Frank Simmons stashed in the crown of the old grandfather clock, by unanimous vote, Pine Apple's City Council gifted it to the city treasury. The

$242,000 was added to the reward money collected for the capture and return of the three Talladega prisoners, and it took every penny to pay the Bellissimo for the contents of their garden, buy new bleachers for the high school gymnasium that would never recover from the goats, and pay for the demolition of the old funeral home. After Roy Howdy moved out. Which was after the root cellar remains were laid to proper rest.

Courtney and Roy Howdy expanded the voodoo candle business and took it to TikTok. They added candles they called Boo that would rid homes of ghosts, candles they called Rabbit's Foot that would bring good luck, and their bestseller, marketed to newlywed couples, Dirty Twister candles. Within three months, they'd hired a staff of three, and two months after that, broke ground on a barn behind Courtney's house for candle production. They named the new business Rydell High Candles. Because, Courtney said, "Get it? Roy Howdy Carter has a R, and a H, and a C, and that's the same as Rydell High Candles, with a R, and a H, and a C. Get it?"

Six long fraught-filled months after Cole Simmons met his Pine Apple family for the first time, Fifteenth Judicial Circuit Family Court Judge Sadie Hayes, finding Fiona Simmons unfit and Eddie Crawford incapable, awarded surprise and sole custody of Cole Simmons to his sister. My lost and found friend Florida.

DOUBLE WHAMMY

Gretchen Archer

A Davis Way Crime Caper (#1)

In case you missed how it all began...

One

A little unemployment goes a long, long way, and after more than a year of it, applying for every available position in L.A. (Lower Alabama), I took a right and tried Mississippi. At the end of the road I found Biloxi, where instead of applying for fifty different jobs, I applied for the same job fifty different times.

My final interview, like the dozen before it, began in a posh corporate office with an executive assistant at the Bellissimo Resort and Casino, Natalie Middleton. From there, the others had gone in several different directions. There'd been a marksmanship test with long-range pop-ups (I aced it), ink-blob and dot-to-dot psychiatric profiles (not sure how I did on those), and an extensive photo shoot with costume changes, tinted contact lenses, and wigs. I couldn't wait to hear what my last interview act would be.

"You'll be meeting with Richard Sanders," Natalie said, "our president and CEO. The final decision is his, and it will go quickly."

I'd applied for the job six weeks earlier. It was two hundred miles from where I lived. Most of the interviews had been all-day ordeals. It had already not gone quickly.

Richard Sanders' office had museum qualities: everything was quiet, valuable, and illuminated. Natalie directed me to a leather chair. "He'll be right in."

Right in, for the record, was almost an hour later.

I'd just helped myself to a fifth Red Hot cinnamon candy from the crystal bowl on Mr. Sanders' desk when a hidden door on the right side of the room slid open and a man stepped through, then froze, staring at me as if I was a ghost. I wondered who he was expecting. From the look on his face, not me.

He cleared his throat, then cautiously crossed the room with a guarded smile, hand outstretched. "Richard Sanders."

I skipped around the candy. "Davith Wathe."

He took his seat behind his desk and reached for the folder in front of him. I could see the right angles of a stack of photographs. Of me. The dress-up interview.

I sat up straighter, looking for somewhere to lose the candy. I gave him the once-over while he looked at the photographs, the whole time discreetly working the candy at top speed, the roof of my mouth on fire. Mr. Sanders was in his early forties, six-two, strikingly fit, blond, and either perpetually tan or just back from the Bahamas, since it was the dead of winter and he had a late-July glow about him.

He looked up. Baby blues. "Davis?"

The cinnamon disk burned going down. "Family name."

"Davis Way," he tried it on. "And you're from Pine—?"

"Apple." The hot candy brick was stuck sideways in my throat.

"Two words?"

"Ach." I discreetly pounded my chest. "Garkle."

"Are you okay?" he asked.

I was anything but.

He pushed a button on his phone. Two seconds later Natalie returned. She gently patted me on the back, then landed one between my shoulder blades that almost knocked me into the next week. She poured me a glass of water while he slid the candy dish out of my reach. As soon as it appeared I would live, Natalie said, "Well then," and disappeared, leaving me alone with Richard Sanders again.

"Why don't we start over, Davis?"

"That'd be great."

"Where is Pine Apple, Alabama?"

"South of Montgomery."

Other than the Red Hots, the real-live Monet on the wall, and the expensive Oriental rug under my feet, I was in very familiar job-interview territory. I'd applied for everything with a heartbeat, and the resulting interviews had all had common elements. First, my name threw people off. In my thirty-two years it had been pointed out to me thirty-two thousand times that Davis Way sounded more like a destination than a person. After that, potential employers liked to suggest that I'd written down my hometown incorrectly. My resume clearly stated my credentials, including two college degrees, one in Criminal Justice and the other in Computer and Information Science. As such, would I really forget where I lived? Next, he would bring up my size, because I was considered undersized in general, but especially so for the line of work I was in. (I'm five foot two.) (And a half.)

He surprised me when he asked instead, "How large is the police force in Pine Apple?"

"There are two of us." There were two of us. Surely he'd read that far.

"Is there a lot of crime in Pine Apple, Alabama?" He leaned back, elbows to armrests, his hands meeting mid-chest. He rolled a thin platinum wedding band round and round his left ring finger.

"The usual," I said. "Domestic, vehicular, theft. We double as fire too."

"So you've had EMT training?"

"Yes."

"And you write computer programming?"

"I'm not sure I'd go that far," I said. "Pine Apple's a small country town, not exactly a hotbed of criminal activity. I had a lot of time on my hands and spent most of it on the computer."

"It says here you rewrote the program for incident reporting nationwide."

I hadn't put that on my resume. What else did it say there? "Not so much, Mr. Sanders. I only eliminated the inefficiencies of the old program and it went viral."

"Why do you want to leave Pine Apple, Davis?"

Oh, boy.

"You know what?" He looked at his watch. "Let's save that for later."

Yes. Let's.

He started up with the wedding band again. "I'm going to say something that could be construed as politically incorrect." He made direct eye contact. "With your permission, of course."

"Sure."

"I have a thirteen-year-old son who has at least five inches and fifty pounds on you."

There it was. "Is he my competition?"

Richard Sanders unexpectedly laughed. "Not hardly. Maybe if we were looking for someone to play Xbox."

"For all I know, Mr. Sanders, you *are* looking for someone to play Xbox." I surrendered. "I've been interviewing for this position for six weeks now, and I still don't know what it is."

"I don't either."

Could we get someone in there who did?

"Did Paul and Jeremy not go over it with you?" he asked.

"Who?"

"Paul and Jeremy," he said. "My security team."

I had nothing.

"Big guys," Mr. Sanders said.

Ah. Those guys. I remembered. The two mammoth men from my tenth interview I'd been trying hard to forget. One had no hair and the other had the biggest, brightest teeth I'd ever seen in my life. The bald one wore strange neckties and the one with the teeth dressed monochromatically—everything, tip to toe, the same color. Natalie introduced them as if I had no idea who they were. As if they hadn't been following me around since my first interview. I'd spotted one, the other, or both giants every time I'd been there. They'd jumped on elevators with me, the bald one had been at the shooting range, and the one with the teeth had actually followed me all the way home once. But on the day I officially met them, I played along. Nice to meet you, large total security strangers.

Then they drilled me for three solid hours on subjects far from security. My waitressing skills, or rather my lack thereof, had been heavily discussed. How did I feel about gambling? (I felt like you shouldn't do it with other people's money.) Would I care to explain that? (No, thank you.) How did I feel about hundreds of pounds of dirty linens? (Opposed.) How about scrubbing shower stalls? (Again, opposed.) Did I know or had I ever known or had I ever seen photographs of someone named Bianca? (No. Wasn't that a breath mint?) How many times had I been married? (None of your business.) Could I type? (How many fingers were we talking about?) Had I always been a redhead? (I wasn't one of those pale, freckled, flaming-red redheads. My hair was a coppery-caramel color, and my eyes were the same color, only darker.) Had I ever been convicted of or committed a felony? (Which one? Convicted or committed?) Either. Both. (There's a big difference.) Let's hear it. (I'd like to use a lifeline.) Did I have culinary skills? (Could I cook Pop Tarts? Yes. Do I know what to do with a dead chicken? No.) Had I ever held a customer service position? (Not specifically. More no than yes. Okay, no.) The hairless one asked me if I could operate an industrial vacuum cleaner. I didn't know such a thing existed.

If I thought I knew what the job was before those two, I sure didn't know after. And there I sat in my final interview with the president, and *he* didn't know.

I picked up my purse.

"Wait," Richard Sanders said.

I put down my purse.

"It's a new position, Davis, and a highly classified one. If I knew exactly what you'd be doing on a day-to-day basis, I'd tell you."

Finally, some bottom line.

"You'll be working undercover throughout the casino and hotel, and if you want to know more than that," he said, "you'll have to agree to the terms."

"Are you offering me the job, Mr. Sanders?"

"Do you want the job, Davis?"

I wasn't sure I wanted it. I was very sure I needed it. "The terms," I said, "what are they?"

"In a word? Discretion." He steepled his fingers, then used them as a pointer. "Your job is to be discreet."

"And?"

"Use discretion," he said.

Use discretion while being discreet?

"Don't talk to anyone on or off this property about your job," he said. "And don't reveal your identity under any circumstances."

"When do I start?"

"How soon can you start?"

"I'm good to go, Mr. Sanders. You say when."

"Today's as good a time as any." His hand went for the phone. "You can start now."

My eyebrows shot up. I didn't mean that very minute. I was thinking Monday. Or the Monday after that.

"Do you need time to think about it?" His hand hovered over the phone. "Because the iron is hot now."

Wait a minute. No one had said a word about ironing.

"Davis? Do you need a little time?"

Yes. "No."

"Good." He smiled. "Welcome to the Bellissimo."

And with that, I was well on my way to prison.

Gretchen Archer

Gretchen Archer is a Tennessee housewife who began writing when her children, seeking higher educations, ran off and left her. She lives on Lookout Mountain with her husband and a misbehaving sheepadoodle named Kevin. *Double Blast* is the twelfth Davis Way Crime Caper. You can visit her at www.gretchenarcher.com.